I0639032

MISCHA TUROW

the deadly quest for love

MISCHA TUROW

the deadly quest for love

A novel
by

ALEXANDER GÜNSBERG

Adelaide Books
New York / Lisbon
2019

MISCHA TUROW

A novel

By Alexander Günsberg

Prize-winning author from Basel-Country Canton, Switzerland

Copyright © by Alexander Günsberg

Cover design © 2019 Adelaide Books

Published by Adelaide Books, New York / Lisbon
adelaidebooks.org

Editor-in-Chief
Stevan V. Nikolic

All rights reserved. No part of this book may be reproduced in any manner whatsoever without written permission from the author except in the case of brief quotations embodied in critical articles and reviews.

For any information, please address Adelaide Books
at info@adelaidebooks.org

or write to:

Adelaide Books
244 Fifth Ave. Suite D27
New York, NY, 10001

ISBN-10: 1-949180-93-X
ISBN-13: 978-1-949180-93-0

Printed in the United States of America

Prologue

At the tender age of five and a half, when nature and up-bringing have little girls playing with dolls and drawing red stick-figures in loamy earth beneath yellow sunbeams, she had already defeated her father – a Russian-born, FIDE World Chess Federation master residing in Zurich after taking a Swiss wife – at chess. This does not presume that little Mischa Turow, as she was named, was averse to playing with dolls, she merely took an altogether different approach than others her age. She forewent the cuddling and catering, did not treat them as adored younger sisters or as pampered babies. No, she deemed herself their merciless mistress, inflicting preposterous violence upon them. Once she had clothed and disrobed them, having explained to them the world and customs with a head-master's pedantry, she took her pleasure by punishing their lack of lesson comprehension. Gripping a sewing needle, or occasionally a knife secretly slipped from the kitchen drawer, she impaled their tender parts and then, exerting no little strength, ripped off their arms and legs, ultimately tearing off their heads. She often worked up a sweat, yet her satisfaction at a job well done, if you could call it that, rendered her blissful and left her looking forward to further acts of this kind with eager anticipation.

The origins of her desire to punish and annihilate, as well as of her wholly unheard-of aptitude for chess, lay in shadows, beyond the grasp of those around her, who were not blessed with Freudian reason. No one had taught her The Game of Kings, no one explained its rules and fundamentals. Her begetter, her physical one that is – not the one who sired her dubious gifts, both good and evil – failed to notice her outstanding ability was the sole result of silent observation. Never bored, she stood or sat by the chess board for hours on end without flagging, watching the adults' moves; first with astonishment, then broodingly and finally shaking her head at the players' ineptitude. Her father hadn't a clue of the power surging forth at her conception; a power dimensions beyond his own, incomprehensible to his or to the majority of minds, not excluding those of above average intelligence. It would have been a rare specimen indeed, who, had they known her since infancy, could have foreseen the brilliant achievements and diabolical aberrations emerging from her slumbering faculties and consequently issued humanity due warning. This, however, did not occur. Thus, the fascination of her life and calamity of her deeds narrated here, began inexorably to unfold.

As word of a not-quite-six-year-old little girl's astonishing triumph over a FIDE chess master – albeit not the strongest one – made the rounds, the newly crowned Grandmaster, Roland Moos, who had won the Swiss National Tournament as well as other noted international competitions, announced he would be willing to challenge the child under official competition conditions. No one believed the child had a prayer. It was an entirely different thing to confront a leading national luminary beneath the relentless spotlights of the public domain than to challenge an indulgent loving father amid familiar surroundings in the comfort of her own home. And yet, to everyone's amazement, the Grandmaster also lost. It was not only the fact he had drawn the shorter stick against a completely unknown child in the most demanding of all strategic battles – a child who, standing up, could barely see over the table's rim – that excited interest far beyond the world of chess. It was moreover *how* Mischa Turow had proved her superiority; how she had put him in his place with a brilliant, startling, impossibly unpredictable sacrifice combination; how she had humiliated him with a stroke of genius; how she had defeated him as if he were no more than a bumbling amateur seated at one of thirty or forty chess boards in a simultaneous exhibition by a vastly superior player, that made tidal waves in the oceanic press, drawing the eyes of the world to a genius the likes of which had not been seen since Mozart. Like a star, the *wunderkind* fell from the heavens as if she wished to illuminate the Earth with her radiance, brighter and steadier than all other shooting stars that fly from one corner of the sky, flit East to West or North to South and vanish, taking their tails with them, on the other side of the firmament, leaving no memorable trace of their existence.

The exceptional confrontation between a not-yet six-year-old child, a member of the weaker sex, to boot – allegedly from birth and capacity far inferior to the males of her species when it comes to chess – and a great Grandmaster, much admired for his chess artistry, took place in the Zurich Chess Club before numerous spectators who were astonished beyond all measure. They could not believe, or even begin to grasp, what they saw. Never before had such a very young, obscure creature displayed such talent for the sixty-four black and white squares they so loved without truly having penetrated their mysteries, or perhaps precisely for this reason.

Apparently, Mischa Turow was blessed with a thoroughly extraordinary gift that must have been granted her at birth since she had never systematically absorbed the insights and skills of the game of games, had never studied the countless opening moves, the strategies, tactics, combinations and closing techniques. The *Neue Zürcher* newspaper brought a full-page article on Mischa, after confessing to have recently phased out their ancient chess column due to lack of reader interest. But the uniqueness of this occurrence was such that not only chess enthusiasts were struck with incredulous wonderment. A person attaining singular achievement inspires admiration, even in those people who would otherwise have no interest in the matter. Little Mischa Turow was soon dubbed *Genius of the Century.*

Mischa is actually a man's name, but her mother, Ella Kronberg, the daughter of a deeply pious, thundering bass cantor of the city's major synagogue, had, for reasons undivulged, firmly turned her back on religion. She had married the ne'er-do-well charmer Maxim Grigorewitsch Turow, a player of not-so-high ranking in the Russian chess hierarchy, who, considering the hostility towards religion in the defunct Soviet Union and Stalin's terror in the thirties, ordering mass executions later dubbed *The Great Purge*, knew less about his Judaism than his wife did. She gave her adored daughter Michaela the nickname Mischa that, in non-Slavic countries, certainly had a feminine ring to it. In Mischa's Russian passport, which she held along with her Swiss one since not only did she have a Russian father, she had entered this godforsaken world in his homeland, she was registered as *Michaela Wolfowna Turowa.*

When she was two years old, she and her parents moved to the city of Zwingli and Pestalozzi where she effortlessly absorbed the local dialect *Züridütsch*, had only Swiss friends and felt herself to be utterly Swiss although at home with her father, or when she accompanied him to chess tournaments, she spoke Russian. In later years, she could never say with certainty whether she felt more at home with her mother-tongue or father's language. She was so fluent in both that neither in Switzerland nor in Russia was she ever taken for a foreigner.

Superlatives came thick and fast in the reports and commentaries journalists published on the young chess and linguistic genius. Even the *New York Times* deemed the advent of a female child barely out of diapers conquering a European national chess champion worthy of mention.

Eighteen years have passed since the world press first took notice of her. She had grown into a stunning young woman who not only filled the pages of *People Magazine* and held the chess world in suspense with her triumphs, she had also flung humanity a quantum leap forward with her revolutionary discoveries in the field of Physics, expanding the horizon of human thought farther than ever before imagined, even in times of worldwide communication and of initial discussions on the feasibility of conquering our solar system's planets. Her nature blended intelligence, beauty and grace to near perfection. One year ago, upon completing her PhD in Physics at a mere twenty-four years of age, she was immediately appointed a professorship at the University of Vienna, occupying a new academic chair created specifically for her as professor of *dynamic particle interference*, DPI for short – an unprecedented sensation in the academic world. Her dissertation on the dynamic interaction between the smallest subatomic particles in elementary building blocks and the resulting *dynamo theory*, soon to be known as the *Turowian Theory*, solved the riddle of thus far unexplained phenomena and operative principles, opening new, unforeknown gateways in especially, but not only, space travel technology, creating furor amid all scientific organs and the most prominent symposia around the globe. In professional circles, the importance of her theory's insights into physical coherencies and its impact on future developments was considered equal to Albert Einstein's general and special theories of relativity, Werner Heisenberg's uncertainty principle and Wolfgang Pauli's quantum mechanics. She accepted only a smattering of the countless invitations to lecture, preferring to devote her time to chess and the peculiar passion to which this book is dedicated. To the general public, whose knowledge of Physics was limited to a casually assumed, often-cited Einstein, propounding that everything is relative, making them relatively correct without knowing why – she had long become an icon.

During her studies, for which she needed much less time than her fellow students, she had taken the leap to the pinnacle of world-class chess. She had won nearly all tournaments, had become Swiss and Austrian Master and had won the Grandmaster title in women's chess as well as the more prestigious Grandmaster in men's. She had also qualified for the World Champion tournament, a title currently held by a Chinese woman, which would take place in six months' time. Her winnings and advertising contracts as well as the royalties from her dissertation publication, which had become standard Physics literature with several examples at every university and scientific library, provided her a comfortable and carefree life.

In an exclusive neighborhood, in the center of the old imperial city on the Danube on one of the not exactly cheap Vienna Graben side-streets where only a minority could afford to reside, she inhabited a luxurious penthouse with a high, glass-domed roof and an extensive garden rife with exotic plants.

The apartment offered a breath-taking view of the monuments, churches and newly built sky-scrapers of an aged city reaching for the present day, whose testimonies to the past shine out like old masters' artworks amid the faceless glass and concrete peaks. Casually on foot, she could cover the distance to the university, to the physics institutes and to the laboratories of a multinational corporation – where she earned more than a pittance on the side – as well as to the opera house, theaters and cabarets she so loved and frequently visited.

For reasons known only to herself, but most likely left in the dark, she maintained but minimal contact with her parents in Switzerland, extending obligatory congratulations at birthdays and other occasions as well as paying for her eight-year-younger brother's private trade school since he had failed to reach the minimum grade average at the public school exams. His frequent absence from classes and verbal abuse toward his teachers drew unfavorable attention and he was ultimately expelled from the state-subsidized learning institute. Although they shared a name and a few inner characteristics, Michael neither looked nor acted like his sister. If you were unaware of the strange and terrifying traits, they both embodied, you would never think they were brother and sister. His intellect was a candle to her bonfire and there was no simile to liken his appearance to hers. In the eyes of his doting mother, he was the most beautiful creature on earth; to anyone else, he was the exact opposite. Squat, obese, broad-shouldered and bull-necked, his over-sized head erupted from his shoulders without a recognizable throat and his long, untamed blond hair flew about his head in wild strands. He resembled a dwarfed Neandertal more than the homo sapiens his mother took him for simply because he was the fruit of her womb and love and would remain so despite the evil he wreaked.

While Michael's nature was stingy, suspicious, aloof, secretive and rarely humorous, Mischa was an open, generous and friendly person, trusting anyone who crossed her path. She exuded cheerfulness, was convivial, open to anything new, tolerant of those unlike her in thought and deed, acknowledging and respecting her fellow beings – including the majority who were less brilliant, witty and beautiful than she was. So, it seemed. To the uninitiated observer she appeared to be a singularly brilliant flower, tall and slender, soaring above the endlessly monotonous green grass that stretched to the horizon.

What these miss-matched siblings shared was an inexplicable distaste for their parents, who, especially their mother, did everything she could for her children. As a nurse, she took on innumerable extra night shifts at the hospital to provide her children with the best possible education, while her husband haunted chess clubs and took part in tournaments, albeit without a hint of his daughter's success. He could also be found in certain establishments of which his spouse had no knowledge, as is often the case with unsuspecting wives who sacrifice themselves for their husbands and children without a shred of reward or a word of thanks.

As to the strange aversion the Turow children had to their parents, many ascribed it to cruel and inexplicable Nature. In truth, as dissimilar as Michael and Mischa were, they were both possessed by the same devil, relentlessly demanding his due. An unbudgeable fiend who, even in later years, refused to be exorcised.

Thus, the uninitiated yet keen observer may perceive that although the siblings bore no outer resemblance to one another, their souls were twinned like two peas in a pod. Hideous Michael and handsome Mischa shared a preference for the scurrilous, not to say for the downright revoltingly repellent. Like many men, Michael was a collector. His passion, however, was not rare stamps, mocha demitasses, beer coasters or miniature train sets as is commonly the case. Michael passion was skulls. He gathered them to himself in every size and shape, from macabre key chains to skull-shaped vases to crania of once-living beings. Whether their deaths came naturally or coerced was of no consequence to him. He rummaged for the objects of his passion amid other grotesque curios proffered by unwholesome dealers, at flea markets, bazaars, second-hand shops or wherever such things could be had for a few coins. But for the well-preserved shrunken head from Borneo, still in possession of its skin, hair and teeth, Michael laid his entire savings on the dealer's table, a man who would not hesitate to sell his own mother.

He coddled and cared for his man-made or once of mother born treasures as if they were still living beings, caressing them lovingly, drawing them to his lips and kissing them tenderly. His openly displayed passion for scandalous, moreover nauseating objects expressed boundless hubris, a seething contempt for all social convention and an utter denial of human consideration and compassion. His single purpose in life was to gratify his ego, although he did not take his devotion as far as his sister did.

Mischa staged her unsavory compulsion, the pinnacle of bliss she incessantly strove to scale, in her bedroom. She kept the curtains in her apartment drawn day and night to keep curious eyes from observing her maneuvers. Like her brother, another inglorious trait they had in common, Mischa was incapable of deep emotion. That is to say, it was not the longing for an as yet undiscovered, rarely experienced love igniting her loins, but a sexual drive to possess that sent her, without a moment's hesitation, prowling coffee houses and bars for a certain type of man, whom she immediately took home following cursory introductions where, during foreplay and intercourse, she stoked her passion by mistreating the groveling slave, fueled her fire with his pain and humiliation. Tied to the bed, she inflicted agony with her whip, her stiletto heels (set aside for such occasions), burning cigarettes or, flesh on flesh, with her bare hands and fingernails. Only so, could she satisfy her lust.

No one, not her friends, faculty colleagues, chess players or other acquaintances – and most certainly not the press, who, had they known, would have struck the headline motherlode – knew of her deviant and dangerous perversion. Her predilection had become an incurable addiction, compelling her to interminably hunt down yet another disposable man to bring home for a single night of erotic torture, after which she absolutely forbade him to even attempt to contact her. Naturally, she only selected total strangers that she had never before laid eyes on and who hadn't the slightest connection to her friends, colleagues or acquaintances. Should the hopeful candidate, sitting across from her with palms sweating, eyes gawking and heart racing in expectation, arouse the faintest suspicion he could be somehow affiliated with someone in her far-reaching entourage, she immediately aborted the mission, paid, leaving him in the lurch, baffled and leaking disappointment.

It never occurred to her to let him buy her drinks or pay her bill. She alone held the scepter in her hand, governing countless sexually motivated encounters, each identical to its predecessor. They began the loud crack of her leather whip, slicing the air into brittle pieces and ended with Mischa's orgasmic roar the moment her victim's delirium of pain reached its climax. For most of these men, the humiliation they endured, the pain Mischa inflicted upon them, the torture, was their only path to the peak of sexual deliverance – a mountain they climbed with their torturer. Mischa was adept at spotting this exceptional male specimen the moment she set foot in the venue, no matter how old or young, in suit and tie or jeans and sweatshirt. Her inherent flair for detecting willing victims, or better, for men who take pleasure in Mischa's exclusive brand of torment, was infallible.

Her friends and the many men who had courted the lovely lady's graces, yet were unsuitable as objects of her sexual fulfilment, found her utterly unapproachable. Some rumors claimed her frigid, while others speculated that she had sacrificed a private life for her career, or maybe had a secret lover stashed away, was possibly even involved in a clandestine lesbian relationship. Most of them, however, were stumped by the contradiction between her candid nature and her refusal to establish a rapport beyond the amenities of friendship. Why on earth would she, the most attractive, the cleverest and most desirable woman of Vienna's high society choose to remain alone, bereft of love's bliss? Especially her, who was the uncontested focus and acme of any event? She needed merely enter a room to draw immediate and undivided attention, which she accepted as the norm. It was neither discomfiting nor a source of pride or conceit. It was simply how things were, part of who she was, no more remarkable than her skin or the streamlined elegance of her everyday attire. She was aware of her outstanding qualities, both inner and outer, yet made no effort to highlight or veil them. Precisely this unpretentious demeanor won her the public's sympathy as well as that of anyone she encountered. No one suspected she could be Dr. Jekyll and Mr. Hyde reincarnated.

Technically a Jew, although not a practicing one – another trait she neither stressed nor disguised, as she couldn't have cared less – her split personality likened her more to a Greek goddess on Olympia, ostensibly noble and benevolent;

covertly, and ruthlessly, pursuing the unbridled satisfaction of her egomaniacal, man-eating hunger without the slightest scruple.

She was not unaware of the influence her ancestor's two-thousand-year-long study of sacred writings had on her superior mind but accepted it as fate. Especially since she hadn't the slightest interest in the past or in historical coherencies, even when they affected her own heritage and intelligence. Like many mathematicians and natural scientists, only the future was significant. A thousand time more significant than the past, particularly a past that pre-dates her birth. Without her knowledge, the traits which live on within her, albeit contradistinctively, are contradistinctions that command her character, you could even say shape it, although they are the exact opposite of the Creator's intention and what her ancestors embodied.

With her scientific efforts, Mischa strove to pave humanity's way into a tomorrow of unburdened life by advancing technological progress. A progress, however, as *she* defined it. A definition that had no syntax for mysticism, or anything she could not rationally dissect, nor for the hidden fascination it contained. The same applied to her view of yesterday and the day before, to how she saw what was and what is gone forever; the *passato*, as she scornfully referred to it. There was nothing you could do about it, so it wasn't worth the effort, she contended, nor was religion, poetry and other excesses of the human mind – her term for phenomena the enclosure of natural sciences –impervious to rational explanation and objective analysis. This was her lifeline, the unshakeable foundation of her existence where she securely held all things in control, ruled her own fate instead of falling into the bottomless pit of uncertainty; divorced from all imponderables and powers that eluded her understanding and influence. She believed that anyone stepping from the protective realm of science into transcendental ether would be caught in a web of speculation, trapped in a labyrinth of illusions, lost on the road to surrealism from which there was no return to the nuts and bolts of reality, the only thing that counted. Such people would be wasting the limited time they had until their deaths, and they would be well advised to strive to penetrate the truth of what factually is, and, if possible to advance humanity. This was one of the few fallacies of her otherwise unerring intellect, but a decisive one. What she considered security, was no more than a chimera. Like many worshippers of the God Science, she was a prisoner of rules, formulas and principles that explained the world without emotionally perceiving her. And only those who carry the world in their hearts see her pure beauty and take care not to violate her.

Chapter 1

February in Vienna was bitterly cold that year. Filthy, frozen gray snow glazed the streets and sidewalks. Tram wheels shrieked over tracks. The sun gave but rare appearances as the seamless, heavy cloud curtain seldom lifted. Street lanterns and show windows only faintly penetrated the foggy gloom and where there were none, people groped their way. Shadowy plump figures packed in thick winter coats, scarves wrapped tightly around head, ears and mouths, scurried past. Only one's own and others' clouds of carbon dioxide exiting lungs could be clearly seen hanging on the icy air, could even be smelled in the piercing cold. Extreme care must be taken not to slip on the treacherous ice and break a leg. There were endless accidents. Mass pile-ups let loose a constant howl of police and ambulance sirens. Hospitals were overrun. None of which in the least dampened spirits swept up in the ball season. Bad weather? Who cares!

Tonight was the uncontested climax, the shining star of the meteoric season, the Opera Ball. An annual event since the Congress of Vienna, when not hindered by war, the majestic Vienna Opera on *Kärntnerring* – destroyed by Hitler and fully restored according to the original blueprints – is transformed into the most beautiful and elegant ballroom in the city. Adorned with thousands of red and white roses, the noble venue is festooned, furnished, made a feast for the eyes for the event of the year where the *haute monde* of the old imperial city on the Danube rendezvous with luminaries from Hollywood to Cinecittá.

In the seventy hours following the final performance of the season – this year a Spanish tenor's rendering of Papageno in Mozart's *The Magic Flute* inspired thundering applause – an enormous rostrum is erected parterre upon which a vast dance floor of the finest parquet is installed. It was on this very dance floor in 1815 that Europe's noblest whirled when, as Napoleon was defeated for the second time, ultimately vanquished at the battle of Waterloo, the five mightiest men in Europe – the Russian Tsar, Austria's Emperor and the Kings of Prussia, Great Britain and France – gathered in Vienna to determine the future fate of Napoleon's crushed kingdom. Nine months long, the powerful and reinstated rulers accompanied by retinues of several thousand attendants, the city of Vienna was the center of the world. Not one member of the entourage was left behind to languish in their remote and abandoned castles: cooks, food tasters, tailors, footmen, coachmen, nannies, valets, handmaids, grooms and many more. They celebrated lavishly each night, as never before celebrated. Even then, the Opera Ball outshined them all.

Following the pageantry accompanying the Austrian President's entry – many of the thousands of guests mourned the lack of a Kaiser – one hundred and sixty young couples dressed in black tails and white ball gowns will officially open the dancing with waltzes by Strauss and polonaises by Ziehrer and Chopin. The world held its breath. The music was to be played by the Vienna Philharmonic. Each player was a highly gifted soloist, a music academy professor at the very least. The rich and beautiful of the world flocked to take part in this unparalleled event; to see the most divine waltz dancers in Vienna flying over the parquet in heavenly synchronicity and to hear the successors of Mozart and Beethoven conjure extra-terrestrial harmonies only to be heard here, in this concert hall without equal.

Prominence from the four corners of the world flocked to the event in the capital city of the defunct – but alive and well in the guests' imaginations -- dual monarchy. Decked out in the newest creations emerging from Parisian haute couture and Florentine Avant guard, they gracefully exited luxury limousines driven by liveried chauffeurs, tapped in high-heels carefully, but smiling, over the red carpet rolled out over the snow while a flash-storm of press photographers followed them to the entrance of the Holiest of Holies, their progress captured by television cameras of the world and brought to living rooms from Tokyo to San Francisco, from Murmansk to Tierra del Fuego. The names alone collected by equally renowned journalists and commentators filled the gossip columns and society pages: Hollywood stars, major politicians, sports legends and society lions. One of them, a multi-millionaire industrialist whose numerous marriages to and affairs with the world's most beautiful women are cross-cultural legend, was also noted for his loge guests, having invited over the years such icons as Sophia Loren, Pamela Anderson, Sarah Ferguson, Paris Hilton and other bearers of adulated names.

This year he had asked Mischa Turow, as newspapers and television dutifully circulated. She, however, turned him down, reasoning she held no interest in glamor and glitter. If one could believe the papers and television, this event apparently most fervently awaited by starlets, wannabe jet-setters, nouveau riche and parvenus was definitely not her cup of tea. She stated, allegedly, she had had her fill of publicity and had no desire to be the object of slathering covetousness yet again, thank you. But this she was, as little as she wanted to be, whether she attended the ball or not. This was a fact arising not from her exceptional scientific achievements, but more from her feminine allure, no matter how she regularly tried to dress it down. An outstanding mind coupled with uncommon beauty was a rare combination in a country where only a few decades ago Nazis persecuted and murdered her predecessors, regardless of how intelligent or attractive they had been, simply because of their faith. Even those who had turned away from it, choosing to worship the god of Science, fell.

Nevertheless, a friend and colleague at the university, had persistently cajoled and badgered her until she finally surrendered and reluctantly agreed to accompany him to the Opera Ball. At least she would be spared the ennui in the aging millionaire's loge, enduring his hackneyed advances. None of her friends could fathom her distate. Any of them would have leapt at the chance to bathe in Croesus' glow and bask in the Vienna Opera spotlights.

The man who pressed her into the dubious honor of attending the Vienna Opera Ball went by the name of Richard von Zehlendorff, a German, ten years her senior, but not obviously so. Although a man of the mind, he kept his body young and healthy by training several hours a day in the weight room. A Biochemistry professor at the Vienna University where the illustrious Sigmund Freud is still considered an *unperson* – as he was branded by the National Socialists' absurdly obsessive racial fanaticism upon their triumphant invasion in March 1938 – because he was a Jew, like Mischa Turow and therefore, according to the racial ladder the Nazis had fabricated, stood on the lowest rung although he stood at the top of the intellectual ladder, a place utterly foreign to Nazis. It had no value for the ***Übermenschen*** they believed themselves to be. Yet that was all in the past and unworthy of Mischa's time or mental energy.

So here they were. She and Richard made their way up the broad marble steps, the meeting point of all those seeking a *tête-à-tête* with social luminaries both native and foreign, or of those who simply came to marvel or even hoped to find their future mate among the assembled. There was no better place in this contradictory country, still and all permeated by the Habsburgers, when love plays a lesser role in marriage. As was the case with many this evening. Mischa wore a floor-length black dress, its simplicity a stark contrast to the other women's ornate robes. She wore no jewelry at all and no more makeup than usual – a touch of powder on her cheeks, traced lips and eye lids. She had held her hair underwater and let it air-dry, which only enhanced her ravishing beauty. All eyes were on her; the men desirous, the women envious. She was accustomed to being gawked at but had never been able to take it in stride. She hated the greedy-amorous gazes.

She and the not much less attractive man at her side drew the photographers' attention and they began taking multiple shots. She gruffly ordered them to stop, but the pictures were already taken and would bring an excellent price. Over the next days, they will be published in newspapers and magazines, with or without the subject's consent. They were celebrities, ergo public property, and as long as the photos were not strictly intimate, the viewed personage forfeited the right of ownership granted any other so-called unimportant person.

"Let's go directly to your table," she suggested, "and get away from this constant gaping and flashing."

"Of course," her replied, "we've only a few more steps to take."

He had reserved a table for two in one of the upper galleries that offered a divine view of the parterre and the loges on the lower levels, which began slowly to fill. They took their seats. Richard succeeded in ordering two glasses of champagne from a hastily passing waiter. Before he could return with their beverages, he took her hands, sought and found her eyes and asked her without preamble, without professing his love for her, if she would be his wife. They had no mutual history, no leisurely courtship, no opportunity to become attuned to one another, no mutual experiences, not a moment of intimacy or trust, no secret or secreted converging of sparked emotion, not one shared night. There was nothing but the thrill of complete surprise, the amazement of the thoroughly unexpected, the kindled desire of the immediate moment that also infected her even though he was not one of her customary slaves. And precisely that electrified her, aroused her hopes of finally experiencing the love granted every other woman but seemed denied her. Any other woman would have deemed this precipitous, unforeseeable marriage proposal absurd, would have dismissed it with an ironic smile and casual remark. But she took it seriously, as if it were a new physics discovery that held her spellbound, robbed her of sleep. She perceived unprecedented feelings of excitement, impatience and happy anticipation. Pulsating thrusts of heat flowed from his fingers, firmly yet tenderly closed around hers. Was this the storied tingle she had never known, or merely nervousness in the face of his proposal? She didn't know, didn't really care. She surrendered to the pleasure of the moment, its tension, its spontaneity, the hot wave that began to spark her desire.

It was not the first time a man had asked for her hand in marriage, but she had not seen this one coming. Especially not on this evening at the opera, the first evening they had ever spent together, having never before even approached one another. Richard was a man who had no difficulty winning over women, be it for one night or longer. This was common knowledge at the university. He had already had many affairs, yet no long-term relationships. Mischa had so far rejected all marriage proposals, and they had not been few in number, without a moment's hesitation. The men aspiring to share her life and bed presumed they were her equals, yet in fact were, to a man, intellectually far inferior. But that was not the most decisive reason for her rejection. She simply couldn't imagine finding sexual satisfaction in marriage that she found with her anonymous one-night stands, with whom she could exercise her inherent passion for domination with abandon, reveling in cruelty without consequence or emotional upheaval. She was convinced both were inevitable, should she indulge her sexual preferences with a man she knew, who was a friend or colleague. Aside from her sporadic sexual excesses with strangers, this was the reason, unbeknownst and unfathomable to her countless hopefuls, why she had never entered into a binding relationship. But this proposal was different from all those preceding it. It came from a man who played in the same league she did; a man who inspired admiration. Was he the one? Could he cure her of the sadistic sickness she suffered? The heat that flushed her body when he proposed and continued to spread seemed an unmistakable harbinger of happiness to come.

She did not answer right away. She looked in his face for some time before asking him, in an attempt to buy time and not sell herself off to quickly even though she had already given herself away, "Do you love me Richard?"

"What a question," he replied. "I love you more than I have ever loved a woman before, Mischa. Which is why I want to marry you and spend my life with you."

She was displeased with the latter part of his answer.

"For a moment there I was seriously considering your proposal, Richard," she said, "but I do not want to spend my entire life with a man who only loves me. There must be more, mutual interests and, more importantly, intellectual compatibility."

Her objection did not discourage him. There wasn't the slightest change in his expression, his smile, his confidence or his charm. She admired him for that. Every man she had thus far rejected had either abruptly stood up in disappointment and left or his happy excitement shifted immediately into hopeless despair, turning the rest of the evening into monosyllabic boredom, even once ending in a fiasco of mutual accusation. Richard was cut of a different cloth. He had seen the momentary shine in her eyes when he had proposed; had taken note of her lengthy hesitation before answering. He was confident that this extraordinary woman whom he more than admired would, on this special evening, agree to be his wife. There was no better time or opportunity. A woman of her caliber was worth being asked twice. None of the feminine creatures he had spent time with so far came even close to her. How could he utter such an idiotic sentence when she asked if he loved her? He was angry at himself but didn't show it. Aside from his desire for her, it was precisely their mutual interests; the soaring intelligence they had in common, the prospect of sharing profound conversations after making love – an appetite he longed to satisfy – that had inspired him to spontaneously ask her to marry him. Here, amid the majestic opulence of the Vienna Opera. In any case, she hadn't brusquely rejected him, as she had some university colleagues as they put it when telling their lovelorn tales. He just knew she would be his tonight, or maybe it was him who would be hers, what difference did it make? Whichever, it had to happen tonight!

Meanwhile, the capacious opera house had noisily filled. Intermittent staccatos from violins, violas and trombones occasionally penetrated the din of chatter and trampling feet. The orchestra was fine-tuning their instruments one last time, to ensure each note resounded in crystalline clarity. Not a single free seat could be seen in the loges, except those in the as yet unoccupied Kaiser Loge, which during the unpopular Republic passed perforce into the possession of the red-blooded, not blue-blooded, Austrian Federal President. People were already crowding onto both sides of the parterre in eager anticipation of the hundred sixty debutantes' entrée in their wide, sweeping, airy white ball gowns on the arms of their cavaliers.

Before Richard could speak further and repair his bumbling sentence of a few minutes ago, trumpets blared loudly, announcing the arrival of the Kaiser's surrogate, the Austrian Federal President. He appeared with his wife on his arm, an elderly, frumpishly styled woman. Her black hair was piled high, inciting much subdued laughter. The pair made their way to the last free loge, the best and largest of all, amid obligatory applause. They seated themselves ponderously and waved benevolently at the crowd, which was a bit awkward. Although they were not even a ghostly imitation of the imperial couple and the applause a mere chip of courtesy and respect, the sound of hundreds of cameras clicking could be clearly heard. The wildly flickering flashbulbs now ceased. From this moment an, they were strictly forbidden to disturb the ball and the performing dancers who, any moment now, would proudly step onto the parquet, conscious that half of the world was watching them. Breathlessly, the world awaited their entrance and the sweeping waltzes of Vienna's *jeunesse dorée* that would exhilarate and enkindle the audience as no other dance at this moment had the power to do. This was the ball's absolute climax, direct at the onset of a gala night extending until five in the morning, where the uncontested Vienna master, Johann Strauss, was annually awakened to life.

Mischa was overcome by the frantic excitement in her breast, rising and falling as if she had just reached the pinnacle of a high mountain. She was caught up in wildly coursing thoughts without an anchor as Richard inspired more passion in her than any other man begging her favor. Was he truly different than all the others? She longed to believe it, she yearned for a profound love she had never felt before; a normal life that she had yet to lead.

There they were, following the call: *Let Us Waltz!* Eighty young princes in black tails, unparalleled in elegance, the issue of Vienna's noblest dance schools where they had been meticulously prepared for the greatest event in their young lives, leading their radiantly virginal ladies in white into the ballroom their smiles and grace captivating. They took their positions and at once began to whirl in breath-taking synchronicity to heavenly music that clouded the senses. Feathery light, they flew over the parquet like divine birds, as if the world belonged only to them and there was nothing that could disrupt the harmony and ecstasy of their universe. Their performance galvanized the assemblage, including Mischa and Richard. He led her onto the dance floor, held her in his arms as if she were the most beautiful and airiest of all princesses, transporting her to spheres of ethereal sound and stimuli that literally electrified her. Trembling, eagerness and hunger. The dancing excited her as nothing before ever had. She quaked in anticipation of more, much more; at the prospect of union with this man she felt on her body, whose breath she smelled, whose eyes she met, whose hands caressed her. She had never experienced such erotic yearning, had never been consumed by such feeling for a man.

Now it was her who hoped her would propose again, or least wrest her into his bed tonight. She must have this man, feel him inside her as soon as possible, even at the price of marriage, which, it occurred to her, was not such an erroneous thought. On the contrary. She hoped for it as if there had never been anything more desirable in her life. For over an hour, he whirled and swung her over the dance floor, intensifying her ecstasy at every new turn. He watched her transformation from initial skepticism and resistance to desire and hunger. He touched her randomly, as if unintentionally, in the most intimate places on her body. She not only allowed it, she took deep pleasure from it. Amid the prevailing bliss in the pressing, waltzing crowd, no one took notice of them and they gave their fingers free rein. As they wordlessly returned to their table, drenched in sweat, she pushed him into a corner. She could care less who saw her. Her lips pressed into his and she kissed him passionately, thrusting her tongue deeply into his mouth. It was the first time in her life she had done such a thing.

The ensuing night of love washed over Mischa like a wave of an undiscovered ocean. All that she had hoped for came to be. Immediate and unexpected, her dreams emerged from the realm of fantasy and wishful thinking and became reality, a glorious reality. She had no need for sadistic devices, her senses heaved and rose to the acme of craving and fulfilment. With Richard, she reached orgasm faster and more often than with any of her anonymous slaves, felt euphoria mounting, endless rapture transporting her body to the clouds, far above reality and all that had come before. She arrived at the place she had always hoped to attain, perhaps even going a bit further, a bit higher into the heavens of passion and bliss.

The moment Richard left, she was struck with renewed desire for him. She longed to feel him inside her again, craved the flicker and flames of the endless inferno chasing through her body in a wild hunt. She ached for the ecstasy only he could awaken in her. She was obsessed with Richard and what he did to her, began to feel for him in a way she had always avoided feeling, ever-alert to circumventing complications and consequences before they could arise. But it was precisely these feelings that drew her to Richard, his absence triggering a physical pain, a symptom of unappeased desire. This was not love, not a profound affection or true sense of belonging to him. It was the recurring exhilaration of an addict, the compulsion of an alcoholic, drug user or gambler. Yet she turned her mind from this thought, preferring to believe it was an unbreakable bond that would unite her with her supposed lover forever.

Two months later, they married, much to the amazement of their friends. Richard was the object of endless envy, being the lucky man who had won the heart of Mischa, the most beautiful, most intelligent and most unapproachable woman in Vienna.

As Richard had long before agreed to a lecture tour throughout the U.S.A. and Asia, they were only together one more time between their first shared night and the wedding. He returned on the day of the wedding. They were married by a justice of the peace at the Vienna Registry Office without the presence of their families, yet all the more friends and colleagues. As they stepped from the building, they were greeted by a sea of faces, many of them those cheering gawkers who come out of the woodwork on such occasions, parading their all-consuming envy and jealousy as admiration. And of course, there were the journalists and photographers who gave them no rest, pursuing them at every turn, impossible to shake off. The reception took place at the deeply traditional *K&K (Kaiser & Kaiserin)* Hotel in *Hietzing*, located at the entrance to the

Imperial Menagerie which had become the city's civilian zoo. They celebrated until dawn became broad daylight and no few married men and women were party to infidelity in the establishment's dark side rooms and secluded garden niches. They suffered through it impatiently, deaf to the accolades, speeches, skits and well wishes, only yearning to get away as soon as possible to pursue the sexual joys they had been denied since Richard's departure three weeks prior. They said their good-byes immediately following the second course of the gala dinner, which did not diminish their guests' excesses in the least, rather spurred them on. Quite the contrary, it enflamed them. Aside from the newlyweds, who carried out their physical union fully within the dictates of social acceptability, the night was rife with adultery – a wedding celebration like any other. Although there was no sadomasochism in Mischa and Richard's love-making, neither was there tenderness aside from the heartfelt hugs and fervent kisses, which were more an expression of passion than of love, which they both misconstrued. Many believe sexual fulfilment is the best prerequisite for a lasting marriage, an opinion they both held with conviction.

Chapter 2

Their honeymoon took them to southern California where in the early spring, beneath the hot rays of a lightly veiled sun, they bathed in the Pacific, although or perhaps because, the cold ocean current traversing the U.S. American Westcoast in April kept the water from warming overly much. It tingled on their skin, gave them goose bumps. But after a few minutes in the water, they no longer felt the cold. Nor did the tepid, northeast trade-wind blowing out to sea hinder them. They surrendered completely to their bodies' hunger and believed they were in paradise.

No one knew where they were headed. They rented a car at the airport in San Diego and drove along Highway 1, searching for a small hotel on the beach where they wouldn't be recognized and could enjoy seven delightful days of undisturbed intimacy. Close to Del Mar, they found a boarding house, an imposing villa of Victorian architecture with romantic guest rooms, lathed colonnades, white wooden balconies, ornate iron parapets and struts and a broad roofed veranda on the ground floor. The structure stood somewhat elevated on a boulder bluff. Long, winding, narrow stairs led down to the seemingly endless sandy beach which, at most times of the day, lay abandoned. They believed it was the most beautiful place on earth. They hurled themselves exuberantly into the spraying spume of the waves, swimming far from the shore, coupling ardently in the salty water. They took long, barefoot walks along the beach in the evenings, making love in secluded places witnessed only by an enormous blood-orange sun sinking into the ocean and made love a gain in their room's creaking wooden bed. They ate divine crabmeat with lemon and lobster drenched in melted butter. In short, they enjoyed three marvelous days.

On the fourth day, their delight, isolation and anonymity came to an abrupt halt. TV and press had sniffed out their whereabouts and shattered their peace. They relinquished their room and took off in their rented car, driving North without a specific destination in mind. Yet, the further north they came, the thicker and faster the tourism and crowds they hoped to avoid. The media stuck to their heels, dogging their every move. It wasn't until they had left Oceanside in San Clemente that they could shake off the last mobile camera. They tore through a red light and abruptly turned into the driveway, invisible from the intersection, leading down into the subterranean garage of a large hotel. They had escaped. Taking a room, they fell onto the bed, exhausted. It was the first night neither of them thought about sex, they were simply too tired. Mischa found herself grateful for the respite. She remembered the last time they made love, not twelve hours ago. It was the first time she had not climaxed. She had simulated orgasm, so as not to disappoint Richard. She sought the reason everywhere but in the incipient routine and fading incitement of novel, unchartered waters and was certain it was a one-time occurrence that would not repeat itself.

She was wrong. Instead of being an exception, it became the rule. Richard's hunger for her was unabated, but her desire for him ebbed, especially after they had cut their honeymoon a day short, returning to Vienna and their daily university duties. Her passion decayed into apathetic athletics which she side-stepped, inventing ever-changing excuses. She feigned head-aches, exhaustion or a heavy menstrual flow. Richard was well aware that the tidal wave of her former sexual abandoned had completely receded. He tried to reawaken her passion with in-tensified ministrations and tenderness, with roses, gifts, kisses and romantic dinners. Yet the more he reached for her, the more she escaped him. Instead of giving her time, keeping his distance, which may have reawakened her desire for him, he pressed her constantly, achieving the exact opposite of what he longed for, remembering events of the recent past with yearning.

Since she felt no love for him, and never had; since the ini-tial joys of sex with him had lost their attraction, yes, repulsed her, his constant courting quickly galled her. Richard became more than vexatious. His touch was unbearable, sickened her. She took every opportunity to avoid being alone with him, coming home late, accepting invitations to lectures and con-gresses she had previously habitually rejected, flying here and there. She returned to her chess club, where she was received with enthusiasm – anything or anywhere that served to escape intimacy with her hastily wed husband. Within a few weeks, her hunger had turned to nausea and the love she had deluded herself into believing she felt for him became contempt, bor-dering on loathing. She admitted to herself that her wish for a normal life, a normal marriage like other couples had tricked her into believing she was in love. Now she knew that so-called normalcy meant nothing to her. It repulsed her, disgusted her. What use was a husband she didn't love, for whom she didn't bear a shred of affection, who couldn't even provide the sexual satisfaction she needed like a fish needs water, a bird needs air?

Had she for one moment believed her appetite for submissive men, her craving to punish and torture them was a sickness she could cure by marrying Richard, she was now convinced this was no sickness, but an inherent faculty clearly setting her apart from other women, just as sequestering as her outstanding intelligence and perfect body. Nature had provided her with and selected her to embody these traits, had elevated her above the rest, so why should she not express them, feast on them? She could no longer endure being in the same room with Richard. What she had recently hungered for, his tenderness, his ferocity, his laughter, his stoic somberness, his superiority and his charm, his way of possessing her, all this revolted her, robbed her of her freedom and air to breathe, kept her from being herself, from expressing her nature, from appeasing her hunger which grew with each day of fasting.

During a lecture tour in London, she resumed her old habit. Wearing a long, blond, wig, dark glasses and gaudy makeup – what she never usually did – she prowled the pleasure quarters of Soho. No one recognized her. For the first time since her wedding, she picked up a willing slave, a shy, weedy, pale-faced musician who gave her endless orgasms as she tortured and abused him. From that day on, she wanted only one thing – to dump Richard as fast as she could. As soon as she got home, she announced she didn't love him and wanted a divorce. He was stunned. Only eight weeks after their wedding! He did all he could to change her mind, but she was adamant, her decision was nonnegotiable. She asked him to pack his things and leave her penthouse on the Vienna Graben that very day, which he did, bewildered and suffering to the depths of his being. He had believed she was bound to him, as he was to her, in profound love. He had failed to realize she was only interested in satisfying her lust – she was incapable of love.

The divorce followed through smoothly in mutual consent without division of matrimonial property as the marriage was too quickly annulled and neither of them was dependent on the pecuniary support of the other. The press had a field day, screaming out the news in huge headlines. Professor friends and faculty at the university felt sorry for Richard who could not disguise his abysmal bitterness. They just knew it, they told him, he had failed to realize that Mischa was not a woman for life-long fealty and had married too quickly. He had underestimated the risk he was taking, had blindly delivered himself into the hands of a woman no one really knew, whose nature, when admittedly brilliant through and through, was a mystery to everyone who knew her. Despite the fact that Richard insisted the marriage crumbled shortly after their honeymoon without the slightest drama or altercation, his colleagues were more than incredulous. Many of them thought Richard was lying, that he had abused her or something terrible had happened about which neither he nor Mischa chose to talk. No one, not even Richard, suspected that the sole reason for their separation lay in Mischa's addiction to sadistic sex. No one, unless they had been on the receiving end of her perverse passion, could have imagined it in their wildest dreams.

Chapter 3

In an attempt to put her intermezzo with Richard behind her, Mischa submerged herself in her physics research with a vengeance. She probed for answers to the questions arising from her dynamo theory. Since, as with all great insights into the ways of the world that have revealed themselves to human thought since the times of Archimedes and Pythagoras, the dimension of ignorance behind them is vastly larger. Every two doors closing on a scientific discovery open twenty more, the existence of which no one had imagined. Socrates declared that the only thing he knew was that he knew nothing and the atheistic Jew Albert Einstein discovered God at the end of his research, in whom he had never before believed. The most ignorant of all creatures is the one who claims to know everything there is to know and there is nothing new to discover. There have always been such imbeciles, and always will be. Stupidity is as rampant as weeds choking out the flowers on a meadow. But these flowers will always be sought by those not content with the monochrome of green.

This time, however, and for the first time at that, progress eluded Mischa. All her searching and calculating led nowhere but back to her initial question. Despite endless efforts, she was going around in circles. Was it thoughts of Richard haunting her? Was it the impatient anticipation of new slaves to torment? Or was it the impending World Championship preliminary competition against the leading female chess masters from around the globe that distracted, excited and occupied her mind? She couldn't say. Despite all her renowned analytical acuity, she could not answer find answers to her scientific questions, neither could she fathom and resolve the contradictions awakened in her soul that plunged her into an unaccustomed confusion of self-reflection and purgation, of conflicting thoughts and attempts to purify herself of past mistakes. Outwardly, she appeared to others as she always had, an intelligent, personable yet aloof woman, her reputation and aura untouched by the recently failed marriage to Richard von Zehlendorff. But internally, a battle raged that she had no chance of winning.

Failing to make advancements in her scientific work or to forget her intermezzo with Richard and to quiet the turmoil that had taken hold of her, she decided to turn her energies toward preparing for the chess championship since chess, as she played it, permeated every nook and cranny of her mind, leaving no space for worries, cares, scientific calculation or anything else, for that matter.

Her first opponent would be Grandmaster Tatjana Lewinskaja, winner of the Russian National Championship. Tatjana held the sixth position in international ranking with 2625 Elo points, two places and 15 points above Mischa. Although it was a narrow margin, it spoke of her opponent's comprehensive chess finesse. Ms. Lewinskaja was born into a Jewish family of doctors, artists and scientists in St. Petersburg with a far-reaching chess-playing tradition. She only played mixed tournaments, as the men and women's tournaments brought more prestige and increased the value of her Elo index more

than women-only tournaments. Most recently, she had played
in the highest category of Moscow's legendary Aeroflot Tournament, in which over one hundred of the strongest Grandmasters regularly participate. Tatjana Lewinskaja shared second
place, only a half-point behind the current men's world champion against whom she had miraculously achieved a draw,
extracting herself from a seemingly doomed position on the
chess board. This brilliant game was analyzed, commented and
celebrated as a sensation in all trade journals.

As she always did when preparing to meet a specific opponent, Mischa accessed all of her rival's previous games on the
internet. She studied her preferred opening moves with black
and white, dissected her middlegame and endgame strengths
and weaknesses and sought out the errors that had cost her the
few confrontations she had lost. She discovered a questionable
16th move in the *Sweschnikov Variation* of the *Sicilian Defense*
as well as other, tiny imprecisions in her opponent's game.
Most tournament players would never have noticed them, but
Mischa found them. They were like miniscule holes in a sack of
flour, from which the entire contents slowly but surely trickle.
These tiny holes were enough for her to face the preliminary
rounds with confidence. They were the undiscovered leaks
slowly but surely draining Lewinskaja's chess virtuosity.

The phone rang. It was her friend Rita Sokol, a talented
young doctor specializing in neurology. She was only a year older
than Mischa, had recently absolved her final exams with honors
and now assisted Professor Dr. Eugen Roth, a world-renowned
neurosurgeon who, a few weeks ago, had successfully performed
open brain surgery on China's Communist Party Chairman,
Li Tao Hong, one of the most powerful men in the world. A
news-worthy event the media duly reported in detail. Rita invited Mischa to a casual dinner at her small apartment in the

9th district, a stone's throw from the General Hospital where she worked. Mischa had been there often, could talk to Rita about everything except her sexual fantasies that went beyond the imaginary. Professor Roth, unmarried and a good story-teller, would also be coming, Rita told her, and bringing a friend with him, a young U.S. American brain surgeon who also had a good sense of humor – according to Roth. We'll see, she added.

Mischa accepted the invitation gladly. She was happy for an excuse to escape her work, her chess studies and the persistent thoughts she couldn't divert, no matter how she tried. She looked forward to a relaxed, witty and humorous gathering with delicious food, as Rita was an excellent cook, which she most certainly wasn't. She had always bypassed cooking, baking and other household chores as she had, in her opinion, better things to do. Rita was cut from a different cloth altogether. She didn't cook because she had to feed her husband or family, she cooked for the pure joy of it, magicking the most exotic, ever-changing variations of east Asian specialties, subtly and originally spiced. Her cooking was divine, elevating the senses, their aromas those of traditional Thai street food or Japanese ryokans. Most were her own creations, not to be found on any restaurant menu. On such occasions, her modest apartment in Vienna was transported to Bangkok, Kuala Lumpur of former Saigon, to Shanghai or Osaka. With little effort expertly applied, Rita's profound affinity with the world of Han emperors, of Siam, of Samurais and Geishas brought the origins of the evening's dishes to her dining room. It took only a lotus blossom or bonsai, an artfully placed dragon image on silk or smoking Hikali Koh incense, with lights dimmed and hands folded, and head slightly bowed she received her guests with the request to remove their shoes – and her tiny home in Vienna took on an Indochinese or Hokkaido ambience.

It was already four in the afternoon. Mischa shut down her computer and went down to the Graben to find a gift for Rita. She struck upon the perfect thing in the large, well-stocked toy store offering, over several floors, the most exceptional wares, from pre-Napoleonic tin soldiers to the latest remote-controlled children's cars that were just as frequently bought by adults. She purchased a small robot with the melodious name *Robomax*. *Robomax* could not only speak, move and take care of chores, he could also generously expose himself. Pressing a button on the remote control caused his clothes to vanish, revealing a naked, well-formed, muscular male body. Another button illuminated the inner organs beneath his 'skin.' *Robomax* carried out his duties clothed, naked or as a skeleton, depending on his master's or mistress's wishes. Mischa was tempted to keep him for herself, as he triggered the most bizarre thoughts. But this was not an occasion for titillation, this evening was dedicated to a pleasurable evening with friends in a casual, relaxed milieu.

As was her wont when going out for the evening, Mischa spent little time dressing up. She merely doused her hair in the shower, forewent the blow-dryer, pulled on a pair of black jeans, a black blouse and her everyday heels; her entire makeup consisting of a touch of powder to her cheeks and refreshing her eye-shadow. She didn't find what she saw particularly desirous when she threw a quick glance in the mirror. Bur she didn't give a rap about how she affected men, as long as they panted after her like dogs and satisfied her lust like bulls. She chose her men, not the other way around. She drew them like moths to a candle, could pick her slaves from an arsenal better supplied than the largest army. It was her dominant character, her laughing, superior presence, her confidence, her self-certainty that she could attain and have anything she wanted, that threw the men at her feet, and not only those who served her licentious purposes. And it was by no means a prerequisite that the brain of the latter be no larger than his reproductive organ, there were scholars and academics among them. For many, especially those whose parents refused to feed their hunger for freedom and self-definition in childhood, education does not supplant the greed for being tyrannized, be it by the mother or a dominant sex partner. They can only find love by perpetuating the physical or psychological suffering they have known since infancy. Particularly in Germany and Austria, where Wilhelmine and imperial-royal discipline – the ruling class ethic to ensure continuation of power – was imposed upon the people long after the monarchy's demise, unfortunate children and children's children were brought into this world. They grew up to give Hitler an inexhaustible stockpile of submissive followers and accomplices as well as providing women like Mischa an enormous supply of compliant prey.

True to form, Rita had once more prepared a Lucullan meal. As an appetizer, she devised a leafy, wild herb salad dressed in borage, olive oil, balsamic vinegar and wheat kernels, topped with king prawns over which she had sprinkled freshly grated wasabi directly before serving. The main course was a divinely delicious veal roulade sautéed in butter, the filling and seasoning she kept secret, while dessert was dark chocolate and maraschino drizzled over fresh fruit *palacsintas*, the likes of which are rarely found, even in Vienna, the unequivocal capital of *palacsinta*. Professor Roth was truly an entertaining story-teller, but not the only contributor to the delightful and hilarious mood. Mischa and Rita also did their goodly bit. Only Roth's acquaintance, the young, U.S. American brain surgeon was still for the greater part of the evening. His name was Jonathan Brady, called Joe for short. He came from New Jersey, was around thirty-five, tall and slim with dark blonde hair and an exceptionally attractive face. There was need for timidity, particularly since he possessed razor-sharp wits. Although he rarely spoke, when he did, his intelligence shone through. His silence was not a result of preferred restraint, but an inferiority complex, either inherent or instilled in childhood. Precisely this shy reserve attracted Mischa, awoke her diabolical senses from sleep she felt had lasted much too long.

Joe was the exact opposite of Richard, who did all the talking and figuratively flexed his muscles at every opportunity. Mischa was certain this reticent American would make a wonderfully subservient slave, but squelched the thought at once, trying to suppress her burgeoning desire. They had met socially and now that he had accepted a position at the Vienna General Hospital, she would not be able to banish him from her life after he had served her purposes, as she had with all his predecessors. And yet, the longer she observed him, the hotter the fire burned in her breasts and between her legs. Rita and Professor Roth were too absorbed in their conversation to take note of her stolen glances, but Joe did and turned his face away to escape them. Not because he thought Mischa unattractive, but because he, like all bashful men, feared making an ass of himself, especially in front such a lovely and clever woman like Mischa. As the evening progressed, she had increasing difficulty shaking off her lascivious thoughts. Her distorted fantasy played detailed mind movies of what she would do with him. She had rarely encountered a more apt target for rioting away her sadism, with less restraint and more abandon than ever.

As was so often the case, her compulsion won out over her rationale. She had to have him, damn the consequences, damn the risk of knowing him socially. She would somehow manage to banish him like all the others once she had exhausted her need for torture and fornication. Or who knows? When he's as submissive, obedient and pliable as he is here, maybe she'll use him again.

Professor Roth said his good-byes at around eleven, explaining he had to get up at the crack of dawn to perform a difficult open-brain operation on a wealthy private patient, and wanted to approach the operating table fully rested. The man should get his money's worth, after all. Rita should also get to bed, he ordered, so she could assist him. God forbid they were inattentive or slipped up! The patient, another Russian oligarch, had flown with his private jet into Vienna, bringing along his entire entourage, family, private secretary and God only knows who else, expressly for Roth's talents and will pay exceptionally well. Should all go well, he had promised a respectable bonus. If the operation failed, Roth added, well, he couldn't take his wealth with him to the grave, he had told him at the preliminary examination. His eighth wife, a former bar dancer, would still have more than enough and his brood, with few exceptions, were ne'er-do-wells gleefully throwing his money out the window with both hands, wallowing in luxury they haven't earned and contributing diddly-squat to the well-being of humanity or society although they have the time and money to do so. He deemed his own humanitarian contributions, the source of his immense cashflow and other quickly amassed assets not worth mentioning. His close connection and groveling comradeship with the Russian president Sergej Ivanowitsch Kutin, however, was no secret and was certainly conducive to accumulating wealth.

Rita obeyed the professor's command and rose from her seat. Mischa took the hint, thanked her for the wonderful dinner and amusing evening. She should go, too, anyway and can take Joe home in her car. Joe hesitated to accept her offer, wanted to call a taxi, but Mischa wouldn't hear of it. "Nonsense!" she said. "You're coming with me. I'm not going to let you waste your money on a taxi. You don't have any Russian oligarchy patients like Professor Roth." And reeled in her squirming fish.

Roth jokingly told with his young colleague to keep his fingers off lovely Mischa. But the shy young man wouldn't have dared. Not for wanting, mind you. He longed for the courage to tell her how pretty and attractive he thought she was, but, as his nature dictated, he spoke not a word. If he had overcome his timidity and fear, had smiled at her and begun to flirt, her desire for him would have disintegrated. But he just stood there, abashed and silent, unaware that, thus, he came closer to fulfilling her wishes, but not as he imagined them to be. While driving down the road, she remarked that it was not yet late, and she could make him a coffee at her place, they could talk better there than at Rita's, where the other two had done all the talking. He began to protest but was already malleable clay in her hands.

"You're coming!" she said to him in a commanding tone with no room for rebuttal. He flinched. His obedience, yes, his docility intensified her want. She could barely wait to torment him, to do all the things she imagined to him, knowing it would bring her, when she showed no mercy, to the climax of lust.

They stepped through the penthouse door and without preamble she shoved him on her bed, planted one foot on either side of him and, towering over him, ordered him to strip lying down, don't even dare to get up. He tried to protest, but came no further than, "I thought…"

"You thought wrong!" she interrupted him rudely. "You'll get your coffee, but only if you're a good boy and do everything I tell you to do!"

"I'll do whatever you want," he whispered, never having thought in his wildest dreams that he would embark on a sex adventure with this stunning woman.

"Good," she answered. "You are now my slave. If you follow my orders to the letter, you will receive your reward at the end."

She handcuffed him to the bed and began with scintillating strokes of the whip that soon became keen and biting. She abused him cruelly with the spikes of her heels and in a hundred other ways as her frenzy mounted. He tried to free himself in vain, writhed and screamed in pain, which fed the fire, bringing her closer to climax. No one would have suspected what was happening in her apartment, no sound escaped the soundproofed walls, not even when he wailed in torment and she shrieked in ecstasy, a long and seemingly endless howl that gradually faded to a trembling whimper. She descended slowly from the heights of her climax, feeling the pricks of Eros' arrows along the way.

When, minutes later, she felt them no more, Joe was given his just reward, for her nothing more than an act of duty. She released his bonds only when the coffee was ready, ordering him to reappear tomorrow night at the same time. He agreed immediately and tried to kiss her in his clumsy, awkward manner. She pushed his head away like shooing a fly, merely commenting, "No kissing."

No quite completely dressed, she maneuvered him out the door and into the hallway, closed the door behind him and fell exhausted and satiated in bed. She slept wonderfully that night of divine indulgence.

As she left her house late in the afternoon next day, she ran into two other condominium owners, Dr. Emanuel Gutensohn, leading District Attorney in the sexual offense department and Wolf Mutter, a popular painter of the Vienna School of Fantastic Realism. She greeted both men cordially. Neither of them could possibly know she was a repeat offender and prime candidate for the criminal court's dock and would make an ideal model for a Fantastic Realism painting.

Chapter 4

For the first time, despite all the indwelling risks involved, Mischa had played out her sadistic addiction on an acquaintance, and even planned to repeat the performance. When breaking the law becomes easy, criminals become over-confident and make mistakes. The same applied to Mischa, although she was not a criminal – yet – as every one of the men, predominantly married, had volunteered to suffer her abuse, were eager for an opportunity to satisfy the zenith of their own unexplored sexual fantasies. Their conjugal status served Mischa well, since men obligated, either by the state or the church, keep quiet. They are more than anxious to keep their extramarital escapades a secret. Whether by force of habit, because of the children, to maintain a certain social status or for pecuniary reasons – that latter being the most common – they clung to a marriage that has long ceased anything more than mutual boredom and perfunctory coitus in the dark on rare nights.

As mentioned, this time she threw caution to the winds, receiving her victim a second night, one where she encountered him at a social dinner, and whom she would continue to bump into on occasion at the university. But that wasn't all. After their second adventure, Joe refused to be shaken off and discarded like all the other one-night stands she customarily roped in. Quite the contrary, he professed on bended knee his love and devotion, swore not to say a word to anyone if she would only let him come again. He would do everything for her, whatever she wanted; be her groveling and obedient slave; would wait for her patiently all day in her apartment until she came home at night; she could have him whenever and wherever she chose. She could treat him like a dog and he'd bark, like a pig and he'd grunt, he would lick her feet, just don't turn him away. Mischa was repulsed by this spineless man who, before the nurses and patients at the hospital, poses as the omniscient doctor, but abases himself before her, strips himself of all dignity, becomes a worm she could crush beneath her heels, should she so desire. But she was not out to crush worms.

Hers was not the sort of sadism intent on destroying her victims, determined to rob him of every shred of dignity, nor was she interested in his possessions or envious of his career. The singular purpose of her cruelty was the fleeting gratification of her libido. She could only reach a climax by inflicting pain. She needed a constant flow of new men since, with a few rare exceptions, her appetite for a particular man died after the first night. Only new men, never-seen-before stimuli could engulf her in the flames of passion. This was her only objective in her relations with men. She was obsessed by it, compelled to hunt for new strangers, like any incurable drug or alcohol addict, at the cost of her own body, if that be the price. Unlike drug or alcohol users, Mischa paid it gladly, as a matter of fact, it, along with the insatiable, egomaniacal, sex-obsessed demon in her soul, actually triggered her compulsion.

Loyalty, love, trust, steadfastness or other, similar Jewish or Christian mores were wholly alien to her, she deemed them standards that religion had force-fed the simple-minded, people unable to weigh and make judgments of their own. They did not apply to her, just as they had not applied to kings and queens, ladies and knights of bygone days, who simply plucked their playthings and bedmates from the common folk, claiming their services without a thought to earthly laws or divine commandments, which their chattels should obey to the letter or suffer dire penalties, either in this life or in the one beyond.

On the second night with Joe, Mischa failed to reach orgasm. He incessantly driveled on about love and living together, he be her slave or whatever she demanded of him, but this was exactly what she didn't want. His simpering took her over the edge and she wrestled him, half-dressed out the door, throwing the rest of his clothes behind him, turning the music up loud so as not to hear his pleading and banging on the other side of the door. What a wimp, she thought, what a miserable, pathetic twerp without a shred of pride or honor. She was determined to never look at him or waste her breath on him again.

But there he was the next day, standing at her office door at the university with an enormous bouquet of red roses. She quickly pulled him inside. Several colleagues had already collected in the hallway, wondering if this good-looking, tall man was Mischa's new lover. He was never to do such a thing again, she hissed, she had made it clear enough that she didn't anything more to do with him. If he even whispered to anyone what they had done the past two nights, she would kill him with her won two hands. He should be happy; he should be grateful that she had given him more pleasure than any other woman could ever give him instead of whining like a spoiled child. He's a grown man, should act like one and accept the facts, she added, and not risk his position at the hospital.

Joe could care less. Her harsh warning only served to in-
flame the desire he felt as her devoted, selfless slave. He fell to
his knees, his arms circling her legs and beseeched her not to
send him away, he would do anything, absolutely anything
for her, sign over his house, his bank account in the States;
he would give up his surgeon's practice to be her servant with
whom she could do as she pleased, if only she would let him
stay with her. Revolted, she thrust him away with her feet, one
of her stiletto heels puncturing his upper arm, causing a bloody
wound. Thoroughly exasperated, Mischa ran to get the first aid
kit from the cabinet and bandaged his injury. Joe enjoyed the
attention, was transported back to the nights when her sexual
sadism misused him, and he began to play the part of her
slave again. Mischa was at a loss. How to get rid of him? Any
moment now a student or colleague could come through the
door. She commanded him to sit on a chair, she had to make a
call. In desperation, she called Richard and asked him to come
to her office immediately to remove a persistent admirer who
refused to leave the room. When Joe heard this, he got up and
left her office without a word.

Mischa breathed a sigh of relief, called Richard back
and let him know it was taken care of, the intruder had left.
No, there was nothing more she wanted from him, she replied to his question, it was over between them, but she was
grateful, appreciated his willingness to help her. She hung up,
wiped Joe's blood from the floor, sat down and poured herself
a cognac. She was relieved that Joe had finally left and that
she could shake off Richard as well. As her knight in shining
armor, she probably would have had to repay him with a night
together, which would, for her, be an act of laborious loathing
instead of passionate pleasure. She hoped Joe had finally gotten
the message that he had no chance of winning her over, that

all his professions of love and submissive devotion fell on deaf ears. But she was mistaken, Joe had no intention of letting her go, could not tell the difference between her compulsion and his love. He took her sexual drive to which she surrendered by torturing him as a sign of love he need only reawaken. He thought her words of rejection reflected the kind of relationship she wanted with him, were a coded command that he continue courting her. He waylaid her at every opportunity, in the university corridors, on the street, at café's and at the theater. They were the talk of the university. Everyone assumed they were a couple and were merely having a lover's spat, which was nothing special. Mischa had no one she could talk to about it, no one whose advice she could take. She didn't know what to do, didn't want to involve the police by accusing him of stalking or mobbing as the risk was too great that her secret would be exposed, her sexual tendency to carry our carnal acts of sadism with total strangers would come to light, would make the press and she would lose her professorship, her standing as a scientist and maybe even as a chess player would be forever destroyed.

No, she had to find another way to get rid of Joe once and for all; to banish the latent danger he posed now and in the foreseeable future. There was only one solution, she would have to kill him without leaving any traces that could lead back to her. She immediately ruled out shooting, poisoning and hanging; considered faking a traffic accident, household disaster, an artificially induced heart attack, but dismissed these ideas as well. A boat accident, that's it! That was the perfect thing, the only right way to do it. Anyone could have such a Malheur in a small motorboat, no more than a nutshell in the hands of unpracticed navigators, of falling into the Danube and drowning in the mighty river, swept away in its implacable current with all other debris. Even better, she would fall into the river with him, that would be most convincing, eliminating any thoughts or suspicions that she could have murdered him.

She was an excellent swimmer, had won the Zurich Canton Championship in her high school days; had crossed Lake Zurich in record time more than once. She was certain she could reach the shore from anywhere in the broad and dangerous river, even from the center or from middling white waters, especially since now, in June, the water temperature was less daunting as it had been some weeks ago. It would look like a common accident. No one would think it had been murder. She only had to be certain they were far from any residential area, from any possible witnesses, but that was not a problem. The Danube flowed through Austria for more than three hundred miles. There was a plethora of isolated, unobserved stretches. And it would be child's play to lure the naïve, besotted Joe to such a place. He only had to believe his persistence had won her over and she wanted to be with him again.

She made painstakingly precise preparations, drove southbound along the wide river from Vienna to Linz. Unfortunately, due to lowlands stretching on both sides, steep cliffs or vineyards, it took some time before she finally found a suitable place at a boat rental between Tulln and Krems. Her Swiss motorboat license was still valid from her younger days at Lake Zurich, and she booked a small 75-hp boat for the coming weekend. Joe would certain have time or eagerly make time when she invited him. She called him up that day and asked him. He immediately accepted although he was on duty at the hospital, he would call in sick, which wasn't a lie, he was lovesick for her, after all.

His heart sang when she cheerfully, which he mistook for happy anticipation, made a date to meet him at the above-mentioned boat rental on Saturday morning. She realized, she told him on the phone, her voice convincingly oozing coquette invitation, she didn't want to admit it to herself, but he was right, she did love him, and she was grateful that he hadn't backed down in the face of her idiotic denial. He was the right man for her, in her bed and in her life, she knew that now without a doubt. He should bring two bottles of champagne, so they could celebrate their reunion; she wanted to couple with him on the boat while the irregular waves profoundly enhanced their sexual senses; she had discovered the most romantic stretch to be found on the Danube between Salzburg and Vienna. It would an unforgettable excursion, that they would remember for rest of their lives. Of that, she was certain, if not as Joe imagined it to be.

"Of course, my darling," Joe responded, his heart filled with joy. "You are the love of my life. I will never give you up again. You belong to me and no one else. No, I belong to you, and only you. You can do what you will with me, no matter what this may be. I'll be there with more than champagne in tow, you'll be amazed!"

If Mischa had felt any subconscious compunction about carrying out her plan, Joe's final words erased them from her mind before they could arise to the surface. She belonged to no man, least of all Joe. Wasn't the love-crazed declaration he just made nothing more than a clearly expressed death-wish? He said she could do with him what she will. Most likely he would take unparalleled sexual pleasure, would soar to the summit of ecstasy when his adored mistress not only punished him but transported him from life into death. Yes, he will experience the keenest orgasm in his pathetic life at the moment of his death. What could be more exalting for worm like him, she thought, than to die at the highest heights of sensual excitement. She was now supremely determined to carry out her plan.

Chapter 5

Any minute now, the Danube threatened to swallow Mischa. She held her head above the waves with the last of her strength, gasping and panting, she paddled against the current with her arms and legs. Again, and again, water splashed into her gaping mouth. Completely exhausted, her voice wet and hoarse, barely audible above the soughing river, she rasped and slurred for help, holding on desperately to a willow branch hanging low over the water close to shore. She was at the end of her wits. Not much longer and the river would claim her.

Two joggers, strong men, happened by and noticed with horror the woman threatened by death as they trotted by. Without a second's hesitation, they jumped bravely into the water. Luckily, her body had been momentarily caught between stones and a forked branch still bearing leaves stuck amid the silt and scree. She swung back and forth like a wet towel, no longer having neither the strength to pull herself hand over hand along the branch, nor to heave herself onto the life-saving riverbank. The two men pulled the utterly exhausted woman out of the river, seconds before it hungrily pulled her away, never to be seen again, taking her to some unknown nowhere, pulling her down to a miserable death. Together, they pulled her from the flow. She had swallowed gallons, spitting it out in short thrusts as she sat on the bank breathing heavily, coughing, vomiting, fell flat and pushed herself up with trembling limbs before falling back again. Her chest rose and fell rapidly. Her entire body was a quaking mass, wholly spent, shivering with cold and horror at her ordeal. Her eyes, wide and staring, spoke of terror.

Mischa played her part impeccably. An Oscar-winning actress couldn't have done it better. Neither her saviors nor the gapers who appeared out of nowhere, gathering around the prostrate woman on the ground and the two men, incessantly taking pictures with their cellphones, had the ghost of suspicion. Later, in the privacy of their homes, they would look at the photos, wallowing in delight, retelling the incredible experience to friends and family, posting them on their Facebook sites to get as many likes as possible. Curiosity and sensation-seeking drove them. Not a shred of compassion or helpfulness was forthcoming as they, gesticulating, clicking and commenting, encircled the young woman who had barely survived death by drowning and her two rescuers.

With flashing blue lights and sirens wailing, the gendarme arrived. Three men in uniform leaped from the car, one of them with a wool blanket in his hands. He threw it over the trembling woman, knelt beside her, attempting to dry and warm her until the ambulance could reach them; he spoke to her without pause, to keep her awake, since she was incapable of speaking about the events that led to her rescue. After a while, between recurring attacks of coughing and gasping, she tried to stammer out a message, waving her arms wildly, gesticulating at the mighty river, desperately wanting to tell the gendarme something, but could not put together a coherent sentence. At first, they didn't understand her babbling, but then they did. A second person, a man, was in the water, was drowning.

The shore patrol's rubber dinghy with a crew of four arrived at the scene. One of the gendarme ran to them, ordering them to set out immediately in search of the missing person. The boat turned sharply and sped off into the current, spraying a wave of spume in their wake. The three-hundred- horse power outboard motor had no trouble mastering the river's power. It tacked and turned in all directions as if it weren't on the deadly Danube, but on an innocently quiet lake. They found nothing but a dead muskrat lifeless fish, their white bellies blindingly reflecting the sunlight. There was not a trace of Joe. No one knew if he had sunk or if the unfathomable current had swallowed him or carried him further eastward.

The ambulance arrived. A doctor and two medics ran to Mischa, who was still laying on the ground. After they listened to the little the gendarme could tell them about events, they lifted Mischa onto the portable, wheeled stretcher, placed an oxygen mask over her face, brought her to the ambulance, attached her to various life-saving devices and measured her vital signs. She was incredibly lucky, the doctor said to the gendarme. Aside from the shock, she most likely will have no lasting injuries. But to be sure, they would bring her to the hospital for thorough examination.

Mischa had regained her ability to speak, but was still captured within the traumatic experience, began to cry convulsively, telling the police between sobs how she and Joe had been celebrating their engagement on the boat, showing them the golden ring Joe had brought and placed on her finger. Overjoyed and in love, celebrating with champagne and caviar, they began to dance. Losing their balance, they fell into the torrent, and despite all their efforts were unable to reach the boat which had drifted too far away on the racing current. She barely escaped a vortex and then Joe was nowhere to be seen, had given no response to her cries, screaming out his name. The Danube, the monstrous river had taken her one true love, had destroyed her life, she stammered out in flawlessly feigned despair. The police offered her the services of a psychologist and assured her she could call at any time when the horrible events threatened to consume her. She thanked them and was overcome by a renewed wave of grief, sobbing with abandon. Never before had a murderess portrayed the bereaved widow with such conviction.

The next morning, Joe's corpse was washed up on the shore a mile or so from the Slovakian border. A fisherman had found it and called the authorities. Comparing the identification in his pocket with the photo Mischa had given them, the body was identified beyond doubt and brought to the forensic examiner. The doctor declared definitively that Joe's death was an accident without the slightest third-party negligence. He ascribed the bruises and pressure marks to collisions with tree trunks and other drifting objects in the water, and not to the life-or-death struggle that actually took place. Based on this evidence, the police ended their investigation, declared the case closed and filed it away. Why in the world would the chief inspector, an experienced civil servant, soon to be retired and awarded the privy councilor title, choose to believe the bereaved, who was celebrating her engagement to the man she loved and wanted to marry, pushed the unsuspecting man into a vortex, causing his death? A young colleague, Hans Josef Schmidbauer, suggested this possibility, but no, that was too far-fetched. After all, the woman had fallen into the water, too, and barely escaped with her life.

"You should watch fewer detective stories on Tv and concentrate on the facts!" he had condescended to the young man, adding, "Facts, and only facts make up true police work, dear

Schmidbauer. Make a note of it, if you want to succeed as a criminologist."

He couldn't imagine that, in a few years, this young up-start would become the youngest ever Austrian Minister for Home Affairs, which would also make him Chief of Police, and not without good reason.

A flood of condolences from all her friends and colleagues washed over the utterly incapacitated Mischa who, as soon as she got home, picked up where she had left off her prepara-tions for the up-coming World Champion Candidates match against her imposing rival, the Russian Grandmaster Tatjana Lewinskaja, which would take place in just a few days.

She was convinced she had taken care of the problem named Joe, that had threatened to ruin her life and future, with bravado and was proud of herself, as she was of many achievements in her life. Her days resumed their usual routine, as they had been before her first, fatal encounter with Joe at Rita's. She buried herself in her scientific work at the university and in the laboratory, finding answers to many of the ques-tions emerging from her renowned dynamo theory. She sent her resulting formulas, analyses and conclusions to *Scientific American* for publication. The article was greeted by her inter-national colleagues with amazement. Like Einstein, she had hit upon results not with the usual experimentation, but solely with brainpower; results that seemed impossible, that upended naturals laws assumed to be carved in stone, thereby solving problems which had posed epic riddles to research. Physicians around the world were so enthusiastic about her work that she was put forth as a candidate for the Nobel Prize.

On one of the following Saturdays, after years of absti-nence and despite her openly declared atheism, she visited the synagogue, the Vienna City Temple, the only Jewish house of God in Vienna not destroyed by the Nazi Kristallnacht on November 9, 1938 – which would be better named the *Night of Ignominy* – because they feared the neighboring houses, not inhabited by Jews, may be damaged and also go up in flames. But the Nazis had not spared the sacred Torah scrolls, the Word of the Eternal, and all other scriptures, but thrown them into the fire. They randomly murdered the pious and the lapsed, the old, the young, men, women and children, including Jews such as Mischa who believed it was better to turn their backs on God and join heretical pagans worshipping the gods of mammon or of science.

It wasn't that Mischa was plagued with guilt or pangs of conscience, but it couldn't hurt to say a prayer. What if there really was a God? Even Einstein had believed at the end of his life. She stood in the women's gallery gazing uncomprehendingly at the men below her and women beside her, who in profound contemplation rocked back and forth, reaching out to God from the depths of their souls and their entire bodies, speaking to Him, praising Him, and thanking Him and His mercy for giving them their daily bread, their children. Mischa did not know that God, even when she didn't ask for it, could not forgive her atrocity, as the Christians believed, who confessed their sins in church and were granted absolution by the priests, God's representatives on Earth. Only after her death, when she arrived in heaven, should she ever get there, when she received the forgiveness of the one she murdered – the most despicable sin on creation – would the Almighty, in his boundless mercy and goodness be able to forgive her. That was Judaism, something she had never understood or practiced, as her religion was egotism; her God, Physics; her Bible, the game of chess and her joy, sadism.

Chapter 6

In one of the most opulent salons of St. Petersburg's Winter Palace, the spacious structure residing on one of the Neva's broad estuaries, impressing visitors with its green and white colors and the noble simplicity of the Imperial Hermitage comparable to ancient Greek temples; in the barely comprehensible expanse of the former tsar's residence, the formal ceremony opening the final matches of the Women's World Chess Championship took place, an event occurring every two years under the auspices of the International Chess Federation FIDE.

St. Petersburg, what a mythical name, what an illustrious and infamous past! The city, founded by the ship-builder and the most powerful regent of Russia, became the administrative seat from which he ruled his vast realm, reaching over Poland to the north of Finland, to Caucasus in the south and to the twelve-thousand-kilometer distant Alaska on the American continent in the east, which we call West. This city, through which the mere seventy-four kilometers of the Neva River, issuing from Lake Ladoga, picturesquely snakes around forty-two former islands reminiscent of the Venetian Lagoon's canals, flowing past the most beautiful palaces and mansions – once held by the mighty Eastern Imperium's patricians who were ousted by the Bolsheviks in 1918 and 1919 – before branching off into a plethora of tributaries and today, thanks to a colossal dam, emptying quietly and discreetly into the Gulf of Finland. But before the dam was built, the Neva, its main body up to one thousand, two hundred meters wide, regularly flooded, its waters reaching far inland, destroying harvests, spreading diseases, bringing death to man and animal. Death came to the city, too, during the three and half years of siege between 1941 and 1945 as Adolf Hitler declared he would exterminate the entire Russian population, far more than a million people suffered a barbaric death by starvation when they could no longer find any rats, mice, beetles, worms or other creepy crawlies, which they ate, surviving both revulsion and the poisons in creatures' bodies.

Their triumphs at interzonal tournaments that had taken place around the globe, entitled the eight female Grandmasters at the tip of the international ranking list to take part in this finale, the most prestigious women's tournament in the world. Awaiting the winning finalist was the honor of challenging the officiating Chinese World Champion and of raking in a victory purse of over a million dollars, nothing unusual in tennis or golf – a mere pittance inn these sports – abut an astronomical sum in the chess world, even for the best on the planet. Television stations lay out incomparably much more for rugby, soccer, ice hockey or boxing matches. The moves and tactics in these sports are clear as glass, the games proceed with swift action and even the dumbest spectator sitting at home on his sofa, drinking tepid beer and chewing on greasy chips, can deem himself expert despite his girth banning him from the turf or ice rink and a broken nose his immediate reward for daring to enter the boxing ring. In contrast, there are long moments in chess where nothing seems to happen, at least nothing visible. To the laity, time stretches like a dry riverbed in the endless expanse of the desert and even for good amateur players, the convolutions racing through the brains of the two opponents sitting mutely across from one another remain enigmatic, an unsolvable riddle. In short, chess is only telegenic when Bobby Fisher puts on his Mohammed Ali act, when blood jets from the defeated player's fingers or when superpowers enact simulated wars on the chess board of international politics.

The eight players qualifying for the final tournament were the Lilit Karoljan of Armenia; Jamie Rothstein, a U.S. American; Mehak Sareen from India, Nafisa Chotowa of Uzbekistan; Elena Taschina from Belarus; Marina Radiskiene for Lithuania as well as the aforementioned Russian Grandmaster Tatjana Levinskaja and Mischa Turow representing Switzerland, literally her motherland. In the opening round of nine games, in which the players drew lots to determine their opponents, they were paired off thusly: Radiekiene – Sareen; Taschina – Rothstein; Chotowa - Karoljan and Levinskaja – Turow, whose surname on the list of entrants was errantly given the Russian spelling *Turowa* because none of the tournament organizers could conceive of a Swiss contestant qualifying to the join the elite ranks of the eight finalists, no matter that she was a world-famous physicist.

"Chess is more demanding than physics," Grandmaster Igor Reblov, chief arbiter, opined in an interview with national and international members of the press. He was no amateur violinist, had taken fourth place in the last Crimean chess championship – a tournament widely boycotted due to the conflicts surrounding the exquisitely beautiful Black Sea peninsula – but hadn't the faintest idea about physics, believing vectors were extinct, prehistoric creatures and photons were camera components.

The ostentatious opening ceremony was attended by no less than the Russian president Ivan Sergejewitsch Kutin. His address to the audience, televised in numerous countries, was once again aimed at the urgent need for transnational cooperation, especially with the U.S.A., in the battle against fundamental Islamic terrorism. He termed Crimea, Abkhazia, South Ossetia, Transnistria und the autonomous Donetsk and Luhansk regions as Russian ancestral homelands that need be defended, only by volunteer natives of course, the Russian army was in no way involved and wouldn't dream of interfering, against alien invaders. The small man, an eloquent speaker convincing many of his listeners, wore his blond hair cut short. He had had so much cosmetic surgery, he looked nor more than fifty years old although he would actually soon be hitting seventy. Everything about him was aimed toward image cultivation. He spoke little about chess, the event's purpose, of which he had only a vague idea, but wished all players good luck nonetheless. His shook Mischa Turow's hand first, also mistakenly assuming she was one of the players representing Russia.

Ruslam Maschinow followed Kutin at the microphone. Maschinow was president of both a small Caucasian republic and the FIDE and was rumored to having once been one of the most influential Russian mafia bosses, which he denied repeatedly. The final speaker was Elena Sarokina, chairwoman of the Russian Chess Association and Minister of National Education, a former photo model who was allegedly a trusted advisor or held suchlike relations to President Kutin. She chaired the chess association and other institutions and organizations of which she also hadn't the slightest notion but could nonetheless place her person and her rapidly fading beauty in the much-photographed limelight. Her acumen in the Game of

Kings did not exceed those of a rank beginner and was more likely to be seen at the bar sipping French champagne than to be conversing with one of the players, which would only be source of embarrassment. Yet her speech dealt with the enormous positive impact chess had on youth, the importance of promoting chess in all countries of the world, even in most remote corners of Central Africa and South America, especially with children and young adults. She absolutely adored chess, she explained, fondly looking back on her many tournament triumphs in her early years, she added inventively. Then these triumphs either were so far in the past her memory deceived her or she was referring to tournaments for dogs and cats, who, as a commonly accepted Russian pastime, also played chess when they weren't busy mating or pursuing other activities according to their natures, which were more akin to that of Elena Sarokina.

The following morning at nine on the dot St. Petersburg time, amid utter silence in the tournament hall, the eight players triggered their clocks and began their games. They played on a spacious, slighted elevated platform, upon which the tables of the tournament director and of the chief arbiter and his assistants – all of which were also Grandmasters – were also situated.

The players' moves were simultaneously electronically transmitted to over-sized screens, allowing the seventy rows of spectators – the lucky ones who had camped out in front of ticket outlets several nights in a row or had high-ranking mentors, enabling them to purchase a one-day ticket at the price of three hundred U.S. dollars – to follow events in detail as they unfolded on the four chess boards. Many had brought pocket chess boards, silently and in awe, playing out the moves made by the masters. Grandmaster Anatoli Karpow, legendary former Men's Chess World Champion, provided live commentary. To ensure the players' uninterrupted concentration, commentary was available only over headphones, which could be rented at the entrance for an additional fifty U.S. dollars per day.

On the extensive tournament hall walls, usually serving as Hermitage Museum exhibition space, interspersed between video screens, still hung paintings by Da Vinci, Rubens, Picasso and their contemporaries. A costly collection amassed by centuries of tsars leaving the greater part of the population to languish in merciless poverty, building neither schools nor hospitals for landless farmers or for anyone else, providing nothing for their people but floggings from Cossacks riding by who kidnapped and raped their daughters.

As the event also posed an open invitation to the dark intentions of thieves and terrorists, each painting was guarded by two ferocious-looking soldiers from the Russian army's elite unit, gripping Kalashnikovs and with bullet-proof vests beneath their black leather jackets. Rumor had it that each had personally sworn loyalty to President Kutin and was paid ten times more than regular Russian warriors not privileged to join their ranks and primarily serving as cannon fodder for Kutin's foreign adventures.

Front row seats were reserved for invited guests free to walk past the ticket office without paying and welcome to help themselves to caviar, blinis, lox and champagne at the VIP buffet, free of charge of course, at the end of each game. They were ministers, congressmen of the governing party, ambassadors and the usual, scantily useful yet highly paid members of St. Petersburg's Russian and international *haut monde*. Several had travelled from Moscow or from even more remote cities and regions of this world's largest in landmass political unit as they couldn't possibly neglect to personally witness the highest level of women's chess competition. None of the spectators, not even the strongest chess player among them, excepting, perhaps, one or two of the attending Grandmasters, could hope for even a draw in a match against one of these eight women, whose expertise in opening, strategy and game ending far exceeded the limits of normal mortals. It was said for example that Grandmaster Tatjana Lewinskaja, the local heroine and multiple national champion sitting across from Mischa, had memorized over thirty thousand chess games and their countless bifurcations, analyses and calculations.

Mischa, her collar and blouse adorned with the logos of a deep red sparkling beverage derived from the coca plant and of a knobby, plastic building block for children that she wore at every chess tournament she played, gazed at Tatjana, devoid of such lucrative insignias, brooding over her next move with her head burrowing into her arms as they rested on the table. Any error, even the tiniest imprecision could cost her the match and the prize money she so direly needed.

Tatjana was a handsome and intelligent woman about the same age as Mischa, and there their similarities ended. She had discontinued her Mathematics studies to marry and have two children, since then dedicating her life solely to her family and to chess. "A loyal woman," Mischa thought, suddenly overcome with melancholy. Such happiness will never be hers. She almost regretted having to compete against Tatjana for a place in the World Championship semi-finals. Tatjana was much more dependent on the championship purse, or even the much humbler sums for second and third place, than Mischa, who hadn't the least financial worries and played professional chess purely for pleasure. Winning at least one of the award premiums would allow Tatjana to send her son to college, to pay for her husband's long overdue back operation as well as for care personnel for her ailing, bed-ridden mother.

But here was not the place for compassion. She had been working toward this goal since was a child, the World Championship title. Now that she was only a few steps away, she couldn't let sentimentality cloud or even erase her vision, no matter how much she admired her rival. She wondered how two bright young girls coming from similar environs, with the same interests, regardless whether they grew up in Russia or Switzerland, could turn out so differently; Tatjana a caring wife and mother while she was a restless bacheloress, ever searching for new scientific insights and for men to satisfy her libido. Mischa banished these thoughts quickly and redirected her concentration to the match in progress.

Tatjana had moved her knight, threatening checkmate in five moves, an exceedingly elegant sacrifice combination. It took Mischa all of two seconds to recognize the trap Tatjana had set on the chess board. She had been expecting the move and prepared her response, moving her rook à tempo, averting the threat of checkmate and jeopardizing Tatjana's men.

Oohs and aahs erupted from the rows of spectators when they saw Mischa's move on the screen. No one had foreseen it. Most of them had already pegged Mischa as the loser, which only heightened their amazement at her surprising answer to Tatjana's threat. Anatoli Karpow had more than words of praise for Mischa's unexpected move as his commentary passed through the headphones, shedding light on the murkiness reigning in the spectators' minds. With a loud shhhhh and sweeping gesture from left to right with his outstretched hand, the chief arbiter demanded silence, which set in immediately.

At the three neighboring tables, the Belarusian Elena Taschina had already surrendered her match against the U.S.

American Continental Champion Jamie Rothstein; Mehak Sareen of India was clearly winning against Lithuanian Marina Radiskiene and a threefold repetition in the match between Armenian Lilit Karoljan and Nafisa Chotowa of Uzbekistan was rapidly evolving into a draw. Which then came about.

Now, Mischa and Tatjana sat alone in the spotlight, battling for the whole point. On the edge of their seats, viewers hardly dared to breathe, fearing to disrupt the widely ramified senses of the two Grandmasters, seeking the ingenious victory combination. The tension could be cut with a knife. A chess-obsessed ministry worker from Moscow was sliding back and forth on his chair. The chief arbiter shook a warning finger at him without bearing fruit. It wasn't until the man's neighbor and superior tapped him repeatedly, shaking his head censoriously, did he finally simmer down.

Again, Tatjana threatened checkmate. Extensive brooding brought Mischa no closer to a response that would not hopelessly deteriorate her position. Her phenomenal memory, second only to her rival, came to the rescue. The combination on the board in front of her was somehow familiar, she had seen it somewhere before. Yes, the colors were changed, but the combination was the same as when, in 1943, Luis Roux Cabral, who went on to become Uruguayan Champion, played against a strong rival named Molinari in Montevideo. Back then, Cabral had also thought himself lost until he found a brilliant combination of moves in which he sacrificed both rooks, leaving three other figures unprotected, invoking an undiscernible threat of mate. That was it! She needn't do anything other than replay Cabral's moves from memory, which she knew along with countless others. Viewers believed the first move to be an error, particularly since the illustrious commentator had yet to discover Mischa's brilliant maneuver. Luckily for Mischa, Tatjana was also apparently unaware of the Molinari-Cabral match. There is such a thing as luck in chess, usually rooted in rival's ignorance. Tatjana answered immediately and naively, convinced she would soon end the match in her favor.

Following Mischa's third move, Tatjana fell into deep thoughtfulness, which only a small minority of spectators understood. Why doesn't she make the move everyone was expecting? It's obvious! Suddenly, they bent over their pocket chess boards and began to discover miraculous things. Renewed turbulence caused the chief arbiter to call for silence once more. After ten or twelve minutes of contemplation, Tatjana abruptly stood up from her place at the board, slowly and deliberately extending her right hand while gazing at Mischa in abysmal despair such as she had never seen before, whispering faintly, "I surrender. Congratulations Mischa."

She switched off the clock, signed the tournament form with shaking hands and quickly strode behind the stage. She didn't hear Mischa's words of condolence. As no other game was still in progress, ending the need for silence, the audience leapt up in enthusiasm, cheering, "Michaela, Michaela, Michaela," clapping wildly, shouting *Pasdrawlaie* – congratulations – unable to contain themselves any longer. They tossed bouquets to her, threw their hats and caps into the air, hugged each other, overjoyed by the triumph of a Russian representative. Their jubilation could not have been more effusive had the Russian football team defeated the Americans!

The tournament director approached Mischa's table to collect the formulas with each player's moves written down in clear cursive – an obsolete chess tradition since moves have been recorded electronically for several years now – and shook Mischa's hand warmly. A veritable storm of flashbulbs broke over them. Mischa, exhausted from the prolonged battle, waved to the audience and headed for the exit.

She had taken the first point, but it was only one in a match she hadn't won on her own account, she believed, but had rested on another's laurels. She still had eight grueling matches to play against the outstanding Tatjana Lewinskaja, who would certainly not allow herself to be caught unawares again.

Chapter 7

That evening, Mischa was invited to a palatial dinner with
sponsors and journalists at one of the most exquisite restaurants
in St. Petersburg boasting an incomparable chef held in high
regard even by French gourmet experts. She was bombarded
with questions, many of which made her uncomfortable and
she considered impertinent, especially those inquiring why she
represented Switzerland when she was Russian-born, spoke impeccable Russian and embodied the renowned Russian soul;
but also, those probing into her personal life. Many had heard
of her fiancés' tragic death during a boating excursion on the
Danube and offered their condolences. Mischa replied that she
had more or less overcome the worst of it, she had no other
choice, she must accept her irreversible fate and wanted nothing
more than to concentrate on the World Championship finals
without being distracted by grief or nostalgic thoughts of the
past. Impressed by her stoicism and inner strength, one man
dared to ask if she already had a new partner. A woman of such
exceptional beauty and talent wouldn't be alone for long, he
said. Another man, a certain Pawel Leskow, no relation to the
great Russian writer Nikolai Leskow, jestingly offered himself
up for the role, if she was in the market, which, following
on the heels of his previously proffered condolences, triggered

roaring laughter among the crowd and wholly other thoughts and fantasies in Mischa.

"Why not?" she replied, which was mistakenly take for a joke by the present company.

Pawel was no particular beauty, but also not an ugly man. He was somewhat rotund and bald, but that didn't bother her. Quite the contrary, she mused. Being far from the ideal sex partner of an attractive young woman, he certainly did not receive such propositions often and would be all the easier to seduce. She already had visions of him naked, tied down spread-eagle and moaning in pain on her hotel bed, where she planned to take him. She would have to make sure the room was sound-proof, or simply gag him tightly so his tormented screams were not heard. She would camouflage the crack of her whip, cleverly tucked away in her suitcase between her underwear, and the hiss of leather on skin with Russian pop music on the radio, with singers like Grigory Leps, whose wild bellows were adored by the Russians, by her as well – his statements were often keenly accurate – and his concerts were frequently transmitted live over radio. It occurred to her that she didn't have her whip with her that evening. How could she have foreseen meeting a new plaything here? No matter, she thought, smiling innocently at the men collected around her table, there's something at hand in every hotel room for merrily thrashing a man. Her decision to make Pawel Leskow this man tonight strengthened by the minute.

Although her last excursion into her demonic game of subjugation and torment, without which her lust remained in-satiate, was only two weeks ago, it seemed like an eternity. She couldn't hold out much longer, expressing her manifest car-nality had long since been an addiction without remedy. She planned to come up with an excuse to take Pawel aside after dinner and make a proposition. Which man could resist? Definitely no Russian, and most certainly not Pawel who obviously seemed to have nothing but sex on his mind, she noticed by his words and glances that stripped her naked. Unperturbed, she let his eyes wander over her body, preparing him for the things to come; things she imagined without him or the others at the table having a clue.

She hit upon the notion of offering one of the six reporters at her table an exclusive interview. To avoid playing favorites, they were all very nice, she said, the lucky one would be chosen by drawing lots. This was a trick she and her girlfriend had often played during high school in Zurich, when they wanted to go out with a certain boy without him knowing they had set their sights on him from the start. She took six toothpicks, clamping them beneath her left thumb and shielding them with her right hand. Six equally long tips could be seen. She claimed she had broken off a piece from one toothpick, which she hadn't, and the reporter drawing the short toothpick would win the interview. One at a time, they drew toothpicks from her hand. Before offering Pawel, her evening's prey, the final lot, she distracted them by looking up at an alleged bat fluttering beneath the ceiling and broke the toothpick in half.

Well, well, the bat has flown the coop and it was his turn now, Pawel crowed triumphantly. That the five other reporters had drawn toothpicks of the same length had not escaped his notice, only the short one was left, which he smugly drew from Mischa's hand, evoking a round of friendly name-calling, such as an undeserving lucky bastard. Once the interview had been published in his paper, he should on all accounts send it along to them, maybe they could use it, or at least parts of it in their publications, as long as Mischa had no objections. Of course, she didn't and told Pawel she would give him the interview in the restaurant bar directly following dinner, she may not have time or opportunity in the course of the tournament.

After the last glass of vodka, they left the others to their lively conversations and went to the restaurant bar. Pawel asked her if he could record the interview on his cellphone or if she preferred he take written notes. Mischa looked him directly in the eyes and said he would get his interview only after they left the hotel to which she wanted to go with him right now. Pawel couldn't believe his ears and asked if that was a joke.

"No," she replied without the slightest hesitation, nailing him with her eyes, without batting an eyelash, "that is no joke, Pawel, I want to sleep with you. You are a wonderful man and I can hardly wait."

Pawel swallowed hard. Never had a woman made him such an offer and certainly never so directly and definitely never such a beautiful and sexy one. Before he could say anything, Mischa continued, "However, you need to know, Pawel, that I don't expect the usual kind of sex, it's much too tedious for me and if I have assessed you correctly, for you, too."

"Absolutely," he gushed, without a clue as to what she meant.

"Well that's good," she said. "Because I love hard sex, with handcuffs and whips and suchlike. How about you?"

Pawel would have agreed to anything now, as excited as he was.

"No problem," he assured her, "I'll bind and beat you, if that's what you want."

"You've misunderstood me, Pawel," she corrected him. "I'm the one who will bind you, beat you, and when you're nice and quiet and enjoy yourself, then you will get me as a reward, but only then."

Pawel, who had been married for a long time but removed his wedding ring every time he went to an event unaccompanied by his aging wife, had no concept of the dangers the impending sex implied, and immediately agreed in greedy anticipation. It can't be all that bad, he thought. Also, it's free sex he wouldn't even have to pay for like the prostitutes he frequented when his wallet allowed. He can handle some hot and heavy torture, even though he believed himself anything but a masochist.

"Where do we want to go?" Pawel asked.

"I know we can't go to your place, Pawel," she answered. "Although you're not wearing a wedding ring, I immediately noticed the imprint on your ring finger. You can't hide something like that, as much as you try. Let me tell you, women see things like that right away. Next time leave it on, for some women it's more provocative when you're wearing it. As for me, I could care less if you're married and your wife is at home faithfully waiting on you. I'm anything but a moralist. If you want to cheat on her, then do that, as long as you do it with me tonight. Drive us to a hotel where no one would expect to find us; where you can park the car directly in front of the room, so no one sees me going in and neither your wife nor anyone else hears about us. You live here, you know the right places, just be sure it's not a pay-by-the-hour hotel, I am not a prostitute."

"No, no, you're the most wonderful woman I've met in my life," he ensured her. She understands everything, and it makes no difference! He was exhilarated, how else could he be? What man in his position, hearing her words and with the prospect of a completely unexpected sex adventure with a desirable young woman, wouldn't be? A man like him, who only once in a coon's age, when it can no longer be avoided, and an errant sense of duty calls him to take upon himself the uncomfortable pulling and tweaking of his ever-shrinking organ in an attempt to satisfy his entrusted wife, with moderate success, or whose only other option was intercourse with cheap street walkers who kept their eyes averted and their mouths full of chewing gum while taking care of business as quickly as possible.

"Wait until you get to know me, before you call me wonderful," she warned with a wink, but the not-so-subtle innuendo failed to intimidate him. She had intentionally enacted this little *tête-à-tête* to see just how malleable he had already become and saw he would be putty in her hands. She sat next to him, seductive, like a goddess of love. His eyes kept sliding to her crossed legs, barely covered by her short skirt; ivory, slim and shapely thighs encased in silky nylons, just waiting for his hands. He threw caution to the winds. His final chance to flee his fate, to stand up from the bar stool and leave this place; to close the day peacefully but alive, in front of the TV or reading in his comfortable, albeit without sex, conjugal bed with his wife, was left unused. Naïve and clueless, he accepted the temptation before him.

"I know a charming hotel on the edge of the city," he said nervously, afraid of saying something stupid that would cause the woman sitting across from him to rethink her offer. "They have small, unattached dachas next to the main building, each has a bedroom, a great jacuzzi and a salon with broad, comfortable sofas."

"That is just the thing for us," Mischa agreed, "let's go there."

He cleared his throat, unwilling to say that this well-known five-star hotel charged far more than his financial means could afford.

"We can split the dacha costs, if that's agreeable to you," Mischa explained, noticing his hesitation and the reason behind it, "or, if half is too much for you, your newspapers probably don't pay very impressive honoraria, I can cover all costs. Money means nothing to me, I have more than enough."

Mischa beamed. Really and truly, he had never met such a woman.

They returned to their table where the men were indulging in increasingly crude jokes and conversation which equaled their intake of ice-cold vodka, and said their good-byes, which were but blurrily perceived by thick impeded tongues and glassy eyes gazing lasciviously at Mischa. To those still semi-conscious she explained she was somewhat tired this evening; wanted at least eight hours' sleep before her next match against Tatjana Lewinskaja and was deeply grateful to Pawel for his willingness to drive her to her hotel. They should please forgive her and begged the ones who were already deep in their cups not to get behind the wheel tonight. They promised, but of course didn't hold to it, doubtlessly causing the already dizzyingly high number of traffic accidents in St. Petersburg to rise over the next hours, which, thanks to the commonly accepted cultural practice of paying brides to policemen waiting for just such an opportunity, perpetrators could escape legal consequences and had only to cope with scratches, bruises, a broken rib or leg and a thoroughly demolished vehicle. There would be no deaths to mourn tonight, at least not on the streets of St. Petersburg.

Mischa accompanied Pawel to his small, battered Moskva on the restaurant's parking lot, lodged between the sleek luxury cars of German and Italian provenience like an impoverished relic of days long past. But his escort seemed impervious to the fact although she was certainly accustomed to a different class of car, as Pawel assumed, yet obsessed and benighted with gnawing carnal expectations and rampant fantasies, he remained blissfully unsuspecting.

They drove out of the city, heading east toward Lake Ladoga and arrived at the noble hotel after about thirty minutes. Mischa placed two hundred-euro bills in Pawel's open hand. Money in hand, he strutted to the hotel entrance, a freshly-baked Croesus, sashayed to the reception desk and booked one of the dachas for the night, or what was left of it since it was already past twelve. Mischa remained in the car, unseen, unrecognized.

Barely through the door of the dacha, Mischa began her usual game. She pushed a startled Pawel onto the bed and commanded him, her voice sharp and cutting, her facial expression unrelenting, to remove his clothes. She, however, remained dressed.

"Aren't you going to get undressed?" he whispered.

"One thing at a time, you'll see," she retorted. "If you want the reward I promised you, you must obey me without question. Otherwise the game is up. Do you understand Pawel?"

"yes, yes, of course," he sputtered quickly, and did as he was told without another word that might risk the sex of a lifetime, as he thought.

Once naked, she ordered him to stretch out on the bed. She tied his hands and wide-spread legs to the metal bedposts with towels from the hotel bathroom, pulling them so tightly, they cut into his flesh, invoking his first cry of pain. She found a roll of twine in the large desk in the salon, cutting long snakes to secure his binds and knotting her victim firmly in position without a prayer of escape.

"Is that really necessary?" Pawel dared to stammer out in fearful expectation.

"Yes, that's the deal, remember?" Mischa snapped back. "You agreed, so stopping asking stupid questions and behave or you can forget your reward."

Pawel abruptly closed his mouth. Mischa returned to the bathroom, when she returned this time, she wore nothing but her high heels. In her hand, she held a shower brush she had found in the bathroom. The fifty-centimeter long handle would serve nicely in lieu of her whip. Never before had Pawel shared intimate space with such a shapely young woman. At the sight of her pearls of sweat broke out on his forehead and upper lip and he blushed deeply. His member, however, swelled but slightly, much to Mischa's contempt.

At first Pawel took no notice of the shower brush, but as she began to beat him with it, unleashing her madness, he realized what she intended, if not yet fathoming the final consequence. He bellowed in agony. She immediately stuffed a washcloth in his mouth and bound this, too, with another towel, twisting it around the lower back of his head and knotting it fast. Now, as her strokes increased in viciousness, the only sound to be heard from Pawel were stifled whimpers of desperation. His eyes reflected his terror and torment, flickering back and forth, bulging as if trying to flee his skull. Despite all her efforts and self-manipulation, Mischa was once more denied the pinnacle of orgasm.

Only when she began to torture him with her pointed heels, drilling tiny wells in his skin, did she feel the oncoming wave of climax. Which faded. She must increase her effort, she must push harder to reach the orgasm she needed now more than the air to breathe, or she would die a terrible death, she felt. Slowly and purposefully, she pressed her heels into his sides. Pawel thrashed in panic, exerting the power of his fear of death to rip free of his bonds, but they held. Mischa felt another wave of lust rising, rising, but ebbing away just out of reach. She rose to the challenge. She would put this miserable cur in his place, show him who reigns supreme, punish him for his useless existence.

Kicking hard, she pushed the long, acuminate heel of her shoe directly into his heart. Pawel's head fell as his life left him and Mischa felt a volcano erupt in her body, hot and violent; exploding sensations never before experienced. The incredible gift of orgiastic ecstasy, unfathomed depths and heights, was handed to her by the death she had incurred.

Rigid with titillation, lust and satisfaction, it was some time before she sank, sweaty and exhausted, to the floor. Only now did she become conscious of the impact and repercussions of what she had done. She had murdered a human being in a dacha of an unfamiliar hotel at an unknown location somewhere in the countryside. What could she do? How to avert being called a murderess, arrested and spending the rest of her life in the dreaded dungeons of Russia where prisoners died by the thousands? No matter how she tried to conceal the murder; even if she did manage to get rid of the body without being seen, to clean the room, there were much too many undeniable traces at the scene of the crime that would lead directly the her. Easily assessed, impossible to completely remove vestiges of DNA, both hers and Pawel's, were all over the room.

She took a deep breath and ordered her thoughts, where she hit upon the saving grace. The only justification for Pawel's death was to turn events around to look like an attempted rape from which she – after he had stripped and tied her to the bed – could escape just in the nick of time. This could be the only possible explanation for the multiple wounds on his body without implicating premeditation. Only the contrary, they would point toward desperate self-defense under most dire circumstances. That meant her body would also have to show equally dramatic injuries, battle-wounds similar to those on her victim's corpse, optimally with knife wounds for added effect. She would resolve the lacerations on his wrists and ankles by describing how she had once knocked him unconscious and taken her chance to tie him to the bed, but he had come to before she could flee the room, broke loose from the hand towels, grabbed her and threatened her with the knife he had used on her before and announced he was going to kill her. Thank God, she had seen her shoe laying on the floor next to her. Having used it before to defend herself, which explained away the cuts on his body, she rammed the heel into his heart just before he rammed the knife into hers.

She began to inflict wounds and lacerations on herself, bashed her head powerfully and repeatedly against the wall, pulled towels around her wrists and ankles until they turned blue, gouged her flesh with the knife and fountains of her blood splattered across the room, and abused herself with the shower brush without restraint. Aside from the droning in m her head, she felt nothing. It was not frenzy or panic suppressing the pain, but rather her mind's survival instinct compelling her to obey, putting her senses on hold to ensure she escaped punishment for her deed. Pain was not an option, it would only deter her from her intent. Her body bowed submissively to her mind's vastly superior power. Lastly, she mussed her hair, pulled out a handful, tore her dress and stockings and limped, shoeless, dressed only in slip and bra, severely injured to the hotel entrance. At this late hour, there was only a solitary employee at the desk, who, horrified by her appearance, jumped to aid her, immediately notifying the police and ambulance. Only then did her mind release her. Mischa began to feel the pain of her self-inflicted injuries and fell into the soft protective cocoon of unconsciousness.

She awoke the next day in the hospital to the sound of doctors and nurses discussing her at her bedside. Blinking, she slowly opened her eyes, recognizing, in addition to the white-robed hospital staff, two uniformed policemen and a man in civilian clothing whose silence set him apart from the others. One of the doctors was the first to notice she had regained consciousness. He signaled her to be still by putting his finger to his lips and told her she would be fine, her wounds were not life-threatening, she had been extremely lucky, would fully regain her health and only a few scars would remain to remind her of her ordeal. Few women would have had the courage, the doctor opined, to defend and free themselves from the clutches of a brutal rapist who, years ago, had been found guilty of sexual harassment at his workplace. Most likely, the perpetrator of several other unsolved sexual crimes will now come to light. The police are already deep in their investigation and had some questions for her. Does she feel strong enough to talk to them? She nodded her head ever so slightly but was too exhausted to speak. The doctor turned to the two policemen and the plain-clothesman, shook his head and told them they should wait a few more hours before questioning the witness. She was too weak to answer their questions and in this early stage following an ordeal one had suffered, the memory is often clouded by stress. They should come back later this afternoon, when the victim would be feeling much better.

However, at about two in the afternoon, before the police returned and Mischa was responsive and feeling much better, when not fully restored, Ruslam Maschinow, president of the World Chess Federation FIDE, entered her room holding an enormous bouquet of flowers and several newspapers clamped under his arm, accompanied by two board members. All were dressed in grey suits, their ties messily knotted in tribute to the defunct, yet still breathing and soon to be brought out of hibernation, Soviet Union.

He, speaking not only in the name of FIDE, but for him-self and the entire international chess community, *gens una summa*, Maschinow declared, deeply regretted her troubles and their thoughts were with Mischa. He congratulated her on her heroic self-defense and everyone was overjoyed that she had survived this heinous assault, the chess world had been spared a dreadful loss and the criminal had received his just deserts. Barbarians like Pawel Leskow deserved nothing less than death. Mischa had rendered society a great service, saving the justice department untold grief. That alone was worth a gold medal. He would suggest her name to President Putin. He then spoke of the World Championship Candidates rounds currently in progress. Her nine-game match against Tatjana Lewinskaja, who sends her heartfelt greetings and plans to visit her in the hospital, will naturally only continue when Mischa feels physically and psychologically up to it. The original dates for the semi-finals and championship matches have been cancelled and will be rescheduled as soon as the outcome of her match against Tatjana Lewinskaja has been determined. He also extended his congratulations on her brilliant victory yesterday. Her game was admired by the entire chess world, especially his good friend Grandmaster Anatoli Karpow. The newspapers were full of it, she could read them herself. He laid the bundle of newspapers on her nightstand. He and his two mute loyal assistants wished her a rapid recovery and left as abruptly as the< had come.

Out of the corner of her eye, Mischa spied the flashing cameras of an impatient press waiting for Maschinow and his escort outside her room, literally crushing them to learn more about the incident in the wee hours of the night that nearly cost famous Mischa Turow her life. She could clearly discern through the half-closed door how Maschinow bathed himself in the media's limelight, she heard how he posed as the omniscient, omnipotent and omnipresent president, in stoic superiority, quietly and confidently dishing up a story to the reporters that hadn't a trace of similarity with events as they truly occurred. Mischa wondered how one single person could invent so much twaddle without the slightest preparation and how experienced reporters could be so easily bamboozled.

Shortly thereafter, the two uniformed policemen and mysterious the plainclothes officer who hadn't spoken a word earlier arrived. He introduced himself as St. Petersburg's Chief of Police, presenting a large box of chocolates and a small model of the Hermitage as sign of the city's admiration and gratitude, he emphasized. Unfortunately, he must ask her a few questions, he continued, although based on the facts and overwhelming evidence, he had quite a clear picture of the horrible events at the dacha and what Mischa must have gone through. Leskow had been previously convicted for a similar crime, having harassed a woman some years ago. Individuals like him, parasites, not even human, are incurably diseased, impossible to socially integrate and despite a plethora of modern rehabilitation programs, they should be locked away forever, or, better yet simply liquidated -- he and most Russians shared Maschinow's opinion – instead being kept in prison for decades, living off the state.

Mischa gave a convincing account of events as conjured up by her sharp and ingenious intellect. Shocked and repelled, the three representatives of law and order shook their heads and pitied her for all had been through, pronouncing her a courageous woman, a true heroine who, by putting an end to a life, saved not only herself but many other women from a similar fate. Once again, Mischa had out-witted them all. Once again, aside from a scratch or two, she had maneuvered her way out of a situation that would have brought any other woman behind bars for life, or even cost her head.

Chapter 8

Everyone took it as a sign of Mischa Turow's magnitude as, after only four weeks of recuperation, she returned to her seat before the black and white chess board. Subsequent to the admirably repelled attack she suffered from a barbaric sex-criminal, a convicted sex offender, that could have easily cost her life, her every move was hounded by the cameras of the world, even those who had previously and grievously neglected the chess world, leaving its newsworthiness to languish uncommented. This, however, was something altogether different. Chess, crime and a heroic young woman who not only fended off a rapist and murderer, but brought him down in the process, caused TV viewer ratings and newspaper circulation to skyrocket. Everyone wanted to see Mischa Turow, plumb the depths of her intelligence and courage, but first and foremost they were eager to drool over details on the impact this terrible night in the St. Petersburg hotel had on her being.

No different than in the Spanish or southern French arenas, people wanted to see blood, preferably that of the torero and not of the bull, as they so feigned. Was his blood already crusted, his tears or creases mapping out the suffering on his face would do. Battle wounds titillated them most of all, the fresh marks from the fray on the face of a young and

beautiful woman, all the more arousing as she had her torturer's lifeblood on her hands. She had killed him as once, before thousands of onlookers in the Roman Colosseum, a brave
Christian had dauntlessly and heroically brought down the
hungry lion. Adversity, valor, acuity and beauty, Mischa Turow
embodied all these attributes, at least in the eyes of television
viewers, who worshipped her. Her moves on the chess board,
however, were of no interest to anyone but chess enthusiasts.
Her true chess challenge was played out in life.

Yet, to great disappointment, the Russian Grandmaster
Tatjana Lewinskaja won the upper hand in the next phase of
the match in St. Petersburg. She brought the second game to
a draw and claimed the following game with brilliant aptitude. The ensuing points awarded brought their score to 4:4.
The great Mischa Turow was obviously not fully restored, so
the newspapers. Or were the repercussions of her ordeal more
insidious than she let on to the rest of the world? Would she
ever be the same genius or had her brilliance and subsequent
success been beaten out of her? Many believed so. Traumas do
irreparable damage to the soul, they are comparable to torrents
pummeling away at stone, changing its shape forever.

Now, the ninth game was at hand, the last with a normal
time limit. Should the game end in a draw, the winner was
determined by a decisive game with a sharply abbreviated time
limit. Both opponents were most unwilling to enter into such
a frantic and stressful gamble, running the risk of trivial errors
and oversights far beneath the dignity of their chess finesse.
Thus, each woman brought their entire arsenal of acuity to
decide the game in her favor. It was, to quote William Shake-
speare a day of *to be or not to be.*

Tatjana won the undeniable advantage of white, giving
her the first move and choice of opening strategy. She plied her

advantage wisely, imposing upon Mischa the dreaded Petrosjan Variation Opening of the King's Indian Defense whereby the central white pawns quickly dominate the middle squares, affording the subsequently advancing officers countless opportunities to break through and attack, provided they are commanded by one of Goddess Caissa's successful, victory-accustomed generals such as Tatjana Lewinskaja.

The tension among the chess aficionados and those spectators attending for the above-mentioned reasons as well as amid the breathless crowd on the large Hermitage plaza, had reached its breaking point.

Stakes of up to five hundred thousand dollars had been wagered. Internet gamers and those who had pressed their money into the hands of questionable bookies in illegal betting offices or on the street, aspired to winnings far exceeding the victor's purse many times over.

Each of the five hundred seats in the tournament hall were filled, even though the high demand had upped the price of tickets from three hundred to five hundred dollars, the official price, mind you. On the freshly booming black market, much higher prices for one of the coveted tickets were asked and paid. Outside, a vast crowd of more than ten thousand followed the deciding game on several monumental screens. Commentator Anatoli Karpow gave *the Turowa,* as he called her, little chance of winning. Lewinskaja had never before lost a game where her opponent had allowed the Petrosjan Variation Opening.

"*The Turowa* has made a precarious decision that will most likely cost her a place in the semi-finals," he announced with skepticism. "What a pity, after so many outstanding games, she now serves Lewinskaja a golden opportunity to pave her way to the semi-finals."

The elderly World Champion couldn't have been further from the mark. Over innumerable hours, until deep in the night, Mischa had studied, analyzed and anatomized every game Tatjana had ever played. In the process, she had hit upon a game applying the Petrosjan Variation Opening that Tatjana had played and won against the Czech Master Hanna Oblatowa. In the 24th move, Mischa discovered an error never before unearthed, not even by the allegedly omniscient computer. Up until the 23rd move, she consistently repeated all of Oblatowa's moves, confident Tatjana would also remember the game and repeat the moves she had made back then, which after all had led to her victory.

Karpow's commentary postulated that *the Turowa* was obviously having an off day; she was ignorant of the *Lewinskaja* vs. *Oblatowa* triumph and was running full speed to her own demise. Yet, Mischa's astonishingly unpredictable maneuver on her 24th move, which at first glance appeared incomprehensible and preposterous, abruptly turned the situation on the chess board in her favor. It took some time before Karpow, Lewinskaja and the knowledgeable among the spectators penetrated the idea hidden behind her last move.

The former world champion was the first to revise his fallacy, recognizing Mischa's move as a brilliant chess theory innovation, dismantling white's perspective of the entire opening variation, rendering it ripe for the dung heap, as he so openly declared. Tatjana, who was at first more than amazed at Mischa's apparently errant move, gradually awoke to its true power. Despite her infinite calculations, she failed to find a response which would maintain, or better yet expand, her current advantage. Moreover, she began to grasp that her advantage was nothing but a chimera, that her opponent's genial 24th move hopelessly submerged her position without a chance of surfacing. There wasn't a single response option that wouldn't strengthen her opponent's advantage. Her radiant, confident facial expression was washed away, replaced by deepest despair. Facing this unexpected reversal, she made twelve more weakened moves before, as in their first game, she stopped the clock, rose and once again congratulated Mischa on her triumph and match victory. This time, however, she held herself proudly, did not wordlessly flee the tournament hall, but rather did her best to pose as a good loser, even though this defeat had cost her a year's income and dashed her son's hopes of a good education.

Mischa was well aware of Tatjana's precarious position and whispered to her behand her hand, "Don't worry, Tatjana, I will see to it that President Kutin gives you the entire victory purse as well as my winnings."

Tatjana gazed at her, stunned, and asked how she planned to do that.

"Let me worry about it," Mischa replied, turning to meet the tidal wave of jubilating spectators.

Chapter 9

Mischa was well aware that part of the Vienna University's motivation in offering her the new, customized academic chair, *Department of Particle Interference*, was a ploy to enhance their prestige. Since March 1938, when the Nazis' racial fanaticism eradicated all prominent Jewish capacities teaching and researching there, the Vienna University's international reputation had dwindled to that of a second-rate academy. By engaging the famous Mischa Turow, they hoped to reinstate their former stature within the scientific world. This allowed Mischa to dictate her professorship conditions. Wanting to ensure she had time for other activities, she had agreed upon a maximum of thirty lectures per annum and the right to personally schedule her appearances. As the university curriculum had planned bi-weekly DPI lectures, which were well-frequented from the outset, during both winter and summer semesters, Mischa's surrogate, Professor Hans-Georg Schuster – the son of a priest who called on the church to actively resist Nazi rule and was one of the few Christians murdered at Auschwitz – was to take on the remaining lectures as well as the seminars, a task he took on gladly and carried out with passion. He had been her teacher and doctoral advisor, had followed her development since her university matriculation at the tender age of sixteen and her career with utmost admiration and was there at the inception and development of her *Dynamo Theory*. Hence, there was no better man for the job. Mischa was also engaged by the Viennese research laboratory owned by an enormous U.S. American corporation, where she earned a multi-million-dollar salary for contractually defined, minimal work hours.

Since her Dynamo Theory rocked the world; since she had been compared to the greatest physicists of the 20th century, Einstein, Heisenberg, Pauli; and since she was now the favored candidate for the Women's Chess World Championship, her name had become a household name around the globe. The fact that she was the youngest, most beautiful professor to teach at a European university made her media star status complete. She could pick and choose from the endless flood of highly remunerative offers to speak, advertise and attend, accepting only those invitations also ensuring the presence of celebrities she wished to meet. She was definitely not interested in selling herself too cheap or wasting her precious time on senseless babble and empty chatter.

She could have paid the tuition for Tatjana Lewinskaja's son out of her own pocket without batting an eyelash. The fees would have only made the slightest dent in her wallet, comparable to a Russian high school teacher's visit to the local coffee shop. But she wanted to know if her power over men could hold sway even over the autocratic Russian president Kutin, making him her plaything and instrument; fulfilling her whims; perhaps indeed, if the opportunity should arise, reducing him to one of her devoted sex slaves. True, he had shaken her hand at the tournament's opening ceremony in St. Petersburg, but his interest was limited to his assumption that she was a Russian, representing Russia in the tournament. Beyond that, he had never extended her an invitation to a banquet at the Kremlin as other government luminaries had done. She had dined with the U.S. American president at the White House in Washington, with the French leader in Parisian Elysée palace, but never with the Russian president at the Kremlin. The powerful men of this Earth had courted her, admired her intelligence and ravished her body with their eyes. Only Kutin had merely shaken her hand.

She was not out to amass more fame and honor, since, if the truth be told, her successes were nothing to her. Her sole aim was to confirm her feminine power over men. As long as she could remember, her intellectual superiority had carried less significance than a man's physical strength, she had never felt that boys and men viewed her as their equal, approached her on an equal footing, but, at first, made her the object of their derision and later, the object of their longing and desire. They never showed interest in her for her own sake, in her being and feelings, as a human being and as a woman. This was one reason, albeit neither the only one nor the crucial one, why she now punished men, took pleasure in their suffering and torment whenever the opportunity arose or was purposely invoked.

Collegial or friendly relations with a man were, for her, flat out infeasible. Nor could she, dispassionate and incurious, pass by a total stranger, be it on her way to work or anywhere else, without sizing him up, painting the most vivid pictures in her mind's eye to determine how suitable he may be for her licentious purposes. Neither the least prepossessing nor most nondescript man was spared her abnormal scrutiny. Yes, those strolling, photographing tourists from every corner of the Earth, were also the object of her lasciviousness as they admired Vienna's palaces and mansions. They were as blissfully unaware of this as they were of the appalling events that had not so long ago taken place behind the imposing façades, deeds unimaginably more savage than Mischa's crimes. But it is hers we are concerned with here.

Only her ruminations on physics or chess, as she wandered the imperial city's streets, cursed with their history, did she forget the world around her, paid no heed to her surroundings and men were absolved from her erotic-sadistic fantasies. Otherwise, without having the faintest inkling, they were all subject to her assessing eyes and scurrilous thoughts, at the drop of a hat, any one of them could be the object of her demonic lust. Not a few of the men she saw cast her desirous sidelong glances, yearning for this unapproachable goddess striding past them haughtily, confidently, with what they took for evident disinterest and wouldn't give them the time of day. Not a single one of them could even begin to envision how his powerful craving was instantaneously magnified and potentiated in her mind in the most glaring light, in the most lurid colors and in the shrillest of cries; that her one and only thought was the most abstruse gratification of her body on his. Had they imagined it all the same, not one of them would hesitate to walk into her trap, all aquiver and jubilant, freely and voluntarily, without the least coercion on her part and never giving the tiniest thought to the perils involved, putting their lives at stake.

Friendship or a normal, unspectacular relationship, free of perverse thoughts and emotions, was only possible with women, which is why Mischa had no lack of women friends, both close and superficial. She also could not complain of a begrudgery-deficit. These people nevertheless veiled their jealousy or envy, pretended to be boot-licking grovelers, as is so often the case with women plagued by inferiority complexes or self-doubt, not rarely culminating in corrosive self-loathing.

One small objective she had set her sights on, was to have President Kutin invite her to the Kremlin, using the occasion to persuade him to financially support her chess friend Tatjana Lewinskaja. Appealing to Kutin's nationalist sentiments, she would argue that Tatjana, in contrast to herself, despite, or maybe due to her Judaism, was a staunch Russian patriot. If one could believe his television addresses -- if they weren't merely promotional lip-service propaganda to strengthen his people's loyalty throughout the land – nothing was more precious to him than the glory and honor of the Russian Nation. She will see if she could instigate an invitation to dinner at the Kremlin.

Should she manage to take this first step, Kutin himself would be worth a try, a goal that was naturally much more ambitious than the first. Even the most powerful men in the world were only men, she thought, men whose thinking is subordinate to their sex drive and, for women like her, are as malleable as wax in her hands, as easy to pilot as toy cars. All of her analytical skills notwithstanding, she was unaware, or refused to concede, that much of what she thought applied to herself and was nothing more than a Freudian projection. Sometimes, it is not a person's ignorance of her failings that refuse to spare her mistakes, but her subconscious aversion to accepting herself.

As to Mischa, she considered herself one of the rare, completely autonomous beings on Earth, thoroughly independent of any other human being. Factually, though, she was one of the least liberated creatures on our restlessly racing rock, flying through space toward its inevitable end, as she was chained to something much more ominous than most people, she was a slave to her urges, most particularly to her deep-seated compulsion, injected by the devil, her special need that made her a ruthless murderess.

She now had President Ivan Sergejewitsch Kutin in vizier, the sovereign ruler of the largest country on Earth. He ruled with an iron fist. Ministers, judges and oligarchs were the chessmen, his folk the pawns he moved, more adeptly than any Grandmaster, over the chess board named Russia. He had never lost a game, no one could best him. Effortlessly, he had frustrated even one of the best players of all time, a genius on the sixty-four squares, the legendary World Champion Garri Kasparov, who challenged him for the Presidency and for his impudence was ultimately banned from the country. From New York and Zagreb, wherever his overzealousness landed him, his rival raged against him like a flushed-out gander honking at the wolf from a safe distance, but no one paid him any heed. The more Mischa thought about it, the more improbable it seemed that she could dig her claws into the great Kutin, although he was just a man. But a man like no other. Maybe he was the one who could turn the tables on her and make her his slave. Suddenly, the idea of getting an invitation from him was no longer so very appealing.

It was but six weeks since Pawel Leskow had met his unhappy end, and the long-awaited semi-final matches of the prominent tournament in St. Petersburg to determine who will challenge the incumbent chess world champion will begin tomorrow. Mischa was paired with the thus far very impressive player Lilit Karoljan of Armenia. In the last eight rounds she had defeated the manifold Asian Continental Master from Uzbekistan, Nafisa Chotowa with a sensational result of 7:2, justly earning her accolades in the press.

At the neighboring table sat Marina Radiskiene of Lithuania across from the U.S. American Jamie Rothstein. Marina had eliminated India's Mehak Sareen, the 3rd best female chess player on the globe, according to the world ranking list. In the

ninth and final game of her duel against White Russia's Elena
Taschina, Jamie Rothstein took the laurels, just as Mischa had
done against Tatjana Lewinskaja.

The FIDE had altered procedures in the semi-final round.
Instead of the nine games played in the quarterfinal, the first
two women to win five games would be announced the winner
of her respective match. Draws were no longer counted, so
each new confrontation between the two rivals will predict-
ably be a bitter battle for victory. Every game, including those
played with black – which, among Grandmasters, promises
much less certainty of success – must comprise a winning
strategy. Once again, the encounters took place in the large
Winter Palace tournament hall and were not only broadcast on
the tournament hall monitors and open-air large screens on the
vast Hermitage plaza, but were aired, along with Anatoli Karpow's commentary, in many cafés and in all larger chess clubs
in St. Petersburg and throughout Russia, a land inflamed with
chess fever from the Polish border in the West to far reaches of
Wladiwostok in the East. The highly infectious virus spread to
other countries as well, with many families falling prey to its
pathogen, losing fathers and sons to hours on end before the
idiot box or the chess board.

Since Mischa, *the Turowa*, as Karpow and all other Russians fondly called her, was the only remaining native Russian,
the entire nation stood firmly behind her. Each player had a
small flag of her country placed on her side of the chess board.
Mischa's seat had two flags, one Russian, one Swiss. Their
colors were quite compatible, although the people and political
systems they represented couldn't be more divergent. However,
appearances veil realities, colors stand out brighter than politics
and fabrics make a folk, as a renowned Swiss poet would have
put it, were he still alive and writing a play on the subject.

But Mischa was not the epitome of his naïve, kindly imposter Wenzel Strapinski and the St. Petersburg metropolis was not Goldach, his fictitious, small town in Switzerland, although much of what occurred there could easily come about in the even smaller town of Seldwyla. Both here and there, people placed bets on the winners, for most of them this could only be Mischa Turowa and Marina Radiskiene. Karoljan and Rothstein were given only an outside chance. The odds quoted for Turowa were 10:3 and 10:7 for Radiskiene, the former quote finding its foundation first and foremost in bettors' national pride and patriotism.

Yet, both matches began differently. Not only Mischa, but also Radiskiene lost their opening games. The newspapers put this down to initial lapses on the part of the two favorites; they had underrated their opponents and would show them who's master in the second game. But this game, too, left a bad taste in the mouths of the press and bettors. With enormous effort, from a poorer position and less two pawns, Radiskiene managed a draw with perpetual check her opponent could not deflect. Mischa, however, went down without a whimper. The petit sports teacher with black curls, Lilit Karoljan from Jerewan, a year younger than Mischa, belied all prognoses, leading 2:0 after just the second game. Mischa's chances faded in the far distance, when, after three games ending in a draw, which according to the rules did not count in the final reckoning, she made an incomprehensibly stupid error in the sixth game, to the horror of all watching.

Thus, the situation was the precise opposite of all expectations. Karoljan led against Turowa 3:0, needing only two victories to enter the finals and Rothstein, at 4:1, was but one tiny win away from contending for the championship. Many bettors feared for their stakes, the media spoke of a black cloud hovering over Russia and Lithuania, giving up both candidates as a lost cause. Spectator interest went out with the tide, the Winter Palace tournament hall was but sparsely filled. Many cafés discontinued live broadcasts and the people turned their interest back to the Russian athletes participating in the track and field World Championship in nearby Helsinki.

No one in Russia wanted to watch an Armenian chess victory, and most decidedly not one taken by a U.S. American. The latter prospect called up memories of the arrogant Bobby Fischer as he dethroned Russian world champion Boris Spasski in Reykjavik in 1972. Fischer's disrespectful comments enraged the entire Russian population, triggering substantial political tension between Russia and the U.S.A., similar to the 1961 Cuban Missile Crisis that threatened to escalate into World War III. Only the prudence of the contemporary Soviet leaders, who refused to walk into the trap set by the eager U.S. American capitalistic agitators Nixon, Kissinger and Fischer, averted the outbreak of an atomic war which had surely destroyed the entire world. Many still believed this fairy tale initially propagated by the Communist Party despite the fact that the Soviet Union was long dead and buried, primarily thanks to President Putin, a KGB Officer in the former communist GDR, who dragged it down from the attic, dusted it off and made it presentable again.

Two days later, an agonized Radiskiene was completely out of the running as Rothstein's outstanding strategy took the last point in the duel, giving her a score of 5:1 and making her the first finalist. Jamie Rachel Rothstein was a slender Mathematics student from New York whose antecedents, prior to WW I, fled from the South Russian Cossack's anti-Semitic pogrom, instigated by the haughty Tsarina Alexandra and maneuvered by the diabolical monk Rasputin, and immigrated to the U.S.A.

In another game, Mischa manager to shorten her opponent's lead by 1:3, but after several draws, lost the whole point in the eleventh game, falling back to 1:4, a loss that was nearly impossible to recover, everyone agreed.

The night before the next confrontation with the diminutive Lilit Karoljan, whose artful strategies gave little room for maneuvering, Mischa slept poorly. She racked her brain for some way to turn the tables in her favor at the last minute, some way to penetrate the machine-like precision of her Armenian opponent. After so many years of preparation was she to stumble just when she could feel the World Championship title at her finger tips? So much would be lost, including an invitation to the Kremlin. President Kutin had no time for losers.

Which of Karoljan's weaknesses had she overseen? She sat at her computer far into the night, clicking through all of her opponent's recent games. They were truly admirable, evincing comprehensive opening insight, brilliant strategies, and infallible instinct for pressing even the tiniest advantage and perfect closing game techniques, especially with pawns and rooks.

But then, Mischa espied something in a game that Karoljan had perhaps won, but there was something there that her opponent, the German Master Jana-Marisa Schmidt and all commentators had missed. Twice, Karoljan had made imprecise moves with her knight, one of which was wholly superfluous and had cost her entire tempo. Analysts had discarded this as inessential to the game's result, but Mischa immediately saw that had Schmidt responded courageously and correctly to Karoljan's second muffed knight move, she would have regained the initiative, improved her position and, playing accordingly, have won the game. Apparently, without any of her opponents noticing, Karoljan suffered from what Grandmasters called knight-indulgence. If the game tomorrow did not turn out to be the last in the semi-finals, Mischa would have to impose an endgame upon her rival that was with knights instead of her usual rooks, with which she was nearly invincible. For the first time in days, Mischa slept well.

The next morning, the tournament hall was once more filled to capacity. Many St. Petersburg cafés had also resumed broadcasting to watch what most considered to be the last game between Turowa – Karoljan. On the heels of her many victories, everyone expected the Armenian to win this game as well and they wanted to see the defeat on the face of their former darling Mischa Turowa, were eager to see her crushed after she had so sorely disappointed them, costing them their confidently laid stakes.

You could have heard the proverbial pin drop as the competitors took their seats at the table and the chief arbiter pressed the button which would set the electronic chess clock in motion. Each player had one and a half hours at their disposal for the first forty moves, plus an additional thirty seconds for each move made, in the hopes of circumventing, or at least limiting, the dreaded shortage of time at the fortieth move. The rest of the game must be completed within thirty minutes, also allowing the thirty-second supplement per move made. Should one of the players not complete the required number of moves within the time allowed until the first time-limit, or her clock runs out before she has finished the game, she may have to forfeit the game, regardless of how promising her position, even if she was but one move away from checkmate.

Time is a significant factor in every chess game, especially those on a Master level. Contrary to the widely held belief among non-players, master players use more study time during a game, not less, than amateurs do, although, or because their knowledge is so much more comprehensive. It's as if they are leafing through a thousand-paged book they have committed to memory. But there were exceptions, and Mischa was one of them. Another *rapid chess player*, as it is called, was Viswanathan Anand of India, former World Champion and six-time Chess Oscar winner; worshipped by over a billion Indians, his face looked out from giant posters on houses from Kashmir to Kerala, but he could walk anonymously through Central European city streets, mingle among the crowds unrecognized and unmolested and drink his coffee in a summer street café without being hounded by photographers, journalists, fans or sensation hunters.

Karoljan led the white chessmen, with the right to make the first move, an opening advantage not to be underestimated. She played 1. e4 e5 2. Nf3 Nc6 and 3. Bb5, Spanish, her ominous, preferred opening. Much to the surprise of Karoljan, the spectators and commentator Anatoli Karpow, however, Mischa did not respond with her usual countermoves, as they knew from many of her previous games, but with a quick exchange of rooks and queens. Karoljan was convinced these were desperate, last-ditch attempts to try something new. She believed Mischa had resigned herself to losing and she would be easy prey, but her opponent was superbly applying the strategy she had worked out last night. Mischa also exchanged knights, bringing about the difficult, incalculable endgame with knights and pawns she had intended. As expected, Karoljan soon made an imprecise move with one of her remaining knights. Imprecise, that is, to someone unable to fathom the position's depths, as if she were on the ocean's surface and could clearly discern what lay on the ocean floor thousands of meters below. Not even the great Anatoli Karpow realized the weakness of Karoljan's move, but Mischa, employing both her foresightedness and painstaking preparation, saw the error of her overconfident rival and exploited it mercilessly. Wholly unanticipated, she sacrificed two pawns. A murmur whizzed through the tournament hall. Has Turowa gone mad? Has she forgotten the elementary chess basics or was this a crude error, a flub made only by beginners? Yet, following additional startling moves, she launched her endgame with an implacable attack, culminating in the conversion of her last pawn on the board into a queen, which her opponent was utterly defenseless to avert. With dawning comprehension, the crowd's head-shaking became nodding, their eyes lost their disappointment and contempt and glowed with amazement and overwhelming respect. The game was decided.

Karpow bellowed his excitement into the microphone, here was a combination that would go down in the annals of chess. What a pity, he added, that *the Turowa*, his nickname for her, found success so late in the semi-finals. Even after this win, the points were still distributed 4:2 for Karoljan, who then only needed one point to enter the World Championship finals.

Confronted with Mischa's unstoppable last pawn, Lilit resigned the game and gave Mischa her hand. Still, she couldn't hide the small smile on her face. She was certain she could regain the lost point in one of the next games and, despite today's defeat, win the match. Some spectators were rather disgruntled. They had been certain they would see the match decided today but would now have to purchase another disgustingly expensive ticket for tomorrow were they to witness Turowa's ultimate defeat; their revenge for her, aside from two exceptions, so bitterly disappointing them.

Only Anatolij Karpow was uncomfortably reminded of his adversary Viktor Kortschnoi, yet another one of these Jews as well as a dissident of and defector from the mighty Soviet

Union, who, in their World Championship duel on the Philippines in 1978, regained a three-point deficit within four games, but ultimately lost to Karpow, who won the following game and match. Hence, Karpow verbalized what many refused to believe, namely, that in the light of *the Turowa's* convincing victory today, the match was by no means in Karoljan's hands, her lead notwithstanding.

And it came about that Karpow was right. Over the next two days, Mischa won both games, and suddenly the match was tied 4:4. Not only all of chess-obsessed Russia, but the entire chess world was in an uproar. Even in far-off Switzerland, the country Mischa actually represented, the chess community began champing at the bit. Was it possible that a Swiss woman would be the first in the centuries-old history of chess to enter the finals of the World Championship Candidates tournament? The reputable *New Zurich Newspaper* referred to the event on the front page, albeit in a small framed box on the lower righthand corner, giving a somewhat more detailed report in the Sports section.

Not only the St. Petersburg cafés were bursting at the seams. One could hear the cracking voices of exuberant Swiss sports reporters, broadcasting from St. Petersburg. Public opinion of Turowa had taken a complete turnaround and they could hardly contain their exhilaration. Every heart in both Russia and Switzerland beat passionately for her in patriotic frenzy, similar to that in soccer stadiums. The pro-regime Pravda went out on a limb by publishing an unusually bold political caricature of President Kutin, his biceps flexed, sitting at a chessboard across from a knight-wielding Mischa Turow. The caption read, *Who's the strongest and most celebrated now?*

Western television also took a sudden interest in the tournament in distant St. Petersburg, although the chess match itself was secondary. The main impetus for this visual media's interest was the two women. Both were the same age, highly talented and shared similar backgrounds, yet, in appearance, they couldn't have been more disparate. Voyeurism and spitefulness were behind the sky-rocketing viewer ratings. Viewers, especially those without a clue about chess, and they comprised the majority, wanted to see two young women at each other's throats; wanted to witness their determination to annihilate the other's ego, observe their vicious battle live and in the flesh. Whether they fought with chessmen or other weapons was immaterial, they wanted to see blood, or at least a goodly flow of sweat and tears. Most people sided with Mischa based on her, by far, superior good looks. They shared her suffering and excitement. As she fell back in seemingly irreparable deficit, they cursed her, switching off their TVs in angry disgust. But now, now that she had made the apparently impossible possible, coming back to even the score, audiences praised her to the skies and couldn't get back to their boob-tubes fast enough. Not a few of them craved to see more than Mischa's victory, they wanted to see her diminutive, homely opponent, whose name they could barely remember, utterly destroyed; to feast on her agony and despair. Mischa's sadism was but the tip of the iceberg in the unfathomed depths of humanity's ocean. The greater part drifted unseen beneath the surface, encompassing millions of so-called fine, up-standing citizens in all countries, in every social stratum, from day-laborer to CEO. They would never dare to do what Mischa dared in broad daylight, but their nightly dreams were full of such deeds.

The imminent game, which would be the last between these two aspirants should one of the World Championship rivals win, was destined to be earth-shattering. When, three days ago, the Armenian had entered the self-assured and confident of winning, she now seemed overly nervous and taut to the breaking point. Her shaky demeanor was clearly visible in the tournament hall and on the television screens. Her eyes were sharply fixed on the chess board, her will and mind powerfully intent on mobilizing every modicum of the enormous chess talent slumbering within her, waiting impatiently to be reawakened. Today, she must reconnect to her initial match successes and tip the scales of this intellectual combat in her favor. She must win this game at all costs, losing was not an option. Today, it was all or nothing.

In contrast, Mischa sat easily, one could almost say cockily, at the table. She seemed cheerful and even lovelier than usual, leaving no doubt as to who would walk away the winner today. She had dressed for the occasion, having exchanged her usual turtleneck sweater and faded jeans for a comely blouse and miniskirt, exposing her thighs and accenting her impeccable figure.

The tension, in the tournament hall, on the Hermitage plaza, in cafés and clubs and in private homes in front of televisions, had reached immeasurable proportions. The air in many venues was thick with smoke and alcohol fumes. Commentators brabbled thick and fast, bringing more sensationalism, idiocy and bias than knowledge and objectivity. Nonetheless, the restlessness was by no means built on an uncertain outcome of the game, as no war could be won with the naked panic and despair in Karoljan's eyes, certainly not one on the chess board. Audiences were on tenterhooks to see her humbled, surrender her weapons, give Mischa her hand and drown in the misery of her defeat. They panted for the ultimate rapture of hallelujahing their idol and for the deluge of contempt and derision they would pour over her opponent. They longed for both. This was the only reason most of them followed the match.

They had suffered and trembled for and with Mischa, she was their secret lover. She was battling a forest fire on a wooden board, the flames shooting sparks into the sky. Thousands of kilometers away, people felt the scorch of its white-hot heat, causing beads of sweat to break out on their upper lips, drip down their backs, clouding their thoughts and judgement with billowing smoke, kindling their emotions to a fiery red.

Devoid of any objectivity, they were all the less capable of recognizing the true demon lurking behind the lovely face of their darling. A demon far more insidious than the ones they carried in themselves. A demon that incited her to torture and murder for the fleeting reward of satisfied lust. Especially blind were those, although they would never admit it, not even to themselves, who dreamed of gaining power others, without having the slightest idea where power could lead them. Had they a suspicion or even evidence, their enthusiasm would peter out, at least for those who expressed it openly. Then, much of what is permitted in dreams is forbidden in real life. Law and order put a limit on our cravings. Had they known, the guards in the tournament hall would have laid Mischa in chains and removed her from the place like a mangy cur. Yet, there would still be some who even at the moment of her arrest, would forgive her diabolical deeds – men driven by the specious delusions of their suppressed libido and women by their frustrated need for power over men. The world not always as it seems. Most particularly not on that day as people, not only in Russia, made their idol's triumph their own, although they contributed nothing to it, not a modicum; although they could not imagine what lay beneath it, from which abyss of darkest human wickedness it arose, an abyss they sometimes plumbed in thought, but never ventured as deep down as the heroine they worshipped, Mischa Turow.

Chapter 10

In the two-week hiatus before the finale between Jamie Rothstein and Mischa Turow, the winner of which will gain the right to compete for the World Championship title against the Chinese incumbent Pinyin To Can, Mischa had been invited to give lectures and take part in events in St. Petersburg and Moscow, among others at the Faculty for Physics at the Lomonossow University, where she was to speak on special aspects and new applications of the Dynamo Theory.

In the four years since Pinyin To Can had seized the title from the Ukrainian Nadeschda Lavrenko, literally declassifying her, she has held absolute sovereign rule over the Olympia of ladies' chess; has never lost a single game and rose to number two in the overall world chess rankings, a position never before attained by a woman in the thousand, six hundred years since chess emerged from its home in India to enrich the world with the most beautiful, most complex game of games; since Scheherazade, with chess and fantastic tales, moved her father, Persia's mightiest Vizier, who was also her lover and father of her children, to spare her mother's life who he had falsely accused of infidelity, an act he exercised daily.

Mischa's arrival at Scheremetjewo Airport was greeted by photographers, journalists and television reports demanding interviews and stories. Flashbulbs blinded her, questions rained down on her. She blinked, denying them any information but asked them to postpone their questioning until the press conference scheduled that evening prior to her talk at the university. The Aeroflot flight from St. Petersburg had been rather bumpy, accompanied by turbulence arising from a strong thermal draft caused by the summer heat. Especially unsettling was the extended descent and landing over the vast Russian capital. Mischa had clearly seen the tips of countless newly erected skyscrapers, glassy and glittering, glaring in the sun, they broke through the clouds covering the city. Normally she was impervious to flying, but this flight had worn her out. She was tired and depleted and wanted to use the more than one-hour taxi ride to rest before the impending evening, which promised to be straining. But her plan came to nothing.

The university had sent a car driven by a wheezing chauffeur and escorted by an elderly professor remarkable in his ugliness and vapidity. She couldn't make out his name when he introduced himself. Aside from a couple of inappropriate and embarrassing comments, he spoke not word during the entire drive. She closed her eyes, but sleep evaded her as the awkward silence was punctuated by the chauffeur's irregular snorting and gasping. It was obvious that the professor felt horribly ill at ease, as he wagged his head back and forth continuously staring with feigned concentration out of the windows, first right, now left. He did his utmost to disguise the hunger in his salacious glances. Mischa could have cared less, and he was much too shy, to cowardly, too inhibited to speak or even make her a compliment. Conversation was not his strong point. He strained his brain for something to say, some anecdote but for the life of him, he drew a blank. He just didn't have anything to say. That suited Mischa perfectly. She ignored the restless eyeballing of the apparently mindless man sitting next to her in the back seat of the car. She closed her eyes and invited sleep to come again, but with the chauffeur persistently grunting like a snoring bear and the low-lying sun blinding her, she didn't stand a chance.

In the gloaming of the setting sun in the West, she could make out, even from this distance, the imposing university structure atop the Sperling Mountains. The building spontaneously brought to mind a many-layered wedding cake, and she had to smile. Correctly so, the expansive, bizarre, baroque edifice had once been called on of the *Seven Sisters*, the, in the none-too-distance past, seven highest buildings in Moscow. At the tip of the acuminated tower rising two hundred and forty meters high in the structure's center, she could just as easily imagine a bride and groom instead of the Soviet Star Stalin had personally and expressly commanded. The Star swaggered before the red fireball sinking below the horizon like a memorial commemorating the pervasive communist arrogance and power, perfectly in accordance with the kitschy-opulent confectionary architecture so loved by the depraved dictator.

Although many Russians shared her opinion, she refrained from voicing it that evening. Of all places, the university was full of influential persons still mourning the seven-decade Communist Era which had eradicated the cruel tsarist dictatorship, placing the more insidious tyranny of the proletariat, or more precisely that of the Central Committee KPDSU in its stead. Persistently and inexplicably, they mourned the Committee's General Secretary, *Youssef Bessarionis dse Dzhugashvili*, who dubbed himself Stalin, and longed for a return of the good old days, when everything was allegedly better. This nostalgic, transfigured reactionism was ultimately inspired and embodied by President Kutin who was no less powerful than Stalin was, governed Russia no less absolutely, repressed, as Stalin had, the slightest opposition and eliminated his opponents with similar ruthlessness. Kutin was simply better at hushing up his crimes than Stalin had been. The rumors leaking to the public on his excessive sexual habits he left uncommented; rumors being below his dignity. With few exceptions, his people regarded him as welder and defender of Russian culture; protector of the poor and weak. To women, he was both loyal, caring husband and lover who they would, without a second's hesitation, passionately and happily take to their beds. To men, he was both esteemed national leader and feared disciplinarian, from whom no one was safe.

Eleven Nobel Prize Laureates issued from the Lomonossow University. Six were physicists and three – Vitali Lazarevich Ginsburg, Lew Davidovich Landau and Boris Leonidovich Pasternak – were Jewish, like Mischa. The great Russian chemist and author, whose first and only novel, *Doctor Zhivago*, was to touch the hearts of people and would do so as long as humans inhabited the Earth and were literate. Pasternak's inimitable narrative depicts the magnitude and tragedy of an impossible love amidst the civil war chaos of the young Soviet Union and ending in death. For some strange reason, at the moment, Mischa identified powerfully with Pasternak's suffering heroine, although she had nothing at all in common with her. Mischa would much rather make people suffer, especially men.

The man next to her was, however, thoroughly inappropriate for the role. Weak men, yes, they suited her monstrous urges; for boring men she felt nothing but loathing. Why bother to punish someone, gift someone with sexual torture, even if he was a professor at the Lomonossow University, who was utterly unable to enjoy life; who spent his days in unchanging monotony and didn't have the guts to tell her he desired her, even when his eyes made this undeniably clear? In his excitement at the airport, and later in the car, he had forgotten to give her his card. If he had, she would have seen that his name was Leonid Ivanovich Sacharin, university rector, dean of the physics faculty and well-known author of numerous, ground-breaking physics publications which had become standard reading at all universities on earth. During her studies in Zurich, and later while teaching in Vienna, she had used and cited them often. All this had no meaning during their drive. Here, he was an awkward nobody, worth less than any common joe on the streets, who would at least have had the courage to look her in the eye.

The car turned into the drive reserved for faculty and privileged visitors. Still ignorant of her escort's name, Professor Sacharin accompanied Mischa on the elevator to one of the upper floors where canapés and drinks had been prepared for her in a room with an amazing view of the city's countless glittering lights as night took hold.

She was awaited by approximately one hundred people. In contrast to Professor Sacharin, the university's vice-rector was a jovial, lively and amusing contemporary. He greeted her warmly, introduced her to his colleagues exuberantly and gave a short introductory, welcoming speech. There as little time until the press conference, which would take place before Mischa's lecture in the university's main hall before over a thousand listeners. She drank soda water, ate lox and Russian salad, her favorite foods since childhood. To keep her senses sharp for the long evening ahead of her, she avoided the sedating effects of alcohol. She had made no particular preparations or notes. As always, she would effortlessly ad lib her lecture on her physics theories and discoveries. She carried her knowledge in her head and would be speaking to people who believed they knew something of physics. This, of course, was a fallacy. In truth, most of them had grasped only a fraction of her theories. Furthermore, the greater part of her audience would be men, governed by their animal instincts, incapable of resisting her or of denying her demands. They would hang on her lips – her breasts, her legs – like starving maggots. At least that is what she thought until she met a man who would teach her to revise her oh-so-certain convictions, if only for a fleeting moment.

The press conference was delayed. Media representatives waited impatiently. In the meantime, Professor Sacharin had been finally introduced to Mischa in all formality as the university's headmaster, which didn't impress her in the least, nor change her opinion of him. To running television cameras and the usual flashbulb fireworks, he strode by her side through the rows of media, swelling like a peacock, sticking his nose in the air to make him more imposing than he actually was, strutting his position and importance. As a scientist, he was an icon, as a human being, a puling pittance, or even better, a sponge, occasionally soaking up water. Two additional physics professors followed them to a table at the far end of the hall with four seats, each equipped with a microphone. As the others sat down, turning their faces to the audience, he remained demonstratively upright, shrieking for silence in a squeaking falsetto. He waited until all conversation had ceased and quiet settled over the hall. With due ceremony, he opened the official press conference, proudly presenting the evening's guest of honor – here he introduced an eternal, theatrical pause to underscore his words -- the youngest scientist of world repute since time began. Naturally, she was a native Russian, what other national could bring forth such genius? Aristoteles, Aristarchus, Archimedes, Ptolemais and other mathematicians, physicists and philosophers of antiquity would have swooned at the sight of her, paled upon hearing her lectures, stunned by the beauty and wisdom creation revealed through her, abashed by her insights exceeding the limits of their own thought, leaving them far behind in the dust. Had she lived in their times, the Pythagorean Theory would be now called the Turowian Theory, western civilization would have been inspired by Russia instead of by Greece, and the mom and Mars would have long been peopled.

It was rumored that his appointment was primarily due to President Kutin's intervention, allegedly in gratitude to Sachrin's family for hiding his Jewish grandmother from the murderous, pillaging SS troops during the rapid German advance in World War II when Nazi Germany invaded the Soviet Union. This, however, was only unproven rumor and had no impact on Kutin's popularity. After all, many of Russian anti-Semites stemmed from Jewish Khazars.

Once the rector had completed his polemic, throwing in a few dry bon mots received with dubious smiles, he cleared the stage for journalists to question their illustrious guest. Mischa answered even the most obscure questions amiably and stoically, glad she was spared going into any probing or personal issues before her scientific lecture, which was to begin in a few minutes.

But her relief was short-lived. After several questions referring to the new Dynamo Theory and its possible impacts, a man, introducing himself as Pierce McFraser, correspondent for *New Glasgow Herald* the took the floor. Speaking Russian, his Scottish accent could be clearly discerned. Contrary to the other journalists, he spoke quietly and slowly, choosing every word with care. Were all other previous questions practically shouted at her to be heard over the general tumult, McFraser's calm voice reached her clearly, commanding the audience's silence and attention. It was not that he looked so much differently than the others, it was his manner of complete composure, self-assurance and superiority. She had rarely met a man of this caliber. She perceived him as a boulder, firmly, immovably planted in the center of a sea of pebbles. His face was impassive as he asked the first question. It sounded like a skeptical statement, bordering on an accusation.

"Professor Turowa, despite my deepest regrets, is it not highly unusual and conspicuous that within the shortest period of time two men of your acquaintance met their deaths. Setting aside how they died, what can you tell us about this rare accumulation of unnatural demise in your immediate surroundings?"

Mischa blanched internally but maintained her cool demeanor.

"Yes, it is odd. First, I lost my fiancé and then I was kidnapped and attacked by a sexual offender. There has been enough press on both incidents. I would kindly ask you not to remind of it. Both experiences were shattering. The next question, please."

An Iswestija reporter made a bid for her attention, but McFraser's quiet voice overrode her.

"I realize that Professor Turowa, but allow me another question, as you seem to have recovered from both traumata quite quickly. How did you come to dance, of all things, on a small boat smack dab in the middle of the Danube's stronger rapids? And how could an allegedly serious criminal drive you thirty kilometers from St. Petersburg without you defending yourself or attempting to jump out of the car or calling for help? You must have been able to open the car door easily."

Instinctively, Mischa recognized her enemy. His accusing questions were delivered calmly, without the slightest aggression or animosity, as if he were posing a simple, rational theory. His doubts hit the bull's eye, could cost her existence, putting her in prison for life. McFraser was better at putting two and two together than all the policemen put together who had questioned her and swallowed the feast of lies she had set before them. She suddenly wondered if he was a good chess player. It would be interesting to play against him. But first she had to deflect the looming danger he posed. Her best bet was to feign an emotional crisis and gain the audience's sympathy. She must deflect his questions before they took on the air of a police investigation where she would run the risk of contradicting herself, or even worse, expose herself as a two-time murderess. She shook head sadly, brought tears to her eyes, allowing one to trail down her cheek. She gazed at McFraser in despair.

"How could you, Mr. McFraser ask a woman who had been through so much such insinuating questions? Haven't suffered enough, losing a man I loved more than my life? Wasn't it enough to have my life threatened by a convicted sexual perpetrator trying to rape me? Do you think, just because you're a man, you can treat a woman like that?"

She began to tremble and sob, playing her role beautifully. This man, this cur, this miserable paparazzo dared to challenge her, to defy her, the great Mischa Turow, world famous and globally admired? He must be humiliated before all these people, in such a way that he would never again dare to, would be too ashamed to ever renew his questions probing in the right direction.

Indignant muttering arose throughout the hall. A wave of pity cascaded over an excellently performing Mischa, while the Scotsman was viewed with scorn, became the butt end of loud disrespectful and contemptuous remarks. The rector laid his hand comfortingly on Mischa's shoulder, took the microphone and, when the voices quieted, scolded the Scottish reporter.

"Have a minimum of respect Mr. McFraser for one of the greatest scientists of our time and a wonderful young woman who has suffered terrible trials through absolutely no fault of her own. She would otherwise not be sitting among us tonight. Investigations by both the Austrian and Russian police have cleared her name beyond a shadow of a doubt. Professor Turowa has earned our compassion and admiration, certainly not unfounded suspicions or accusations. As you can see for yourself, your inappropriate questions have reawakened those traumatic experiences she was forced to endure. Experiences we would wish upon no man or woman. Shortly, she will be giving a highly complex lecture. Be so kind and grant her a few moments of rest. I hope we are all in agreement when we end this press conference at this point to spare Professor Turow any further discomfort which may endanger her lecture that the entire world has long been waiting for, not only the world of physics. Those of you with reserved seats are warmly welcome to hear Ms. Turow's lecture. The rest of you, and specifically you Mr. McFraser, are asked to refrain from disrupting the talk. Ladies and gentlemen, I wish you a pleasant evening and thank you for your understanding."

Mischa had done it again. Without the slightest effort or pleading, the rector had served her purposes, defended her, protected her from an appalling enemy, spared her his accusations. That was one of her strengths. Men, particularly those who were weak and insecure, attempted to gain the lovely lady's favor by defending her interests. Little did they know their endeavors only increased their attractiveness as potential victims.

Covertly, still somewhat atremble, she looked over to McFraser. Apparently unaffected by either the uproar he had caused or the rector's reprimands, he stood up, as casually and confidently as he had posed his questions – the only worth-while questions during the entire press conference – he strode toward the exit. She had always been a warrior, Mischa thought to herself. And now, finally, she had found a commensurate opponent. A man. Not a weakling and bootlicker like Sacharin and not a duel on the chess board, but a real challenger, here and now, in real life. Her opinion of him altered. She observed him from afar. He began to appeal to her, as the only person here who could call himself a man. She hoped she would see him again, later on in the lecture hall. Maybe he was the one. Maybe he could put an end to her compulsion to torture men. Maybe he could sooth her endless longing to experience normal love and happiness. He attracted her more than Richard had done when they had first met.

Chapter 11

Applause for her lecture was endless. For one and half hours she had stood at the lectern and spoke about her Dynamo Theory as if it were the easiest thing in the world. She had scribbled formulas and curves on the whiteboard behind her that only a select few in the vast, lecture amphitheater, filled to capacity, understood, even though most of them called themselves physicists. One thing was clear to everyone, though. Very soon, this young, genial woman standing before them, demonstrating coherencies none of them had ever dreamed of, would soon be accepted into the illustrious circle of Nobel Prize Laureates. Fascinating, almost unbelievable new possibilities for communications technology, the transportation industry, data transmission, aviation, space travel and even medicine emerged from her theory. She was literally intoxicated by her lecture, had swept her audience up and away with her enthusiasm for a marvelous, impending future.

Particularly one listener who had never seen the attraction of physics or mathematics, lost his disinterest in dry, pedantic and unworldly matter during Mischa's illustrative, albeit incomprehensible in its details, demonstration. This one person was Pierce McFraser, the Scotsman, sitting in the third row. Mischa had only spotted him near the end of her lecture. In the hour and a half of her talk and gesticulated explanations, his face had lost its aloofness and was brightly open. She was relieved to see him, gave no thought to his ominous questions during the press conference. Had he even smiled at her? She thought she had seen a curving of his lips and expected to see him among those who came to the lectern to congratulate her. Maybe he would even apologize or invite her out for a drink. But he didn't. He was not one of the many who rushed the stage to shake her hands worshipfully, to give her flowers and other gifts. Neither did her come to the subsequent reception. Had her performance been too much? Too good? Had she chased him away? She would have loved to have met him personally, but, that's her luck, she thought, true love will never find her anyway. It would be better to never see him again. Who knows, he might be the one to bring her crimes to light. She tried not to think of him anymore, to banish him from her mind, but he haunted her. She thoughts refused to detach themselves from him, although she knew she was playing with fire and would most likely get burned. If anyone could expose her, he could. Was it the thrill of danger, her regard for his acuity or the man McFraser that drew her? She couldn't formulate her fascination with him, had no explanation for why the thought of never seeing him again made her stomach seize up nauseously.

She spent another three days in Moscow, strolling through the city, buying useless things like a purse, a leather jacket, purple lipstick, but also two sensible things, a painting by Isaak Brodski and an El Lissitzky sketch. Both would be outstanding additions in her Viennese penthouse, despite the fact that they were complete opposites. But opposites had always attracted her. She visited the Kubinka Tank Museum, the Tretjakov Gallery and the flea market, where she found and purchased an old Russian chess set that had obviously been played often and suffered plenty. The wooden men were extremely worn and faded, the paint barely discernable. She liked that.

In the evening she visited the Bolshoi Theater with newly won friends from the Lomonossow University physics faculty. A great lover of Tchaikovsky, she admired the half-naked men twirling and flying over the ballet stage, ever invoking the same thoughts. But this evening, her mind was only filled with images of the man who caused panic and terror to course through her body. In every sadist lives a masochist. Without admitting it to herself, the fear he triggered excited her, just as the fear she inflicted on other men.

After the performance, they took a taxi to an exquisite, small cellar restaurant where they ate well and sumptuously, but mostly laughed, joked, sang Kalinka accompanied by domra and balalaika, and Mischa allowed herself to be swept into the dancing. Swan Lake, Crimea champagne, borscht, Ukrainian varenyky stuffed with cherries, delightful Russian folk melodies, hands on hips, mouths whooping loudly, legs kicking wildly in Cossack style, altogether a marvelous, inimitable combination only to be found in Moscow if you are not one of those who such pleasure would cost a month's salary or more. But for her and her university colleagues with access to lucrative, supplementary income, this was not the case. Baksheesh flowed steadily into their ever-open pockets for matriculating near-illiterate sons and daughters of the city's many nouveau riche, or for issuing top-grade exam certificates, diplomas and other attests to the wealthy, graced with little more intelligence than an earthworm or fruit fly, future elite of Russia, who are, of course, loyal members of President Kutin's party with only the country's, or at least the party members', best interest at heart.

On the third day, Mischa flew back to St. Petersburg, and there he was, sitting a few rows behind her in economy class, reading a newspaper. Apparently, he hadn't noticed her. For the first time in her life, her heart beat as wildly as any normal young girl's would for a man. But not for any man. Of all men, her heart thundered for Pierce McFraser, the only man out to destroy her. Yet, her attraction was founded in the danger he posed to her, in the angst he triggered in her, in the power he held over her without her having the least notion of it, which was certainly not the usual heartthrob of a normal young girl.

Once in the air and the seatbelt sign switched off, she made her way through economy class to the rear toilets instead of the ones in first class. When McFraser still didn't look up, but kept his nose in his newspaper, she accidently on purpose knocked her knee on his armrest, yelping quietly as if in pain, as if a suddenly jolt of the airplane had caused her to stumble and she had hurt herself. Finally, he looked up and caught her in free fall. A hot shudder bolted through her body. Never before had a man touched her so.

"It's okay, thank you," she said. "Oh, it's you! What a coincidence, I nearly didn't recognize you."

"Hello, Dr. Turow," he said, "nice to see you here. Is everything all right or should we call the stewardess?"

"No, that won't be necessary. I just need to sit down for a moment until the pain subsides. I banged my knee."

"Of course. The seat next to mine is free. I'll just slide over, so you don't have to climb over me."

He slid onto the center seat, leaving the aisle seat free for her.

"I hope you've forgiven my questions at the university press conference," he began conversationally.

"Well, I can't say your questions were exactly kind, but you weren't the first person to ask them. The police wanted to know the same things during their investigations," she lied, since it had occurred to neither the Austrian gendarme and inspectors, nor their Russian colleagues to probe in the right direction, as he had done. The surrounding circumstances and her reputation as a serious and world-renowned scientist had caused them to swallow Mischa's lies without question. A professor at the Vienna University had once told her that anyone disliking Beethoven's music or doubting Einstein's statements is a philistine and a moron. Which was one of the reasons why, in 1938, when Austria was annexed by Nazi Germany and all Jewish professors at the Vienna University were ousted, the once noble institute sank into mediocrity. It was the same complacency and conformity of those swimming with the tides, those discomfited by criticism of the powerful, those cringing when commonly accepted, chiseled in stone truths are questioned, with which the Austrian and Russian police led their investigations. They shrank from the possible repercussions of doubting one such as Mischa Turow.

The conversation the Scotsman brought Mischa no closer to him. He was polite and attentive, showed interest in her research, but not in her person, regardless of her efforts to show him her interest in him. He was different from all other men she met so far, composed and aloof, and remained composed and aloof. Although he understood little of chess and physics, not saying much, it was he who navigated their conversation. Despite her genius, she felt like a schoolgirl confronting a teacher. He asked all the right questions as if he already knew their answers and simply wanted to discover if Mischa had learned her lessons well. He was ten or twelve years her senior. Everything about him attracted her, not only his deep, warm and thoughtful voice, also his enigmatic smile – was that agreement or disapproval? – his self-assurance, his wit, his humor, and yes, even his smell. That he was shorter and much less educated in natural sciences than she was didn't seem to bother him in the least. She was certain he had a diploma in journalism, history or languages, subjects that held no interest for her. He had a response to her most intelligent remarks, clearly expressing his opinion that there was more to life than physics, chess, art or the Bolshoi Theater without hurting her feelings or bringing his profession to the forefront. He gave her no footing on personal ground, if he was married, had a girlfriend or children or about any other people close to him. In any case, he did not wear a ring or have any tell-tale signs of having worn one, which was not conclusive evidence. Men more adept than Leskow knew how to skillfully disguise their marital status when stalking women, which McFraser obviously wasn't. When she suggested they might get together for a drink one evening during the World Championship elimination finals, his reply was a monosyllabic "We'll see." Any other man would have been charmed, willingly seduced, becoming putty in her hands. But she couldn't get a hold on him. It seemed as if her were used to women swarming around him, that he only needed to wait until they threw themselves at his feet and begged for his affections. But this was all in her head. He didn't give her a second thought, at least not yet. He was not a flirting man, and certainly not with a woman in the public eye and involved in two deaths, one following on the heels of the other. He kept up the conversation on the airplane to be polite and to amass more information on her for his article in the *New Glasgow Herald*, which would not be only flattering. This, however, he kept to himself to keep his source from abruptly running dry.

The seatbelt indicator lit up and the pilot announced their approach in St. Petersburg. Somewhat disappointed, she bade

McFraser good-bye and returned to her seat. She did not get his telephone number and he did not ask for hers. In any case, she knew he wrote for the *New Glasgow Herald* and assumed he was also correspondent to other English-speaking media in St. Petersburg. She was certain she would see him again or knew where she could find him. Seldom, if ever, had she been so captivated by and drawn to a man who was everything else but not an object upon whom she could unleash her sadistic sex-drive. She simply felt the need to be close to him, to come together with him. No matter that he was shorter than her, he was obviously the stronger of the two. True strength lies in the character, not in height or muscle mass.

Chapter 12

The final match between Mischa Turow and Jamie Rothstein to determine the World Championship candidate was talked up in the media as a battle between Russia and the U.S.A., almost as if time had traveled back to 1972 when Bobby Fischer confronted Russian title holder Boris Spasski in Reykjavik, Iceland. Suffering from paranoia, Bobby Fischer was long reluctant and only agreed to play after Henry Kissinger's personal intervention yet went on to storm the chess field and snatch the crown from the Russian's head. Fischer's extravagances, escapades and provocations kept the world breathless for weeks on end, the global chess community population exploded, sales of chess boards and chessmen reached unheard-of highs and every day chess made headline news, for once outshining soccer, tennis and ice hockey. That all four protagonists, then and now, were Jewish was hardly mentioned. Yet particularly appealing to many was the fact that Robert James Fischer, as he was properly called, was an ardent anti-Semite, his Jewish descent notwithstanding. This was his saving grace.

The highest American and Russian politicians plunged into the freshly declared war on 64 squares, loudly and fervently supporting their champions on television and in the press with arguments that had as much to with chess as the

egg of Columbus with a Russian hen. The American president, an aging playboy and millionaire with blond hair and
falsetto voice declared Jamie Rothstein, in titanic ignorance of
who she really was, a brave defender of Christian civilization
challenging the untamed hordes of the East, which of course
triggered a roar of indignity in Russia, closing the ranks behind
Mischa even more firmly.

President Ivan Sergejevitsch Kutin made a demonstration
of presenting Mischa with high medal, normally reserved for
Russian army generals. At the presentation ceremony in the
Winter Palace a few days prior to the battle's onset, he announced he was certain Mischa Turowa would put the arrogant, megalomaniac Americans, who want to control the entire
world, in their place. Mischa took the opportunity, as soon as
the cameras were turned off, to tell Kutin it would be a great
honor to be invited to dinner at the Kremlin, as she had already
dined at the White House with the U.S. president and with
the French leader at the Elysée Palace. Kutin laughed, tickled
by her directness, and said it would be his pleasure to invite
her, whether she triumphed over the American or not, but she
should. This was her patriotic duty and should not be put aside
lightly. She fought for Russia and should show the Americans
once and for all who was the stronger. Mischa's mood darkened
at this. To Kutin, she was nothing but a soldier, a chess piece,
when not the lowliest, that he moved as he chose on the chess
board in his match against the U.S.A.

Furthermore, McFraser seemed to have lost interest in
her. He had not contacted her since their conversation on the
plane. Even if he didn't have her telephone number, as a journalist he would know where to find her, if he chose to seek her
out. Lately, her compulsion to enslave a man had mysteriously
vanished. Kutin and McFraser haunted her thoughts, which

was by no means an indication that her character had changed, but only temporarily wandered from sadism to masochism, the other side of the Janus face. Subconsciously, she no longer desired a weak man, but a strong one. She dreamed of becoming putty in his hands, of being the shape of his desires.

The stage in the Winter Palace tournament hall had been raised higher for the grand finale of the St. Petersburg World Championship elimination round, it was an old psychological maneuver, giving the impression that the two aspirants had climbed to Olympic heights. Mischa Turow and Jamie Rothstein should appear as goddesses to whom the audience should raise their eyes in worshipful admiration. Heightening histrionics to heady hyperbole, the small flags before each protagonist had been dispensed with and replaced by giant Russian and U.S. American flags, on the walls behind each player, held taut with poles. The flags now dominated television and press cameras, framing the players as if at political summit meeting. Some people had the impression that the two chess Grandmasters were no less than ambassadors representing Kutin and his U.S. American adversary.

Bustling, dwarfish Ruslam Maschinow, the gaunt FIDE chairman, rumored to be a former mafia boss, an office commonly held part time or full time by influential Russians, gave a rambling and exceedingly boring speech heeded by no one. Subsequently, the first, restlessly anticipated game began.

Mischa led white, choosing the Queen's Gambit opening, failing however to achieve a winning edge, despite her not negligible efforts. After five hours, the game ended in a draw, as did the second and third games. Again, the victor would be the player with the most points after nine games. Should the score remain tied, four games ensued with only one hour's time limit per player with each given two games leading white and two black. Should there still not be a decisive winner, players entered sudden death blitz games. The Grandmaster leading black receives a one-minute advantage to compensate for her opponents opening edge; white has four minutes for the entire game, black has five. The first player to lose a match or run out of time, loses the entire match. Not a very elegant solution, but better than deciding the winner by lots.

At the close of nine regular games, the score stood at $4^{1}/_{2}$: $4^{1}/_{2}$. Neither of the women had managed to win a game outright, which had a dramatic effect on public interest. Only a smattering of people had come to the last three games, regardless of the championship stakes involved and the alleged patriotic weight of a battle between Russia and the U.S.A. Few seats were occupied in the hall. One stalemate after the other is hardly thrilling, no matter how weighty the consequences. Spectators want to see goals, dueling blood, the Toro's death, or even better the Torero's, or chess victories. Conciliatory finales are boring.

At the onset of the second phase in the competition, the hall filled once again, when not to capacity, in the hopes of witnessing a yearned-for checkmate or surrender by one of the two Grandmasters brought about by the extremely abbreviated time limit. Yet, to massive disappointment, these four games also ended in a draw.

There remained but one, single blitz game to play. Alone the color selection, regulated by the classic fisted choice – the chief arbiter holds a pawn, one black, one white, in each of his fists and the players choose – could have a decisive impact on the outcome. The player leading white had one minute less to reflect than her opponent. She must win the game within four minutes if she did not want to lose all she had worked for, the match and her right to challenge the title holder.

The hall and Hermitage plaza were once again full to bursting. The next nine minutes would determine who was to challenge the incumbent World Champion and this final blitz sortie would decide the victor of this epic battle between Russian and the U.S.A., a sensation destined to draw spectators by the thousands. In addition to the wide screens inside and outside the hall electronically broadcasting moves as they took place on the chess board, television cameras were suspended over the game table transmitting the critical game to viewers all over the world. Swiss media interrupted a live soccer match between Zurich and Basel to see Mischa Turow, who they considered one of their own, in action. Even those without a whit of chess affinity backed her passionately as if the honor or blank existence of their tiny country was at stake.

Less than a meter from the game table, cordoned off with a red rope, sat privileged VIPs, pressing on all four sides to catch every move at close quarters. Inside the ring, standing next to the table where the two challengers were seated, stood Grandmaster and chief arbiter Ivan Reblov. His job was to start the clocks, to implacably, and in the final analysis, uphold FIDE rules and, should the slightest infringement occur, to immediately stop the game and announce his decision according to FIDE regulations. Should all go smoothly, and the game culminates in either checkmate or overstepping the time-limit, it will be his honor to announce one of the players as victorious.

Reblov was a corpulent man ever bathed in sweat, who permanently wiped his face and neck with a sopping cloth handkerchief. To disguise his not exactly enticing body odor, he applied perfume lavishly. Which was not much better. Thus, he exuded a sweet, flowery stench whereby a moldy, sluggish effluvium would have much better corresponded with his obesity. The cordon on his side of the table had to be pushed back an extra meter to make space for his colossal mass. Standing for nine minutes at a stretch was an Olympian act for him, but there was no other option to ensure seamless game supervision. For the first time in the tournament's three-month duration, he was called on to earn the money the FIDE paid him. Nine long minutes he was forbidden to sit, was required to keep his eyes and concentration on the chess board. He must follow the rapid-fire moves with scrupulous attentiveness to discover and mercilessly penalize even the tiniest inadvertence such as unintentionally touching a figure or making an errant move – a frequent occurrence in blitz chess – which, in strict compliance with the rules, would lead to immediate forfeit and defeat.

Mischa and Jamie sat across from one another, both nervous, but without animosity. Their eyes met and held firm. In a few seconds, the infernal cliff-hanger game would begin, the game that would cost one of them the chance to challenge the World Champion, not to mention years of arduous work and effort. Over the past nine days, they had wrestled long and hard with one another, neither of them making a single error in nine games, resulting in nine draws. This game is different. Whatever happens, they can no longer offer a draw, not even when their positions are wholly equal. Within the next nine minutes, one of them has to lose, there is no alternative, unless, before four minutes have elapsed, they have reached perpetual check or a draw because there are not enough men to establish checkmate – a most unlikely occurrence. But, should this come about, they would be forced to immediately launch another unnerving battle under the same conditions, once more risking everything.

Be it coincidence or fate, or whatever you want to call it, Reblov stretched his clenched fists holding the two colors in

Mischa's face. The audience held its collective breath. Slowly, Mischa indicated the right hand. Reblov opened it, revealing a white pawn. She now had only four minutes to checkmate Jamie, a trick she hadn't accomplished in nine previous games. She had spent many painstaking hours preparing for this game, and so had her opponent. With white, she hoped to surprise Rothstein by making moves never played before, even if they weren't optimal. Seeking the correct response would then cost her some of her additional time. Normally, a game opened with three or four standard options; pawns or knights moved center-board; the so-called Indian Defense moving a b or g pawn one square, or with a knight in the third row. In blitz games, a strong player would respond quickly and confidently, relying on her profound theoretical knowledge and photographic memory that recognized the opening and automatically made the responding moves deemed most appropriate. But Mischa planned a sensation by opening with allegedly absurd moves with the two outer pawns, 1. a3 and 2. h3. Because of its double tempo loss, this opening was considered dilettantish and unworthy of developing theories to respond to it. Beginners were expressly advised not to play this opening and a Grandmaster would never play it unless she had five hundred Elo points more than her opponent and wanted to prove she would win all the same.

Reblov requested absolute silence in the hall. He waited until his request was granted, even in the outer-most rows and then pressed the button activating Mischa's second counter. She instantly moved as planned, far-left pawn from a2 to a3. Less than a second later she stopped her timer, which set Jamie's clock in motion. As expected, Jamie was taken completely by surprise by Mischa's opening. She knew it was considered pathetic, but how to respond? At a loss, she hesitated, losing a full ten seconds before, not knowing what else to do, moved her king's pawn two squares forward to center-board. Occupying the center was always recommended, no matter how your challenger opened. With lightning speed, Mischa responded with her second, equally unorthodox move, far-right pawn from h2 to h3. It took her less than a second. Jaime hesitated again, even gripped her forehead and lost another ten seconds deciding to move her queen's pawn next to the king's.

Jamie's beginning position was now stronger than Mischa's, but her time advantage had shrunk from sixty to forty-two seconds, thirty percent, after only two moves. Furthermore, Mischa had expected those moves and had the strongest responses in petto. Thus, her next moves cost her practically no time at all – à tempo as chess players express it – while the unusual strategy pressed Jamie into reflections, her seconds slipping by like an old man's years. In less than ten moves, her time advantage was depleted. She suffered a deficit and was forced to find answers to Mischa's instantaneous, well-prepared moves. Which she failed to do. Her initial position advantage quickly transformed into a hopelessly faulty one. A murmur swept through the audience as she lost her first pawn. Shortly thereafter, she lost another, and then a third. She had lost. Baffled and completely demoralized, she stood up without stopping her clock, gave Mischa her hand and abruptly vanished. As if she had never been there. Mischa alone saturated the space. No one gave another thought to the loser or to the alacrity of her defeat.

Indescribable roaring jubilation erupted. Spectators raised Mischa onto their shoulders, snatched the Russian flag from it anchors and began to wave it as they danced exuberantly. *Kalinka, kalinka maja* was bellowed to frenzied stamping in the hall and on the Hermitage plaza. Tournament officials were powerless against the frantically celebrating mob. Crowd-control police outside the Winter Palace gave up all pretense of doing their jobs and joined in the riotous hullaballoo, dancing, screaming, singing and whooping like Cossacks, throwing their caps in the air, kissing and hugging each other as only Russians do. Television images, more rambunctious than any soccer triumph, detonated on sets around the world.

Although Mischa was not yet world champion, merely vice-world champion, to the Russians she was the uncontested heroine who won the war of the minds against the United States of America. What Jews won't do for the other peoples of this world, particularly for those who had perpetrated the most horrendous pogroms and other crimes against their race! Mischa was in excellent company with Jesus, Freud and Einstein as well as Bruno Kreisky and Pierre Mendès France. But in contrast to her fellow idols, Mischa was a murderess. A double-murderess unbeknownst to the countless newspaper and television journals who photographed, filmed and interviewed her in the wake of her triumph. Detailed reports of the genial scientist and chess player's most recent accomplishment made the media rounds. She was celebrated as a role model for young people. Television aired a myriad of reports and special programs on this much admired and emulated woman. Young and old, talented and mediocre, lovely and homely, prude and promiscuous, everyone wanted to be like Mischa Turow – sovereign and uplifted by the masses.

Zurich city council decided to arrange a large reception for Mischa at the Kloten Airport before she caught her connecting flight to Vienna. They also planned to rename in her honor a narrow lane in Niederdorf, an Old City district directly on the Limmat River. The street in question was well-populated; during the day by business people, shoppers

and tourists; at night by theater-goers, prostitutes and criminals, city elders couldn't have selected a better. Unless, of
course they had chosen the nearby university district on the
upper Rämis Street, which was also home to sex offenders,
murderers and drug-users up to no good, most of them
holding a PhD or professorship, dutifully paying their taxes
and lauded by the general public instead of being locked up.
Certain inborn human impulses that go unchecked will not
shrink from the most heinous misdeed, most of which are
perpetrated unseen and unheard. They cannot be exorcized
from the soul, not even with today's advanced upbringing
and educational possibilities. The war between intellect and
instinct that has been raging since the beginning of humanity
has yet to be decided. It probably never will be.

Alderman Ernst Josef Stämpfli of the right-wing nationalist Swiss party was delegated to call the Zurich professor and
freshly designated World Chess Championship challenger,
Professor Mischa Turow in St. Petersburg and request she delay
her flight to Vienna by two hours. He was also in charge of or-
ganizing the reception, an exquisite buffet and official speakers,
of sending out invitations and of formulating a press release
announcing the event. Few living still knew that it was his
grandfather who, during World War II believed Nazi Germany
would soon rule the world, urgently warned against Switzerland's *Verjudung*, i.e. increasing Jewish population; thundered
against accepting Jewish refugees fleeing Vienna and vehemently demanded a St. Gall policeman, Paul Grüninger, be
discharged and punished for disregarding orders from Bern
and issuing residency papers to eight hundred young Viennese
refugees who had managed to circumvent the bloodhounds
and bayonet-carrying Swiss Border Patrol who would have
handed them over to the SS. Two hundred thousand other

Jews would not survive remaining in their homeland. A gold-framed photograph of the aforementioned grandfather hung in the Stämpfli family's living room, a constant reminder to remain vigilant and defend Swiss values as he defined them.

Highly popular among his people, Swiss Federal Councilman Emil von Stauffenried, Minister for Education and Sports, former successful ski racer and *Fürsprech*, as lawyers are called in Bern, sent a diplomatic note to his Russian colleague. He pointed out that Mischa Turow, without an 'a', thank you, had represented her homeland of choice, Switzerland and not her country of birth Russia, and therefore demanded an explanation for why the Russian flag and not the Swiss flag was on display in the Winter Palace hall. Russian Minister of Sports and Culture, Michail Maximovitch Pavlov, was another close friend of President Kutin's, and an ice hockey, basketball and pretty young ballerina promoter. He financed luxury condos for the latter's discreet use out of his vast fortune, rumored to have originated in the sale of state's treasures at the end of the Communist Era and to be as large as Kutin's. Responding posthaste, Pavlov explained that FIDE, the World Chess Federation was responsible and wholly independent of the Russian government. The Swiss should take up this issue with Federation Chairman Ruslam Maschinow, who has his residence in Geneva and is a generous taxpayer. Let it be known, he highlighted in his dispatch addressed to *My Dearest Colleague Emil von Stauffenried* Russia held Switzerland, its government and its people in the highest regard. Furthermore, to underscore the close bond between the two countries and peoples, he would personally commission his state secretary responsible for sports to be especially attentive to placing the Swiss flag directly next to the Russian flag at all future events with Swiss participation. And just to clear up any possible misunderstandings, he suggested a friendly get-together at his chalet in Verbier in the Valais canton where he will, as every winter, spend his ski holidays. He, his wife and daughter and all of their many Russian friends deeply admire this wonderful location, its marvelous atmosphere, both warm-hearted and discreet. And thus, without further communiqués or diplomatic snags, the topic was washed away in the Rhone River, springing forth from the mountains of Valais, crossing the *lemanischen* Lake to flow through Geneva, the city of Calvin and Rousseau, of banks, clocks, international organizations and tax evaders. Allegedly Russian mafia bosses and dubious Russian playboys, politicians and businesspeople are among them, but this has never been proven beyond the shadow of a doubt.

Chapter 13

A day before her return flight to Zurich, Mischa decided to approach Peirce McFraser one last time. She had discovered he tended to take his lunch alone at a popular cafeteria on Newski Prospect, St. Petersburg's noblest boulevard, not far from her hotel. She put on her shortest miniskirt and highest heels. Shortly before twelve noon, she set out for the cafeteria, her steps accompanied by admiring glances and beckoning wolf-whistles from both young and older men alike, all of which she took in stride, as was her wont. To her disappointment, the Scotsman was nowhere to be seen. She bought a vegetable smoothie and sat at the last free table. And then she saw him, a full tray in his hands, scouring the venue for an unoccupied seat. Feigning surprise, she waved to him, indicating the free chair at her table. McFraser had little choice if he didn't want to appear impolite. He approached her table and set his tray down. Since their acquaintance had a brief history, he greeted her as customary in many countries, but not in Russia, with an inconsequential kiss on each cheek, which she reciprocated.

"You do know," she said, "that's not a widespread practice here. In Russia, only lovers kiss each other."

"Excuse me, please, I hadn't thought about that," he replied.

"There's nothing to excuse," she insinuated with a wink, "maybe you're in love with me."

He studied her for signs of an attempt at approaching him. She returned his gaze.

"I'm not sure how to answer that. Who isn't smitten with you?" he responded, side-stepping a direct answer.

"And you?" she wanted to know.

"Well, to be honest, a bit I suppose. Women like you are far and few between."

She took his hand, caught and held his eyes saying, "You are a wonderful man, Pierce. Any woman claiming you would consider herself lucky."

"Are you serious?"

"I wouldn't say so otherwise."

"You confound me. Last month I separated from a woman I had been with for six years. I'm not quite ready for a new relationship, I need time to think things over."

Mischa withdrew her hand. She didn't want to seem too eager. She her fish had taken the bait and before long would bite hard into the hook as long as she didn't yank of the rod or try to reel him in too quickly. Besides, this was no ordinary fish, but a very rare and special one. Once she had him, she wouldn't ever let him go.

"You should eat something, you look starved," she said, laughing into his eyes. "It looks like I need to cheer you up. After a month's time, you needn't worry all too much about a woman you've put behind you. The world is full of beautiful women, especially for a man like you!"

As he ate, and she drank her smoothie, they spoke together like two people who were deeply in love with one another or were well on their way to becoming so. This was no flirt, but deeply intimate bonding. The brief episode of uncertainty that had afflicted Pierce McFraser upon Mischa's seemingly coincidental re-entry into his life soon faded. He regained his nonchalance, self-assurance and sharp wit that so fascinated her, this time enhanced by a subtle, cryptic humor. If she hadn't known for a fact he was a Scotsman, she would have probably taken him for an Englishman. The longer she watched him and the more she talked, interrupted only by his occasional trenchant, parenthetical remarks, making her chuckle or laugh out loud, the more powerful her desire for him took hold. She ached to lay in his strong arms, to press her lips to his, to feel his muscular body on hers and his lustful thrusts inside her as her tongue thrust deep into his mouth. Oh, how she would love to be the slave for once, his slave. She had only a few hours before her flight, an obstacle she suddenly rebelled against, a boulder rolled onto her path to the man she wanted, the man who was sitting across from her right here, right now. She must make a run for it, take a shortcut and ask him directly if he wanted to go to bed with her before the boulder of her looming departure rolled onto her path and kept her from him. But he wasn't one of her playthings, one of her slaves who would do anything she demanded, answering to her every whim. She held no power over him. she was the one who wanted to sacrifice herself to his will, he was her master. How could she say what she wanted from him? How could she beg him to take her, take her with all the power he was capable of; that she wanted nothing more than to lay herself, body and soul at his command, permitting him, no, pleading with him to bless her as he fancied?

He had no idea what was going on in her mind, that she was only waiting for him to tear her from the table, wordlessly leading her to the next flophouse. She was terrified this magical moment would vanish forever if she did not immediately make perfectly clear to him what she wanted. Right now, today, before she boarded that plane. She took his hand and spoke to him as she had never spoken to one of her slaves. It was more a subtle supplication.

"Pierce, do me a favor. Come with me to a hotel and do with me what you will. I want to be your slave, I want to do what you command. Love me, beat me, I belong to you, but do it now. Tomorrow I will be gone, and we may never see each other again."

Never before had a woman spoken such words to Pierce McFraser, especially never such an attractive woman as Mischa Turow. He was conscious of his effect on women but had never taken advantage of it. In the six years of his relationship, he had been loyally monogamous. Yet, here was one of the most attractive women he had ever met literally begging for his love, for his dominion over her. Pierce was not in the least hardwired for dominance or, heaven forbid, sadism, but neither was he immune to the electrifying impact of her words. He tenderly stroked her cheek with his hand.

"I will love you as no man has ever loved you before, that's a promise. Come, Mischa, my slave!"

His lips curved into a smile at his last words. He hadn't taken her words seriously, didn't believe they were meant literally but rather as the teasing cooing of lovers. But his smile would soon be wiped off his face. Her words were in deadly earnest, she was very demanding slave and expected unrelenting stringency from her chosen master, the same severity with which she used and abused her slaves. If he had known what lay in wait for him, he would never have agreed, but have turned his back on her for good.

He led her to his car, telling her of a small hotel on the city's periphery, where, for a price, they would be spared the embarrassment of showing their papers. They should both wear wigs, so as not to be recognized. The idea of waking up tomorrow morning to find himself in all the newspapers was far from appealing, particularly when depicted as the scorned lover of the famous Mischa Turow, should she not want anything more to with him the next day.

"Your wish is my command, my master," she answered, misinterpreting his suggestion as an initial behest in his role as her lord and master.

They stopped at a store offering inexpensive wigs made in China. He chose one with short hair and midnight black, under which he hid his blond curls. She pulled a long-hair wig, ash blond in color, over her naturally lush brown mane. She also bought shoulder-length opera gloves made of black silk and a tightly-fitting velvet black choker with a golden buckle. Pierce asked if that was really necessary, he would love her without it, but Mischa held two fingers to his lips and said,

"Yes, it is. I want you to be my overlord, I want you to own me. You should see that I am your subjugated slave."

They drove to the hotel at the edge of the city. He paid in advance, discreetly giving the man at the reception desk an additional fifty-dollar bill. The key exchanged hands wordlessly.

Once in the room, Mischa expected her new master to treat her with the same contempt as she treated her slaves. He should look at her sternly, punish her, beat her for the tiniest inattention or hesitation. He should abuse her with whatever came to hand, inflict pain that made her cry out in torment and lust.

But Pierce McFraser was not the man for the job. He tried to mime the master but kissed her after every little smack on the butt, to take away the suffering she didn't feel. She asked him to hit her harder, to pull on her hair, to smash her breasts.

He gave it his best shot but found the situation more idiotic than stimulating and soon stopped.

Finally, she told him, "If you want to have sex with me, then you have to handle me like a ruthless slave-driver would deal with a worthless, truculent slave, otherwise it's just boring. I didn't come here with you for the fun of it, or to have you whisper sweet nothings in my ear. I came here solely for the torment that will give me endless orgasms."

Pierce tried again, hitting her harder on her backside. He pulled his belt from his pants but was unable to hurt her with it like she demanded. She urged him to hit her in the face, but he could only caress her cheek. Finally, as she knelt in front of him, head bowed, saying she awaited his commands, he couldn't help himself and burst out laughing. This humiliated Mischa far more than any beatings or torment possibly could, but not the humiliation she wanted from him. She screamed at him, calling him a coward and a pussy, not having the slightest idea how to handle a woman. Furious, she snatched up the knife accompanying the fruit basket by the bed, pressed it into his hand and stretching out her arm, roared at him,

"Here, cut me if you're a man! Show me you're strong and not a wimp like all the others!"

Pierce stared at her in horror. Was she mad? What was going on? Did she really want him to slash her? That had nothing to do with sex! She may be a genius, but she was obviously mentally disturbed and belonged in a psychiatric clinic. He no longer felt a spark of desire. His only wish was to calm this banshee, take the knife from her and bring her to her senses.

"Easy now, easy now, Mischa, no one is going to get hurt, especially not you. Please, give me the knife, then we can talk. Nothing has happened, and nothing is going to happen. Let's get dressed and go to the bar, have a drink together and forget the whole thing. Sometimes the chemistry between two people just isn't right."

Mischa's eyes narrowed as he spoke until they were the mere slits of a wildcat fully focused and ready to leap on its unsuspecting prey. Who was this piece of shit talking to her as if she were sick or disturbed? He knew nothing, was a worm, a cockroach like all other men. She wanted to give him one last chance and hoped he would use it.

"Either you cut me, or I will," she hissed.

Pierce was shocked. This woman was completely around the bend, was psychotic and a threat to him and herself. The knife in her hand was a dangerous weapon he absolutely must take away from her. He acted as if he was going to fulfil her wish and took the knife from her trembling, outstretched hands. Instead of slashing her with it, he carefully buried it in his small, black handbag.

That sent Mischa over the edge. Every fiber of her body was suffused with loathing for this stupid, stupid man who was incapable of enslaving her. He must be destroyed. He had degraded her more than she had ever degraded her slaves. She stood up slowly, as if his words had taken hold and she had come to her senses. She turned around and snatched up the first thing that came to hand, a heavy crystal-glass ashtray on the night table, spun with all the momentum of her fury and crashed the ashtray into his head. Pierce didn't have a nano-second to preparation for the attack and fell to the floor un-conscious without a sound.

Mischa took the knife from his bag, straddled his limp body and began slowly sinking the knife into his flesh. She gouged his legs, his arms, his belly. Blood erupted from the wounds. She began to moan, rocking on the lifeless body beneath her, felt the gathering force of an orgasm. She thrust the knife into his kidneys, his stomach, his face, his balls, his neck and into his heart, again and again. With the knife's final penetration, the tsunami of ecstasy crashed over her, an orgasm gathered from the depths of the ocean with the uncompromising power of her implacable nature. In tiny increments, the waves of bliss ebbed from her body. Exhausted, depleted and satiated, she sat on the floor next to the corpse, now barely recognizable as human.

It took her while to collect herself. She had to think rationally. There was no question of removing the sack of bones and blood. She could only remove herself. Luckily, she had kept her gloves on the entire time, there would none of her fingerprints in the room or hotel. Certainly, there would be a multitude of DNA, but who would ever think to compare it with hers? No one! The porter at the hotel reception hadn't seen her face, only the back of a woman with long, blond hair and sunglasses. She went into the bathroom and washed the blood from her clothes, stockings, shoes and wig, wisely keeping on her silk gloves. She blow-dried everything until it was only a bit moist, put her wig back on and the knife, the instrument of her lust now cleaned of her victim's blood, into her handbag. She made a minute search of the room, centimeter for centimeter, finding an earring she had lost and made an inventory of her handbag's contents. Everything was there. Nothing was missing. She left the light on in the room and slipped quietly out. The corridor was empty. She took the elevator down to the subterranean garage. No one in sight. She walked through the exit gates and blended in with the passing crowd, walking the entire way back to her hotel in the city center. She made no eye contact with anyone, spoke to no one. Taking a taxi or bus could have given her away. It took her less than two hours to cover the ten-kilometer stretch. Shortly before arriving at her hotel, she went into a department store and found one of the many ladies' toilets. Here, she used her tiny manicure scissors to cut the wig, gloves and choker into miniscule shreds, flushing them bit by bit down the toilet. She washed her hands at the sink, freshening her face powder, fixing her hair and reapplying her lipstick. Thusly, she returned to her hotel as if nothing spectacular had occurred. As if she were not coming from her third murder.

Her dress, shoes and undergarments would also have to go. Unfortunately, she must also dispose of the knife, the lover that had triggered in her a tidal wave of ecstasy she would have otherwise been denied. It was full of the Scotsman's DNA, a man who proved he was no man, not worthy of her and therefore forfeiting his life. It was his own fault. She left the hotel and went into a department store to buy new clothes, changed in the ladies' room and stuffed her old things into a shopping bag. For a long moment, she held the knife in her hand, caressing its shaft with her fingers, kissing it as other women kiss the living object of their passion. She broke her skin, watching the blood flow and licked the wound clean with her tongue. She felt a returning wetness between her legs, held the knife's blade more tightly in her hands, closed her eyes and revisited the scene, hoping to ride again the endless wave of orgasm that had flooded her as she drained the Scotsman of his life's blood.

She concentrated hard with the knife in her hand, with the warm blood from her hand on her tongue, but she could not relive the ecstasy. It was her own blood, and that was insufficient to sate her diabolical hunger. She wrapped her newly purchased silk scarf around her wound, threw the now useless knife into the sack with the other articles and went out onto the street. What to do with the damned bag? How to get rid of her shoes, the knife and the other things? Not a toilet in the world would swallow them for her.

As chance would have it, a trash truck crept slowly past her. It stopped at the side of the street in front of large garbage containers. The two workers jumped down from their running boards to roll the container to the truck. Mischa seized the moment and threw the shopping bag into the devouring maw at the truck's rear and walked away casually, without being observed.

Relieved she returned to her hotel. In her room, she threw herself on her bed to rest a while. She was overcome with pride in a job well done. No, perfectly executed. Once more, she had found an outstanding solution, as she always did. She had not only experienced the most intense orgasm in many moons, but she had permanently silenced the one man who posed a threat to her. The fool. How could she have ever admired such a pathetic twat, have believed she was in love with him? Well, he will not betray her now. He had gotten his just desserts for not taking her seriously, for thinking she was out of her mind. Who did he think he was to judge her, the cleverest woman in the world? He was nothing compared to her, he wasn't worth the air he breathed, and so he won't be breathing anymore. He was thoroughly ignorant of what he was missing: sexual fire of untold radiance. He had spent his life in undignified mediocrity, never climbing to the pinnacle, the only place worth living for, no matter in which field. Athletes, industrialists, inventors, artists and even politicians, when they weren't thinking of only themselves, have achieved glory, meandered through her addled synapses. Glory, that was the right word. Life must be glorious. Glory must be achieved, or life was not worth living.

Look, she had left the little hotel on the edge of the city without being seen, she had removed all evidence that could lead to her, except for the DNA, of course, but no one would connect her with that. She swelled with pride and a touch of what you could only call cheerful satisfaction. No one had recognized her. No one would suspect her. She had committed yet another perfect murder. What genius she was! Not only in physics or chess, but in everything she put her hand to! Not for nothing was she the best physicist on earth and would soon be world champion in chess. No human intelligence in the world could hold a candle to her.

She slept a few hours, went down to the hotel restaurant and, famished, ate a salmon salad with pine nuts and crisply toasted bread, accompanied by a dry French wine. She savored her glorious existence.

Tomorrow she would land in Zurich and be greeted jubilantly at the airport, the moment she got off the plane, by those who wouldn't have dreamed of treating her as an equal in her childhood and youth. Now, she towered over them. They lay at her feet, threw themselves on the ground at the sight of her, as vassals once did when a mighty king came by, only to be trod upon as if they were dust. What could be more fitting?

Chapter 14

Not only Zurich's entire city government peopled the spacious arrivals hall at Kloten Airport, there were also many city council members, canton council members and the cantonal executive branch led by their ever-present puppeteer, Social Democrat Esther Wyberg-Scheuch. Born into a filthy rich family of brewers, livestock traders and stock market speculators, she was married to a Swedish expat and ophthalmologist and had been mourning Marxism since her college days at Zurich University, where she studied architecture. Her first political objective was to reinstate medieval architectural conditions throughout the entire Canton of Zurich, from Schaffhausen and the German border in the north to Knonauer Amt, colloquially known as *Säuliamt*, with the exception of the monotonous, vacuous skyscrapers designed and built by her architecture offices, which lent the buoyant verdant Upper Zurich hills an air of tristeza and bland artificiality – which she considered the epitome of modern architecture – whether the inhabitants liked it or not. What do they know about architecture? Her second objective, as she lived in carefree luxury from her employees' profits and on the interest of her inherited capital, was to raise taxes to astronomical heights for all other Swiss citizens to finally make a breakthrough in her propagated equality for all peoples and countries. The ensuing poverty, from which she was naturally exempt, also threatened the unique Swiss social and economic reputation for which it was much envied by its neighbors.

Mischa Turow was by far not the only psychotic in these parts of the world.

Over a thousand fans, countless journalists, bloggers and youtubers had also turned out to extol Mischa Turow's return from Russia, putting her on display to the entire country. Never before had a Swiss citizen risen to number two in ladies' chess world ranking; never before had a Swiss woman earned the right to challenge the chess world champion, a chance to reign supreme over the most important, complex and difficult intellectual sport.

A sea of Swiss flags undulated over the hall. Not a single Russian flag in sight. Patriots will be patriots, everywhere. Cow bells rang, the Zurich volunteer fire department's horn orchestra took up its position, ready to launch into deafening action the moment their heroine appeared, drowning out airport announcements making final calls for passengers to please come to the gates or their flights to Hong Kong or New York would start without them.

Finally, the green light on the information board next to Swiss Air flight 312 from St. Petersburg lit up, announcing the plane's successful landing. An edgy murmur passed through the crowd, cow bells rang out louder, conversations quieted, but only for a brief moment. All eyes were on the large sliding glass doors through which passengers were exiting, astonished at the enormous reception but quickly realizing it was not intended for them. With roving eyes, they sought out family members, waiting friends or husbands making a pretense of their devotion who were trapped somewhere in the mob, trying to draw attention to themselves by waving energetically.

On the plane, Mischa had scoured every newspaper to find some mention of Pierce McFraser's death but found nothing. Either his body had yet to be discovered, which she thought unlikely, or the event was not newsworthy enough for media attention. Local authorities probably assumed the murder was the result of a mafia vendetta, an everyday occurrence in Russia. Few of these cases were ever solved and were usually closed without much ado. There was no overwhelming public interest, people were glad to have one less gangster amongst them, and there were certain people who knew just how to put a rapid and discreet end to any necessary investigations. Baksheesh, the magic word. Practically every Russian civil servant responded to it. Its enchantment filled the pockets of policemen, district attorneys and judges, many of whom were mafia members deeply enmeshed in criminal machinations, organized crime and assassinations. They lived in fearful suspense should a member of their shady circle be indicted and pressed into revealing information that contained their names, posing a threat to their position and standing.

On the other hand, the papers were full of large-font headlines shouting about her victory at the St. Petersburg World Chess Elimination Tournament and Russia's triumph over the United States of America. The decisive blitz game against the unfortunate Jamie Rothstein, who was portrayed as representing insatiable U.S. capitalism although she had far more need of the prize money than Mischa for whom it was but a drop in the deep well of her enormous fortune, was exhaustively commented and analyzed, hyped as one of the best blitz games ever played. There were many portraits of the radiant victor, of the congratulatory hand-shaking with FIDE President Ruslam Maschinow and many other VIPs as well as a photo of President Ivan Kutin who called from the Kremlin and congratulated Mischa on the telephone.

She put the newspaper aside and readied herself to leave the airplane. She was one of the first to enter the gangway, enthusiastically applauded by her co-passengers, stewardesses and pilots. Many curious and admiring eyes followed her through customs and passport control, which proceeded without a hitch. One uniformed customs officer, a stocky man with poor teeth in his mid-fifties gasping and sweating in his excitement, accompanied her to the exit so he would be photographed with her by the waiting journalists and, with his picture all over the next day's papers, could proudly present his moment of glory to his wife, children and colleagues. Yet, back to the exalted moment when Mischa stepped from the plane that had just landed in Zurich Kloten carrying her incomparable triumphs and undiscovered murder she had brought with her from St. Petersburg and a customs officer escorted her to the waiting masses beyond the exit doors. The cacophony erupting from wildly wielded cow bells just about drowned out the wind orchestra's welcome. Mischa was plunged into an eternal light-show of flashing camera's. She shook thousands of hands and her shoulders began to ache from well-intended, enthusiastic pats. She didn't know which microphone to speak into first or into which camera she should smile.

Eventually, a pair of broad-shouldered policemen, equipped with bulletproof vests, heavy black leather jackets, bobby sticks, and bulging gun holsters managed to propel her away from the ecstatic crowd, shielding her from frenzied fans and escort her to the politicians impatiently waiting on the sidelines. Before running cameras, Josef Stämpfli, Esther Wyberg-Scheuch and other state officials shook her hand with beaming exuberance, taking their time to hug and kiss her, presented her with flowers and congratulated her, eloquent and telegenic, on her exceptional achievements of which all Switzerland, but especially Zurich was extraordinarily proud. What they truly thought was inaudible. Of primary importance was television time with the amazing Mischa, which was sure to earn them votes in the up-coming elections. Heinz Stauffiger, former not-so-hot ski racer and current sports reporter representing Zurich in the upper chamber in Bern, whispered discreetly that she was nominated for Athlete of the Year, most likely to receive even more votes that Roger Federer, the world's best tennis player. And he was from Basel. It was high time a Zurich athlete took the cake.

Hundreds of albums and photos were pressed onto her, the least of which she managed to adorn with her autograph. A little girl had her heart set on giving Mischa her teddy bear. Mischa took both in her arms, hugging and caressing the child. The photographers went wild, knowing full well that these photos were a veritable gold mine. Magazines and newspapers the world over would pay for them handsomely. The little black-haired girl was four years old. Her name was Ramona and she was the daughter of a Spanish-Portuguese couple, itinerate workers who had recently received their residency papers. The portraits not only displayed Mischa's heartfelt warmth, they moreover proved beyond doubt Swiss liberality and generosity to the entire world. It is common knowledge that pictures often speak more than words, no matter if what they say reflects the truth or an illusion. Then little has changed in Switzerland since 1938 unless one considers that the meager number of refugees they have taken in, today known contemptuously as asylum-seekers, are no longer forced to build roads or work in rock quarries where many died of black lung back then but are rather paid by the state to idly languish on the streets for months on end.

Mischa's allotted time passed quickly and the local politician's speeches, which no one paid any heed to anyway, had to be radically abbreviated. A member of SWISS, a German dressed in a dark blue suit with matching club tie whose name was Hans von Ostenroth, came to retrieve Mischa, or *Professor Doctor Turow*, as he reverently addressed her. The flight to Vienna was prepared for take-off. They had gladly given her more time for the reception but could wait no longer and really must be off now. His car would bring her directly to the airplane waiting on the runway. He had spoken to security and customs and attained a special permit, allowing her to circumvent all procedures. Would she be so kind and tell him if she had hazardous objects or liquids? After all, he was responsible for her.

Mischa laughed and raised her arms, answering he was welcome to frisk her here, in front of all these people, that would make for excellent press photos. Who knows? Maybe she's a criminal, no one really knows her. The German blushed deeply, unsure of how to respond before the live cameras and microphones ready to broadcast his words and gestures to the world. As ambassador representing Zurich, Frankfurt and Munich airport executives, he had had many an encounter with luminaries of all kinds, but Mischa Turow was unique and perhaps the most beautiful, popular woman that he had ever had the honor of escorting to her first-class seat on a SWISS airplane. The standard response, that he was only concerned for her safety and that of the other passengers, was out of the question as it would come across on television as ridiculous and could even cost him a dress-down by the supervisory board president for generating negative PR, which would in turn hinder his further climb up the corporate ladder. Who could possibly suspect Mischa Turow, a famous physicist and predestined to challenge the incumbent world chess champion, of being a criminal or terrorist? Mischa politely took leave of politicians and press, waved to her fans one last time and hurried away down a high-security corridor. The obliging German escorted her to his car, which brought them one minute later to the airbus waiting solely for her. Its colossal rotors already spinning and roaring, making any attempt at conversation impossible. Less than three minutes later, they were in the air and on their way to the Imperial City of Vienna, her second, or more precisely, her third, homeland.

The trip to St. Petersburg had been rewarding for Mischa in all respects. She had achieved every goal she had set for herself: she had won the World Championship elimination tournament; had experienced the most excruciatingly ecstatic orgasms with the lowliest of slaves, whose worthless lives were the price; had eliminated all threats to her existence and was now the most envied woman in the world. She reclined in the broad, first-class seat, raised the footrest to a nearly horizontal level and drank to superbly delicate French red wine the obsequious stewardess had decanted with blatant worship. It was a 2005 Chateau Lafite-Rothschild Grand Cru Classe from the Pauillac vineyards on the Medoc Peninsula by Bordeaux, costing 1,200 Swiss francs the bottle, without value added tax. Yet, who's counting added value tax with all the honor befitting a three-time murderess?

Chapter 15

As soon as she was sitting comfortably in the taxi which would take her the 18 kilometers from Schwechat, home of the Vienna Airport, to her home in the city's center, Mischa called her friend Rita Sokol, the young doctor and assistant to Eugene Roth, a renowned neurosurgeon. She made a date for the following evening, there was so much to tell her about the countless adventures and exciting events she had experienced in St. Petersburg and on excursions to Moscow and the Baltic Sea. Naturally, she didn't waste a word on her deadly encounters with Pierce McFraser and Pawel Leskow, but she hardly thought about them anymore, anyway.

The warm blanket of oblivion smothers many terrible things, but it takes a goodly time before they are completely enveloped in its cocoon. Never completely, to be honest. There is always a small remnant peeking out and causing pain, or not, depending on the suppressing soul's nature. Mischa's soul was of the sort that did not repress her atrocities because she regretted them or was ashamed, rather because the men she brutally murdered were of no consequence, weren't worth a place in her memory. Her sexuality had no past, only a future, striving toward the next overwhelming orgasm she could only reach in a murderous fashion. She was not plagued by a guilty conscience. She did not have a conscience at all.

Nature has a balancing character. When she gifts a human too generously with one attribute, she takes from another with abandon. Mischa was granted a mind far more perceptive than any of her species. In exchange, she had no insight into the evil corrosion residing within her, knew nothing of the demon inhabiting her since birth. She accepted it as her inherent right to decide over life and death. For her, right and wrong were defined by a lexicon unread by her fellow humans who left such definitions to the generally valid laws and the moral teachings of Judaic-Christian or other recognized ethical codes. Right, for Mischa, was whatever served the fulfillment of her desires, regardless of the shape it took, and wrong was whatever stood in the way of said fulfillment. She did not bow to laws or morals or any other societal conventions, was allegiant only to her striving for power, recognition and sexual satisfaction.

Rita Sokol, the best and truest friend Mischa had and the only one she considered her confidant, although, of course, she couldn't tell her everything that propelled her life and being, was a of wholly other nature. She was only a hair less beautiful and attractive to men than Mischa, a bit shorter and not quite so willowy, but her intelligence was merged with a warm and caring heart, her kindness was authentic. Rita had no interest in holding power over anyone, certainly not over men, or in using her sexuality as a weapon. She did not strive for honor and fame and hadn't the slightest sadistic or masochistic tendencies. It was Rita who took Mischa along to the synagogue on high holidays and while Rita asked God's forgiveness for sins not committed, Mischa boasted to Him of those she had committed, not believing in His existence, thus fearing no retribution. Like two opposing electrical poles attract one another, so were Rita and Mischa drawn to one another.

Rita's last relationship with a man lay two years behind her, having fallen apart due to his notorious infidelity, about which, as is often the case, she was the last to know. He was a tall, good-looking man, ever-ready to play pranks and joke around, extremely popular among his fellow students. She had met him in the university lecture hall, fallen head over heels in love with him and, against her habit, slept with him the first night. His name was Max Wieder and, once completing his studies, took on a position as assistant doctor in the pediatric ward at the Vienna General Hospital, the same place she worked. Seeing him nearly every day was a constant source of pain and sorrow, as, even though she insisted on separating from him, she had yet to get over his treachery. She had planned to spend her life with him. Yet, after discovering his alleged first infidelity, she found out that his by far not the only case, and her dreams shattered like thin glass. Max was a desired man and despite his love for Rita, he was rarely capable of turning down the endless parade of offers made by worshipping women. For Rita, this made marriage completely out of the question. She was not prepared to be the constantly deceived wife, spending her life in perpetual heartache. Still, she couldn't get him off her mind, out of her thoughts and heart. He feelings for him were simply too strong, too deeply rooted the ties that bound them. At least that was her perception. It was not in her nature to find solace in another man. Her disappointment in Max gnawed at her and made her distrustful, uncertain and doubtful of other men.

But things had changed recently, changed dramatically. While Mischa was spending her days at the tournament in St. Petersburg, Rita had met a young, French painter named

Fred Lavalle at one of the coffee houses on the Ringstraße. His father worked for the news office at the French embassy, not far from the Belvedere Palace by Schwarzenberg Place, one of the most beautiful palaces among the not exactly few palaces and neoclassic residences once inhabited by the powerful upper echelon of the defunct Austrian-Hungarian Habsburgian kingdom, which was still one of the most densely populated and prominent cities in the world up to the beginning of the 20th century. It was commissioned by Eugen, Prince of Savoy, *the noble knight* as Viennese still sing of him today, commemorating the overwhelming 1715 victory over the Turks by Belgrade. How must Louis XIV, the Sun King of France, have felt when shortly before his death he received the shocking news that his repudiated protégé who, due to his dwarfish stature he had deemed unfit to serve in his own army, had achieved the greatest triumph of all time on the battlefield for Louis XIV's arch enemy Carl, Emperor of the Holy Roman Empire of the German Nation, who ruled in far-away Vienna with same opulence as he did in France?

But back to Fred, Rita's new beau. He was a quiet, reserved, brooding man, completely different from all those who pushed themselves on her, seeking to conquer her even though she was not looking to conquered. She was still suffering under her separation form Max. Fred did not possess Max's flamboyance, he demanded nothing from her, offered her nothing, not even himself. This is what attracted Rita most. He had taken her heart slowly, probably without even intending to, during low-key meetings full of talk and harmony of thought and feeling. This was wholly new to her. She soon knew that he was the man of her dreams, the man with whom she could talk about anything and he would listen to her, as she would listen to him, a man who appreciated her work and goals, just as she appreciated his artistic ideas and creations. When he wasn't with her, her heart filled with longing. She could hardly wait to see him again, to gaze into his brown eyes, glittering with enthusiasm for his painting, for the things he saw and rendered in his unique style; shining also for her own dreams and hopes. He looked at her as if she were a gift from heaven. Even before they had found each other, she had known they belonged together, were made for each other.

He was so different than Max, the man she was so sure she loved, even though their relationship, after the initial infatuation, had dwindled to tender habit, something she was only beginning to admit to herself. Fred was not only quieter, more prudent than Max, more thoughtful, Rita loved the tinge of melancholic sorrow in his face, his discretion, his earnestness, his striving for truth and authenticity in all things he approached, for their meaning and their essence. She loved these things as she loved his thickly curled black hair, running riot over his head like an eager mushroom. She loved everything about him.

Shy and hesitant, it took him a long time to declare his love for her. She was enchanted. She was the one to kiss him for the first time. He would never have been so forward. Together, they delved into newly created world all their own. Their love-making, from the first time onwards, from the first delicate kiss, was a whirlwind of sensual experience, the deepest physical and emotional bonding. His gentle caresses on her long-untouched body; their lips, tongues and hands so eager and desiring, broke the dam of passion, flooding her with endless desire for him. The two-year phase of suffering and mourning dissolved into nothing. All at once, she felt as if Max had never happened, as if she and Fred had always been together.

Rita wanted to tell Mischa all about it, about her new, great love. She could hardly wait to share her inner most thoughts and feelings, exactly what Mischa didn't share with her. She wanted to introduce Fred, her wonderful new partner, to her and show her the beautiful pictures he paints. Bright colors, landscapes flooded in light and springtide scenes brought to mind Cezanne and Renoir, Fred's compatriots from the not-so-distant past. But the barbarous events separating then from now: two World Wars, mass murders, the cruelest atrocities humans inflicted upon humans, had changed the very substance of not only Austria and France, but of all Europe, giving the Impressionism reflected in Fred pictures an age-old appearance of a long-lost epoch.

Yet, before the two friends could meet and open the floodgates of their respective narratives, Mischa was obligated to give one of her contractually stipulated lectures at the Vienna University. Lectures that were given to capacity halls at the institute. And now, after her three-month sojourn and her celebrated victory on the enigmatic black and white battlefield in Russia, the lecture hall was inhabited not only by her usual students. Guest auditors and former students who had become engineers, teachers and researchers had gathered, as well as professorial colleagues from her own and other faculties who had yet to penetrate the Dynamo Theory all too deeply, taking the opportunity to hear its conclusions and expansions explained directly from the mouth of the great scientist from whom the ground-breaking theory had first issued. As she spoke, gesticulating sweepingly, scratching curves, diagrams and formulas on the whiteboard, many were put in mind of Amadeus, that young genius and the greatest musician of all time, playing a symphony on the piano, a symphony he had just written, a symphony that was more exciting, more illuminating and closer to the divine music of heaven than anything their ears had yet to perceive.

One listener, however, took no pleasure in Mischa's words. He found her lecture obviously more than distasteful. This listener was Professor Heydrich Sinkfuss, a grey-haired, haggard, soon to be an eighty-year-old physicist sitting in the first row. Despite his age, Professor Sinkfuss still taught at the Vienna University. He is said to harbor sympathies for National Socialism and the neo-Nazi scene, which has never been proved. Like so many other related issues in Austria, this too, remained in the dark. As the speaker, not so many feet away from him, shared her newly developed theory, the Professor's face went to stone, occasionally twitching in undeniable anger. But when she came to speak of the so-called *butterfly effect*, an idea well-known to physicists describing systems that can be profoundly influenced by and dependent on unforeseeable, unpredictable factors, creating a chaos that is an integral part of the nature's order, the professor could no long contain himself.

Furious, he stood and bellowed at the young professor, "So, Ms. Turow, you are also one of those who credit the completely idiotic thesis that a single, meaningless flap of a tiny butterfly's wing in China can influence the weather in Hamburg! Well, I say you should burn your doubtlessly dearly-bought professorship and come down from there right now instead of forcing such idiocy on our respectful students that could only have come from witless, mendacious minds!"

Upon receiving this thoroughly inadequate remark, a storm of indignation swept through the over-filled lecture amphitheater. Many, professors and older people among them, jumped up angrily and demanded Professor Sinkfuss be immediately removed from the hall.

Mischa only shook her head at the Professor's narrow-minded backwardness whose intellectual growth was apparently arrested in 1938 when it latched onto the Nazis' psychotic ideology, as they seized power in Vienna and plunged Austria and all of Europe into destruction.

Although Mischa had renounced Judaism to the extent she could be considered more God's enemy than ally, yet her renown and public position provided certain people a perfect target for open attacks, as Professor Sinkfuss promptly proved. Had he called her a murderess, he who have be right without knowing it. But calling her ignorant, accusing her of buying her professorship was so obviously untrue and solely an expression of his hatred that he made himself a target of ridicule, exposing himself as an irrational fanatic who was no longer welcome at a modern university. The rector personally ushered him out of the hall and Mischa could continue her lecture once the applause had settled. No charges were brought against Sinkfuss. His sparsely attended lectures were simply discreetly struck from the university's weekly schedule.

That evening the two disparate friends, Rita and Mischa met as usual in Rita's small apartment. As Rita met Mischa at the door, they greeted each other with exuberant hugs. Rita's new partner, Fred, was also there and exactly as Rita had described him. His bushy black hair also charmed Mischa and she was immediately overcome with the many wild and obscene things could do with him. She would hardly find a more devoted and submissive slave, but she quickly repressed these thoughts. Fred was Rita's beau and therefore taboo.

A couple of Fred's gouaches and aquarelles stood on the commode. Mischa went over to examine them. They were truly good, wonderfully tender, radiant neo-impressionistic paintings full of poetry and visions of a magical world. At the same time, they revealed profoundly precise observation, excellent technique and the gift granted to but a few artists – to paint reality not only with the hand but with the soul. In each picture, with all of its buoyancy, there was also a touch of the melancholy and sorrow Fred embodied. Mischa felt as if she had traversed eons, finding herself at the end of the nineteenth century standing before one of Picasso's earliest works, which in those days could be had for the cost of a decent meal at one of the cafés on Montparnasse.

"I like your paintings," she said to Fred. He blushed but said nothing.

"Your Fred is a true artist," she turned to Rita, "do you think he will sell me one or two of his works?"

"You're going to have to ask him yourself," Rita replied.

"I'll try, but will he answer? Your brilliant French painter hasn't had much to say thus far."

"That will change. Give him time to warm to you. He's the kindest and cleverest person in the world, present company excepted, of course," she laughed.

"Here goes: Monsieur Lavalle, would you allow me to purchase this picture of a field of tulips?" Mischa turned back to Rita's beau.

At first, Fred didn't know what to say. After a short hesitation he answered with a clearly discernable French accent, "I am not so sure, Professor Turow. I would prefer to give the painting as a gift. You are Rita's best friend and she has told me so many wonderful things about you. You doubtlessly deserve it."

"Stop being so formal!" Rita interrupted. "You are both my friends, so act like friends, give each other a kiss on the cheek and relax. Otherwise I'll start feeling awkward, too."

"Fine with me," Mischa agreed and pressed a kiss on an addled Fred's face. "You can call me Mischa if you like, and if it doesn't embarrass you into wishing the earth would open up and swallow you."

"Don't be so harsh, Mischa," Rita warned her. "He's sensitive and can't handle such rough treatment."

Fred felt horribly uncomfortable between the two attractive women, especially so close to Mischa who literally reeked of sex. No timidity or shame could hide such things from his finely tuned perceptions, and he reddened anew.

"C'mon Fred, you're not usually like this," Rita encouraged him. "Give Mischa a kiss and sell her the painting. She doesn't want it for free and has enough money anyway, definitely more than you by all accounts."

"Hey, Rita, don't ruin my deal!" Mischa laughed. "but I really would like to buy the painting, if it's affordable."

Fred return Mischa's kiss at the most awkward moment possible; as she was turning away, haven given up on the greeting. In his ineptitude, his chin collided with her cheekbone painfully.

"Ouch!" she yelped, but immediately saw the unfortunate randomness of the mishap. She held her cheek and joked, "You're Fred's a real tiger!" Turning to the chagrined painter, she said, "Now you have to give me a fair price, otherwise I'll sue you for inflicting personal injury!"

"Okay, okay, I'm truly sorry! I'm just a touch bewildered," he replied. "Two such lovely ladies at one time is a bit much for me."

"Well, well," Mischa said to Rita," your dear Fred can be a charmer when he wants to."

And then to Fred, "So, tell me, what does the picture cost?"

"Are two hundred euros too much?" he asked uncertainly.

"Are you out of your mind?" Rita interrupted, "You never sell a painting for under two thousand. You worked an entire month on that picture!"

"I'll give you two thousand five hundred," Mischa bid. "A deal?"

She offered him her hand.

"Of course, that's very generous of you," Fred replied and shook her hand, blushing yet again.

Mischa felt a gentle tingle. Pity he's Rita's beau, she thought, he would have been a wonderfully submissive slave with whom she could do the most wonderfully damaging things.

Rita had once more done wonders in the kitchen. The three of them sat at the table, feasting and joking. Mischa and Rita couldn't get enough of the reports and descriptions of all they had experienced during the three-month separation. Without Mischa mentioning her last murder in St. Petersburg, the conversation went on and on. It was long past midnight when she said good night to the lovers, who, as soon as she was gone, made love in such a way that would have only frustrated Mischa. United, they soared in the highest bliss of lovers unsullied by the madness and compulsion governing Mischa's being.

Chapter 16

The call reached Mischa at the nuclear laboratory she had been directing for several months which belonging to a multinational corporation operating out of Vienna. She was working with physicists, engineers and computer scientists on a costly international experiment which entailed transferring enormous amounts of data real time, i.e. less than a fraction of a nanosecond travel time, via a liquid crystal cable to the CERN *Large Hadron Collider* not far from Geneva. The LHC is a subterranean particle accelerator measuring twenty-seven kilometers in circumference, the largest of its kind on earth. Its purpose is to hurl massless particles at one another at nearly the speed of light to simulate processes in space in the hopes of understanding them and produces particles of matter and antimatter from which heavenly bodies were and continue to be created. Over three thousand respected scientists from twenty-two-member nations work at CERN, not only with the Hadron Collider, the most elaborate CERN apparatus, but on several other facilities whose construction devoured many billions of euros in the hopes of navigating humanity's future toward better waters, if their multifarious fanatics don't destroy it first. Among them – the profoundly complex facilities to aid human life, not the destructive fanatics – are the proton and heavy ion linear accelerators, the proton synchrotron booster, the low energy ion ring, the antiproton decelerator and the ISOLDE, Isotopes Separator Online Device. More were being built and by the time you read this report have doubtlessly been completed and in operation. That is, of course, when, as said before, our world still exists, and the Earth has not become a contaminated wasteland decimated by holy warriors, doomsday apostles, self-proclaimed califs, race propogandists, or other deluded demagogues in the name of some idol they errantly consider the shaper and mover of our world.

Against all company regulations, since interrupting an experiment in progress costs millions, a secretary charged into the laboratory. There is an important phone call for Professor Turow, she declared anxiously. By the director's express order, since the call is not private in nature it has been channeled over the house speakers and everyone should hear it. She asked Professor Turow to please allow this and abort her experiment this one time, as the director had approved it and the company would assume all accrued costs.

"Now that's something new. What's the flap about?" Mischa asked.

"The call is from Stockholm," the secretary answered all a-quiver.

Aha, Mischa thought. She relayed the cancellation report to Geneva and took the call in English.

"Mischa Turow, to whom am I speaking?"

"Good morning Professor Turow. My name is Löre Andersen, president of the Royal Swedish Academy of Sciences in Stockholm. It is an immense pleasure to speak with you and I have been given the profound honor of informing that the Physics Award Committee has unanimously voted to confer this year's Nobel Prize upon you in recognition of the *Dynamo*

Theory development which has rendered a great service to furthering the science of physics. My heartfelt congratulations! To present the award, we request your presence at the Academy in Stockholm on December 10th."

Before Mischa could respond, every person in the house began to clap, bang on tables, whistle, shout and make as much jubilant noise as possible. Some danced and jumped around wildly. The Nobel Prize! Their boss, Mischa Turow, was going to receive the highest honor given on the planet. An honor that reflected prodigiously on the institute and laboratory; an afterglow shedding recognition and prestige on them as well. First and foremost, however, the Nobel Prize Laureate herself must be properly celebrated. Mischa vainly attempted to calm her people, at least long enough to respond to Löre Andersen who was still on the phone awaiting her answer.

"I can hear that all hell has broken loose, as they say," the president of the Swedish Academy of Sciences and Nobel Prize Committee could hardly be heard over the loudspeakers. "Is it possible to speak to you, Professor Turow?"

Mischa gave a sign for the people in the room to pipe down, so she could speak, but it took some time before the high spirits and acclamation throughout the building settled to a dull roar.

"I'll give it a try!" Mischa shouted over the din. "I thank you from the bottom of my heart, Professor Andersen. I am totally overcome by your wonderful news. I didn't dare hope. Of course, I will come!"

"I can hardly hear you Professor Turow," the Swedish Academy chairwoman's deep alto sounded from the speakers, "but I'll assume you are coming. I will send you an official email from the Academy with all the details concerning the Prize and award ceremony. You may call me back if you like when you have time and your colleague's exuberance has calmed somewhat. But first, celebrate with your people, you have more than earned it. I congratulate you once more from the bottom of my heart and am looking forward to meeting you personally. That will be a special honor for me. Good day and see you soon, Professor Turow!"

Mischa was barely able to close the telephone conversation before the connection was cut and colleagues and co-workers raced toward her. The laboratory door was thrown open and people from every nook and cranny of the capacious building stormed the room. Everyone wanted to be the first to congratulate her. She was smothered in hugs, kisses, compliments, good wishes, pats on the back and congratulations. Her hand was wrung so often and enthusiastically she feared it would be damaged. Director Michael D. Berenger, a large, broad-shouldered U.S. American in his late fifties was bubbling over like the head of beer in a schooner. He was the only corporate executive without a PhD, yet was more than a master of humor, joviality and assertiveness. He charged into the laboratory with a magnum of champagne, wielding the bottle triumphantly, ran to Mischa hugged her and lifted her up dancing and swinging her around in a circle. Two nervous secretaries in high-heels followed in his wake, trying desperately to bring the trays with champagne glasses they balanced in their hands safely through the noisy, exhilarated and wildly cheering crowd. Which they naturally failed to do. They constantly bumped into people spinning around erratically, gesticulating, laughing and joking. The glasses swayed like a nutshell on a restless tide, finally taking water and crashing to the floor. The shattering glass was a fitting partiture for the spirited atmosphere. Berenger shook the magnum and twisted the metal casing holding the cork down. The cork flew out with a loud bang and landed on one of the secretary's head. Her yelp was drowned out in the general tumult as the champagne shot from the bottle, raining over Mischa and those closest to her. Another bottle and more glasses were quickly fetched. They toasted one another, drank, celebrated and gave no thought to the high price paid for this particular Nobel Prize, unaware of the sinister urgings lurking within the recipient they so joyfully celebrated with such abandon.

"Broken glass brings good luck!" someone called out.

"For she's a jolly good fellow!" another began to sing, soon joined by all.

Berenger's enthusiasm knew no bounds. He spread his great arms and took Mischa in a bear hug, nearly squashing her. She gasped, trying to draw a breath.

"Let her go Michael," someone warned him. "You're going to kill her!"

Which the diabolical three-time murderess had doubtlessly earned much more than an honorary celebration.

Continuing work on this day was unthinkable. Mischa got home quite late that night. To her colleagues incessant cheers and applause, she read the promised email from the Academy chairwoman in Stockholm out loud. The Nobel Prize was accompanied by an eight-million Swedish krone endowment, which came to nearly a million euros. Mischa had promised to spend a part of the endowment to invite every institute employee and her friends at the university to a Lucullan lunch at the acclaimed *Backhendlstation* in Thallern, a small hamlet south of Vienna where nuns cultivated wine on the gentle slopes.

Hilde Ofenberger, Mischa's forty-five-year old administrative assistant was seen only impeccably dressed according to the latest fashion. She was nobody's fool, as they liked to say about her, with a razor-sharp mind. She called the cloister restaurant in Thallern and reserved the entire culinary temple which consisted of several dining rooms simply and comfortably furnished with light wooden tables. The restaurant manager, Margarete Haldinger, Grete for short, promised to attend to festive decorations and prepare for the expected media circus. She was not one of the cloister sisters, in fact, did not believe in God at all. She was thrilled about the free advertising, then she prayed to the God of Commerce and her smile that of a card shark. Her many guests hadn't a clue, though, they came again and again to enjoy the juicy, crisp chicken and pour oceans of red or white spritzers down their gullets, increasing their risk of heart attack. But that, too, remained a secret no one really cared to know.

Mischa found no rest that night. In the coming days as well, there was no hope of getting any work done. She was hounded by journalists day and night, gave interviews, was photographed and filmed. Austrian, Swiss, German, Russian and even U.S. American, French and British television stations broadcast in-depth reports and specials about her career, her scientific achievements and triumphs on the chessboard. There was an Israeli reporter as well since Mischa, at least on paper, was still Jewish although her conversion to Catholicism was pending. Naturally, that her conversion was not an issue of faith, but more a means to an end and social acceptance; that her sadistic excesses, her compulsive libido and barbaric torture and murders found no mention in the many reports since no one besides her voluntary slaves and murder victims knew of it, and they, with one exception, obviously kept quiet.

This exception was Hans Bierbaum, one of Mischa's one-night stands. A man she used, abused and then ruthlessly cast aside. Hans was well-built and athletic, had a handsome face and longish blond hair that had a feminine quality about it. He was taller than Mischa and few years her senior. There was absolutely no visible reason for his timidity, yet her blushed every time a woman looked at him directly, even if she was less attractive, less sexy than Mischa. He stammered whenever a woman spoke to him and looked away when she spoke the obvious body language of a woman interested in a man: she ran her tongue over her lips, played seductively with her hair as he watched, or discreetly hiked up her short skirt, sending a visual invitation to feast on her thighs. His glaring inferiority complex had plagued him since his youth, barring him from any sexual union with a woman of his species until Mischa's one-time, brutal intervention.

Although he had completed his studies in National Economy, his shy, hesitant demeanor deterred him from advancing any further than assistant accountant at a small corporate bank. He lived alone, had few friends. His parent had died years ago and there were no brothers or sisters. He had grown up as a sheltered, pampered single child. His timorous mother kept him fearfully away from anything that, in her opinion, could hinder his well-being and advancement, achieving the exact opposite of what she had intended. It wasn't until he entered the Vienna University of Economics and Business that he came in contact with the opposite sex. Much too late for casual interaction, never having practiced talking to girls in his childhood and youth, as all his other fellow students had. They went to parties together, gathered to just hang out at student bars and drink beer, dated, laughed and flirted with female students and other women they met at the university or in the city, made love and did all those things young people do when two of them are alone and undisturbed and feel the desire to explore their bodies. For Hans Bierbaum, all these pleasures were forbidden fruit.

His meager assistant accountant salary didn't allow for extravagant escapades. It was just enough for his annual hiking vacation in the Styrian Alps where he rarely encountered anyone who may want to converse with him. He was endlessly anxious of saying the wrong thing or embarrassing himself in some other way.

Mischa had picked him up at a coffee house in Vienna. She had found him with his head buried in a newspaper, drinking chamomile tea because he had heard it was good form him. She immediately recognized her victim, sat down at his table uninvited, gazed over the edge of his paper and told him without preamble that she would sleep with him for free if he was willing to be her obedient servant, fulfilling all her sexual desires without question or resistance. Crimson to his hairline, he immediately agreed without an inkling of what was in store for him. He endured her usual abuse and torture, and then finally, for the first time, became one with a woman. The moment lasted but a few seconds. In his profound inexperience he had no control over his body and immediately climaxed, which led Mischa to bombard him with derision, laughing at him spitefully, cursing him a worthless, pussy, not a man at all, and he better not dare show his face here again.

He took home this and other verbal abuse she battered him with, as well as the countless wounds and bruises inflicted by her whip, high heels, shoe tips and other instruments of torture. For weeks he suffered pain and discomfort. The experience had intensified is inferiority complex and he hadn't contacted her since that night, even though his climax, as quick as it may have been, had also been a revelation in pleasure he would have gladly repeated.

Another thing he took away from his painful, torturous evening, this without Mischa's awareness, was a video he had secretly made with his cellphone, having placed it on a cupboard without her knowledge. He had captured the entire evening on video until his cellphone battery died. Thus far, he had only used the video, or more precisely the parts of the video that showed Mischa naked and him less groveling, for personal satisfaction of an evening. But this morning, while listening to the radio, he heard his flagellatrice was to receive the Nobel Prize. Later, he saw her picture in the papers and read she would also receive almost a million euros, and it occurred to him that he could secure a sizable portion of the prize money for himself. He simply had to threaten to publish the compromising video on internet.

He was too much of a coward to call her directly, so he sent her a text message with scenes from the covertly recorded video. She saw the message while having lunch with reporters from the *Times*, *American Scientific* and other journalists of acclaimed British and American newspapers and magazines. She immediately recognized the danger and, excusing herself for a moment to call the browbeaten man from the ladies room, asking him what he demanded in exchange for the video. Nervous and stammering, Bierbaum wanted to sleep with her again and also demanded three hundred thousand euros to destroy the video. Mischa didn't hesitate a moment. She calmly agreed on all counts without giving away a hint of her agitation, saying she had long desired to see him again and would call him this afternoon to suggest a discreet trysting place. Her apartment was out of the question since the journalists were literally camping on her doorstep. He should bring the video material with him and she would give him the money directly. The sum was no problem for her. By the way, she added sanctimoniously, he had earned every cent. She was intent on making him feel secure, so he wouldn't smell the trap she was setting for him. She was happy to give him the money, she continued flatteringly. She would bring it in cash since a check could give rise to uncomfortable questions at the bank and lead to tax problems, too. The naïve man was thrilled about receiving so much money so easily and looked forward to meeting her without knowing what awaited him.

Mischa had to act fast. To her self-obsessed, diabolical mind, there was but one option to banish the danger of this video's publication – Hans Bierbaum must die. As quickly as possible. If she spared his life, he would just come back for more, like all blackmailers do. He could have easily copied the video and was ready to post it on the net even after she had paid him in full. He would always have a hold over her, and that was the last thing she wanted. She, the great Mischa Turow, at the mercy of a reeking, repulsive cockroach for the rest of her life? Not an option! That must be stopped no matter what. And it would be necessary to properly punish his colossal arrogance in blackmailing her, catching two tigers with one lamb. Not only would he not see one cent of her money, in his throes of death he would be the one to pay the glorious price for her soaring sexual satisfaction. A climax she had not reached since Pierce McFraser's death in St. Petersburg. Since meeting Rita's new beau, an electrifying experience, her lust had been mounting, but had yet to find release. Finally, here was a golden opportunity to release it. But she must be clever and find a way to dispense with him without there being even the remotest indication connecting the two of them. No one knew of their acquaintance so far, and that's the way it should stay. She must dispose of him somewhere isolated, where there would be no witnesses and she could easily and completely cover her tracks. Who would suspect her? Why would Mischa Turow, the most loved and admired woman of the day, murder a mosquito like him? she was miles above such a worm, a connection between the two is simply ridiculous.

For a moment, she considered the Danube, the muddy waters hungry for life, not so long ago taking Joe Brady's like a child takes a piece of candy. But a second boating accident was unthinkable, it would trigger too many suspicions and awkward questions. She discarded the idea.

She remembered taking a walk once through the wetlands east of Vienna. It was after one of those rare occasions when she had less than cleaned up at a chess tournament and she was brooding on what went wrong. She had seen the semi-ruins of a fisher hut hidden behind high reeds. As far as she could remember, the hut stood on stilts over the water, a good bit distant from the path. She had wanted to hike over to it and explore, but gave it up after a few steps, her feet sinking deeply into oozing silt. The toe-path leading to the hut had been long abandoned and ended just a few meters in swamp-land, teeming with weeds and high bushes. No one would ever think to use it again.

She had to drive out and see if the hut was still standing. She pulled on a warm jacket and rubber boots, took the machete from the wall that she had brought from Borneo last year, and got in her car. It took her over an hour of searching before she found the hut. There it was, barely visible in an impenetrable jungle of the Danube wetlands! There was no better place for her purposes.

Not a person was in sight. The only sounds to be heard were croaking frogs, singing birds and the swish of the Danube flowing past. She traversed semi-solid ground to the edge of the wetlands for about a hundred and fifty meters from her car. From there, the further she went, the deep she sank in the slick. The high reeds shot up, blocking her way, about two hundred meters from the hut. Good thing she thought to bring her machete along to cut through the dense growth. Otherwise she could go no further. With strong, sweeping strokes she sliced through the compact greenery, forging a path between the pliant, in part arm-thick ligneous vegetation. Finally, she reached the narrow wooden planks leading to the hut. It was very old, eaten away in places, rotten in others and she had to be extremely careful not to fall in the water since the bank offered no hold to get out again. Step by careful step, she reached the hut where obviously no one had been in many years. The wooden beam someone had nailed across the door was riddled with worm holes and a single stroke with the machete divided it in two. Built on high stilts, the dilapidated interior looked better than she had hoped. Cold, yes, damp, yes, but not water-logged. A few layers of wool and down blankets, a little gas heater, sweep out the cobwebs, dust and wood shavings, clean up a bit. An hour's work would transform the hut into an especially titillating, inviting stage. She was sure of it.

On the way home, she called Bierbaum again as promised. She told him she had found a wonderfully romantic, hidden love nest where they would be free to explore their passion without being disturbed and gave him detailed instructions on how to find the isolated place. She instructed him to bring a powerful flashlight, rubber boots and warm clothes. They will meet at ten o'clock, and, naturally he should bring the video, so she can give him the money for it. No, she unfortunately couldn't get away earlier. She will bring candles and champagne and was looking forward to seeing him. It was going to be an unforgettable, wonderfully effervescent night at an exciting place. Of course, she will have the money for the video with her, he had earned it, even without the video. She realized she had gone too far the last time they met and would like to candidly apologize for that. It was just that she was so crazy about him, and still was. She will be more gentle tonight, although she does prefer hard sex. He was just the right man. When nearly everything else she said was a bold-faced lie, the last sentence was the pure truth, but not as gullible, naïve Hans Bierbaum understood it.

Ten o'clock on the dot, as is the wont of all pedants, timid and submissive people who fear reproach should they be even a few minutes late, he stood dripping wet at the door of the eerie fisherman's hut with a bouquet of short-stemmed roses in the hand. He had found his way through the moonlit desolation of the wetlands guided by faint candlelight and the shimmering blue glow of the gas heater. The utter silence was broken only by a few crickets not yet fallen victim to the encroaching winter and the soughing Danube, impervious to the changing seasons.

He tapped hesitantly on the wooden door, as if in apology for his coming, fearful of disturbing the non-existent neighbors with his noise. Mischa opened the door. The sight of her sent an immediate charged of sexual shock throughout his body, sweat broke out on his face where a year ago a moustache had sat. He had shaved it off when he discovered it made him more noticeable.

Mischa opened the door. Never before had a woman stood so invitingly before him. He heard soft music wafting in the background. His eyes rushed to the feast she offered, devouring, devouring. She wore a little nothing negligee, black and transparent, reaching just to her hips without covering her mound of Venus, accentuating her seductive nakedness. Her breasts seemed to dance in the blue gaslight and warm, yellow candlelight. Her perfectly formed, long thighs shone pale and succulent. She wore knee-high black leather boots.

Without greeting, she pulled him to her, quickly closing the door against the coolness of the night. She tore his clothes from his body, pressing him down on the layers of warm, soft down blankets and kissed him on the mouth, something she had expressly forbidden him to do last time.

"So good to have you here, my darling," she cooed, lulling him into a false sense of security.

He opened his mouth to reply, but she gently stroked his lips, indicating he should be still.

"You don't need to say anything, Hans," she whispered. "I know you're crazy about me. I want you as much as you want me."

"Is that true?" he asked.

"But of course," she lied fluently. "Do you think I would go through all this trouble, coming here and dressing like this if I didn't?"

He felt this was an invitation to begin feeding his hunger and touched her in forbidden places. He went about it so clumsily she involuntarily shuddered.

She sat up and asked him, "Do you have your cellphone with the video? The three hundred thousand euros are yours for the taking. Let's take care of business first, okay? Then we can concentrate on having fun, all night if you want, without having to think about money. What do you think?"

"Yes, of course," he answered meekly, thoroughly lost in her enchantment. He took his cellphone form his jacket pocket and gave it to her. She gave the compromising video a cursory view, went to the door and opened it, throwing the device in a high arc into the Danube. Even if a police diver should ever find it, the device and all its data would be destroyed beyond repair by the patiently corrosive waters.

"You can buy yourself a new one!" she said, knowing at that moment that he hadn't made any copies of the video since he didn't have any other electronic devices to copy it on to, no computer, no laptop, no tablet. He would rather spend his money on beer and sausages and the rare trip to a bar, where he sat alone without talking to anyone. It was precisely in one such bar that he had had the misfortune of being approached by Mischa, of being her chosen victim for the night and for what was in store for him now.

"No need to worry, Hans," Mischa soothed him. His concern about the three hundred thousand euros was written all over his face now that he had played his trump and had no more leverage in his hand.

"I keep my word. Here's the money!"

She took thick bundles of notes from a suitcase and handed them to him. Visibly relieved, he took them, gently caressing his paper-dream come true. He had never held so much money in his hands before and didn't know that it wouldn't remain his for long.

"Let's have a drink before we settle in," Mischa said, picking up the bottle of champagne she had set on floor and opening it. The cork flew from the bottle with a loud crack, bouncing against the wall and spraying foam. She decanted the effervescent beverage into two glasses. While he clung to the bundles of money, his mind far, far away, he failed to notice the finely ground, odorless and tasteless sleeping pills in his glass. Most of the powder dissolved at once. She made a show of gaily swirling the glasses to increase the bubbles, but in truth dissolving the last dregs of the sedative at the bottom of the glass she held ready for Hans. But her innocent victim was much too captivated with the money to become suspicious. He was already far away in Hawaii, lolling on the beach sipping pineapple juice, surrounded by lovely hula girls, eager to satisfy his every need.

"This will make things even better," Mischa said. You could never know if the ugly, lecherous, money-obsessed ass sitting next to her had other plans. "That makes it even frothier and I love frothy champagne, especially before sex!"

After they had drunk the first glass, she poured him another, and yet another, while only to pretending to sip on her own glass.

Bumbling and crudely, Bierbaum pawed at Mischa's breast with one hand while the other hand still held one of the wads of bank notes. The rest of the money had fallen to the floor. Mischa allowed him his fun, he should get the most out of life while he could. She led his hand to other places under her negligee but that was too much of a good thing for him and he tensed visibly. So she took his hand away.

"Don't come so quickly tonight like you did last time. You have to hold back, or you'll ruin everything for both of us!"

"I'll try, but it's not that easy," he murmured. "You're just too sexy!"

She tolerated his fumbling without letting on just how huge her boredom and how miniscule her desire was. Not even she would deny a condemned man his last meal. His pathetic attempts to hold back his orgasm were, of course, useless and thirty seconds after he had entered her, he fell back on the blankets next Mischa, exhausted from his acrobatics, champagne and the slowly unfolding effects of the sleeping pills. He barely noticed when, four or five minutes later, she spread his arms and legs wide open and tied his wrists and ankles to nails she had hammered into the wooden walls. She stuffed a cloth in his mouth and bound it tightly to his head. She abruptly slapped his face hard with her open hand to see if he was still conscious. He winced slightly from a distant place in the world of dreams. Red heat flooded his left cheek where her hand had struck.

Gripping the large butcher knife she had brought specifically for this purpose, she sank it into his thigh, making the first cut. Blood splattered over her negligee and gloves. The sleeping wounded bucked in pain, moaning loudly despite the gag in his mouth and drugs in his body. His protests were nonetheless not loud enough to merit her tightening the cloth around his head. His subconscious mind led him to believe he was observing torture in some bizarre nightmare while his consciousness was already far, far down the path to the nothingness of death, fading beyond return to the light of life.

She gouged him again with her right hand, boring deeply into his shoulder while touching herself with her left, rubbing her most sensitive spot as women do whose men fail to satisfy them fully. She cut and slashed and gored the massively muscular man. The strength and power in Bierbaum's body spoke a completely different language than his weak and helpless character. Mischa bathed gleefully in his blood and gore, saving his heart for the moment she peaked on the orgasmic wave rolling higher and mightier, ever closer. She plunged the knife into his heart, extinguishing his life just as the wave began to engulf her. At the thrust of the knife her body bucked wildly, lightning struck in her sex, sending shock waves in all directions and threating to tear her to pieces. She howled and begged for mercy. Orgasm followed orgasm. There was no end to the divine torment. She folded herself in half against the pain of endlessly undulating currents of ecstasy she had so long awaited. Half of eternity passed before the orgasm finally washed out to sea and the cramps in her womb receded. Completely drained, heaving and glutted, she lay next to the corpse that was barely recognizable as human. She had murdered again. She felt like God. Although in truth, the Devil is the true master of life and death.

She rose gingerly and came to her feet. Barefoot, clad only in her bloody negligee and the gloves she had worn since her arrival, she went out into the frozen night, oblivious to the icy wind blowing against her skin. Holding tightly to a strong branch hanging over the Danube, she glided into the current to wash away the blood. After some time, when the cold finally penetrated her senses, she pulled herself hand over hand to shore, climbed up to the hut, went inside and rubbed herself dry. She dressed and collected everything, the blankets, the butcher knife, candles, champagne bottle and glasses, the gas radiator, her suitcase, Bierbaum's pathetic gift, his short-stemmed roses and empty plastic briefcase – of course, she had repossessed the money – and threw everything into the Danube which carried it all away to Slovakia, to Hungary, to Romania or even to the Black Sea. She left the fisher's hut with the packets of money in her jacket pocket and drove home. No big deal.

The following day, she threw the negligee and shoes in the garbage. She washed and vacuumed her car like countless other car owners in one of the myriad automated carwashes in Vienna. She returned the three hundred thousand euros to her safe at the bank from which she had taken it.

Once again, Mischa felt she had found the perfect solution to an annoying problem. A solution that had the added bonus of satisfying her blood-thirsty libido, that otherwise could not be quieted. Serene, sated and confident, she looked forward to the Chess World Championship playoff against Pinyin To Can that would begin in a few days in Las Vegas.

It was more than a half a year later, in early summer, when the corpse was found by a hunter's dog that caught the scent of decay. Barking loudly, it strained for his shared of the re-mains. And that wasn't much. Worms and insects covered what muskrats, ravens, ibises and other hungry creatures had torn to shreds, having feasted on flesh, sinew, nerves and organs, gnawing on bone. What was left was little more than pieces of a skeleton, its species unrecognizable to the unschooled.

The *critters* had had enough time to help themselves according to Fritz Smetana, criminal inspector of the Lower Austrian detective squad, who was leading the investigation. The only usable tissue they had to work with was scant, heavily decayed, miniscule skin particles that had resisted the decomposing process.

There were, however, conspicuous slashes, deep holes and clean cuts in the bones that could only arise from premediated use of a sharp knife. And there were further indications that what had happened in the fisher's hut was murder: frayed ropes tied to the victims hands and feet; wilted leaves and crumbly thorns from short-stemmed roses; the wax particles they found came in all probability from candles that must have burned on the floor of the dilapidated hut. No, this was not just murder, this was a downright execution. Without a single clue as to the perpetrator. The wetlands and the Danube had swallowed all traces, if there had been any in the first place.

The cadaver could only be identified by his teeth. He was an assistant accountant at a cooperative bank by the name of Hans Bierbaum. Mr. Bierbaum had lived alone and had no known relatives or friends. No one had reported him missing, not even the bank he worked at. His superiors reacted to his months-long unannounced and unexcused absence only months later, and then by merely sending him a termination of employment notice in the mail. This, however, could not be delivered since his landlord had canceled his lease after the rent had failed to be paid several months running and, as was his good and legal right, had dissolved the meager apartment

Alexander Günsberg

inventory, selling anything of worth to recompense for the lost income and discarding the junk. He had assumed the tenant had flown the coop without leaving a forwarding address to escape his debts. Not a rare occurrence in Vienna or other cities in the Balkan region.

The police suspected the brutal killing was an act of organized crime. There was no lack of Hungarian, Polish, Russian and Romanian smugglers, drug dealers and human traffickers in the Austrian capital, taking advantage of the untamed borderland through the Danube wetlands and the Lake Neusiedl in eastern Austria. These people were unforgiving when it came to renegade members, traitors or delinquent payers. Still, it could have been a crime of passion in the homosexual milieu. Failing to unearth clues or evidence pointing to the perpetrator and the motive for such barbarity remained unclear, the case was closed after just a few weeks of investigation, the file marked *unsolved* and stored away.

"At least that's one less gangster on the streets, even when no one deserves to die like that," Smetana remarked. He had been on the force for many years and soon to retire. One unsolved case more or less was water under the bridge, there was no sense in making unnecessary efforts. They wouldn't turn up anything anyway.

Chapter 17

On December 1ˢᵗ the decisive battle began for the lady's crown in the most supreme of all intellectual sports, chess. Chess, emerging from India four centuries after the birth of Rabbi Jesus of Nazareth, called Christ, spreading through Persia and Arabia to conquer Europe and the world. There is no country on earth where it is not played. No age, from three to one hundred and three, that is too young or too old to play it. No human being too poor or too rich to indulge in it, be they beggar or emperor. Perhaps chess does not draw mass audiences like football, ice hockey or baseball, but it can be played anywhere, and for free. Chess does not require costly equipment, nor does it call for a playing field, spotlights or clement weather. Chess needs but a partner, who can easily be found no matter where you are, and a small, pocket game made of wood or plastic that can be used for you and your opponent's pleasure and edification wherever and whenever you like – on a train clickety-clacking over the tracks; on an airplane high over the clouds; in a café; on a terrace in Vienna, Zurich, Paris or Hong Kong; on the sly at the office; under a desk at school; before or after dinner at a restaurant; on the beach or in the hotel on vacation; in a cozy mountain cabin banked with winter's snow; in the sauna in Budapest, Leukerbad or Abano; at home; at a friend's place or, for those more serious about it, at a chess club. The divine game of kings and pawns will enchant the hearts and minds of humanity as long as these sentient beings, be they good or evil, populate our tormented Earth.

The FIDE awarded Las Vegas, Nevada in the United States the right to host the ultimate duel between legendary incumbent World Champion Pinyin To Can of China and her challenger Mischa Turow. This honor was the work of busy bee Bucksy Meyer, an elderly but singularly agile, small, bald man who was personal friends with FIDE President Ruslam Maschinow and President Kutin, Russia's top man, as well as amiable business associate to several Russian oligarchs. Meyer was the major stockholder and executive manager of the re- nowned casino hotel *Caesar's Palace* on Las Vegas Boulevard. He had not only offered the highest prize money for the players, but gratis lodging in his establishment including additional comforts for the more or less honorable FIDE functionaries and their equally glorious guests of dubious character.

Among these additional comforts was a free choice of the willing, lovely young ladies wearing the shortest skirts, highest heels and most radiant smiles as they sashayed – amid lights blinking in all colors of the rainbow and machines striking every audible tone – through the casino salons, distributing free alcoholic beverages to the countless hopeful gamblers pouring coins into the one-armed bandit or sitting at the ta- bles playing roulette, poker, blackjack and other games, luring them to stay until they had lost every red cent in their pockets to Bucksy Meyer and his cigar-smoking associates, who also partook of the delicious ladies, who were no ladies, whenever the mood struck them and their wives were not in the vicinity. This earned the scantily clad jaded ladies more pocket money than their wages; more than they would earn dancing naked in the sin-city's strip-bars or plying their trade in whorehouses and gave them the *Pretty Woman* Hollywood illusion of happy-ever-after dreams – that on rare occasions came true – of snatching up an absurdly wealthy man who provided a carefree, idle life of luxury, allowing them the freedom to take their sexual desires elsewhere, should they have them, as long as their newly wed and freshly cuckolded husband didn't catch wind of it.

Naturally, these licentious, lusty perks found no mention in the written contract between FIDE and Caesar's Palace corporate owners. They were, nonetheless, a clause clearly defined in the oral agreement between Bucksy Meyer, Ruslam Maschinow and two other FIDE delegates who made the trip to the hot, desert state of Nevada, U.S.A., leaving their legally wedded wives behind. Duty calls, they bemoaned. They were obligated to shoulder the burden of traveling to America, to dull Las Vegas, and there was no need for them to suffer the long, boring flight too, waiting endless hours in the hotel room as they tended to FIDE business. They would have a much better time of it if they took the opportunity to splurge on a wellness weekend, went out with friends to a café and, most importantly, kept an eye on the children who, as soon as papa was in their air, would most likely go looking for trouble. Besides, there weren't enough air-conditioned rooms in the hotel available so what would they do? There was nothing there besides the infinitely dismal casino tables and deplored American automated games of chance that, once you had fed them all of your money, were utterly tedious. They would die of boredom. Better they stayed home.

One and half million dollars would go to the winner of the ultimate chess duel in Las Vegas, nearly five times the prize money awarded in Russian St. Petersburg. Even the

loser would receive half a million dollars, twice as much as
the winner in St. Petersburg was awarded. Never before had
such astronomical sums been paid out for women's chess
tournaments, not even for the World Championship playoffs. Bucksy Meyer could barely remember the rules of chess.
The last chess game he had played was nearly thirty years ago
against a school friend in Brooklyn, which, as was his habit,
he lost. Still, at all costs, he would host the World Championship. It must take place in his hotel. It was a matter of
pride and reputation. He must always be first. And he would
be the first to be able to boast of and advertise with housing
the Chess World Championship in his establishment. His
7-year-old son Jeffrey, the light of his life, had given him the
idea. Jeffrey was wholeheartedly obsessed with chess, having
learned it from a classmate a few months prior and spent
every free moment playing against his computer. He knew
and idolized the best players in the world, both male and
female. Papa would do anything for Jeffrey, even when it
cost him millions. He grossly overestimated the revenues his
luxury hotel would earn by hosting the World Championship
since in the States chess was a poor man's sport played primarily by the employed and old men, meeting in the parks
on warm days. Only a handful of talented young people
were drawn to chess clubs and serious tournaments. Many of
them, however, reside at the top of the world's ranking, such
as Jamie Rothstein, who lost to Mischa in the final round of
the Candidates tournament during their four-minute sudden
death blitz game in St. Petersburg.

Entering this world in the New York borough of Brooklyn,
Bucksy Meyer was the son of lower-middleclass Jews. He had
not been among the privileged who had attended college or
enjoyed a higher education. How he came to his immense

wealth remains a mystery. Some accuse him of a criminal past, owing his rise to the top ten of U.S. American businessmen to the notorious Corleone clan of the Sicilian mafia for whom he had, according to rumor, rendered supremely valuable services. There was, however, no evidence to back these accusations, putting him on an equal footing with his illustrious Russian friends who were just as innocent.

Bucksy Meyer had suffered only one major disappointment in his life. Despite his enormous fortune, his obvious connections with the mafia made him one of the few Jews denied the inherent right, anchored in Israeli law, to return to Israel, from which the sons and daughters of the great kings David and Solomon, of the prophets Samuel, Elijah and Nathan had once been driven out by the Roman general and emperor Titus and their no less bloodthirsty progeny. Israel, the Jewish homeland fighting for its survival. This was a hard blow for Meyer as he had been a fierce Zionist as long as he could remember. The most shattering moment came when he was passing customs on his way back to the States from the Tel Aviv airport and a lowly officer said to him, "Israel needs honest workers and soldiers, Mr. Meyer, not nefarious criminals with ill-gained millions. Our land is built on sweat and bricks, not on money, fraud and delusional glamour. Take your riches and go back to America. You are not wanted here."

He had no other choice than to obey. In Las Vegas, a city planted in the heart of Nevada's desert, replete with tax privileges and a peculiar skyline sketching the bizarre casino and hotel structures, he was one of the most powerful and influential personalities. The street was lined with hotels up to sixty stories high, shaped only by the limits of human fantasy – moated castles of the Middle Ages, Egyptian pyramids and maharajah palaces with elaborate fountains the likes of which have never been seen in India – punctuated by colossal Mickey Mouse and Popeye figures.

The uncontested sovereign, the most lustrous attraction in this soldier-of-fortune city was Caesar's Palace, named for the ever-celebrated Roman Consul who had elevated himself to emperor of the mightiest empire of his times, encompassing all of Europe, Africa and western Asian countries on the Mediterranean Sea, from Scotland in the North to Nubia in the South. Well-paying, gambling junkies from every continent and country on Earth pilgrimed to Caesar's Palace to eagerly and rapidly throw their easily come by or hard-earned money into the insatiable maws, parading as casino cashiers, of Bucksy Meyer and his Jewish, Christian and Native American colleagues. The biggest, gaudiest and most seductive casinos on the planet.

Four thousand rooms in six different hotel towers. Gambling salons in Roman décor cover fifteen thousand, five hundred square meters, one an arena replicating the Roman Colosseum. Caesar's Palace, where cameras are perpetually flashing, women seductive and inviting and the air is filled with the shouts, moans and yowls of winners and losers alike while boxing World Championships in all classes blare from the speakers and the most prominent stars in and beyond Hollywood – such as Frank Sinatra, Judy Garland, Liza Minnelli, Diana Ross, Dean Martin, Janet Jackson, Rod Stewart, Mariah Carey, David Copperfield, Elton John, Cher and Celine Dion – play before vast audiences.

It is also worth mentioning that Caesar's Palace boasted more Roman columns, halls and fountains than could be found in most Italian cities, sheltered shopping arcades proffering the most expensive and least useful luxury articles, illuminated by an artificial Roman sun by day and artificial Roman stars by night. The parking lot alone, not counting the many subterranean levels, was large enough to host the Formula 1 races.

Despite its unparalleled luxury, Caesar's Palace was not the largest hotel in Las Vegas. Not by far. The Venetian had over seven thousand, one hundred rooms, the MGM Grand nearly six thousand, nine hundred, the Mandalay Bay and the Wynn each held four thousand, seven hundred and fifty rooms. But, tirelessly scheming, Bucksy Meyer had plans to build a new hotel on the world-famous Vegas Boulevard – bigger and more luxurious than them all, putting on spectacular show events that leave all previous extravagances in the dust.

In a Caesar's Palace salon, a small room adjacent to the humongous casino halls with maximum seating capacity for a mere three hundred guests, the decisive encounter in women's chess, so eagerly awaited in the chess strongholds of Russia, Germany, China and India, finally began. As the challenger Mischa Turow was due to fly to the Nobel Prize ceremony in Sweden on December 10th to accept the Nobel Prize in Physics, the organizers had installed a four-day hiatus in the match schedule running from December 7th to 13th.

The winner and new, or repeat, women's chess world champion, was the player with the most points after fifteen games with the standard time allowance of one and a half hours for the first forty moves and a half hour for the rest of the game including a time bonus of thirty seconds per move. Former world champion Bobby Fischer suggested the time bonus to spare players the dreaded time pressure before the chess timer ran out. This, however, profoundly diminished spectator enthusiasm since it also suddenly did away with exciting endgame massacres arising from intense time pressure. The time bonus first became socially acceptable after Fischer's death. It was precisely this endgame battle that inspired many spectators to buy expensive tickets or to sit in front of the television munching tensely on their chips. They felt cheated out of a time-pressure blood bath.

Should the match remain undecided after the fifteen regular games had been played, the same procedure was applied as had been in St. Petersburg, i.e. five condensed games would ensue allowing only a half-hour's time per player, plus time bonus. Should this not suffice to declare a winner, the deadlocked players would move on to a four-minute sudden death game, with the player holding black receiving an extra minute's time. This final option will clearly determine which of the two Grandmasters will have earned the title World Champion and will walk away with Bucksy Meyer's one and a half million dollars in prize money, the greater part of which will be devoured by a hungry Austrian or Chinese tax collector, depending on which woman takes it home.

True, Caesar's Palace had inside and outdoor screens broadcasting the games live, but Las Vegas' interest in chess games, even those on the highest level, did not come anywhere near the passion displayed in Russian St. Petersburg. Save a handful of truly exceptional spectators – yes, the United States had its share of top-ranking chess players – to the average American, chess was a game for old men to be played on folding tables in the park, taking their time, playing long into the summer nights for a dollar a game. Thus, spectator interest at Caesar's Palace was meager, to say the least. Baseball, rugby, basketball, football and ice hockey drew thousands to stadiums, yet guests, in their haste to get to the gaming tables, gave the live chess games on casino screens as much attention as they would a detergent or maple syrup commercial.

Some paused in puzzlement, eying the unusual game with curiosity. They tried to fathom its secrets but failed when attempting to grasp the pieces movements. Only a few mavens had traveled from major cities on the east and west coasts, but there was also a smattering of chess aficionados from Chicago, Huston and Atlanta as well, who had come to take part in this rarest of events in the United States, a Chess World Championship between the best two players on the planet. This, they had to see.

Very few thought Mischa had a realistic chance against Pinyin To Can. Betting offices and internet put the odds 7:2 for Pinyin To Can, who has held the title for four years now and not a woman on the planet has defeated her since. Known as simply *Can* in chess circles, pronounced *Chan*, she holds second place in the world's overall ranking, only a few points behind Magnus Petersen, the men's World Champion and former Danish *wunderkind* who had attained his Grandmaster title at a mere twelve years old. He was the only one to prove her inferior, coming out triumphant in their bitter battle at the Aeroflot Tournament in Moscow.

Many claimed she played like a machine, exacting and precise, never making even the tiniest, humanly recognizable error, mercilessly pressing her advantage no matter how veiled the opportunity to attack may appear to be. Her last game, played in Tiflis shortly before the World Championship play-offs, was against the Georgian Grandmaster Nina Gopariani, another globally admired chess miracle and number four in the women's world ranking. Using an inspired combination, Can took her down in only eighteen moves, proclaiming checkmate in seven moves, but needed only five when Gopariani failed to find two of the best defense moves, accelerating in her doom.

The profoundly abbreviated opening ceremony in Las Vegas had none of the extravagances seen in St. Petersburg. There were no political luminaries present, no music to be heard, no armed guards in the salon. The only speech was made by FIDE president Ruslam Maschinow, who did not even have the time to relay Russian President Kutin's greetings because the hotel director and chief stockholder, Bucksy Meyer – sitting front and center in the half-empty salon between his son Jeffrey and his omnipresent, striking ash-blond private secretary Nancy-Ann Taylor – had expressly requested he not speak longer than five minutes.

The first game proceeded as generally expected. Although the champion led black, giving her challenger the opening advantage, she outmaneuvered her, thanks to an innovation in the sixteenth move of the French defense, which she had chosen in part for the arbiter, and won the game easily. Three moves before checkmate and deeply disappointed, Mischa surrendered. 1:0 for the title defender. Betting odds rose from 7:2 to 9:1 in favor of Chan, not only because of her victory, but also because of the ease with which she had wrested it from her challenger who had, after all, proved in St. Petersburg that she was the second-best player in the world. Newspapers spoke of Pinyin To Can's talent and drew parallels to the deceased Bobby Fischer, propounding that Mischa was nothing but a sparring partner for the champion. At an interview with the *New York Times*, when the reporter asked Can what chances she thought Mischa had as the match progressed, her answer was a single word that said more than any lengthy analysis could have done. That word was "*None.*"

Mischa went to bed late that night. She had imagined the World Championship playoffs differently; had calculated with better chances against Can. Far into the wee hours she researched every one of the title holder's games she could find in the net, combing them for the slightest error and finding nothing. Nothing at all. How was she to gain the upper hand against a player who was a machine, as everyone claimed her to be. Mischa decided to use her most powerful weapon in the second game, which would take place in a few hours. Assuming Can opened with the queen's pawn as she usually did, Mischa would reply with the Volga Gambit. She had a more than seventy percent success quota with this strategy, raising her confidence in the coming game despite her opponent's genius.

Confidence deserted her at the chess table when the champion chose not to open with the queen's pawn as Mischa expected. Once again, Can surprised her challenger by implementing the King's Indian Defense which she had very rarely used at important tournaments in the past. Hence, for the second time, it was Can who seized the initiative, gaining a superior position.

Mischa gazed at Can for a long time, who sat motionless on her chair, her face utterly devoid of expression, her head tilted slightly downward, completely absorbed in the game as she considered her next move. Not for one second did she turn her eyes from the chess board. There seemed to be nothing that could distract her thoughts from the game, nothing that could interrupt her concentration. Mischa did not find this unusual since Can was an unattractive, yes, truly ugly woman. Had she not known it, Mischa would have been at a loss to guess her age. An uninitiated spectator could have just as easily placed her at seventeen as at thirty-seven. Actually, she was thirty-two and had never had a man before in her life, Mischa knew from reliable sources. Not surprising, then Can did nothing to camouflage or beautify her repulsive appearance with flattering clothes or concealing makeup. Her complexion was nearly ashen pale, her face disfigured by two large, black warts on her chin and forehead. Thick black hair sprouted from her warts, grew on her upper lip, arms and legs, which she didn't even bother to shave. To make matters worse, her legs were thin and bowed, a malformation easily discernable beneath the table despite her knee-length skirt. Her entire body, including her extremely oversized head, couldn't weigh more than forty-five kilos, as her figure was small and boney like an undernourished child. She wore her thin, dark hair extremely short and beneath the thorny growth you could see the poor skin on her scalp densely populated with acne and moles, peeking out through her butch haircut. All in all, she looked like an East Asian ascetic from another, earlier century. Obviously, chess was her only option for gaining self-assurance and recognition. From a very young age, and because she was exceptionally gifted, she had immersed herself in chess, pushing aside any and all other distractions, learning, studying and practicing, often as many as fifteen hours a day, the theory of this most difficult game of games until there was no other woman in the world who could defy her.

Deep in these contemplations, as Mischa sat before the chess board, staring at her weak position with little hope of improving it, wracking her brain for something she could do to turn the tables in her favor, she had an idea. It was not fair and certainly not sporting, but it may have the de-sired effect. After all, she had not dedicated so many years and so much effort to arriving where she was only to lose everything shortly before attaining the World Champion-ship title. She was Mischa Turow, Nobel Prize Laureate, the cleverest woman in the world; clearly more intelligent than this revolting, untouched and introverted Chinese woman across the table from her, intent on blocking her path to the crowning title. If she can't defeat her with the weapons of chess on the battlefield of forty-sixty black and white squares, then she would have to resort to the weapons of a woman that would have the same impact on those squares as brilliant chess moves could have.

Mischa would find a man. A man to distract Can's concentration on chess and make her think other, new thoughts. Can was a virgin and convinced she would remain a virgin for the rest of her life. Since no man had ever expressed interest in her, she was resigned to never having sex – at least the kind of sex that calls for a partner – although, like any other woman, she has her dreams of love and relationship, Mischa would bet her life on it. And now she knew what she had to do. Continuing the hopeless chess game in front of her was an exercise in futility. She would be better served to spend the rest of the day and the coming night to find an appropriate man, willing to endow upon ugly Pinyin To Can her first sexual experience, granting Mischa the World Championship title. She knew what she had to do. No other woman knew it better than Mischa Turow, slave to the demon she bore in her body. Her master in things libidinous and licentious.

Smiling, Mischa stopped her clock and gave her opponent her hand, surrendering the game. Can accepted her capitulation without expression, taking her victory as a matter of course. No one in the salon could explain why the challenger had thrown in the towel so early on in the game without even attempting to turn it around, which was surely in the realm of possibility. Nonetheless, the World Championship playoffs now stood at 2:0 for the title defender. The odds rose to 15:1 for Can, of course. The entire community of chess commentators and all press and television reporters already saw Can as the decided victor, the new and repeat World Champion in women's chess. But their sight overlooked Mischa Turow, who had yet to play her trump cards.

Without giving a moment's attention to the journalists or invited celebrities, she took several elevators down, down, down to the subterranean garage where she had parked the car she had rented at the airport. She got in and drove out onto Vegas Boulevard, its sidewalks surging and pulsating with masses of people. Most of them knew nothing about chess as they dashed from one casino to the next; were completely ignorant of the fact that here, in this city, the women's Chess World Championship was now taking place. Their sole intent was to find the next available gaming machine as quickly as possible, to get the last tickets to the evening's entertainment, or, when they had not yet had their fill of steaks offered in the iniquitous gaming dens – for free or at a chip price of three dollars, drinks included – they hustled into fast-food joints or bought hamburgers or hotdogs at the many street stands, stuffing their guts with junk.

Mischa drove westward the entire length of the Boulevard, stopping at one of the last casinos, not far from the desert that encircled the gambler's city on all sides. Here, far from Caesar's Palace and the city's center, there a much greater probability that she would not be recognized. No one here was interested in Nobel Prize Laureates or Chess World Champions. This end of the city was the realm of boxers, showtime, film and baseball stars, jazz giants, rappers and poker players. A huge billboard on the hotel offered double rooms for $19.99, luring gaming addicted guests. The interior, however, was a replica of all other casinos in the city, with the single exception that its audience was composed of members of lesser social caste than that at Caesar's Palace. But Mischa was not looking for a rich man. Quite the contrary, she was scouting for a man who could be bought with money and was willing to sleep with the ugliest woman in Las Vegas.

Dressed in work clothes, far removed from the world around them, retirees of both genders were sitting at one-armed bandits and other colorful, glittering and loudly pinging gaming machines, their bloodshot eyes locked onto the flickering, spinning numbers and symbols that rolled ad nauseum as long as they fed the insatiably hungry, addictive machine with the chips that kept them clacking and whirring. Each automat bore a sign at the top in glaring neon letters propounding the ever-increasing millions to be won. Everyone jockeyed for the machine with the highest number, believing that they would be the one to crack the jackpot and the millions would pour out and over their waiting hands. But the reality none of them was willing to accept was that the chances of snatching up those millions were as likely as the possibility of being bitten by a sand flea at the North Pole or eaten by a polar in the Amazons. Still, each person playing here was firmly convinced he or she would be the one to take home the millions, all they needed was patience and to feed chips into the slot within comfortable reach from where they sat.

An elderly woman, perhaps she was once a cleaning lady working for minimum wage and was now retired, sat sweating profusely at one of the ravenous, profiteering slot machines. Nervous, chawing madly at her chewing gum she held her last chips tightly in her fist as if by the power of her sweat they would be enchanted and finally grant her the longed-for blessing of riches. Trembling, she inserted the chips one after the other into the slot machine until it came down to her last chip, the one to make her a rich woman at the very last moment. But, of course, it did not. In less than fifteen minutes she had offered up her entire savings and lost everything she had worked so hard for over so many years of scrimping and saving. She had never treated herself to anything, no vacations, no evenings out, not even a half-hour's respite in a coffee shop. She had denied herself all joys for the one-time chance of playing the slot machines in a casino and winning the jackpot. These last few minutes of her life had transformed her from a humble, but not wanting woman into an utterly destitute pauper. Too old to work, she was doomed to spend the rest of her life begging on the streets. In the land of the rich and beautiful, there was no humane place, no dignity for men and women like her. Her pension was too small to even feed her on a daily basis, not to mention the rent on her tiny apartment or, heaven forbid, the doctor's fees should she fall ill or have an accident.

Searching for a fitting candidate, Mischa walked through the rows of gaming junkies, who, like the retired cleaning lady, were sitting at the glittering, flickering automats obsessed with their unfulfilled illusions and, also like her, played away their hard-earned money. Mischa entered a salon where the gamblers playing poker, roulette and blackjack seemed somewhat better situated. None of them seemed appropriate until she spotted a young man sitting at the roulette table. He was about thirty she guessed, dressed in well-tended, elegant clothing and placing his chips in a curiously bored manner. He stood out among the other players who seemed to be hired hands in their Sunday clothes, frantically distributing the chips over the felt as if they would miss something if they weren't quick about it. The elegant man had several stacks of purple chips stacked neatly in front of him. Before each spin of the wheel, he set about half of them on a wide variety of numbers and number combinations. Mischa watched him for while from a distance, careful not be noticed. He had an attractive face and a trim physique; had deep brown, nearly black hair and brilliant blue eyes. His demeanor was very self-confident yet fell short of arrogant. She couldn't determine his height but towered over his neighbors, so he couldn't be short. He seemed an intelligent player as his stacks of chips of grew more steadily than they shrank. Obviously, he was alone. Several women in his vicinity, even younger ones with escorts, repeatedly shot stolen glances in his direction, which did not escape Mischa's sharp observation. The longer she watched him, his game and the other people at the table, the more she was convinced he was the right man for her purposes.

While the greater part of players set their chips haphazardly, quickly losing them all and soon thereafter getting up and leaving the roulette table, he appeared to have either a golden touch or a successful strategy. His cache of chips grew consistently more abundant. Mischa also detected the rotating camera over the table was immobile, fixed on him, but the croupier kept his face turned away as if making a point of not looking at him. No one besides Mischa noticed this oddity. The other players were too busy placing their chips in all possible combinations before the croupier expertly set the roulette wheel in motion. It was fascinating to watch how he deftly put the small metal orb into play at the rim of the wheel in precisely the same manner and after several turns of the wheel, as the ball began to detach itself from the rim, called out, "*Rien ne va plus*." All eyes were glued to the tiny, rolling ball, following its circulation, waiting impatiently to see where it would land before exclaiming oohs and aahs or other sounds and comments, depending on whether Lady Luck had been true or unkind to them. Only the elegant young man remained calmly seated without uttering a word. Taking stately steps, drawing the eyes of those gathered, Mischa walked over to him and placed herself behind his chair. He smelled exceptionally good. She bent over the back of his chair, holding five chips in her open hand that she had bought at the cashier's upon entering the establishment for five dollars per chip.

"Would be so kind as to set these for me?" she asked him.

He turned around to look up at the alluring woman and said, "Certainly, madam."

He set her five chips and a few of his own, primarily on the simple combinations PAIR - IMPAIR and ROUGE - NOIR. One of Mischa's chips, however, he set, apparently casually, on the number 18. This was the only chip on this number, while the other placements were loaded with chips. Suddenly, the lady next to him set two of her chips on the 18 as well. The croupier set the roulette wheel in motion, but before her could call out "*Rien ne va plus,*" the man Mischa had given her chips to slid them from 18 over to 34, another unoccupied square. His neighbor had neither time nor quick enough wits to follow suit. The rotating number wheel slowly came to halt. The croupier called out, "34, PAIR, ROUGE."

He then placed the small plexiglass chip on top of Mischa's chip, swept nearly all others and paid out the winnings. Mischa retained a total of forty chips for the five the man had placed. He turned to her with a smile and handed her the winnings.

"Would you like for me to set them for you again?" he asked.

"No thank you," she replied, believing she saw a suggestion of a smile on his face. Nice, she thought.

"But I would be happy to buy you a drink to express my thanks, if I may," she added formally.

As if it were the most natural thing in the world to receive an invitation from an absolute stranger to, a breath-taking one like Mischa to boot, he smoothly segued to collecting all but two of his chips, which he slid over to the croupier as a tip and rose from his seat. He was even taller and more impressive than when seated. Even in her high heels she was shorter than he was. A well-dressed monument, Mischa thought, unshakeable in his smiling self-assurance. His self-confidence matched her own.

They went into the bar and ordered two martinis. The barkeeper was overly generous with ice cubes and both of them asked him to remove all but one or two.

"You must not be an American," Mischa said to the man beside her, an unknown quantity as of ten minutes ago.

"You mean, because of the ice?" he asked, adding with a laugh, "I know Americans have the bad habit of adding too much ice without asking, but all the same, I'm a died-in-the-wool Yankee from Detroit. I'm an architect. I hope you have nothing against Yankees from Detroit and unemployed architects!"

She laughed with him and replied in a slightly cutting tone, "Not when they're as adept at roulette and so witty as you are."

He introduced himself as John Dwight Donaldson and invited her to simply call him JD, as all his friends did. He was amazed to discover that she had come to Las Vegas from far-away Europe to play chess, not poker or roulette.

"How many players in your tournament?" he wanted to know.

"Only two," she answered, "The World Champion and myself."

"Wow! You must be really good, Mischa, to play against the World Champion!" he exclaimed. "It's all right if I call you Mischa, isn't it?"

"You can do more than that, JD. Besides making jokes, you can sleep with the World Champion. I don't mind of you make jokes while doing it, she might even like it."

"What? That's the craziest offer I've ever had, that calls for a drink."

"I don't expect you to do it for free. I'll pay you twenty thousand dollars if you succeed in getting in her bed, but I have no doubt that you will."

"Aside from the fact that I have no idea why I should do this, what makes you think she will get in bed with me?"

"That's easy. Because she's most likely the ugliest woman you will find in Las Vegas at the moment; because she has probably never been in bed with a man before and you are exactly the attractive, charming man she dreams of on sleepless nights."

"Thanks for the compliment. Do you at least have a picture of the ugliest woman, so I know what's coming at me?"

Mischa took a newspaper clipping she had the forethought to bring with her from her handbag, unfolded it and handed it to JD.

"The one on the left," she explained. "That's me on the right, obviously."

After looking at the photo and handing the clipping back to her, he offered her another laugh, saying, "I have a much better idea. Instead of sleeping with the woman on the left, I sleep with the one on the right for free and you keep your twenty thousand dollars. What do you think of that?"

"Sounds like an option," Mischa replied, looking him in the eye. "But business before pleasure!"

"You're about the craziest woman I've ever met."

"I'm much more than that. I know what I want and that's more than most women know."

"Joking aside, are you serious about this?"

"I'm always serious."

"Show me that clipping again, I want to read the article."

She gave it to him a second time and he scanned the print.

"Oh, I get it now. You want me to distract her so that you can win the match and become World Champion in this weird game I know nothing about."

"It's not a weird game, but the most divine and unfathomable game there is. But you're pretty much right about the rest."

"I love swindlers, especially when they are as lovely as you are."

And I love swindlers, especially when they win at roulette," she grinned.

"Then kiss me, or the game's up."

The man fascinated her. He was just as direct as she was, funny, good-looking and charming. Not in the least submissive like her slaves. He was up for anything and best of all he smelled fantastic. She brought her lips close to his and kissed him quickly, without opening her mouth.

"That was a nice beginning," he said, "but not nearly enough."

"We can't make out her in front of all these people."

"Then let's go up to my room. I live here on the eighth floor. We can close the curtains, and no one will be the wiser."

She looked into his eyes. Why not, she thought. Sex was something she could use right now, especially after the two devastating losses she had suffered at the hands of her Chinese rival. It might not be the sex she usually enjoyed, but she found this man highly attractive.

"Come," she said to JD throwing a ten-dollar bill on the bar to pay for the drinks and taking his hand.

In passing, they exchanged their chips for dollars. Mischa's chips were two hundred dollars' worth, JD's a bit over a thousand. She winked at him, understanding that his winnings were not completely honestly gained.

"You're no babe in the woods," she ventured.

"Look who's talking," he shot back. "If there's some here who's not a babe in the woods, then it's you. That's what I like about you."

"We'll see about that," she implied slyly.

The sex was wonderful. He was a fantastic lover, strong, demanding, superior, dominant and commandeering, never uncertain or doubtful, yet sensitive, understanding her and leading her to the pinnacle of pleasure as if it were the most natural thing in the world. He knew what she wanted and expected without her uttering a word of direction or pleading. He knew her better than she knew herself, although he had never seen her before, although they had met less than an hour ago and were in bed together for the first time. Whatever he did, it was the right thing. Whenever he did it, it was the right time. He was violent, plunging her into a madness of desire. He held back the moment her moans and trembling told him the waves of lust were deepening and widening, bringing her close to the edge. He molded her entire being into one huge orgasm, eliciting wild and uncontrollable throes and loud ferocious screams.

Mischa came quickly, again and again, whining, groaning, roaring, limitless and untethered. She hadn't the slightest urge to torment or torture him. No, no, she loved to surrender to him and his desires, freely, voluntarily falling into the depths of novelty and the unknown without a clue as to where she will land and what will happen to her there; to become a slave herself, feeling endlessly dominated and safe instead of seducing weaklings and making them her slave, abusing, maiming, killing them to reach a climax, as was her habit until JD came along and showed her the natural, unblemished path to a sensual paradise of desire and emotion.

They kissed and made love until deep in the night. Without him demanding it, without him taking advantage of it, she surrendered to all his wishes, becoming his servant. The more and longer they made love, the more Mischa doubted she could surrender him to her opponent. Would she feel the same for him afterwards, be able to make love to him like this? He was the most fantastic man she had ever been with. For the first time in her life she believed she was in love. Her feelings were so much stronger than what she had felt for Richard or any other man at the onset of their relationship. Maybe she should simply walk away from her duel with Can, forget the World Championship title and simply hold on to this man, be happy, have children with him like any other woman.

Hours later he fell asleep beside her. She looked down on this quietly snoring man, on his completely common chest as it rose and sank, on his utterly normal stomach and its curled belly button in the center, on his finger as it jerked when his breath rasped in and out, and she suddenly doubted her plan. But one look at her watch and her doubts dissolved. She had not come to Las Vegas and this cheap three-star hotel to be seduced by fleeting sentimentality brought on by, admittedly deeply satisfying, sexual intercourse only to give up on her goals. What does she want with a new husband, with children and a life as the little woman at home when she could be World Chess Champion and the best physicist in the world? No, she was not made for a life led by millions of oppressed women tied to the kitchen. She was made to soar. Why else had nature given her a brain and abilities far exceeding the common mean?

She shook JD awake. Laying a five-thousand-dollar down-payment for the seduction of the Chinese woman on the night table, she asked for his cellphone number and gave him hers. She explained her plan in detail. Tomorrow morning, at ten on the dot he was arrive at the salon, as elegantly dressed and preened as he was today, and take a seat in the center of the front row, using the VIP ticket she gave him. He should sit as close to the playing table as possible and directly attempt to make eye contact with Can. At that time there will be more than enough free seats since the big shots, as she called them, usually turned up toward the end of the game, when at all, to catch the most exciting part and not have to wait too long for the champagne, lobster, steak and caviar buffet served to players and officials backstage after the game. This, too, was an unwritten clause in the agreement between the disparate partners and friends Bucksy Meyer and Ruslam Maschinow. The latter was clearly obsessed with food and could go but a brief time without eating or stuffing something into his mouth, as long as it was edible.

JD was to come to the VIP buffet as well and speak to Can, plying her with compliments and asking her to dinner. Of course, it should go further than dinner when all went well, and Mischa was certain it would. The following day, after fulfilling the sexual contract, which she assumed would be Can's deflowering, he should call her before ten o'clock and the next game in Caesar' Palace. They would then decide together what to do, depending on Can's state of mind following her night's adventure and its impact on her chess game. If she had fallen head over heels in love with him, he was to abandon her, and lost and lovelorn, her chess precision will suffer accordingly. On the other hand, if she was not yet completely hooked on him, he should sleep with her again to make sure she swallows the bait whole, and then ditch her. It was essential to cause her agony, distracting her from her chess game. Triggering emotional trauma was not a criminal offense, neither in the U.S.A.

nor in Switzerland, so this time, Mischa was not breaking the law for once.

She kissed him tenderly good-bye, leaving him in an emotional turmoil and returned to Caesar's Palace. It was far past midnight before she could sleep. She could not decide if she was in love the man she had just met or if he had only given her the illusion of love. Was even capable of love, or was it merely a fleeting emotional outburst that had come over her? Men came and went, but her passion and extraordinary gifts for physics and chess were inherent qualities and will dominate her thinking until the day she died. Of this, she was certain.

Was JD the man who could make her happy? Could he free her of her addiction to capturing and torturing slaves, an addiction dealt out to her by the devil? She had felt so wonderful with him, like she had felt with no man, no person at that, before. She ached to lie in his arms again, to feel his strength and power, to hear him laugh, to feel his manhood inside her, allowing the waves of passion and lust to wash over her, waves he knew how to incite better than any other, driving her to the highest heights, to hear his words and the silence when he was still. Why on earth did she leave him? Why did she hire him to seduce the ugly Can tomorrow?

She felt longing in her body and in the core of her soul, but also the insistent, loudly vehement commands of her mind, daring her to be so stupid as to throw away everything she had worked for since she was child on a man. She took a sleeping tablet to silence the battle between her feelings and her thoughts that was worse than any chess defeat.

Chapter 18

When Mischa stepped on the stage in the tournament salon the next morning shortly before the third round of the World Championship playoffs, her opponent was already seated, her arms resting on the chess table, her eyes gazing immobile at some boundless something far, far away. Mischa scanned the salon and saw JD immediately. His long legs were crossed comfortably, and he looked better than he did yesterday in his dark blue, slightly wrinkled linen suit without a tie, his white shirt with the top button casually open, a silk scarf draped around his neck, a natural leather belt and designer shoes. His tanned face, his hairy chest, his smile, his blue eyes, his dark hair, everything reminded her of yesterday evening. The entire day yesterday came alive in her mind's eye. She thought about the wonderful hours in his arms and couldn't banish him from her thoughts. She felt so powerfully drawn to him, her entire being wanted to jump up and run to him, wanted to hold him and profess her love to him, shouting it out to everyone present. She still had time to call the whole thing off and not serve him up to the ill-favored woman sitting across from her silent as the tomb and with pursed lips like an old witch.

But, she realized, if she remained entangled in these thoughts and feelings her plan would turn against her instead of against her opponent. She had to pull herself together and focus solely on the World Champion title that was just within her grasp but over the last two days had slipped from her fingers. She forced herself to concentrate on the current game for which, playing white, she had prepared a treacherous response to Can's preferred Caro-Kann defense. Once more, she played out her moves in her mind, hoping her rival did not know the variation she had rehearsed. Should she make a single imprecise move, her position against black would quickly collapse.

She scanned the salon, deliberately overlooking JD. A remarkable number of spectators had come today, expecting the incumbent World Champion to wrest a third devastatingly rapid victory to follow the two previous ones. Mischa was well aware that no one gave her even the ghost of a chance. Can had simply been too phenomenal at the last two encounters.

As the large clock on the wall told her it was ten o'clock, she joined her opponent at the chess table. Moving to give Can her hand, she immediately retracted it as it was obvious that Can had no intention of taking it or even acknowledging Mischa's presence with her eyes.

The French chief arbiter stepped onto the stage, greeted the players and requested silence in the salon. He spoke a few words to the audience and then set the chess clock in motion. The third game had begun.

Mischa was amazed and profoundly disappointed when she discovered that Can was not only perfectly aware of her chosen variation, she appeared to have memorized each detail although she had never encountered it in any of her tournament games. Obviously, she had studied it and learned it by heart along with all other four thousand, eight hundred classified chess openings. She knew every aspect, every derivation. Without giving it much thought, she responded correctly to every move. It was Mischa who made the first tiny blunder when she found herself in a complex position after the eighteenth move in the middle of the game. Can immediately took advantage, a smug smile curling her lips. Her move was not Grand masterly, it was world masterly.

Mischa was on the brink of a third catastrophe when, at that moment, the World Champion, without knowing it, made her first false move. But not on the chess board. Her slipup was raising her head to bask in the audience's admiration. Her eyes landed on JD. He smiled at her, gave a thumb's up and winked. *What a man, she thought! The kind of man I will never have. I'm so ugly. That's the kind of man who could have the most beautiful women in the world, all he had to was snap his fingers and they'd come running. Women like this inept Mischa Turow sitting across from me, who has the temerity to challenge my World Champion title, me the best player on earth!*

With diabolical pleasure, she watched her shameless challenger as she desperately sought an advantageous response to Can's last move. But Can knew there was nothing she could do to save herself, she had calculated the strategy from opening to checkmate during her endless study and analysis hours at home.

And then, Can made yet another blunder, and this one was decisive. She stole another glance at the elegant man in the first row. His eyes were still locked on her and he gave her a subtle nod. She turned her head away, but not so far that she couldn't keep her eyes on him from an oblique angle. Only women have this ability, their peripheral vision's reach being much broader than men's. It wasn't just the man's outer appearance, his entire habitus reminded her of the handsome Hollywood actors she idolized, those manly lovers radiating youthful energy, strength and charm in the films she watched when, after night-long chess studies, she turned on the television in the early morning hours to transport her thoughts to a fantasy world where reality will never take her -- to the luscious images of a man's undying love – in the hopes that these images would follow her in her dreams. The elegant spectator in the first row was actually looking at her, not at lovely Mischa sitting opposite. Were his eyes expressing admiration for her chess prowess alone, or could he be interested in her person as well? No, that was just wishful thinking and out of the question. How could such an Adonis possibly be attracted to her? Yet, she had no experience with men. She had been saving herself for Mr. Right or Prince Charming who would one day come along and awaken her, like Sleeping Beauty, and carry her off to his castle, making her his queen, showing her the most beautiful things in the world. This had been her dream for many, many years. A hope that had yet to be fulfilled. Could it be that it would come true today, that the man in front of her is the one for whom she has been waiting an eternity? Or was she just fantasizing again, hanging on an ephemeral illusion that would vanish into thin air like all others before, leaving her more bereft than ever?

She had to know if his interest was in her or simply in her chess game. She turned her head again and looked him directly in the eyes. He seemed to have been waiting for just this opportunity and discreetly blew her a kiss. She felt as if she had been struck by lightning. Never before had a man done such a thing, especially not in the middle of a tournament game. She felt heat rise to her chest and tried to smile back at him, resulting in her face and lips screwing up into a grotesque grimace. She hadn't a whit of experience in smiling at a man, let alone flirting with one. The man gave her a small sign. Apparently, he wanted to signal to her that they could meet at the bar after the game. His hands barely moved, so no one else in the audience caught their exchange. Can was thoroughly addled. A man wanted to meet her. And not just any man, but the best-looking man she had ever seen, an American in a VIP seat, probably the owner of an inherited fortune or some huge corporation or some other obscenely wealthy capitalist who travelled the world in his private jet, hosted opulent parties on his yacht, and basked in the sun with friends beside his swimming pool at his mansion in Texas or California. Could it be that she would soon be among them? Her heart began to throb in her chest, her thoughts roaming throughout a fantasy landscape, exactly where Mischa, who had already made her move, wanted them to be. No one besides her was watching the drama playing before her and which she took in with divided feelings, yet also followed with satisfaction as she waited for the Chinese woman's response. She was not in a hurry, it was her opponents time that was slowly running out.

The audience became restless as minutes ticked by without the World Champion giving the chess board her undivided attention. She seemed focused on something completely different. The arbiter stood up and broadcast a loud *shhhh* in the salon, looking sternly at the public and giving an unmistakable hand signal for silence. The room fell abruptly still, the murmuring cut short as if turned off with a switch. The sudden quiet shook Can from her reverie. She gave herself a shake to bring her back to reality but succeeded only in part. Her thoughts were obsessing with the exciting man not ten meters away from where she sat. He had smiled at her, winked at her, signaled to her and blown her a kiss, here, in the middle of the World Championship playoffs! Longing burned in her breast.

She looked down at the chess board. Her opponent had already made her move and it was her turn. Her clock ticked away coming to the end of her time limit. She feverishly sought to find her way back to her strategy, to remember the move she had prepared and knew was right, but the more she wracked her brain the further away it skittered. Her thoughts were on the man and only on the man. The man in the front row seat. She tried to tear herself away from him, to scan the variations she had studied the night before and that she knew were stored in her brain. But a short foray into the labyrinth of her mind brought her abruptly to a dead end. She was lost.

"Bah," she thought, "then I'll have to do it without relying on my memory. I'll have to find the move myself." She considered, combined and calculated as quickly as she could. The time remaining was dwindling rapidly. She came up with a thousand possibilities, discarded them all as none of them was the move she had planned to lead her rival into hopeless entanglement and certain defeat. "Well, then," she assumed, "the second-best move will have to do. I'm going to win anyway." This was a gross misconception.

Once again, a murmur swelled and fell in the salon. The World Champion, who had thus far played with calm sovereignty made a thoroughly incomprehensible move with one of her pawns. Was this her first inaccuracy? Only a few minutes remained until the first time-control. Quickly and without hesitation, the challenger responded with her knight on the right-hand edge of the board. Can couldn't believe her eyes. One move had completely dissolved her so carefully constructed position. It was now her opponent's turn to threaten her, gaining the upper hand and, by making a sacrifice introducing an indefensible checkmate. Frantically, the World Champion searched for a strategy save her skin, to fend off the darkly looming defeat as minute after minute swept past. Calculating at top speed to find an option, perhaps a hidden interim move that her adversary had not considered. Good heavens, there it was! A solution that would at least bring a draw! Sighing in relief, but also in disappointment she moved one of her rooks between the attacking figures, offering up both rooks to capture. Mischa was forced to accept the dual offer if she didn't want to risk taking a loss again. Can saw Mischa in the ye for the first time since the match began, waiting for her to offer a draw. But Mischa let her stew, enjoying the first signs of weakness in her oh-so-superior opponent. Finally, it was Can who had but a few seconds on her clock. Reluctantly, the Chinese woman offered her hand, stammering, "draw?" this time it was Mischa who refused to meet Can's eyes, only nodding curtly and turning off the clock. She signed the game protocol, rose, smiled widely at the audience and took her leave. Thus abandoned, Can could only shake her head in disbelief.

The audience began to clap enthusiastically. Defying all expectations, the challenger had maneuvered the World Champion into a draw, robbing her of half a point. The score was now 2½: ½. Can was still well in the lead, but Mischa Turow had shown them that she was an adversary to be taken seriously and not a lamb being led to slaughter. She was capable of resistance. The odds in favor of the Chinese player sank from 15: 1 to 12: 2.

Grandmaster Bastien Lacrotte, the heavyweight, in the most literal sense of the word, French chief arbiter came to the table and collected the two protocols. He attempted to comfort Can, but in vain. The stage was crowded with audience members, mostly amateur players keen for once in their lives to bathe in the glow of a true chess coryphaeus, to touch her perhaps even or shake her hand, to catch a word falling from her mouth, giving them a tale to proudly tell their children and children's children, to have their picture taken with her, giving them the illusion of being chess players of the same caliber. Can let herself be hauled over the coals. Not a single one of them would last ten moves with her without suffering serious figure loss or checkmate. Only Mischa Turow had done this, but she had already vanished behind the curtain.

As the distraught Asian was bombarded with journalists' questions, she saw the elegant man from the front row amble past the media mob and go into the bar. What she didn't see was how he accidentally on purpose brushed her opponent's hand behind the curtain and how her opponent not only tolerated the contact but returned it tenderly in kind. The fleeting incident was witnessed by no one.

Journalists were primarily interested in discovering what had so fully captured the World Champion's attention after the twenty-fourth move that she seemed miles away, allowing her clock to nearly run out and giving the impression she was no longer interest in the chess game in front of her. She explained it away by saying she had been momentarily nauseous, but it had fortunately passed in time for her to find what may not have been the best move, but good enough to save the game with the double rook sacrifice. Although she did not win today, she was satisfied with her performance and confident she will gain the required six points in the subsequent games without have to play out all fifteen games. Her adversary is certainly an outstanding physicist who has no doubt earned the Nobel Prize, but chess is decidedly more complex than physics. Chess demands an artist's genius, not the arts of a scientist. In this respect she is far more advanced than Mischa Turow. The World Champion title is hers and she is not going to surrender it to anyone as long as she is able to move the chess men, which will hopefully be many decades to come.

But you would please excuse her now, she would like to go the bar and drink a glass of juice in peace, she's sure the journalists would allow her this.

She went to the VIP bar that had been set up behind the curtain and sat down wordlessly next to the fascinating man who had, she believed, arranged this encounter and nearly cost her the game.

"What do you want from me?" she asked brusquely and gracelessly.

The man looked at her. He had never seen a more repulsive woman. Her aggressive, crude greeting would have normally caused him to get up and leave without a word, but he had promised his dear Mischa – the woman he thought he knew although he had yet to meet the demon behind her beauty – and he intended to keep that promise, regardless of the hurdles he would have to take. Besides, there was twenty thousand dollars to be had and that was worth the effort.

"Not here," he replied. "I would like to get to know you. My name is John Dwight Donaldson, my friends call me JD, and I come from Detroit. You are a truly exceptional woman. Do me a favor and come with me to a café, where not everyone is staring at us like they are here. If you would be so kind, I will be waiting for you at the garage exit in fifteen minutes. You can't miss me. I'll be driving an antique, light blue MG convertible, one of those tiny British roadsters that make you feel like you're sitting directly on the street, inundated by the wind, vibrating with the motor, there's no more exhilarating vehicle! I'm sure you will love it."

"Do you really want to be with me or are you simply out for an adventure?" Can whispered the question, her eyes lowered, afraid of both driving him away and appearing to be an easy conquest.

He smiled at her and replied, "Life is nothing but an adventure. As Chess World Champion, you should know this better than I do. You can't take everything seriously. Let us take this one step at a time. We can simply have a cup of coffee together before we talk about being serious and other things. I promise you I will do nothing you don't like or wouldn't want me to do."

Tiny Can was hanging on his every word. She was so absorbed in watching him speak, in listening to the warm melody of his voice that she hadn't really understood his words. More than anything, she would like to just throw herself into his arms. She believed she had never met a more charming and candid man, whose feelings for her were replete with honorable intentions. Can knew all there was to know about chess. And absolutely nothing about men.

"Give me twenty minutes and I'll be there at the garage exit," she said in quiet embarrassment. "Please don't make me wait. Please be there and don't make a fool of me."

He pressed a tender kiss to her cheek, "Don't worry, I'll be there."

In a gleeful tempest of emotional turmoil, Can went up to her room to dress for her him. She put on a bit of power and makeup on her face, combed her hair and changed into another dress in the misguided conception that it suited her better. She slipped into shoes with slightly higher heels, traced the outline of her lips with lipstick and left the room for the first rendezvous in the thirty-two years of her life.

That night, Mischa had a very difficult time falling asleep. She was plagued by the certainty that the coffee date her new lover had with the woman she could not otherwise defeat would lead to more. It was her idea and she had even paid JD to do it. Mischa was neither prudish, jealous or possessive. With any other man she could have cared less who he went to bed with. Especially not when it happened because she requested it to happen and the woman in question was so hideous and repugnant. Mischa was even more than aware of how Can revolted him and the he was doing it solely for her. But with JD things were different.

Mischa imagined them having sex. This man in whose arms she had felt so divinely complete, with whom just yesterday she had had the most stimulating and satisfying love making. She imagined him penetrating no one other than that hairy, bow-legged bag of bones wrapped in pimple-plastered skin, hardly more than a skeleton and stinking from all pores. She saw him touching her yellowed teeth with his tongue, kissing her bloated head and warts. Of all the slaves she had had in her life, none had been so abominable as this tiny Asian. In her travels she had seen the most enchanting, desirable Asians and Eurasians in the world, in Peking, Hong Kong, Singapore and Tokyo. She would have happily seen JD indulge himself in a lust-filled night with any of them, but the thought of him being intimate with the likes of Can was excruciating and nauseated her. Would they ever be able to come together again, she asked herself? She could no longer decide if she should love him or hate him, no longer knew how she felt about him. Maybe this was why they seemed to ideal for one another.

Chapter 19

The following morning, Mischa was one of the first to enter the tournament salon. She wanted to see the expression on her rival's face when she walked through the door; wanted to get an impression of her emotional state. As agreed upon, JD had called her an hour ago. He reported that the deed had been done just as she had commissioned although it had been a trial for him to even touch the creature. Mischa did not let on in any way how she felt about this, but merely promised to bring him the rest of the money after today's game.

Completely uncharacteristically, Can entered the stage with a lighthearted step. She was accompanied by a photographer and two journalists armed with portable recording equipment. Another member of the party was Jorge Manuel Lopez Martinez, a high Argentinian government official – he was also a member of parliament, amassing offices and titles as if they were collector's items to proudly show off and trade or designer clothes donned and changed to fit the occasion – and freshly elected FIDE delegate who had just arrived in Las Vegas. Due to frequent detailed reports in U.S. American newspapers and on television, the American public also knew Jorge Manuel Lopez Martinez as JMLM, as the media dubbed him.

JMLM had been entangled in a scandal concerning a significant construction contract on the outskirts of Buenos Aires commissioned to a Russian syndicate, which had cost him his lucrative position as delegate to FIFA, the international soccer association. Despite overwhelming evidence of his involvement, massive bribes bogged down the investigation in Buenos Aires to the point it vanished in the morass. The district attorney charged with the inquiry was fired on trumped up charges of incompetence. The Russian consortium awarded the commission valued at two billion dollars was led by none other than FIDE president Ruslam Maschinow, who had immediately arranged for his friend JMLM to cloak the no less lucrative FIDE delegate position. This man in dark grey pinstripe suit hadn't a shred of knowledge about chess but was an expert on catchpenny performances. He was undoubtedly the center figure of the group as they entered the stage, answering the reporters' questions thoroughly and with serene condescension leaving no doubt as to his personage's importance. The Chinese World Champion beside him seemed no more than an afterthought, but as she was in an unusually good mood – most likely the result of her experiences the night before – she was most welcome to be a character actor in the career-crazy Argentinian's theater, appearing with him on the press photographs.

Yet, when he espied the remarkably lovely championship challenger standing at the chess table, a woman who will be accepting the Nobel Prize in physics in the very near future – a fact he had researched thoroughly – he left Can where she stood and approached Mischa with arms flung wide, as any future president would do, clasping the wholly unknown to him and perplexed woman to his chest and congratulated her in the name of Argentina, with or without the right to do so, on her Nobel Prize. He disregarded the fact that his government saw him as anything but their representative but had rather summoned him to appear before a senatorial committee in a few days to answer question on his participation in the construction contract scandal. He was not overly concerned about this, he was quite equal to a senatorial committee. Flashing cameras let loose a storm over Mischa and him. JMLM knew just how to make the most of publicity, be it with an ugly Chess World Champion or a picture-perfect Nobel Prize Laureate. Tomorrow, the photos would be printed in all the most important Argentinian newspapers, nudging the construction contract scandal and its accompanying senate committee inquiry even further into the background aa well as giving his campaign for re-election a gratis boost. He knew better than most that being seen with beautiful women, no matter how ignorant or clever they may be, won votes in Argentina and JMLM was very good at that.

The corpulent French chief arbiter arrived and submitted himself to the cameras as well before he escorted the Argentinian, whose dignified pseudo-presidential aura enhanced the international significance of the Women's Chess World Championship, to his seat in the VIP section of the audience. JMLM found himself seated between the recently crowned Miss Vegas, a large-bosomed, peroxide-blond with a permanently gaping mouth revealing sparkling, highly-polished horse teeth and the two unoccupied seats reserved for Bucksy Meyer and his son Jeffrey. The Meyers usually waited until the game was nearly over to take their places, unwilling to waste their time with what they considered, in their abysmal ignorance of chess, as an insignificant preamble.

The blondie took the Argentinian sitting next to her for an influential politician with weighty money bags and immediately began to ply her charms, making a play for his affections. She applied breasts, legs, hair and asinine remarks she considered amusing, as she had no access to other, more demanding attractions. Tournament director Bastien Lacrotte, however, put an end to her flirtations, which she would no doubt re-assume at a later date, by placing his finger to his lips, demanding silence in the salon which today was filled to capacity. When there was not a sound to be heard, the Grandmaster and chief arbiter declared the fourth round of the Chess World Championship playoffs opened. The Chinese title defender played black and chose the Spanish Opening, also the favorite of the great Bobby Fischer who suffered from delusions of persecution later on in his life. The initial moves proceeded according to theory and neither player made an error.

To Mischa's enormous satisfaction, she observed how frequently the World Champion eagerly and expectantly scanned the audience. She was obviously looking for JD who had promised to come, but he wasn't there. Mischa knew he wasn't and wouldn't turn up either, because that was part of their agreement. Can, on the other hand, was unaware of the intrigue at work against her. The more time that passed, the more impatient she became. Her behavior at the chess table was unrecognizable. Had it been the third game, before JD and caught her eyes and attention, throwing her into confusion, she would have been thoroughly concentrated on the chess board in front of her, her head buried in the hammock of her hands braced by upright arms, her elbows resting on the table, utterly immersed in calculations and combinations without looking right or left to avoid the tiniest distraction. But things had changed, and she was now more interested in the audience than in the chess board. She sought the man who had awoken her from her virginal Sleeping Beauty coma, loving her, she hoped, and ready to take her way to his palace where they would live happily ever after. Her game's quality deteriorated accordingly. Just as in the previous game, she barely managed to scrape by with a draw. This time she exchanged all of her pawns and once again sacrificed two figures, leaving Mischa with only her two knights with which checkmate was not possible.

The chess world puzzled over what could have led to such a change in the World Champion's behavior. Why did she suddenly neglect obvious opportunities to attack? How could she miss making the best moves? And why did she need so much more time than usual to consider her moves, appearing uncommonly nervous and unfocused? Endless speculations, possible and impossible explanations, were postulated and published in the newspapers. Some proposed a serious illness, others poor sleeping habits. There was talk about her agitation arising from threats posed by the Chinese communist party should she lose her title and some even suggested she was under the spell of a telepathic witch the challenger had engaged and for whom she had reserved a seat in the audience.

The odds fell again slightly, from 12: 2 to 10: 3, naturally in favor of the title holder who still led the match with 3:1, although not as indomitable as expected. She kept wondering why her new beau had not come to the game as promised, answering the journalists questions distractedly while constantly glancing toward the door to see if he may come after all. But he didn't. She made her excuses and went to the ladies' room. Turning on her cellphone, which was forbidden to carry and must remain turned off during the tournament under threat of forfeiting the game and called JD. Was he suffering some kind of physical malady that kept him from attending the game, she wanted to know, still hoping and believing he had slept with her out of love and sexual attraction. Not wanting to give her the cold shoulder and hurt her unnecessarily – although Mischa had told him to do precisely that should she call – JD said that after such an intoxicating with her, lasting until far past midnight, he was simply too tired and needed time to rest. She shouldn't be disappointed in him, he will certainly be there tomorrow and take her back to his hotel again after the game. Can swallowed his lies whole, she was starving for them, having fallen hard for this man who had opened the floodgates to a world she had never imagined. She was in love and could hardly wait until tomorrow. According to Mischa's malicious plan however, JD was to cast her from the heights of divine bliss into the abyss of abject misery.

Early that evening, Mischa went to JD's hotel to bring him the remaining fifteen thousand dollars. She had sworn to herself she would not sleep with him today, but after he greeted her with a passionate kiss, her firm intentions melted like snow in the sun's warmth. He told her that what he had done for her yesterday was a one-shot deal and he wouldn't do it again for even a hundred thousand dollars. Mischa threw herself into his arms, tears in her eyes for the first time in years. She would never find a better man, the feeling hit her with rock-solid certainty at the very moment. A man who would do anything for her, a man she loved, that she raised to the heavens. A man who could give her the sexual satisfaction she needed like air to breathe without her having to torture and murder for it. She would begin a new life with him, maybe even have his children. With him, she could find her way into a normal life without having to surrender chess or physics. God, in whom she did not believe, had forgiven her sins and sent her the man of her dreams.

She spent the entire night with him in his hotel. Over breakfast she invited him to accompany her the day after tomorrow when she would fly to Stockholm to accept the Nobel Prize in physics. He needn't give a though to money, she had more than enough and would cover all costs, their love was the only thing that mattered. JD couldn't believe his ears. He hadn't known she was a globally recognized physicist about to receive the highest award, the Nobel Prize.

"What could a woman like you, Nobel Prize Laureate and maybe even Chess World Champion, possibly want with a common man like me?" he asked, adding, "You should marry a scientist, a professor or author, and not waste your time with the likes of me."

She silenced his mouth with a tender caress, kissing him lovingly.

"Does that answer your question?" she asked in turn.

"But love is not everything," he interjected. "I'm not fit to hold a candle to you. You'll eventually get bored with me."

"Never," she stated firmly. "You are the man I have dreamed of all my life. I want you and only you. Never before has a man so fascinated me. Never before has a man made me so happy. We don't have to get married right away, we have all the time in the world, but if, one day, you should choose to ask me, I am telling you now, yes. We have known each other only two days, but I feel like we have known each other since we could think, as if we loved each other before we even met. I know that you are my man and that we belong together forever. Don't say anything right now, just kiss me."

"What are we going to do with that oddball Chinese girl waiting for me to come and fetch her at the tournament salon? How are we going to get rid of her?" JD wanted to know.

"I've already thought of that," she replied. "Find yourself another hotel in Vegas, throw away your SIM card and get a new cellphone number. She will search for you and find nothing. She will cry her eyes out over you, unable to concentrate on her chess game and lose her World Champion title to me. Thanks to you and only you. So you see, it's not you who's nothing compared to me, it's me who's nothing compared to you!"

"Imagine, a nothing holding the Nobel Prize," he laughed, "is kind of nothing many would like to be. But okay, since you seem to have a plan for everything, you should also get a Nobel Prize for scheming. We'll do it as planned. I'll send you my new number and hotel via SMS. Just be sure I never have to see or meet up with that horrid Asian again."

Don't worry, my darling, you won't." Mischa told him. "And what about Stockholm, will you come with me?"

"What a question! I'd fly with you to the end of the world!"

Mischa had difficulty tearing herself away from him, but time was running out. It was already nine o'clock. In less than an hour, the fifth round of the World Championship playoffs would begin at Caesar's Palace. She would have to hurry. She gave him a final, tender kiss and said, "I'll see you tonight and buy your plan ticket in the meantime." Then she left.

The next two games, round five and six, went to Mischa, her victories most convincing. Can seemed to have forgotten how to play chess. She was disjointed, hyper-nervous, totally lacking concentration. She couldn't remember strategies or positions, failed at every combination, couldn't calculate beyond three moves and played at least five hundred Elo points below her average level. She kept getting up from her seat, searching the audience frantically, made one inaccurate move after the next, blatant boners such she had never made in her entire career. She was constantly going to the toilet, obviously ill. Only Mischa knew what kind of illness had befallen her. Can was desperately heartsick, and there was no medicine to cure that disorder.

The day Mischa left for Stockholm, the World Championship score stood at 3: 3. Mischa had not only balanced the score, due to her easy victories of the last two game and to the title holder's inexplicable decline she had won an edge with the bookmakers. The odds were now 7: 5 in Mischa's favor.

Chapter 20

Mischa would never have believed she was capable of experiencing such consistently divine bliss as she did with JD. She could care less whether there was a God or not, the main point being He had forgiven her and sent her JD. JD and Mischa not only harmonized on an intellectual level, they trusted one another implicitly in all matters. They laughed and joked, took long, rambling, romantic walks through snowy Stockholm, meandering over its bridges and countless canals. They couldn't keep their lips, tongues and hands off of each other. With blithe generosity, they allowed the pack of photographers trailing them like wolves or lurking in corners to catch them unawares to take their picture, any one of which would bring the paparazzi an excellent price. To Mischa's relief, her anxious worry that the sexual attraction would wear off quickly, turning to revulsion as it did with her first husband Richard, did not come about. Each time they made love, she was even more fulfilled than the time before. Three or four hours was the maximum they could bear before returning to their hotel bed. There was not a trace of routine nor ennui.

Much to the organizer's woe, the traditional schedule of events surrounding this year's Nobel Prize presentation had to be altered when the Swedish king, who attended nearly all presentations, fell ill with a feverish intestinal flu. The lectures Laureates were to give on their awarded works at the university's Aula Magna, scheduled for December 8th and the December 9th banquet at the king's palace, as well as several other events, had to be cancelled and rescheduled a few days later. In recompense, Mischa and JD, along with the Laureates in the categories Medicine, Chemistry and Literature as well as the winner of the Alfred Nobel Memorial Prize in Economic Sciences and their escorts were guests of honor at the Royal Opera where they enjoyed Mozart's *Magic Flute*. In honor of the occasion, Mischa bought a deep red evening gown of brocade and velvet for herself and black tails for JD.

One exceptional alteration in the presentation ceremony on the following day was its relocation from Stockholm Concert Hall on Hötorget to the Royal Palace as the comprehensive Concert Hall renovations were unable to be completed in time for the event. Also, the King of Sweden, in defiance of his doctor's express warnings, insisted on presenting the Prizes despite his health issues.

But a Bernadotte heeds no man's advice, not his doctor's, nor his ministers' or advisors' when he is intent on doing a thing. Yes, not even Napoleon could influence his best friend and most able commander Jean-Baptiste Bernadotte, *Maréchal de France*, when, in 1810 the Swedish Reichstag elected him to succeed the last of the house of Holstein-Gottorp, King Karl XIII who was left childless. The chosen King went so far as to oppose Napoleon when it came to retaining Sweden's independence, a loyalty that earned the Swedish people's gratitude and respect until this day.

The taxi drove Mischa and JD over the Norrbro Bridge crossing the Norr River to the square named for the Swedish war king renowned for his equestrian skills and tactical prowess, Charles XII's Torg, which was located in Norrmalm Stockholm's central borough. At the age of fifteen, Charles XII placed the Swedish crown on his own head, a feat imitated by other pretenders to the throne, among them the great Corsican himself who for nearly fifteen long years suffused Europe with war as well as the precepts of the French Revolution. Like Napoleon, Charles XII spent his entire reign in battle. Although outnumbered by nearly four to one, he conquered Peter the Great's Russian army during the legendary battle of Narva in 1700. Yet the Swedish Empire lost most of its power and much of its territory to Russia following the disastrous defeat at Poltava in 1709, which forced Charles XII to flee to Turkey, finding asylum with the Osman Sultan Ahmed III. When Ahmed, however, came to the conclusion his royal Swedish guest was no longer of use to him against his arch enemy the tsar, he had him captured by Janissaries and incarcerated in Adrianople. King Charles III fled his captors, riding over the Austrian wilderness, through Hungary, Germany and what today is known as Poland, a fifteen-day forced trek covering over two thousand kilometers, arriving home in the Swedish Pomeron accompanied by one single officer. He immediately joined the siege of Stralsund but lost his life three years later during one of his many attempts to conquer Norway when one of his own soldier's bullets bored into his head, putting an abrupt end to his earthly existence. Today, we would give this occurrence the more than odd epithet *friendly fire*, but what is so friendly about war's gunfire? Especially when it puts a hole in your head. The term must have been coined by people who already had so many holes in their heads, another one more or less made no difference.

The imposing structure of the Royal Opera, delicate rose and white, could been seen from a distance. The massive three-part entryway was held up by six Greek columns over which the large covered balcony presided on the first floor, its roof held up by three gracious archways. Further in the distance yet highly visible, standing behind the Royal Opera was the Jacob's Church tower with its four over-dimensional church clocks and tapered, domed copper roof with a small bell-house at the tip, conjuring up more images of erotic Greek temples.

The Laureates and luminaries were received by milling crowds of journalists, photographers, gaffers, officials and invited guests who had traveled from all over the world to take part in this annual event. Photographers of Mischa and JD standing before the Royal Opera as well as the plethora of shots taken over the past few days, depicting them deeply in love, holding hands and kissing in the parks, on the streets and canals of Stockholm, would doubtlessly appear the following day in not only Swedish and European newspapers and magazines but also in American and Chinese publications, perhaps even on television, especially since two Americans and one Chinese were among this year's Nobel Laureates. There was no escaping the fact that Can would see the photographs and tumble into the abyss of deepest despair. Neither JD nor Mischa could care less. Mischa found her chess adversary's dejection most opportune as it increased her chances of wresting the World Champions title from her. It was comparable to the fortunate deaths of her slaves. But now she had found her liberator, the man who had broken the chains of her murderous compulsion.

The performance at the Royal Opera was outstanding, rousing the audience as it swept them away to a world of unlimited creativity; the world of a man who prematurely met his death, remaining an eternally youthful musical genius, the world of Joannes Chrysostomus Wolfgangus Theophilus Mozart, who called himself *Amadé* and was dubbed *Wolferl* by his friends and adoring Constanza. The screamingly colorful costumes alone – Tamino's Sarastro's, Papageno's and Pamina's bird and dream robes, the garb of priests, pages, slaves and knights in armor, the Queen of the Night and her ladies in waiting – addled the audience's senses, enveloping them in Mozart's divinely childish dreams. The Swedish State Opera choir sang in unearthly tones and as the tenors and bassi, sopranos and mezzo-sopranos let loose the unrelenting power of the arias *The birdcatcher am I, This Image is Enchantingly Beautiful* and *Hell's Vengeance Boils in My Heart* that reverberated through the sacred halls of Stockholm, all spectators fell victim to their beauty, JD and Mischa included. They were enchanted, untethered, soaring in spheres beyond earth's gravity. They failed to recognize the parallels in plot and music, as if Mozart and his librettist Emanuel Schikaneder had composed and written the piece solely for them and those they had so sorely abused.

The evening could have become a truly unique and unforgettable enchantment for Mischa as she bathed in the sounds of the best Swedish royal singers, a Japanese woman comparable to Maria Callas and an Italian boasting a girth only centimeters less than the late, great Lucian Pavarotti, if she hadn't been sitting next to the Mexican Laureate in literature, a small man in his mid-seventies whose corpulence rivalled that of the Italian tenor. The poor man could hardly breathe in his constricting formal shirt, gasping, panting and clearing his throat without pause, until Mischa turned to him and, smiling kindly, her dexterous fingers untied his bowtie and opened the top button of his shirt. Relieved and charmed, he thanked her profusely. From then on, he did not leave their side, followed them throughout the intermissions between the acts, speaking incessantly about his new bestseller, a novel of a melancholic ninety-year-old's unrequited love for a timid fourteen-year-old girl that ends not in the death of the old man, but of the young girl. Wildly gesticulating, he told his tale to the seemingly innocent couple, not knowing that they had committed misdeeds a thousand times more despicable. People simply enjoy writing, reading and doing terrible things, particularly in the land of Brothers Grimm, who proclaim their lack of vice no less lucidly than Mischa Turow and are yet like single-celled twins in their iniquity and crimes, fathered by Satan and born of Messalina.

Fortunately, the unaccompanied literary left the opera house directly after the performance, returning to his hotel, leaving Mischa and JD alone – even the journalists left them in peace -- to partake of a romantic dinner in the *Operakäl-laren*, a restaurant rich in tradition, with justified claim to the Bibendum-Man awarded by the French tire manufacturer and the housed directly within the Royal Opera. They delighted in delicious maatjes salad, steamed lobster, caribou filet and the famous Swedish princess torte. Even more delightful was the discreet play of their hands under the table, undetected by the other guests. They could hardly wait to return to their hotel and finish what they had begun in the restaurant. Their thrilling and satisfying love-making continued until the break of dawn. This was to be a climax in Mischa Turow's life that very few scientists attain.

That morning, prior to the Nobel Prize presentation, Mischa gave her postponed lecture in the large lecture hall of the Stockholm University. Luminaries in physics and other scientific branches had travelled from all corners of the earth to hear first-hand how she had arrived at the theses and for-mulas of the *Dynamo Theory* which was in the process of rev-olutionizing civilization and opening the floodgates to a new, never-before-imagined future for humanity. Whether better or not, it would certainly be more progressive- Since humanity is known to prefer progress to improvement, she promised a golden future, or at least one that glittered like gold. Thanks to Mischa's theory, Mars and other planets in our solar system could now be promptly populated, not to mention the theory's many other technical applications that until that point had been fantasies found only in science fiction novels. Not one of the coryphaeus in the audience worried their noble minds with the fact that the theory did not put an end to humanity's false idols, the perpetrators of nearly all Earth's havoc and disasters, but it would serve to export them into space, expanding their power even more. No, they ignored this in their eagerness to celebrate the greatest among them Mischa Turow.

Mischa gave her lecture the title *The Impatient Gluons*. Anyone familiar with physics had thus far assumed gluons -- eight species of which had been discovered to date -- were mass-less subatomic gauge bosonic particles with a neutral charge and spin of 1-. Gluons are charged with color and anti-color. Previous experiments, primarily those carried out at the nu-clear research institute CERN in Meyrin, Switzerland, had provisionally concluded that the theoretical zero mass did not reflect reality but had to be assumed in calculations or it would lead to falsified results. It was Mischa who had developed a for-mula to unknot this apparent paradox, allowing gluon mass to be measured in millielectronvolts, since Einstein had made it common knowledge that energy is only another form of matter into which it can be transferred. Mischa dubbed the gluon characteristic of vacillating between mass and energy *impa-tience*, the irony of which seemed to escape her since this phe-nomenon attributed to the smallest particle in the universe also applied to certain more massive objects and subjects, namely

Mischa herself and perhaps to every living thing in the galaxy. But as long as this is not scientifically proven, it will remain a philosophical question, philosophy being the uncontested queen of science, also called the Science of Sciences by many.

Mischa did not limit herself to the gluons and their impatience, but also spoke of the characteristics, interaction and newly discovered phenomena of other particles. She talked about leptons, fermions, bosons, quarks, muons, electrons, neutrons, photons, charms, tops and several others. She gave them explicative adjectives that elucidated her theory but had little to do with Mischa herself, so would make little sense and go too far afield enumerate them all here and explain their functions. This is a report of Mischa's deeds and misdeeds and not of events in this world's natural or divine anarchy, perpetrated by whomever you choose to blame.

Mischa's lecture was received with thundering applause. Those who had understood it clapped in enthusiasm, the others clapped to veil their ignorance. Löre Andersen, Swedish Academy of Science chairwoman and physics professor as well – one of the worldwide leading researchers in the particle physics field – and Erik Johan Rydberg, university rector and biophysics professor, thanked Mischa warmly for her lecture which, as Rydberg expressed it, was testimony to the young woman's outstanding mind and a shining example for all humanity. A typical accolade of a man mistaking intelligence for character.

Finally, the long-awaited moment had arrived. The Nobel Prizes would now be presented to their Laureates in the Royal Palace's grand hall in the center of Stockholm. Seats were placed in narrow, tight rows to accommodate all two thousand guests attending the most important occasion in Sweden, royal weddings and coronations aside.

Next to Mischa, who was to receive the Nobel Prize for physics, on her right-hand side, sat Tokihashi Sudaka, the Japanese Nobel Prize Laureate in Mathematics whose groundbreaking theory on the dissolution of paradoxes of the infinite shed much light on the previously inexplicable mathematical enigma. On her left-hand side sat the Israeli biologists Ronen Har Zvi and Esther Weinstein, teachers and research scientists at Weizmann Institute in Rehovot together with Hansjürg Stauffacher, Swiss director of the Life Sciences Institute at Basel University. The trio had dedicated years of international collaboration to developing a new strain of organic insecticide, contributing to substantial boosts in crop yields without detrimental impact on the environment thus ensuring sustenance for billions of people in the developing countries of Arica, not to mention numerous regions in southeast Asia and South America. Mischa was filled with no small portion of pride to have a fellow countryman representing Switzerland among the Nobel Prize Laureates today. The rest of the Laureates were from the U.S.A., China, the Philippines, South Africa, Romania, Belarus, Norway, Japan and Mexico. Fortunately, the corpulent Literature Laureate Raoul Francisco da la Vega of Valparaiso sat huffing, puffing and polluting the air around him at the other end of the row. Mischa had had her fill of him yesterday.

The only damper was that the Nobel Peace Prize Laureate, Mohammed El Rahimi, was to receive his award in Oslo, Norway simply because the awards founder Alfred Nobel had decided as such, without giving any clue as to why. Admired by Mischa and millions of others around the world, Rahimi was a not quite forty-year-old Muslim who had defied all resistance in Islamic countries and founded an organization championing human rights, women's and girl's rights, the physical and emotional integrity of all people, the abolition of the death penalty and corporeal punishment as well as the enforcement of the Geneva Convention to protect prisoners of war. Mischa held him in high esteem although she hadn't the slightest regard for the physical and emotional integrity of others, like many people who claim to cherish precisely that which they themselves defile.

The orchestra began to play the *Kungssången*, the King's Song or Royal Anthem of Sweden, announcing the ceremonial entry of the royal family. With the utmost respect and eager anticipation, the public came to their feet. Led by the famous opera singer Inge Larsson, the Swedes among them joined in singing the melody composed by Otto Lindblad in 1844 and five-stanza lyrics by Carl Strandberg that expressed the love and honor the Swedish nation held for their King, although he originally came from France. Yet he had always placed Sweden's interests above all others, including those of Napoleonic France, a loyalty Swedes have never forgotten. Mischa was accustomed to great displays of patriotism in Switzerland, but this moment surpassed anything she had ever experienced with the exception, perhaps, of when she had heard the Hatikvah, the Hebrew song of hope, sung by thousands of Holocaust survivors' children and children's children in Tel Aviv when they had gathered before the Habima National Theater to celebrate their young nation's Independence Day. The unforgettable lyrics echoing throughout the night; the melody held strong by the descendants of terror also touched the hearts of those who had not suffered the Holocaust, such as Mischa Turow. Despite her family being one of the few spared the horrors of the Nazi regime; despite her turning away from Judaism and soon to convert to Catholicism; despite her bearing the devil's darkness in her breast instead of God's light, that night, beneath the starlit heavens, among dedicated Jews on Habima Square in Tel Aviv she felt she belonged, just as she felt she belonged among the Swedes gathered in the Royal Palace in Stockholm. She wished she could hold JD's hand right now, but he was standing with the other invited guests, his eyes filled with love as they gazed at her.

With stately, regal steps, the royal family entered the hall led by the King decked out in the gala uniform of a high Swedish cavalry officer bearing the red royal sash and the numerous medals and insignia he had been awarded over the many years of his constitutional reign. The King was followed by the Queen, also wearing the red, royal sash indicative of her status. Neither King nor his Queen wore a crown. Behind the royal couple came their adult sons and daughters and the Queen Mother together. The hymn came to an end, the orchestra fell silent and the royal family took their designated seats, which was the signal for all those attending to follow suit.

The chairwoman and various Nobel Prize committee members who had selected the Laureates, all of whom were Swedish Academy of Science professors, addressed the royal family in the guttural, wonderfully melodious Swedish language. They expressed their gratitude to the King for attending despite his illness and wished him a quick and complete recovery. They paid homage to the Laureates' accomplishments for which they had been chosen. Finally, one by one, the Laureates' names were called out -- either in their native language or in English since none of the professors spoke Japanese or Romanian – upon which they stepped before the King and received the Nobel Prize medallion and certificate from his hands. When Mischa shook hands with the sickly, elderly King she had a premonition that this was the last time she would see him alive, should she return to Stockholm and once more be invited to the Royal Palace. The sentiment intensified her emotions on this momentous occasion. She felt as if she had arrived at the summit.

The banquet presided over by most of the royal family – the King had excused himself – was an exquisite dinner served by four hundred liveried attendants and allowed Mischa to sit once more beside her beloved JD. Their blissful dancing, his caressing hand in her lap, his passionate kisses and other unbridled delights when they stole off to the ladies' room; the ensuing sleepless night and the following day – the last before their return flight to Las Vegas – when she gave another lecture at the Academy and swapped notes with the other Laureates; her visit to a children's home that was to be named after her; but mostly the moments of intimacy she shared with JD, their passionate love-making made her time in Stockholm a profound experience deeply imprinted onto her memory in this life and the lives to come, for there will be more. But let's not get ahead of our story.

Chapter 21

On December 14th the battle for the Chess World Championship between the Chinese title defender Pinyin To Can and her
Swiss-Russian challenger Mischa Turow, freshly elected Physics
Nobel Prize Laureate, resumed. The current score was tied at
3: 3. Besides these facts, everything had changed, especially for
the incumbent World Champion from China. Like everyone
else, she had seen in the newspapers the countless photographs
of her adversary and the man who was obviously her lover.
She had watched the reports from Stockholm on television.
Initially, she couldn't believe them, but her incredulity soon
gave way to devastating disappoint and heartache, which was
eventually replaced with growing outrage, fury and poisonous
abhorrence for the two of them. The wounds to her soul hadn't
even begun to heal before they were festering, oozing the primal
instinct of exacting vengeance. She will see them punished,
those two villains who so cruelly ill-used her. She so desperately
wanted to see JD suffer, she wanted to slap him publicly, spit in
his face. Mischa would get her just deserts on the chess board.
Can will annihilate her so thoroughly in the next game that the
entire chess world will see her as the nobody she is.

When Mischa entered the salon the next morning, she
saw Can sitting at the game table, he eyes narrowed and her

lips pressed together so tightly, her mouth was but thinly drawn line. Before the game began, the French chief arbiter and FIDE officials offered brief speeches congratulating Mischa on her Nobel Prize achievement. Imposing as ever, Argentinian Jorge Manuel Lopez Martinez gave his address particularly entertainingly, both jovial and amusing. He was most adept as presenting himself before the cameras flashing and rolling for all they were worth. Equally photo and tele-genic, stood Miss Vegas stood, chesty, long-haired and sensu-ally-lipped. Her partially open mouth revealing unmistakably bleached horse teeth, she smiled, cooed and snuggled up to JMLM, showing off her wares to the media, heaving her open-hearted décolleté and generously displaying the alluring flesh of her longs legs between hot pants and high heels. Obviously, in the interim between Mischa and JD's Stockholm trip she had become JMLM's lover and already saw herself as a jetsetter and supermodel.

Proud, not to say arrogant, she introduced herself as Jennifer-Ann Page, made idiotic remarks about weather and men, made a great effort to clarify her relationship to the sig-nificant politician next to her holding an important speech and that she had now made her entry into the upper echelons of society, the rich and beautiful, of whom she had dreamed since she was in high school. In her books, only grumpy, ugly, bow-legged Pinyin To Can was the only one on stage who did not belong to the chosen elite, who cares if she's World Chess Champion? Holding a World Championship title, and in chess of all things – such an incomprehensible game! – did not grant her a ride up to the top of society's skyscraper, where Ms. Page believed she now resided in JMLM's company. Money and glamor were absolute prerequisites, she believed, an arena re-served for men who knew how to bring in money faster than their women could throw it out, who cruised the boulevards in Ferrari or Bentley convertibles, flew first class, lived in mansions with huge swimming pools, wore Rolex watches, ate at the most expensive restaurants and bought their suits at Harrod's of London – not at Macy;#y or Sears or J.C. Penny like the common rabble – and provided their women the comforts appropriate to their wealth and status.

Jennifer-Ann had succeeded in seducing and capturing the pompous Argentinian, yet neither his sky-rocketing political career nor her dreamed-of life of luxury was to come true. But she didn't know that then.

Her next goal was to marry JMLM. He had lied to her, though, telling her he was divorced. In reality, his wife and five teenage boys were waiting for his return in a cheap apartment in Buenos Aires. His meager civil servant salary barely kept them in food and clothing. The substantial bribe money he took in was, in his infinite wisdom, transferred to a bank account on the Cayman Islands, concealed from his family and fiscal authorities, reserved, in part, to finance his collection of playmates of which Jennifer-Ann was but one example. As long as she kept her figure without going to fat from a diet of hamburgers and Coca-Cola as so many American women did; as long he found her entertaining and was not elbowed out by one of the countless silicon-breasted, injected-lipped, horse-toothed smiling volunteers in the glittering city of Las Vegas or elsewhere in the Land of Opportunity who throw themselves at well-situated men; as long as she complied to his whims she was welcome to bask in his resplendence and dream her doomed dreams.

Mischa abruptly turned her back on the frivolous woman whose brain was apparently smaller than a four-toed jerboa in the desert, and went to the game table, taking her seat across from Can. The Chinese woman thoroughly ignored her, acting as if the newspaper photographers and television reports hadn't fazed her in the least. But Mischa could clearly see her roiling below the surface, spitting and clawing like an infernal wildcat. Can was hellbent on winning today, would prove to Mischa that she was the better woman on the chess board, if she didn't stand a chance with men.

Mischa smiled, well aware that her adversary's craving for blood would work in her favor since any emotions, especially powerful emotions like hate and lust for vengeance, profoundly influence the complex thought processes involved in judging constellations, in comparing positions with those stored in the memory, in calculating and selecting possible responses – a highly disruptive influence offering Mischa a plethora of advantages. Mischa had learned this lesson as a child and since then, at least in chess, has never allowed her feelings to lead, or more aptly mislead, her game.

She had also seen what this brings in other aspects of her life, particularly when it came to fulfilling her sexual desires. Every time she deviated from her precept of rationality, with Richard but especially with Pierce McFraser, letting her emotions get the better of her mind, it had ended in disaster. She hoped, no, she was certain that things would be different with JD. Never before had a man so intrigued her. Never before had she admired a man like she did him. Never before had she felt so whole and comfortable as she did with him. Never before had sexual attraction steadily intensified – without her enslaving and torturing him to reach a climax – not rapidly degenerating to a repugnant routine as it had with Richard and Peirce McFraser.

The certainty that he loved her in return gave her the necessary quiet serenity and clear mind for the impending battle on the chess board, while Can was obsessed with sinister emotions, embroiling her thoughts and incarcerating her soul in a tiny cell with massive walls. Chess, though, knew no boundaries, tolerated no walls against which a player's copious calculation and combinations are abruptly pulled up short. In chess, thoughts must fly free and not be held captive like a bird in a cage. Can was under the thrall of her will's powerlessness; Mischa set free by the power of her new love that allowed her to forget her inner demon.

Mischa let her gaze wander over the audience as the seating area slowly filled. She recognized several Grandmasters across from whom she had once sat, the chess board between them. There was the amiable, ever-joking, Polish-born Alex Yerkontinsky, recurrent U.S. American Master. All four games they had played ended in a draw. Over there was the former German Master Thomas Muther, the modest thalidomide baby whose physical handicap had no influence over his kindness, joviality and lust for life. And just entering the salon was the magnificent Icelander Johann Börnesson, who in the Men's World Championship Candidates tournament of 1987 made it to the quarter final before falling to Anatoli Karpow. Mischa waved at him and he gave a cheerful wave back, curling his four fingers for a thumb's up, letting her know he was backing her to win.

Mischa thought back to 2005 when, thirty years after the legendary World Championship match between Bobby Fischer and Boris Spassky, Fischer was wandering the world to escape arrest for incursions on the United Nations embargo on Yugoslavia in 1992 and the Icelandic Prime Minister granted him Icelandic citizenship out of gratitude for putting Iceland on the map by holding the *Match of the Century* in Reykjavik in 1972, thereby saving Fischer from extradition to the United States.

Paranoid and egocentric, Bobby Fischer had made plenty of other enemies in other countries. When a journalist asked the Prime Minister why she brought, of all people, the obviously insane Fischer to Iceland, she replied there were already three hundred thousand crazy people in Iceland, one more made no difference. A smart woman, Mischa thought.

Finally, Chief Arbiter Lacrotte silenced the rustling, murmuring audience, welcomed the two players and the public to the second half of the World Championship duel and started Can's clock, thus opening the seventh game in the Women's Chess World Championship. Can, playing black, had prepared a notably aggressive opening in lieu of the cautious Caro-Kann defense – the so-called Marshall Gambit. In 1918, legendary American Master Frank Marshall introduced the Gambit in New York during a game against José Raul Capablanca, a Cuban player who went on to become World Champion between 1921 and 1927. With the Marshall Gambit, black sacrifices a pawn after eight moves, opening promising attack strategies. Mischa, like nearly all Grandmasters, had detailed knowledge of the Gambit and the threats it poses, having analyzed it hundreds of times. She eluded the Gambit and launched the Anti-Marshall counterattack as preferred by former World Champion Garri Kasparow, political opponent and rival of Russian President Kutin and, some say, the strongest chess player of all time.

As Can realized the game was developing in a direction she had not reckoned with, her already taut nerves were wound even tighter. Inner turmoil, tension and rage brought blotches of red heat to her usually pale cheeks. She wracked her brain to somehow uphold her attack. She simply had to win this game no matter what, but in chess, as in life, force, adamancy and defiance are doomed strategies. Can ignored the veiled traps Mischa's counterattack held and promptly fell into one. She couldn't believe her eyes when, Mischa unexpectedly sacrificed her queen at the twenty-eighth move, she saw herself confronted with the choice of either being checkmated in five moves or losing all of her remaining men. At the end of her rope, she stood and through half-closed eyes looked poisoned daggers at Mischa, shrieking with infinite hate, "Fucking whore!" so loudly it was heard in the furthest corners of the salon. She smashed her fist down onto the chess clock, overturned the chess board, pieces flying every which way, and stomped from the stage without giving the arbiter, officials, journalists or spectators a second's thought.

The audience jumped from their seats in outrage. Even the Grandmasters and journalists sprang up. The chief arbiter frantically called out and gestured for order, trying to restore the former dignity but his efforts went unnoticed, were drowned out in the exhilarated din of people stampeding the stage, were swallowed whole by the reigning chaos triggered by Mischa's victory and Can's insulting exit and blasphemous scorn of all proper protocol. Photographers sent a hailstorm of flashing cameras over Mischa and the rampant crowd.

Grandmaster Börnesson from Iceland was the first to clasp Mischa's hand in both of his in congratulations. He raised his fist to the heavens, the gesture meaning *bravo*, *break a leg* and *to hell with Can* all at once. Mischa's fans surrounded her, patted her on the back, gave her their hands and asked for her autograph on photos and game forms where they had noted the moves of the abruptly ended game. Many already saw Mischa as the new World Champion.

Finally the chief arbiter managed to push his way through to Mischa and congratulate her as well. He related his intention of suggesting to FIDE officials that Can not only surrender the point for today's defeat but also lose an additional point for unsportsmanlike behavior, the extra point going to Mischa. In exchange, he requested Mischa forego charging Can for defamation of character, which would only damage the honorable reputation chess enjoyed, as he put it. *Gens una sumus*, he added, quoting the FIDE motto well-known to every player and meaning so much as *We are one family*.

A fitting description in this case since the bitterest battles and most heinous crimes take place in family circles, as history has proven often enough. Cain murdered his brother Abel in a fit of jealousy, Oedipus killed his father Laius so her could marry his mother Jocasta and Agrippina, Mischa's predecessor, tortured and killed her sex slaves and poisoned her spouse, the weak and sickly historian-poet Emperor Claudius, so she could carry on with her wicked sexual excesses as well as put her son Nero on the throne. Nero thanked his mother by killing her. For his part, Claudius had his young, beautiful wife Messalina executed for her orgiastic infidelities. Agrippina was sister to the maniacal Emperor Caligula who made his favorite horse Incitatus a Roman Consul. The son of their incest, Nero, was a pathetic whiner who also had his popular half-brother Britannicus assassinated to eliminate competition for the throne. Nero, with his thick, red beard and sideburns, will always be remembered for setting fire to Rome which he did for the most varied reasons, depending on who you are reading at the moment, Seneca, Pliny, Statius, Juvenal, Suetonius or other chroniclers of the time. One claims the inferno was revenge for Gaius Calpurnius Piso's assassination plot, another was Nero's simple desire to sing and play fiddle in the delightful firelight and yet another said he wanted to blame the strengthening Christian sect for the fire, giving him due cause for throwing them to the lions in the Colosseum.

Whatever may have occurred in the *Domus Aurea* during the first century after Christ in Rome inside Nero's hundred-hectare golden Emperor's Palace that was so immense a thirty-five-meter high marble statue of himself found space in the entry hall, in the twenty-first century in Bucksy Meyer's much larger Caesar's Palace the current score in the Women's World Chess Championship was 5: 3 for Mischa. To seize the title, she needed but two more points.

The betting odds rose from 7:5 to 10: 3 in Mischa's favor, but as she was quietly celebrating her victory with JD over a romantic candlelight dinner in a small Italian restaurant removed from the casino throngs, she received an unexpected call from FIDE President Ruslam Maschinow. Calling from Havana where he was putting in an appearance with the new Cuban president, he wanted to be the first to congratulate her on winning the World Chess Championship title. To Mischa's utter amazement, Pinyin To Can had surrendered the match, automatically losing her title to Mischa. Maschinow would be coming to Las Vegas the day after tomorrow to present the title to her, so Mischa should please stay for another few days. In two days' time, Mischa and her escort would be invited to the World Championship celebration and gala dinner at Caesar's Palace which promised to go late into the night. Many illustrious guests are expected, among them the Russian and Swiss ambassadors in the U.S.A., Michail Grigorewitsch Saitschew and Hans-Ulrich Vonwilen respectively, Kentucky's Senator Ricky F. Staunton, the former governor of California Harald Schwarzenfelder as well as many other luminaries and Hollywood stars. Naturally, hotel director Bucksy Meyer would be there to present her not only with the World Champion trophy and certificate, but also a check for one and a half million dollars. Would it be possible for Mischa to buy a small gift for

Bucksy's son Jeffrey, who was a great fan of hers? It needn't be anything expensive, perhaps a small pocket chess set with her autograph, or something similar, as long as it came from her personally. Jeffrey would be thrilled, and so would his father, our generous host who may be willing to sponsor future events, as Maschinow could not omit mentioning.

Mischa was stunned. It took her moment before she jumped up and flung herself at JD covering him with a hundred kisses. She had achieved everything she had aimed for in life; she had won the Physics Nobel Prize, she had become Women's Chess World Champion. It was if she had been subconsciously carrying an enormous weight all these years and it suddenly was lifted from her shoulders. She felt as light a feather. She closed her eyes and heaving a heavy sigh fell back into her chair.

That night, for the first time, she did not make love with JD. She simply lay beside him, wandering fully satisfied through a reverie, cuddling close to him as his hands journeyed over her body. She responded but little to his caresses, enjoying the moment at the pinnacle of her life, wanting nothing, missing nothing, hungry for nothing. This bliss she felt, this fulfillment she perceived, this pride that elevated her, this man by her side, all these things transported her to ultimate happiness. She kissed him tenderly. Her travels were over, she arrived in paradise. Her past lay behind her forever. She had no compulsion to torture men, to see them suffer, to watch them die. JD had healed her addiction, had awoken her from the nightmare, leading her to a new, fabulous reality. Her future with him opened up before her, amazing and full of promise.

They spent the next day lazing by the hotel swimming pool, working out in the fitness room, surrendering their sweat bodies to the staccato drumming of Thailand masseurs, sashayed carefree and happily through the streets, casinos and shopping centers of Las Vegas. The bought a chess set for Jeffrey, no piddling thing but an expensive standard-sized set with hand-carved maple figures and valuable inlaid board. The bought a radar sensor device for JD and daring sexy underwear for Mischa. In the evening, they took in a music show, more or less, since they hardly took in anything as they were too busy being in love, kissing and caressing, oblivious to the show on stage. They made love in a small broom closet they found next to the toilets in a hotel corridor and, without giving Mischa a chance to try out her new underwear, again and again in bed until the wee hours of the morning on the day the entire world would watch as she received the Women's Chess World Champion title.

Bucksy Meyer had requested she not appear at the gala dinner before nine o'clock since, he said, the salon in which the World Championship match had taken place must be completely converted and prepared for the evening's event. A few minutes after nine, Mischa and JD stood at the salon door, opened it only to be met with total darkness. All at once, blinding light exploded, the orchestra played a fanfare and a thousand sparkling eyes gazed at her from merry faces, erupting in exuberant applause. As they passed the threshold, they discovered the conferencier standing a few steps away, an approximately fifty-year-old man dressed in extravagant grey and white tails, his heavily pomaded hair done up in an Elvis Presley do. He motioned the guests and orchestra to silence and spoke into the microphone.

"Ladies and gentlemen, please welcome the new Women's Chess World Champion who only a few days ago also received the Nobel Prize in Physics. It is our immense honor to have with us this evening one the most exceptional, intelligent women in the world, Professor Doctor Mischa Turow of Switzerland!"

Thundering applause erupted accompanied by an unending chorus of bravos, the rumble of feet stomping and the strobe-lights of flashing cameras. The conferencier approached Mischa and JD, who felt somewhat out of place and looked to make a retreat but was commanded by the conferencier's unmistakable waving and gesticulations to stay.

"Stay with us please John!" he called out, obviously having taken his name from media reports. "The man who has won the heart of the woman desired by every man on planet Earth, myself included," he added impishly, "has earned the right to celebrate with her."

Amid the sound of We Are the Champions by Freddy Mercury and the Queens, sung by the entire audience, the conferencier ushered Mischa and JD to their table. Also seated at their table and greeting them with smiles and applause were the Swiss and Russian ambassadors with their wives; hotel director Bucksy Meyer, his wife – a somewhat worn-out woman in her mid-forties – and their son, eight-year-old chess enthusiast Jeffrey; the elegant Senator Staunton posing like a Hollywood star in the company of his latest reproduction of the woman he ditched two days ago; FIDE President Ruslam Maschinow and the Argentinian Delegate Jorge Manuel Lopez Martinez with his faithful Miss Vegas who dogged him like a shadow. The neighboring table was filled with well-known faces from Hollywood turned toward Mischa grinning and applauding as if they were at the Oscar Awards.

The evening, however, put one more in mind of a fundraiser for an American presidential candidate than of the Oscars. The pattern was the same; intervals of music and shows, speeches dripping with accolades, steak, lobster and crab dishes, the adored guest of honor rising to face her worship-pers and the presentation of an over-sized, nearly one square meter large symbolic check. The actual sum had already been transferred to Mischa's Swiss account. And then there was the giant trophy, filled with champagne, and the World Cham-pion Title certificate framed on gold and signed by Ruslam Maschinow and JMLM – which they presented to her with pomp and grandeur.

Though it may well be that many marriage vows were broken this evening, the bond between Mischa and JD held fast, seemingly welded in eternity. Rarely had one seen a hap-pier, more in love couple in Caesar's Palace.

Chapter 22

JD had rescinded his lease on his apartment in Detroit, sold his furniture and move to Vienna with Mischa. Unlike her times with Richard and McFraser, their union did not degenerate into a love-annihilating routine, not even after months of living together. Every time they made love, JD aroused Mischa even more than the times before. He only had to touch her, and she was electrified, only a moment together and she was panting and screaming for more. It was a magical relationship, the magic of love, of harmony of lust and of satisfaction. Their mutual attraction lost none of its freshness, as is usually the case, but grew steadily. Mischa appeared to be free of all evil impulses. She led a normal, yes, marvelous life of a young woman basking in the special glow of a happy relationship and sexual fulfillment. She and JD were an ideal couple, admired and envied by all they encountered.

They were often invited to visit Rita Sokol, the young neurologist and her French partner Fred Lavalle the painter, but also frequently hosted highly popular parties and dinners that were the talk of Vienna. They went to the National Opera, the Castle Theater and Academy Theater, enjoyed themselves in Cabaret *Simpl*, in *Ronacher* Theater; visited the Secession at the Vienna *Künstlerhaus* and the Concert Hall. They were invited to receptions given in Mischa's honor by the Federal Chancellor, the President and other leading members of the Republic. They appeared on talk shows, gave interviews, were available for documentaries and paid calls to chess clubs in Vienna, Zurich, London and wherever else their travels took them. Everywhere they went, they were received as if young British royalty or the protagonists of a smash hit Hollywood film had just walked in the door. Many compared Mischa to Romy Schneider or Lady Di. She and JD were the center of every event they visited, be it in or out of a chess club. Their activities filled society columns and internet fora, offering endless topics of conversation to their admirers in Vienna and around the globe. Mischa no longer had time for chess tournaments, which had no tarnishing effect on her halo. Quite the contrary, it gave it an even higher shine. Since she never lost a game, she had become the invincible Goddess Caïssa.

In just two years' time she would have to defend her title against a challenger who must first run the gauntlet to get so far. She would have to take the same hurdles Mischa took, the same qualification tournaments, the same process of elimination where a tiny lapsus could destroy the dreams and work of decades. Mischa didn't wish that on any of the talented up-and-coming chess players who with evident ease overtook the old guard of grandmasters, making them look like dilettantes and claiming their right to the title with cast-iron determination. And yet, only one of them could be challenger. Mischa was relieved to have survived it all and was free of having to confront those who were just waiting to defeat her and put insurmountable boulders on her path to Chess Olympia.

For two years hence, the place just a hair from heaven was reserved for her without her having to lift a finger to defend it. She could simply bask in the light of fame shining down upon her, lending her an aura of invincibility and genius, even more than it had with Pinyin To Can, who had sat on the chess throne for four years before Mischa had massacred her. Can had not appeared at the World Championship closing celebration in Las Vegas nor had anyone heard anything from her since then in China. She had not participated in any chess tournaments and there was no mention of her in newspapers and magazines. She was nowhere to be seen at chess events nor at any other public occasion. It seemed she had vanished into thin air.

It was rumored her unexpected defeat to Mischa Turow, but also her crass behavior at the final game, had caused irreparable damage to China's reputation and the Eastern Giant's almighty Communist Party had punished her severely, stripped her of all privileges, forced her to relinquish the entire prize money amounting to five hundred thousand dollars to the Federal Treasury, sent her to live in a remote agricultural cooperative village somewhere in Manchuria where she toiled in the fields or factory twelve hours a day, after which she must give gratis chess lessons to the children there. Contact to the outside world, especially to journals was forbidden, the rumors say. But no one knew for certain.

The source of all Can's woes, JD, on the other hand and not without Mischa's kind and effective mentoring, had quickly found a well-paid position at a large German engineering office's branch in Vienna. He was given free rein to accompany his famous wife on her lecture and research travels. They would never have guessed that the seed of their first encounter in a cheap, three-star hotel in Las Vegas would so quickly blossom into profound love, the greatest love that either of them had ever imagined, that this would become a bond for life. But this was not a gift from heaven as they believed, but bait from the

Devil who gives nothing without calculating the price, and most certainly gives no gifts.

Of this they were blissfully ignorant.

They flew to Tokyo, to Rio and Amsterdam, to Kuala Lumpur, Singapore and Bangkok. They spoke at congresses, in universities and before the highest executives of mega-corporations. They flew to national receptions, to birthday or engagement parties given by Hollywood stars, were top-dollar guests at media events or took a flight to Sydney just for fun to enjoy an unforgettable evening at the opera. For more than half a year that lived in a paradise of science, work, pleasure and sensual delight.

Without a doubt, one of the highlights of this time was the invitation to the Kremlin, extended by the Russian President Ivan Sergejewitsch Kutin, with whom Mischa had always had a special relationship. During the Candidates' Tournament in St. Petersburg, seducing this powerful, apparently unapproachable man had been one of her primary objectives. That she was now coming to him with her husband seemed to spur him on to prove to her just exactly who was the single most desirable male being on Earth.

Late that night, after dinner, Kutin took Mischa and JD in his helicopter and flew with them to his dacha deep in the forest far outside of Moscow. Accompanied by only a handful of bodyguards they went bear hunting, an entertainment not without its perils. With one well-aimed shot, Kutin nailed a huge bear at close quarters. On an open fire, they grilled and ate fresh bear meat, drank heavenly Crimea wine and listened to the songs Kutin sang, playing the domra, the Russian lute. His playing was unparalleled.

Although he could easily be Mischa's grandfather, Kutin's body was as strong and well-trained as a young man's. With his upper body bared, he chopped wood in the cold night, fired up the fireplace that could have easily held three oxen and allowed himself to be unabashedly served and pampered by six young Russian girls who were permanent installations in the dacha household. Later in their room, before Mischa and JD had even begun foreplay, they could hear the screams of unbridled lust, pain and abandonment coming from Kutin's suite, echoing through the Olympic swimming pool in the next room.

Following a late breakfast next morning, they boarded his jet, a re-constructed four-engine Tupolev, a comprehensive military and government center and an apartment with whirlpool and movie theater for his own entertainment. The jet was equipped with state-of-the-art weapons systems and had space for than one hundred guests. Most of those on board were bodyguards, but there were also a few ministers and oligarchs with their wives and children. Kutin sat at the helm, instructed his co-pilot and kept up constant communications with his ministry presidents and other loyal servants who held the largest land mass on Earth in an iron grip, making people dance like marionettes on a string when they chose to do so, not to mention the other, more life-threatening activities in which they engaged.

There came a call from outside of Russia. It obviously aroused his anger as he roared into the telephone, his face red with wrath, he abruptly cut the call. Mischa and JD sat directly behind the cockpit and the door was wide open. In his jet, Kutin fear nothing and no one. They distinctly heard his furious bellowing. Mischa had never seen him like this, neither at their personal encounters nor on television where even the most provocative questions from western journalists failed to rattle him. He was always calm and thoughtful, never allowed himself to be put on the defensive, but rather inimitably, quietly launched his attack with natural authority, presenting brilliant, well-researched insights and arguments, never raging and violent as he was now.

It was some time before he had regained his composure.

"That was the Syrian president, a slaughterer of his own people," he said to Mischa. "He does not hesitate to wipe out entire cities and villages in his own country, to gas people like the Nazis once did. He is truly a mass murderer."

He motioned her to join him in the cockpit, so he could show her his city of birth Sotschi as they approached for landing and the stunning view of the Black Sea and of the snow-capped Caucasus.

"One day I will have to drop the mongrel," he continued, "and let the vultures eat what the wolves have left over. But at the moment I need him to help against the terrorists and unfortunately against the Americans, too, who know about as much about Syrian politics as an elephant knows about water-skiing."

He laughed. His anger had dissolved. He was back to himself, prudent and clear-headed. HE was a master of facial expressions, never letting on what went on behind his façade, even when many believed they could intuit his thoughts, feelings or intentions. They were mistaken. It was typical for him to work with a man he detested and considered an unscrupulous mass murderer.

Mischa didn't know what she should think of this and forced herself to think of something completely different. She told him it was wonderful to be flying with him over Russia, it stirred very special feelings in her.

"You have inherited a Russian from your father," he rejoined. "Only Russians feel that way when flying over Russia, or when they wander over the vast expanse of the Russian taiga with no more than a backpack and a gun, or ride over them on horseback like Michel Strogoff, the courier of the tsar, made immortal by a Frenchman's tales, or like the heroes brought forth by Pushkin, Tolstoy and Dostoyevsky or the simple people of whom they tell. For anyone else, the land below us is merely land like any other, but for us, it is the keeper of our most inner awareness, it's what makes us who we are, it is the soil for which we live and die. A few weeks ago, I met the Israeli Prime Minister and he said the same thing about his country. But Israel is miniscule and vulnerable, Russia is huge and indomitable. Be proud to be a Russian Mischa and represent your fatherland in the future, not that tiny Switzerland that wouldn't be there if it wasn't for its banks. Otherwise Hitler and his cronies would have overrun it a long time ago as Napoleon once did!"

Mischa was at a loss for words. Kutin spoke with such conviction and enthusiasm that responding with logic or rational arguments were just so much spit in the wind. She truly felt like a Russian at the moment. She had never heard such words from a Swiss minister nor been offered them.

It was her first time in Sotschi. The architecture presented a cityscape of contradictions, Fin-du-Siècle mansions and sanatoria; Russian Orthodox churches with their imperial roofs; modern high-rises; nondescript, concrete-box hotels and the harbor building in Stalin's Zuckerbäcker style. Yet the palm trees, beaches, marinas, terrace restaurants, lightly clad girls, joggers, roller skaters and skateboarders could just as easily be found in Cannes or Nice. Most of the signs and lettering were in Cyrillic script. For the occidental tourists who flooded the city every summer, this one being no exception, there were also many signs in Latin letters, especially those bearing the insignia of luxury boutiques, or the menu boards on the street outside the restaurants or advertising announcing special sales on useless things of all shapes and sizes that are the same anywhere on the globe.

President Kutin and his entourage gave little time and but cursory attention to the large reception – orchestra, flower girls, municipal officials and an entire school class of children -- waiting to greet him at the airport. He deigned to shake hands with the mayor, a few people in immediate proximity and the children closest to the front. He spoke a few words and then vanished into one of the twenty black stretch limousines waiting to carry him and his people away. With a police escort, one in front and one bringing up the rear, the presidential cavalcade took off at high speed from the airport tarmac toward the city center. Speed limits, traffic regulations or right-of-way, for example yielding to on-coming traffic, were repealed for the duration. They barreled through downtown of the densely populated city at one hundred and eighty kilometers per hour and faster. No one thought it unusual. It was taken for granted as part of the commonly accepted reality in Russian cities.

The traffic lights naturally were all green. Military had secured the pre-planned route and pushed passers-by, natives and tourists, young and old alike, abruptly out of the way, partially for their own protection, but also to ensure the president's undisturbed passage. Upon seeing the blinding, blinking lights of the signal trolley announcing the approach of the cavalcade, private cars, trucks and busses were to immediately clear the road, which meant driving onto the sidewalk into the milling crowds. A collision could easily mean death, and if not, then a life sentence for the driver holding them up, not seldom ending in his disappearance for good. Better to risk scrapes, broken bones and screaming children than to land in Siberia or in the secret police's dungeon. Four jet propulsion helicopters armed with live rockets kept pace with the tapeworm dashing through the streets, monitoring and protecting it from the air.

A taxi brought Mischa and JD to the university where they were heartily greeted in corpore by the assembled faculty, first and foremost Rector Nikolai Armandovitsch Sarkissian, professor of literature and well-known author of Armenian stock, whose humor, warmth and impishness were immediately evident. His gripping tale based on true events, *The Legacy of Musa Dagh*, is an impressive sequel to the Armenian national epos surrounding cosmopolitan Franz Werfel, originally from Prague and one of the countless Jewish literati during the pre-WWII and Nazi Vienna era. The story tells of the tragic yet hope-inspiring fate of an Armenian family during the barbaric forced exodus and death marches organized by Young Turks in 1915. Hundreds of thousands died of exhaustion or starvation, were beaten to death or shot by soldiers and sympathizers. The book became an international bestseller but was banned in the land of Ataturk that was torn between newly revived Islamism and modernism. The ban triggered a veritable flood of under-the-counter sales to dissidents and all those who refused to be browbeaten by the Islamist government's intimidation campaigns and waves of arrests issuing from the demagogic, dictator-president.

Following a small aperitif, during which Mischa was bombarded with questions and comments, the entire party was led to the largest lecture hall in the Physics Institute where the first two rows were reserved for them. The remaining seating, numbering several thousand, was filled to capacity with students of all fields who were waiting with bated breath to finally see and hear the famous Nobel Prize Laureate and creator of the Dynamo Theory, not to mention the fact that she was an attractive young woman they had been long expecting since the lecture had been announced months ago.

JD sat among the predominantly male audience and watched as they hung on her lips, devoured her with their eyes and, he imagined, dreamt of her in lonely hours, painting the most adventurous pictures at night as they lay next to their faded or wilted wives. JD thanked his luck stars to be the man at her side. And this feeling of singularity, the blessing of having been chosen by the other, of being loved and respected filled his soul and expanded his heart, just as it did Mischa's. Although she could have her pick amongst the most desirable men in the world, she never doubted her choice. JD was the man of her life. She could talk and laugh with him as with no other, he knew what moved her, he understood what she wanted, he was her accomplice, her best friend and her lover, he was the man who aroused her lust, who gave her the most exquisite sexual pleasure, wherever and whenever she so desired. And, best of all, he was the man who had cured her sadistic compulsion and paved the way to a normal and happy life.

Their carefree summer days Sotschi melted away like ice cream in the sun. One day, President Kutin gave Mischa an unexpected call. He told her she was an exceptional woman and Russia was very proud of her, he thanked her for her visit, although Mischa felt it was she who should be thanking him for the exciting night at the dacha, for the bear hunt and campfire in the forest, for the unforgettable flight to Black Sea. He casually informed her, as if she were one of his ministers, that the North Korean dictator's constantly fluctuating atomic madness requires him to fly immediately to Peking and meet with China's party and government head, which means he will not able to meet her and JD for dinner in Sotschi as planned, but, he specifically mentioned, the date was only delayed, not cancelled. He would always be there for her, should her life take an unexpected turn. Russia is her true home he stressed, speaking slowly and clearly so she would remember his words and the depth of their meaning. Russia would never leave her in the lurch, would protect her, should she ever need protecting. Mischa took his words to be the usual platitudes and would never have thought that she would remember and gratefully make use of them in the not-too-distant future.

Those who have surmounted the highest mountain in the world, basking in the brilliant sun at the pinnacle so close to heaven, rarely reflect on the depths below and take the precaution of stretching a safety net to catch them and save their lives when they fall. Kutin was stretching a safety net for Mischa without knowing she would one day be in desperate need of it. He was the President of all Russians who were not among his enemies or victims. Where they lived, in Russia or in another country, and which passport they held alongside a Russian one, was all the same to him.

Chapter 23

On the flight back to Vienna, Mischa made her usual one-night layover in Zurich which turned out to be unexpectedly longer. She had heard that her younger brother Michael was once again in trouble and she was called on to help. The police had obtained a search warrant and turned up hard drugs in his apartment. Michael had not only verbally abused one of the officer, he had also slapped him around and was now in custody.

At the police station in Zurich, she met up with her parents for the first time in many years. With trembling hearts and hands, they hugged her and JD, but Mischa felt not the slightest stirrings of love or of any other warm affection toward her parents. As her mother practically begged her to come home for just one cup of coffee, Mischa curtly refused, much to JD's confusion. He felt sorry her parents. Mischa's only explanation was that she and her parents had disparate interests and objectives in life, they were not on the same wavelength, as she put it. He should accept this once and for all and ask no further questions. She regularly sent her parents large sums of money, much more than they had ever spent on her, and that must be a sufficient show of gratitude for the fact that they incidentally put her on the planet. She was not prepared to do more than that, would rather spend her precious time with him or other people that she appreciated, that she got along with, with whom she could have fun and get something out of the exchange. She had no desire to waste a single second with people who did nothing for her, even if they were her parents. Discovering this sudden, sharp coldness in Mischa startled JD and he put it down to a small, grey shadow on her soul arising from a childhood trauma that had yet to heal over. But there had been no such trauma in Mischa's childhood and the shadow was much larger than JD could know. It wasn't grey, either, but the inky black Devil he had failed to exorcise, who was coiled inside her half-asleep, waiting his chance to return to life and wreak more havoc than ever before.

Procuring the help of a friend who was both professor of law and *Fürsprech* in Bern, applying both plausible arguments and his personal influence on the District Attorney in Zurich, Mischa managed to get her brother released for the nonce as long as he complied with certain conditions. She gave him a check with a long row of zeros and bid him to put an end to his drug consumption and dealing, especially in parks to minors. He should use the money to establish himself in an honorable business, computer services, for example, since he had a talent for IT and spent his nights sitting in front of the computer; or he should prudently invest the money in the stock market, she implored him. Michael merely nodded, but Mischa took this meager assent for a promise, primarily to convince herself and her conscience and get her off the hook, releasing her from her duty to look after him. He had already taken up much too much of her precious time, regardless of her feelings for him. And, yes, she did have feelings for him, more than she did for her parents, but she also believed her money would make everything right, solving any difficulties or problems. She was incapable of supplying the kind of help he really needed, incapable of listening and guiding. When it came to her family, the enormity of her brainpower and abundance in her wallet stood opposite of the absolute vacuum in her heart, although she did her best not to let her brother, or herself for that matter, see this discrepancy.

There were a few people who touched her heart, some even profoundly – JD, Kutin, her friend Rita and a handful of others – but these stirrings arose from her egocentricity, her self-centered orientation and craving for recognition.

Mischa and JD had taken a room at the best five-star hotel Zurich offered, the *Baur au Lac* across from the pier where paddle steamers docked to take on shiploads of tourists and ease them over Lake Zurich to Pfäffikon, Rapperswil and the picturesque Au peninsula where the city of banks melted into the snow-capped Alps. Here, not only the mountains are higher, so are the prices, catering to landowners both Oriental and Occidental who have relocated far from the roar of battles, tax investigators and others looking to snatch away their money.

The district near Bahnhofstrasse and the Lake is the best in Zurich if you don't count the Alp paradise at the other end of the lake, which isn't within the city limits anyway. The noble hotel was founded in 1820 by a bakery journeyman, an immigrant from Vorarlberg, Austria who had bigger plans and was willing to take greater risks than his professional guild colleagues who looked no further than the inside of their ovens. He had already bought a restaurant hard by a shop owned and run by a certain pastry chef and chocolatier David Sprüngli, as well as an older hotel on Parade Platz, the *Savoy Baur en Ville*.

Empress Elizabeth of Austria-Hungary, the renowned Sissy, had spent many days in *Baur au Lac* as well as Ludwig of Bavaria, William II of Germany, Haile Selassie of Ethiopia, Richard Wagner and Walt Disney. Mischa's ears perked up when she heard that it was in *Baur au Lac* that Bertha von Suttner convinced Alfred Nobel to establish the Nobel Foundation and it was also here that Thomas and Katia Mann spent their honeymoon. These two tidbits touched her particularly not only because she had received the Nobel Prize in Physics just over six months ago, but especially because before they left for Moscow, at a dreamy dinner in a fish restaurant on the Danube in Vienna, by candlelight and gypsy music, JD had asked for her hand in marriage, which she had joyfully accepted. Unfortunately, the receptionist did know exactly in which room Mr. and Mrs. Mann had occupied. They simply imagined it was the one they were in right now and that they would spend their wedding night in the very same bed, which began immediately after they had checked in early that afternoon. Their bodies ached for one another, their lust untamable. They just couldn't wait until nightfall.

Misfortune struck Mischa, no, an outright debacle such as she couldn't possibly imagine, crashed into her world on the third evening she and JD spent in Zurich. They were sitting in the hotel restaurant, a pavilion-style addition to the original structure filled with lush greenery. In the twilight before true darkness fell, Lake Zurich lay open before them glittering with reflected lights, candles and a single, long-stemmed rose on the table spoke of love and romance. Her hand lay in JD's, her eyes gazed at him with love, her heart pulsated in anticipation of another stimulating night. The wine she had drunk ignited her passion and she felt a-tingle and aroused.

There was no forewarning to prepare her for the coming events, no hint of the incomprehensible and chaotic drama about to unfold.

The door crashed open and out of nowhere Mischa's brother stormed into the restaurant bellowing followed by two Canton police officers, both with their weapons drawn. Without a doubt, they would have fired if it weren't for the crowd of restaurant guests who could get in the way of a bullet. Michael was desperate to escape his pursuers. He plowed into tables and diners. Tables turned, glasses and plates crashing to the floor and bursting in a shower of splinters, flinging their delectable contents onto the guests who jumped up in horror and confusion. Michael resisted wildly, his arms and shoulders thrashing out as the police battled to restrain him. The two policemen lunged and caught hold, crashing their captive to the ground, brutally wrenching his arms behind his back to lay the handcuffs around his wrists. Michael shrieked in pain, babbling incomprehensibly, his voice pitching and falling like a ship in a storm. He writhed and bucked, kicking out in unleashed fury to free himself from his bonds, overturning more chairs and tables as he twisted his body across the floor. He cursed the uniformed law enforcers, spat and frothed at the mouth. Tableware crunched, glass shattered. Straining and pulling, the cords of veins bulging at their necks, the policemen finally succeeded in dragging Michael, kicking and screaming from the establishment. A large candelabra swayed and fell to the floor. They jostled a service trolley tumbling whiskey and cognac bottles that exploded and poured their contents onto the costly Persian rug, blending with the wine and coffee in Meissen carafes and cups that had most recently graced the tables and now lay in shards on the floor. An oil painting by Carigiet, the Bündner artist, fell to the floor, it's frame splintering and breaking into pieces. The elegant restaurant was reduced to utter chaos, splitters, food and broken furniture were scattered everywhere.

With the exit blocked, the restaurant guests had sought shelter in the corner of the room. They stood there fearful, mute, addled and helpless, bent over with their arms over their heads, pressed against the wall without a clue as to how to act. They were too cowardly anyway to get involved, to help the police by holding down the criminal. They hadn't the courage to even protect their wives, so who cared about anyone else, they weren't going to risk their skin for another. And why should they? Rubbernecking or turning away were safe alternatives to courage they did not possess. Their dresses and suits were ruined with stains, their hands trembled.

Mischa, too, had jumped up in horror, quaking and confused. She had no idea why her brother was being arrested so violently. What crime had he now committed? What was he accused of and how could she help him? A bundled of nerves, she hastened after the civil servants who were wrestling Michael brutishly into the cruiser and buckling him in, the police car standing in front of the hotel, sirens wailing and blue lights flashing, which had drawn a large crowd of gawkers. She asked the men why her brother was being arrested once more, he had just been released yesterday. They gruffly told her they weren't supposed to talk about the case, but since she was his sister, maybe she should keep him under control, maybe she should prevent him from criminal activities before they occurred instead of worrying about him now, when it was too late, and she was only keeping them from their work. There was nothing she could do for him now. This morning two plainclothes officers had caught him selling ecstasy to teenagers in Platzspitz Park behind the train station. It wasn't the first time, either. He had been carrying a bag full of money and all kinds of drugs, cocaine among them. He had punched one of the officers in the face and broken his nose, nearly pushing him into the Sihl. He pulled an illegal switchblade on the other cop, gashing him in the arm before running off like a madman, leaving his bag of money and drugs behind. He is an incorrigible violent criminal, a dealer rotten to the core, seducing children into taking drugs. He is a threat to society and must be stopped at all costs to protect society from his evil-doings. She could hire even the best lawyer in the world, but it wouldn't do any good. The man belongs behind bars and that's where he will be, nowhere else.

The first cameras were flashing. Mischa wondered where they had caught wind of the tumult so quickly, racing to the scene of the crime. She could only hope her face would not be in the newspapers the next day, linking her to the scandal. She hoped in vain.

Mischa screamed at her brother through the police car window that was open a crack. She hadn't given him the money to buy drugs! That money was intended for him to establish an honest business! His body full of drugs, Michael was oblivious to his sister's wrath. Hashish or cocaine made no difference, he was lost to this world, rolling his eyes and babbling incoherently. Unsettled, Mischa returned to the mercilessly battered restaurant to find the guests shaking their heads and making their way to the door in high dudgeon. Now that the danger had passed, they became courageous, albeit only verbally and in their facial expressions. While the waiters were milling around, busily collecting shards and cleaning up, the guests exiting, making snide remarks about Mischa and her criminal brother, staring at her as if she were the criminal, without knowing how close to the mark their accusations actually were.

Mischa wrote a check for ten times more than the cost of the dinner they did not consume. She begged the maître d'hôtel not to press charges against her brother for damages, he had more than enough on his plate without additional charges, which would probably make no difference anyway. She apologized profusely for him and would naturally recompense the restaurant for all the damage he had done, would pay even more if the check did not suffice. He should please not hesitate to send her the bill for everything, she would transfer the money immediately.

As quickly as possible, she left the restaurant with JD. She had but one objective – to get out of Zurich as quickly as she could.

Not two hours later, they sat in the last flight to Vienna. Mischa held fast to JD's hand and for the first time in a long while, she cried.

Chapter 24

The next day, Mischa asked JD to marry her as quickly as they could. She snuggled up close to him saying she had never known a better man, would never find a better one since there was no better man than him in the world, she loved him, worshipped him, wanted to spend the rest of her life with him, be his one and only, have his children and finally, finally, have a normal family. JD took her in his arms, covered her face in kisses, gently wiped away her tears with his fingers and suggested they go to the registry office today and order the intention to marry papers, setting the process in motion.

Mischa hugged him tightly to her body, bade him to make love to her right now, she couldn't wait another second, he could do whatever he wanted with her, just do it now, she needed him, wanted to feel his skin on hers, couldn't wait bear to be without his touch, without him inside of her. He gladly complied, leading her to what seemed like eternal orgasms. Mischa felt the most powerful, painfully pressing waves of lust and bliss crash over her, she begged him to stop even long after he had. She writhed and twisted in ecstasy, sinking but slowly, her body twitching again and again in the afterglow, into serene satisfaction. She hugged him to her, kissed him from head to toe, wallowing in heavenly happiness, the greatest she had even known.

Before driving to the registry office, they decided to have a bite to eat. JD said he had always thought how nice it would be to take lunch on one of the restaurant ships cruising up and down the Danube, to feel the gentle current of the majestic river beneath him, to gaze at the old Emperor's City of Vienna and the beautiful Austria landscape as they glided past. Today would be an ideal day, being the day when they would make their marriage intentions official. Mischa, of course, agreed. JD could have asked her anything at that moment. He could have asked her to fly with him to the Brazilian rainforest to eat snake meat with the Yanomami tribe; to the Dayak in Kalimantan, Indonesia or to the Batwa pygmies in the Congo, she would have immediately agreed without a second's hesitation, would have said yes to everything he requested, to anything that would give him pleasure.

In the car, Mischa told JD that after the wedding at the registry office, she wanted to arrange a huge wedding in white at the Saint Stephan Cathedral and invite all of Vienna and her friends around the world. She had an appointment next week with Vienna's new archbishop – he had been recently ordained by the Pope in Rome – to discuss her long-planned Christening and could talk to him then about the wedding. According to what she knew about Catholicism, her first marriage to Richard was invalid since it was only consummated by the Justice of the Peace. So, there should be no problem with a Catholic wedding in Saint Stephan's Cathedral, at best directly following her Christening. The would have the celebration of their lives, of this she was convinced.

Mischa gazed out the window, dreaming of a wedding in the cathedral in which the Austrian Kings were once crowned, including Franz Joseph and Elizabeth, the royal couple still inhabiting Austrian hearts. Movies had been made about them, their wedding and biographies filled books, their portraits could be seen on all Viennese brochures and posters. There was no longer an emperor in Austria-Hungary today since ninety percent of his realm was lost when Italy switched sides and the United States entered World War I in 1917. But there was Mischa and there was JD. She was certain the media and gossip columns would flood the event with hyperbole as if it were a n emperor's wedding. But she would have to Catholic, of course, then who in Vienna would care about a Jewish wedding?

The divine late summer weather in Vienna was warm, just degree or two away from hot. The sun was shining in an azure sky with only one or two clouds for company. They drove to a spot just a stone's throw from where the Reich Bridge, one thousand two hundred meters above, spanned both arms of the Danube and the island between them. Here was where many restaurant ships laid anchor, awaiting their guests. Mischa and JD were the last to board one of them as it was casting off, its ropes already hauled in and the signal horn giving its third and final blast to announce its departure. They were just able to jump on deck as the ship's rump separated from the quay walls.

"Whew! That was close," JD panted. "Good thing I didn't fall in the water. My swimming talent is more than minimal."

Mischa laughed and reassured him.

"No worries, my darling," she said, "I was once Zurich Swimming Champion. You can be sure I would have pulled you out. I'm not going to let the only man who makes me happy and wants to marry me drown in the Danube!"

"Lake Zurich is not the Danube," JD replied. "I could probably save myself in a lake, but definitely not in a river as mighty as the Danube."

"Then I am going have to teach you how to swim," she countered with a mischievous twinkle in her eye. "You'll see. There are so many wonderful things we can do in the water!"

"Can't we do them at an indoor pool where I can stand up in the water with my feet firmly on the floor?" JD asked, adding, "You'd have a much better grip for doing all those wonderful things going around in your mind again."

"What in the world would we want at an indoor pool with thousands of people milling around?" she shot back. "Would you like them to watch?"

Playfully flirting, they made their way to the upper deck where an abundant buffet of appetizers had been arranged for the many guests already busy filling up their plates. A waiter in white livery greeted them and ushered them to the last table on the railing from which they had a stunning view of the city as it slowly sailed past. They saw the huge Ferris Wheel in the Prater, Vienna's capacious recreation park and Saint Stephan's Cathedral with its serrated tip in the background. There were many new high-rises and the enormous green dome of Karl's Church. As they travelled eastward, the endless sea of roofs stretched to Kahlenberg in the north, to Wienerwald in the south and, on their left, nearly to Schwechat.

The ship was bound for Bratislava, the first city on the Slovakian border, where they would make a short stop for those wishing to go on land for a shopping spree before turning around and heading back to Vienna. They took their seats and ordered a bottle of Austrian pearl wine to be followed by a fine, white Hungarian Tokay to go along with the main dish, a mixed fish platter with baked carp, pikeperch and perch filets in buttery parsley sauce and catfish swimming in garlic, mushroom and sour cream. The waiter informed them that the main dish will be prepared fresh, taking about a half an hour, so they should help themselves to the buffet in the meantime. Mischa took only a small portion of shrimp salad, while JD piled his plate with everything offered from marinated herring in dill sauce, to crabmeat, mixed Italian shellfish and lobster tail. Mischa laughed when she saw the mountain of food on his plate when he returned to the table.

"Make sure you don't fall in the water," she teased him, "even the Zurich Swimming Champion can't pull a whale out of the water!"

The table next to theirs was occupied by an elderly couple, German, judging by the language. They both wore the same baroque wedding ring and seemed disgruntled, hardly speaking a word to each other as they focused on ingesting as much food as possible, taking no notice of the city as it flowed by. The man's eyes roved repeatedly over to Mischa, snatching stolen glances. He was a large, fleshy man in his seventies with sparse blond hair and a leathery pale pink face liberally pockmarked. As Mischa caught him staring, she returned his gaze sternly, forcing him to look away. But the moment he thought she wasn't looking, he resumed his peeping. The woman sitting across from him was a much smaller, rotund gourmand, ceaselessly stuffing more than bite-sized portions into her mouth, the overload falling from her lips onto her plate. She scraped it back onto her fork or spoon and shoved it in. She paid no mind to her husband's wandering eyes, after so many years they could do what they pleased, she could care less. With each mouthful, her upper lip curled as if the meal she bared chewed and quickly swallowed was not to her liking, but she was obligated to clean her plate. After all, they had paid good money for it and there would be no wasting it.

At the table across from them sat two women in their mid-forties. They were enjoying a lively conversation in Viennese dialect, making jokes and having a lovely time as opposed to the mute German couple. It was immediately clear they were gourmets instead of gourmands. They ate with delightful pleasure, praising the delicacies before them, licking their lips and rolling their eyes in epicurean ecstasy. They, too, paid no mind to the scenery around them, but not because they were dispirited like the Germans but because their spirits were soaring high in a totally other realm.

Once they had finished their appetizers, Mischa took JD's hand, gazing deeply into his eyes, prefacing her declaration of endless love. But just as she wanted to speak, the waiter brought a large chafing dish that he placed in the center of their table and their fish dishes on top. Mischa's declaration would have to wait.

"Eat quickly, my love," she whispered, "I can't hold on much longer without you. Hopefully the toilet cabins are big enough for the both of us."

He discreetly slid his hand under the table and caressed her knee, stroking higher. She moaned with lust.

"Stop that JD," she warned, "or I will have to devour you here in front of all these people."

JD smiled at her. How did he deserve such a fantastic woman? Not a single woman he had known had given him a fraction of what she gave him – the feeling of being loved and desired without limit, unconditionally, of being respected and appreciated without the slightest reserve. This woman was a world-famous physicist and Chess World Champion and he was nothing but a common, dime-a-dozen architect yet she never made him feel the tiniest bit beneath her, as if they were on the same level. She introduced him to everyone as her most admired husband, often claiming he was the cleverer of the two; she could never build houses like will build.

The backed carp was a dream, the pikeperch and perch smothered in parsley butter, the catfish in garlic, mushrooms and cream all deserved verses sung in their praise. The drank the fruity Hungarian Tokay and were more in love than ever. Already nine months had passed with them claiming every new day as the most beautiful day in their time together and Mischa felt not a shadow of diminishing sexual attraction as she had with other men over time. Her appetite for him grew and grew, her lust and the stilling of her lust heightened and deepened every time they made love. He was simply the man for her, a match literally made in heaven as she had learned as a child in religion lessons, although she had long lost her faith.

"Hurry, you've had enough to eat," Mischa urged him, her hunger for him threatening to burst its restraints.

"Just let me finish the catfish, its divine," JD answered. "You never get food like this in the States, they only serve shrimps, shellfish, salmon and sweet-water crab."

"If you do not stop eating this very second, I will personally throw you in the Danube, so the fish can eat you!" she demanded.

Unintentionally, she had raised her voice, causing the two elderly Germans and the Viennese gourmets to abruptly raise their heads and stare at her in amazement. Mischa paid them no mind.

JD took one last sip of his Tokay, stood up and followed her. The went down the stairs to the lower deck where the toilets were located. The German and his wife shook their heads.

"Some people are nuts, without the least sense of decency. They act like the ship belongs to them," he said angrily. It was the first thing he had said to his in some time. Mischa's loud remark was a godsend, giving him at least something to say. He knew no other topics of conversation that would interest her.

On the steps, JD saw the ship's bow cutting through the bucking waves. It remined him of James Cameron's epic film.

"Come," he said to Mischa, "let us be Jack and Rose tasting the wind and freedom on the *Titanic*.

Mischa followed him. He climbed up onto the tip of the railing, holding tight to the rigging, closing his eyes and taking a deep breath of the headwinds. He stretched out his hand to Mischa, pulling her up to him. They stood there like Leonardo DiCaprio and Kate Winslet, high, at the very tip of the bow's railing on the moving ship. Carefully, JD let go of the rigging and spread his arms wide. Mischa was in the act of doing the same, one hand already free, when suddenly there came a blast from the foghorn, most likely to draw the attention of a swimmer of small boat, urging them to clear the way, pronto. Startled, JD lost his balance, swaying precariously over the deep drop to the Danube below. He waved his hands wildly, searching for the ropes or any other hold but found nothing. Mischa immediately saw the danger he was in, clawed one hand into the rigging and tried to pulled JD back with the other. Several people behind them spotted their quandary and began to call and scream for help, running to the pair to pull them both back on deck, but they came too late. Mischa felt JD's leg slipping out of her grasp. He wind-milled his arms desperately, frantically trying to regain his balance while Mischa tugged on his pants with all her might. Useless. Without a word, JD fell directly in front of the ship's bow which promptly plugged on over his body. Mischa went mad with fear and worry for her loved one. She raced from one side of the ship to the other, hoping to catch a glimpse of him but found nothing. She climbed over the railing, preparing to jump in a look for him, but an attentive sailor saw what she intended to do and held her fast, lifting her back over the rail. She tore herself away, running crazily around the deck, searching for a hint of JD in the water. But there was no sign of him amid the frothy, mud-brown water churned up by the still rotating giant propellers, even though the helmsman – he had seen a passenger fall from his glass cabin – had immediately initiated an emergency stop by putting the engines in reverse propulsion. Now every person on the ship, passengers and crew alike, were bent over the rails, searching the waters for the man overboard. Mischa screamed and screamed and screamed his name in the frenzied hope he was still alive, would hear her cries and raise his arm to show where he was in the murky waters. Only several hundred meters upriver did the ship finally come to halt. The captain immediately had the lifeboats launched, jumping in one himself and roaring the motor to life, racing back down river with the other boats to the place where JD had fallen. Mischa had also jumped into one of the boats. It would have been better if she hadn't. One of the officers noticed red discoloring on the water's surface and motioned to the others. A nightmare of bloody flesh, skin and bone floated on the surface, drifting in the current. Fish hungrily snatched up the unexpected banquet, pulling large pieces beneath the surface, defending their catch from less fortunate of their species. The scene took on the likes of feeding time at a crocodile farm or of a piranha's catch in the Amazons.

Apparently, when JD fell overboard he was sucked into the propellers at the back of the ship, tearing him to pieces. Mischa held her hands over her eyes, sobbing, crying and howling, pushing anyone away who dared to try and comfort or calm her. She tore out handfuls of her hair, pounded her head with her fists and tried again and again to jump into the water and chase off the fish to hold on to at least one piece of her dearly loved man, who was dead, who had left her forever, who never return to her. Once again, strong arms held her back. She bellowed, screamed as she had never screamed before. From one moment to the next, her life had been demolished, she had lost everything, her love, her hope, her future.

The lifeboats could do no more and motored back to the ship that immediately turned around and was back in Vienna in little more than an hour where an ambulance and the police were already waiting on an utterly demolished Mischa. The captain had radioed Vienna with the news. He brought Mischa from board first, delivering her into the care of the medics and emergency doctor. The police boarded the ship to talk to eyewitnesses and reconstruct the course of events with firsthand reports. Mischa was given a sedative and brought to the General Hospital at the Vienna University Clinic for psychological treatment.

Chapter 25

Eight days had passed since JD's death. After her release from the hospital, Mischa closed herself in, only leaving the house when absolutely necessary. And for JD's funeral mass. She had called in sick at the university and laboratory where she worked and did her research. She found no reason to keep on living. All of her hopes and dreams had been annihilated. One brief moment of distraction had demolished everything, her shared life with JD; her wedding and all the plans they had made together; the children they wanted to raise together. The boundless joy she had found, her entire existence that she had reveled in over the past nine months of bliss had become, from one second to the next, boundless misery. Why had she allowed JD to climb up on the railing? Why had she kept hold of the rigging when he needed her help instead of using both hands to pull him back up on the ship's deck? Why couldn't she hold onto his leg? Why had she grabbed only one leg instead of grabbing hold to both? Why hadn't she climbed up to join him on the railing fast enough to prevent him from falling into the water? Why hadn't she immediately jumped into the water after him and pull him out of the ship's path? Why had she gone with him, of all men, who was so different from all the cowardly, despicable slaves, to the Danube, this horrible, hungry river? Why did she go on a ship with him when he was hardly able to hold himself above water? She tormented herself with thousands of unanswerable questions that gnawed away all of her pride and shattered all of her joy in life, snatching away any desire she had to draw another breath and continue to live. She accused herself and found herself guilty. From the absolute pinnacle of her blessed existence she had been catapulted into the damnation of a bottomless abyss and continued to fall endlessly. There was no way to return to the light. JD was dead and with him, her future died.

The devil slumbering within her had reawakened. He had had his fill of driving her to satanic acts. Now, he was out for her soul, blanketing her in the most insidious of tortures, destroying everything she had lived for, wrenching away her happiness, the love of her life and the most valuable of all conceptual assets, her hope. She found no sleep at night and no comfort in the day. Food and drink were of no interest. She sat or lay unmoving, was overcome by ever-renewed attacks of wrenched sobbing. She drifted in various states of vegetation or aimlessly roamed about the apartment, making no effort to tidy up or open the windows to allow fresh air to clear the stuffy and stale rooms. She lived in darkness, unable to summon the strength to turn on the lights. The death of her lover, the man she had adored and was closer to her heart than any other creature on Earth defeated her. The concept of his death failed to penetrate her clever mind. She could neither believe it nor accept it, nor find a way to begin to get over it. The worst of it was how he had died. The terrible shreds of his body that could not be recovered but were eaten by fish like garbage vagabonds had carelessly thrown into the Danube. This was more atrocious than anything she could imagine. The images revisited her, were permanently before her eyes; how they had driven to the blood-tinted waters with the lifeboats, the minced remains, no longer recognizable as a human body she had loved, chopped by the ship's propellers as they rotated, driven by a thousand horse-power. The pictures haunted her persistently, were glued behind her eyes. She could no more erase them, or think of anything else, than she could put them behind her. Day and night, her mind was filled the instant replay of memory.

She mutely attended the funeral mass at a church in the second district enveloped, completely in black with a veil over her face. JD's mother had flown in from Detroit. Mischa was deaf to the priest's words of comfort. She shook hands apathetically with an endless line of acquaintances and strangers. She recognized or made eye contact with no one. She was unable to absorb what was going on around or to take in the soothing comfort JD's mother offered her, having heard so many wonderful things about her form her son. Mischa left as quickly as possible to return to her dark apartment and the even darker carousel of her obsessed thoughts.

On the ninth day after JD's death, as Mischa continued to hole up in her gloomy, silent penthouse, the doorbell rang. Mischa approached the door dressed in her bathrobe, bereft of makeup and her hair in disarray, and looked through the peephole. Two men stood at her door. One looked like a pop musician, a fast-draw cowboy, a burglar or cruel primp from Prater or the red-light district. His head was shaved, he wore jeans, a brown t-shirt, a black leather jacket and had a red silk scarf tied tightly around his neck. His feet were clad in sinister, white and brown snakeskin boots and looked like they meant brutal business. They frightened Mischa. As she was regularly besieged by press and paparazzi, Mischa had long ago installed an intercom system with which she could speak with visitors at her apartment house door. She had programed the device and installed speakers outside of her penthouse to also communicate with those who had managed to slip inside the building.

"Who are you and what do you want?" she asked.

"Police inspectors. We have a few questions to ask you Professor Turow. Would you open the door please?"

Mischa was alarmed. Were they really police inspectors? And if they were, why were they here? Was she under suspicion? Of doing what? Did it have something to do with the slaves she had tortured and killed? No one knew anything about that, did they? She felt queasy.

"Please show me our identification. Hold them in front of the peephole so I can see the photographs."

"Of course. Gladly."

One after the other, the men held up their IDs. She meticulously compared the ID photos with the men standing outside her door. They were definitely who they said they were. Without warning, she had the police standing at her door. Mischa began to tremble. So, this is how the Jews and dissidents in Vienna had felt, she suddenly thought, when the gestapo came to get them in the spring of 1938. Although, back in the Nazi era the gangsters before the door were dressed in gray suits and long, black leather coats. In her comparison she forgot to account for a tiny difference: back then, the people wrested from their homes were innocent of any crime. They were not murderesses as she was and had not won a World Championship title by waging emotional warfare on her rival as she had.

"Okay, I'm opening the door," Mischa said, carefully swinging the door open to allow the two men to enter.

"Good day to you, Professor Turow. Hans Stankowski, criminal investigation, central Vienna," the man in the conspicuous snakeskin boots introduced himself. He was the larger and more muscular of the two but spoke with a high falsetto that clashed dramatically with his martial appearance.

"Robert Fiala. Head of the police commissioner's office, Vienna East," the smaller man greeted her. Fiala looked much more like a typical police investigator, corpulent, neatly styled hair, freshly pressed beige slacks and beige checkered jacket. "We are working this case together."

"Good day to you, too, gentlemen. You come at a very inconvenient time. You can see I am not feeling well. Only a few days ago, my fiancé died in a horrible accident on the Danube. But you probably know about that."

"Our presence is always inconvenient," Stankowski responded.

"And what brings you here? What case are you talking about?" Mischa asked, adding quickly, "But I'm forgetting my manners. Please, have a seat and excuse the mess. I'm still in shock over my partner's sudden death. Can I offer you something to drink?"

"Don't go to any trouble on our account," Stankowski replied, "but we'd like to sit down. Don't worry about the disorder, it's no problem."

"If you like, I have beer or Coca cola in the fridge, if you'd like to drink something," Mischa offered.

"I'd gladly take a Cola, you know how it is with beer while on duty...," Fiala, the smaller and

friendlier of the two spoke up.

"One moment please."

While Mischa went to the kitchen, the two men inspected their surroundings.

"Do you mind if I turn on the lights?", Stankowski called after her.

"Would it make a difference if I said no?" came out of the kitchen.

Stankowski pushed all the buttons on the strip by the door. Magically, the darkened room transformed into a brightly lit hall crowned with a large glass dome. The officers were amazed.

"Never been in such a noble palace," Fiala whispered to Stankowski. "Looks like chess and physics are very lucrative."

Mischa returned with a large glass of Cola with ice cubes swimming in it and handed it to the civil servant.

"Thank you," he said and took a long pull.

"Now you can tell me which case you're talking about that led you to my door. I can't imagine what it could be," Mischa

From that moment on, Stankowski had the floor. Fiala sat next to him, casually looking around the spacious room, admiring the paintings on the wall, the sculpture of the Greek demigod and the many other antiques and works of art scattered about as if they had been there forever. It seemed as if the conversation bore no interest for him, but he was attentive to every word. When questioning suspects, it was his task to surreptitiously observe the man or woman in question, studying their gestures, facial expressions and body language closely to discover lies and misrepresentations of the truth.

"I'm talking about the alleged accidental death of your alleged fiancé and two other unresolved deaths in the Danube," Stankowski quietly said to Mischa, watching her reaction intently.

Horrified, she jumped ab in agitation. "What do you mean *alleged* accidental death and *alleged* fiancé! Everyone knew that John Dwight Donaldson and I were a couple and everyone on that ship were witnesses to his death. Are you suggesting that I intentionally pushed my own fiancé into the Danube? The man I had hoped to marry in just a few days? That's utterly ridiculous!"

"Not quite so ridiculous as you may think, Professor Turow. Several witnesses on the ship have attested to seeing you argue with Mr. Donaldson after your lunch on the upper deck. They claimed they heard you angrily threaten to throw him into the river. Other witnesses insist that instead of pulling him back when he lost his balance, you held onto the rigging, so you could push him even harder, but made it to look like you were trying to pull him back up."

Mischa's face went white as chalk and she began to scream hysterically that that was nothing but lies, slander, not a word of it was true; she had loved Donaldson with all her heart, his death had demolished her; the police should have compassion with her instead of believing the warped versions given by witnesses who obviously misread the events on the ship; who dreamed up farcical fantasies. The more she screamed, the more hysterical she became and the more Stankowski and Fiala were convinced of her guilt.

"There are two other things. These are easier to prove than your murder of Donaldson," Stankowski continued.

"Stop accusing me of murdering my fiancé!" Mischa shrieked at him. "What possible motive could I have to kill the man I loved more than anything?"

"Well, we've done our homework Ms. Turow. Last December you were in Las Vegas, where you beat the presiding Women's Chess World Champion and became her successor."

"So, what about it?" Mischa barked at him. "That's why I murdered my lover? To destroy our wedding and our whole future together? That's utter madness, utter madness!"

Thus far, the policemen had allowed Mischa her theatrics, but they had had enough of it now. Stankowski looked at her sharply and ordered her to get a grip on herself if she didn't want them to continue questioning at the precinct. Once Mischa had calmed herself somewhat, he continued.

"Let me finish without interrupting again! We issued a request for cooperation and the help of the Chinese police in Peking, who allowed us to question the Chinese woman with the unpronounceable name you conquered in Las Vegas. She was by far unmistakably favored to win the match, but contrary to all expectations, she lost. Now, according to the Chinese lady, she lost because you had stolen her fiancé out from under her nose and she was so distressed, she could no longer concentration on the chess game. Her fiancé's name was John Dwight Donaldson, known as JD. What do you have to say to that?"

Stankowski kept his eyes peeled on Mischa's face as he watched the impact of his words sink in. Mischa shook her head emphatically.

"This is what I have to say," she answered sharply, "it was the other way around. JD had slept only once with that ugly toad, I admit it. Why else do you think he stayed together with me and not with her?"

"Maybe for the money, you have more than enough of it. And he took a liking to the luxury, the travels in first class, the meetings with presidents, professors and artists. He enjoyed catching a few rays of radiance in the glow of your fame as Nobel Prize Laureate and Chess World Champion."

Mischa attempted to interrupt him, but he sternly bid her be silent. She can say her piece when was finished.

"But most recently, Mr. Donaldson came to his senses, remembering his true love, the Chinese woman from whom you had snatched him away. He had called her many times and told her he wanted to come back to her. She told us this quite clearly in Peking and when she heard he was dead, she insisted you had murdered him in cold blood, premeditated, to keep him from returning to her!"

"That lying, scheming hellcat!" Mischa spit out bitterly. "She's out for revenge. She had put her hopes on JD, but he wanted nothing else to do with her and chose me instead."

"That's your version. The witness tells a completely different story. But that's all circumstantial evidence and hunches. It's even possible, when not probable, that all the witnesses on the ship are mistaken and the Chinese woman in Peking lied to avenge herself."

Mischa brightened at these words, seeing the lifeline that would pull her out of the muck and mire that threatened to swallow her whole. But the lifeline slithered from her grasp and floated away as Stankowski continued.

"We cannot prove you murdered Donaldson, even though we are convinced you killed him. But there are two other murders you thoughtlessly also committed on the Danube and we can prove without the slightest doubt that it was you."

Mischa blanched.

"As you know best, we are talking about the murders of Jonathan Brady and of Hans Bierbaum. You made Brady's death look like a boating accident and you lured Bierbaum to an abandoned fisher's hut where, with countless knife wounds, you downright executed him. You really shouldn't have planned and committed the third murder on the Danube. If you hadn't, we would never have made the connection to the other murders; would never have dreamed of suspecting you, of all people, the world-famous Professor Mischa Turow. It looks like criminal investigators are sometimes just as clever as physic professors or chess World Champions. During the three days you were recuperating in General Hospital after Donaldson's death, we took the liberty of taking your DNA. We sent yet another team of specialists to the fisher's hut where we found Bierbaum's remains and had them scour the place again, centimeter for centimeter and guess what they found? Your DNA! We then exhumed Brady's body and had the pathologist examine him for wounds that may have been caused by something other than collisions with objects drifting in the river's current. Now, what did the pathologist find on Brady's skull this time around? Naturally, this you also know Professor Turow, the imprint of a heavy object. A heavy object, most likely a stone, that knocked Brady's unconscious before he died. Since the boat rental clerk once again expressly stated that Brady was completely unharmed when the two of you left the pier, and you were the last person to see him alive, no one but you could have inflicted the wound to his head on that boat on the Danube. Once unconscious, you pushed him into the river to drown, jumped into the water yourself and swam to shore, allegedly exerting the last particle of your strength. But you're an excellent swimmer, aren't you Professor? You're even a champion swimmer! But to the police and witnesses you were the picture of traumatized exhaustion, artfully covering up the murder you had committed, erasing all doubt at the scene of the so-called accident. Back then, the officers paid no mind to the dent in the corpse's head, they didn't even mention it in their report. The body was covered in contusions and lacerations from collisions with all kinds tree trunks, car parts and what have you drifting in the Danube, and they were convinced it was an accident. But now we know better, don't we Professor Turow?"

Mischa spoke not a word, but merely sat there, her head bowed. She trembled slightly.

"Better for you when you don't speak, Professor Turow," Stankowski agreed. "There's no need for you to implicate yourself. You're within your rights to remain silent, but keep in mind there is no perfect murder, even when you and many others believe there is. At some point, every murderer or murderess comes to light, especially with the modern investigation methods and tools available to criminalists and pathologists today. Especially you, a significant scientist, should have known that, Professor Turow!"

Stankowski couldn't know that Mischa had committed two other unsolved murders on Pavel Leskow and Pierce McFraser. How could he? They were not committed on the Austrian Danube, but far, far away in remote Russia, where Mischa is adored far more than she was in Austria or Switzerland, especially by the Russian President Ivan Sergjewitsch Kutin.

Fiala thanked Mischa for the ice-cold Coke that he had enjoyed very much, he stressed, and expressed his pleasure at having seen such a fantastic apartment since he had never before had the opportunity to experience such a thing. He explained she was being taken into temporary custody as a primary suspect in the murders of Jonathan Brady, Hans Bierbaum and John Dwight Donaldson, and it would be better if she were fully dressed as it was improper to go out on the streets in her bathrobe, and she should pack a few things while she was at it. He put her in handcuffs and led her away, conscientiously turning off all the lights in the amazing apartment before he and Stankowski sealed it.

Chapter 26

The news of Mischa Turow's arrest as the principal suspect in three separate murder cases erupted in international media, bombarding their readers, viewers and listeners. Very few were prepared to believe the reports and assumed they were just another case of hype and fake news that everyone was talking about. When the inconceivable turned out to be true, which quickly became evident, opinions were divided. While, on the one hand, it was obvious that the rich and famous, no matter who they were or how much they were admired, no matter where they came from or what they had achieved, behind the mask of splendor and glory lurked a vicious criminal ready to do even murder when it came to defending their advantage. Others, however, for a wide variety of reasons, spoke of a lurid conspiracy against an innocent young woman who had become too successful and too renowned for the less talented Chinese Chess World Champion determined to regain her title, or for the men unwilling to allow a woman among their ranks, especially not one whose intelligence infinitely outshone theirs and whose utter independence was utterly inacceptable and out of line with their mediocre concepts of decorum. Still others claimed that the incompetent Austrian police were simply desperate to name a perpetrator for the three murder cases they had failed to solve.

Screaming headlines announced, *Nobel Prize Laureate Accused of Triple Murder; Is Mischa Turow a Triple Murderess?; Chess World Champion Commits Murders of Passion; Mischa Turow, Genius and Mass Murderess; The Dark Side of Mischa Turow; How Many Murders Has Mischa Turow Committed?; Three Danube Murders Solved!* And more of the same.

Announcing from Moscow, President Kutin let it be known he was absolutely convinced that Mischa Turow was innocent. He was a personal friend of hers and knew her only as highly principled and incapable of hurting a fly, as he expressed it. This was obviously a new intrigue cooked up by the West, led by the United States. The fact that a Russian-born could be the cleverest and most adored woman in the world so damaged their bloated ego, they construed the most absurd accusations to tumble her from her throne and, most likely, planned to replace her with an American even though not one of them could hold a candle to Mischa Turow's beauty and intelligence. Should she so desire, Russia stands ready to take her in and provide political asylum, all the more so as she already possesses a Russian passport, he added implicitly. Kutin harvested applause for his address from both the Left and Right wings in a wide variety of countries – strong men and strong words exercise an irresistible attraction on people longing for someone to clearly establish law and order or for someone to stand up for the underdog against the omnipotent United States.

Naturally, the only one to know the whole truth was Mischa Turow herself. That of all the deaths she had been party to over the last two years, it would be the one she was innocent of that triggered her disastrous fall was a horrendous irony she was both unwilling and unable to accept.

She requested one of the most honored and successful lawyers in Vienna, Dr. Harald Farbmann, to act in her defense.

Farbmann was the son of a Jewish pediatrician and poet who survived the Holocaust in the cellar of a Viennese actress and the daughter of a high-ranking Austrian Nazi functionary whose complicity in vile war activities were never proven, nor disproved and thus advanced to General Director of a large government branch in post-war Austria. At every possible opportunity, he elaborately praised his Jewish son-in-law to the skies as if to maintain his innocence of participating in Nazi war crimes and his sympathy with their victims, which crassly contradicted, however, his affiliation with a former Nazi officer organization. But, in those years following the war, he was by far not the only one torn between Nazi-nostalgia and the shame, admitted or not, of the crimes committed. The vast majority of citizens who had enthusiastically greeted Hitler's invasion of this historic country on the Danube and had prepared him an extravagant reception were thereafter plagued by the conflict between pride and regret for the Nazi past, between knowledge and conscience, between forgetting and remembering, between craving for and coping with their cultural past.

Dr. Farbmann, as also a prominent Vienna parliament representative of SRA, a right-wing political party bearing the ostentatious name *Society for the Rebirth of Austria*. The party's chairman, blond, blue-eyed, anti-Semite Hans Streicher was careful to never mention the Jews by name but thundered all the same against the bearded vermin contaminating his people, leaving no doubt as to who he had in mind. Contrarily, he also prominently publicized his sympathies and support for the courageous and resilient state of Israel, which he believed to be infested with a population of Hottentots, Apaches and Navajo Indians, and not only Jews.

Mischa Turow had met Steicher at the vernissage of a painter of Jewish origins who had converted to Catholicism.

The event had taken place in one of the leading Austrian galleries in Kärntner Street nearby the Opera House and Hotel Sacher – Streicher's preferred venue for after-party retreats with his female or what have you escort. He expounded his respect and admiration for Mischa's decision to convert to Catholicism, congratulating her profusely as, in his words, she would thereby prove without a doubt her bond with the European culture. Mischa did not deign to respond. She had rarely heard such outright idiocy coming from the mouth of a politician although she had certainly heard plenty.

In contrast, Dr. Farbmann was a highly intelligent, profoundly humorous defense counsel, feared by the district attorney for his ability to attain acquittals for defendants confronted with apparently water-tight evidence and doomed from the start. Not one representative of the state could match his knowledge of the law, his cleverness, wit and powers of persuasion. He had no scruples in saving serious criminal from their just punishments. He held the conviction, sharing it freely with his clients, that the most perfidious criminals occupied the most powerful positions in the Republic, yes, also in the government, and he saw it as a challenge to take on so-called hopeless cases rejected by all other lawyers, especially to protect from Justitia's dictates those defendants proclaimed guilty before the process had even begun.

Prejudgment was the preferred slogan and argument he often flung in the face of helpless district attorneys in court, harvesting the judge's support, especially the judges also belonging to Farbmann's political party, or were at least not members of the current district attorney's. Farbmann was well-versed in Austrian politics and had explored every corner of the political landscape; he held a decisive position in and campaigned for one of the major governing parties, all of which he knew to exploit and served him extraordinarily well. In parliament, where all parties depend on coalitions and pacts with the others in order to push through their proposals -- and their jockeying for position outside of parliament -- Farbmann was an important figure no one wished to confront unnecessarily, risking his disfavor or even wrath, particularly when it came to a trial that had nothing to do with politics. This is Austria. Never step on anyone's toes unless it's really worth it Although this certainly does not only apply to Austria, it is a hallmark of the country bringing forth the music of Johann Strauss and Franz Lehar, the satires of Karl Kraus and Karl Farkas, and the statesmen Franz Olah, Bruno Kreisky and Kurt Waldheim.

To look at him, you could conceive of Dr. Farbmann's outstanding qualities as an attorney and defense lawyer but would never believe he was a National Council senator. Under-sized and weedy, he was forty-five years old and a childless, confirmed bachelor, never to be seen other than elegantly and fashionably clad with his part precisely parted. When not in court, in parliament or at a meeting with politicians, colleagues or clients, he spoke little, rather listened closely to his counterpart, attentive to his surrounding and the people therein. No detail escaped his notice. Even the tiniest thing could eventually prove important. Furthermore, he possessed a photographic memory. Nothing he had ever seen or heard vanished completely from his minds meanderings. It could be years later, but he would still remember the names and faces of people he had been introduced to at an insignificant event, would know every detail of whatever he had been told or had heard. His historic knowledge was legendary. He not only knew the precise date of all major events that had taken place in Europe, America and the Middle East in the past five hundred years, his knowledge encompassed much earlier times and other continents and regions of the world. More impressive than amassing dates and facts was his ability to allocate them and put their coherencies into perspective. His keen judgement, unparalleled knowledge of human nature and his rare talent for immediately recognizing if stories told by people sitting across from him were lies or truth made him who he was – the best defense attorney in Austria.

It took Dr. Farbmann all of two minutes with Mischa at their first encounter in the well-guarded conference room of the Vienna detention prison to become aware not only of her diabolical character, but also of her guilt, which she vehemently denied. He looked at her sternly and spoke in a voice that brooked no dissent.

"Professor Turow, I am well aware that you are one of the world's most intelligent women, but if you want me to defend you, I demand you be absolutely honest with me. You can tell the district attorney and judge whatever you want, or better, whatever we decide to tell them, but you must tell me the truth on all counts. It makes no difference to me what you have done and whom you have murdered, but I must know the truth, every last detail of it, to prepare my defense strategy. I am not here to sit judgement over you, neither in a legal nor moral sense, but am here to ensure you are acquitted. Morals and justice have about as much to do with our legal system and the realities of our country as prophets have to do with God or presidents with their people, namely, nothing. Do not forget this and be assured that I am completely on your side should I represent you in court, no matter what the charges against you may be. The only offenders I refuse to defend are Nazis and child abusers.

Now about your case. My assessment of your current position is that you are a lost cause. Or to use a chess term, you have lost your position. To regain it requires accurate analyses and surprising maneuvers with which our opponent has not calculated. As Chess World Champion, you know full well that an objective analysis is only possible when you have insight into all the possibilities and options the position offers. Personally, I am convinced you murdered Bierbaum and Brady. I'm not so certain about Donaldson but tend to believe you when you say it was an accident. Rotten luck, that a murder that wasn't a murder brought the police to your door. But that's life. Fate is decided by those things one doesn't consider and therefore one doesn't expect. So, please tell me openly and honestly if my assessment of the situation is correct, keeping in mind I am bound by my obligation to maintain secrecy. The only thing you have to lose is my legal support. You risk nothing but losing the best defense attorney you will find."

His words did not fail to impress Mischa. The man was her master when it came to mental acuity and immorality. She no longer felt like a Nobel Prize Laureate, but rather like a censured schoolgirl after a dress-down from her teacher. If there was anything she admired in a man, it was his ability to surpass her. JD had surpassed her in presence, Dr. Farbmann surpassed her in judgement.

"You should have taken the Nobel Prize, not me," she said softly. "Fortunately, you are a lawyer and not a physicist, or I would have been out of the running. Yes, your assessment is correct. You are the first, only and last person to hear that from my mouth. If you get me out of this, I want to sleep with you," she said directly, looking him straight in the eyes.

Farbmann held her gaze. She was the first to blink and lower her eyes.

"Well, I'm not so sure I want to sleep with you, as sexy and seductive as you are, since I intend to stay alive as long as the Lord God chooses," he responded.

"I promise you, no, I swear to you, I will not kill you."

"Plenty of murderers have said that before you, just as plenty of alcoholics who, like you, cannot free themselves of their addiction, Professor Turow. Or should I call you Mischa, now that you have made me such a proposal?"

"Please, call me Mischa. You have me in your hands anyway. My life, my entire existence now depends on you."

"Good. You can call me Harald, but only when it's just the two of us. Before all others we are Dr. Farbmann and Professor Turow. Any personal relations between us could damage your defense."

Mischa's grief over JD was gently pushed aside by her feelings for this small, reedy man sitting across from her who was a giant compared to her. If they hadn't been in a guarded room in prison, soundproof, yes, but under permanent police observation through a thick one-way glass window, she would have immediately stripped naked and seduced him. Farbmann sensed it, too.

"As I said Mischa," he stated, "I will decide whether to sleep with you or not only after I have succeeded in having you acquitted. But don't get your hopes up, we have a long way to go with a lot of arduous work before us, so do not try to seduce me again before I have saved you from a life sentence in prison."

In keeping with Mischa's essential nature, every new man fully erased his predecessor from her diabolical heart. And JD was barely two weeks dead.

She confessed to her now official defense attorney everything she could remember, freely and without a trace of shame; her eternal search for love and sexual fulfilment, her compulsion to torment submissive men, yes, to murder them in order to achieve the pinnacle of lust; but with men she loved, only in unconditional capitulation could she find sexual and emotional fulfilment; her inner conflict between sadism and masochism.

Harald Farbmann, Sigmund Freud's immoral successor, listened without batting an eye. Before he left, he said to her, "I will get you acquitted Mischa, if it's the last thing I do in this life."

Here, he was no Sigmund Freud. Although, as an attorney, he was no less sharp-minded, perspicacious, methodic and successful, he had no talent as doctor or psychiatrist. He did not maintain the necessary therapeutic distance, nor did he have a clue as to how to treat the disease infecting Mischa's psyche, that would heal her and drive the devil from her soul.

All the same, she looked at him with gratitude and complete submissiveness, just as a woman surrendering her heart to her psychiatrist as he listens to her in silence, worshipping him as he were a divine being.

Chapter 27

It was the day the district attorney and defense would make their summations to the jury in the process against Mischa Turow, professor of physics and the *Dynamo Theory* at the Vienna University. She was accused of murder on three separate counts, on Hans Bierbaum, Jonathan Brady and John Dwight Donaldson. The trial was being held in the large state court for criminal affairs in the 8th district which also housed the largest prison in Austria, the Vienna-Josefstadt Penal Institution. It was here, during the 369 weeks of Nazi rule in Vienna – errantly depicted as *Occupation* on a memorial plaque on the building wall – over one thousand, two hundred dissidents, both real and imagined, were executed. However, not one Jewish name can be found on the ten plaques covered in small print with the victims' names since the bearers of such names did not have the privilege of an official trial nor the honor of being immortalized on Austrian plaques. Nameless, they died by the millions in Nazi concentration camps and forced ghettos, were shot by so-called *task forces* in their villages and cities in Poland, in the Ukraine, in Russia and in the Baltic states, or were herded into synagogues built of wood, barred inside and burned alive. In Moscow and Zurich, the forefathers of the accused escape the horrors of the Nazi regime, but not those of her defense attorney, Dr. Harald Farbmann. His grandfather, his great-grandparents and his great aunt, his grandfather's beloved little sister, were all gassed in Auschwitz. The scars and wounds of this past can be found and felt everywhere in Vienna, even when only a few have the courage to look back in compassion.

The trial at the *Big Court*, as it was called in Viennese dialect, had been in progress for more than two weeks during which the district attorney brought forth all hard and circumstantial evidence speaking against the accused, calling on any available witnesses to strengthen his case. The defense had been limited to objections, demanding assertions incongruous with the code of procedure be struck from the record, categorically rejecting all of the district attorney's allegations as construed nonsense, entangling witnesses in contradictions and questioning his own witnesses who had nothing to say about the state's version of events since they hadn't been there and thus did not occur anyway, as he never failed to mention, but attested to the accused's impeccable reputation, her high moral standards and ethics and her loathing of violence in any form. He had reserved his refutation of the state's alleged hard evidence and nonconclusive indicators and of misinterpretations based on witness' statements for his summation.

During the entire process, the accused had remained silent, as she had been instructed to do by her attorney. When questioned, she consistently pled *no contest*, the right of every accused in all democratic, constitutional states, even in the southern successor state emerging from the Third Reich, this small fraction left over from the second largest country on the European continent, after Russia, in which thirty-two nations lived in greater prosperity than we do today in the European Union until President Thomas Woodrow Wilson, son of a slave-owning, Presbyterian preacher from Ohio, divvied up Europe at the Paris Peace Conference in 1919. For this consequential, global political blunder – compounded by imposing sixty years of war reparations on Germany which contributed not insignificantly to the rise of Nationalism which led to National Socialism and hence to World War II, which was incomparably worse than the first – Wilson was presented with the Nobel Peace Prize in Oslo that very same year. As is the wont of American Presidents, they often apply their democratic missionary zeal and ignorance of regional circumstances to exacerbating precarious situations instead of improving them, for their own country as well. Historically, they're not alone. Many potent regional or global powers have followed the same course. Take the emperors of Rome, Carthage, Parthia and China as well as Napoleonic France, for example. Few were so clever and farsighted as Alexander, the Macedonians, King Solomon or Cyrus the Great of Persia who left conquered realms their honor and lands.

But let us get back to the Mischa Turow's trial at the Vienna Federal Court for Criminal Affairs aka the *Big Court*. Dr. Hans Mauerfreund had little experience, having little more than three years ago completed his state exams at the university, was a staunch Marxist and member of the co-governing Social Democratic Party of Austria. Gangly and emaciated, with the immature body of a not quite thirty-year-old young man, his voice had cracked repeatedly in revulsion for the savage capitalist, as he never failed to call her throughout the trial, sitting on the prisoner's dock, working himself into a lather and shrieking wildly, his face turning such a deep red, one worried his arteries would suddenly burst, blood erupting from his cheeks and forehead. Chairman of the judiciary triune collegium, Court President Gottlieb Heldwein, Doctor of Jurisprudence and Theology and twice Mauerfreund's age, was an SRA member, the oppositional, right-wing party to which Dr. Farbmann also belonged. Held-wein reacted to each eruption spewing forth from the angry, excitable district attorney with a grimace and demonstratively clapping his hands over is ears. The difference between his court-room antics and a parliament session were barely recognizable if it weren't for the eight jurist there to decide the guilt or inno-cence of the accused at the end of the trial.

This end was nigh. In his final speech, the district attorney summarized all solid and circumstantial evidence brought forth during the trial as well as a recapitulation of statements made by witnesses for the state. In his opinion, the accused was guilty beyond the shadow of a doubt. Her motives were both base and egocentric, he stressed; she murdered John Dwight Donaldson out of jealousy to ensure no other woman would have him, she murdered Jonathan Brady out of revenge because he had the temerity to leave her and, most vile, she contrived to lure Hans Bierbaum to an isolated fisher's hut and murdered him most cruelly with over thirty knife wounds and punctures out of sexual madness, doubtlessly a premeditated act. Winding up his summation, his tone condescending as he addressed the jury, he was convinced they would come to the only feasible decision, namely to find the accused guilty on all charges. It was their responsibility to protect society from mass murder-esses such as Mischa Turow, he added finally, and not succumb to the foul excuses, evasions and invented, cynical arguments of the defense attorney, known for his lively imagination, not allow his contempt for the truth to influence them but stand firm in their decision. There is but one just punishment for the accused, and that is life-long incarceration.

Judge Heldwein thanked the state representative, but also warned him to forego personal and libelous comments about the defense attorney in the future. He instructed the jury to give the defense attorney's summation the same weight and attention as they did the district attorney's and to arrive at their decision only after carefully considering all evidence and witness statements, both those for and those against the accused. They should put circumstantial evidence aside as it was open to interpretation, only drawing on it to substantiate their decision.

Now Dr. Farbmann would have his say, the small man with a huge intellect and without a conscience. He placed himself before the jury and began speaking to them softly, calmly and politely, also paying his respects to the district attorney and the state's office, despite his displaced attack on Farbmann's character. His unpretentious, poised and factual demeanor was a blatant contrast to young Dr. Mauerfreund's invasive, task-masterly manner attempting to coerce the jury into following his lead, into substantiating his point of view with a verdict of guilty or risk the shame of becoming insidious traitors to society if they did not.

"Ladies and gentlemen of the jury," Farbmann began his summation, "you have heard my young college, the honored district attorney superbly occupying the role bestowed upon him by the state as he gave his best and used all available means to convince you of the accused's guilt. I congratulate him on his profound juristic finesse. The edifice he has constructed from so few and so flimsy nonconclusive evidence, implications and witness statements is truly admirable. No doubt, his rhetoric professor at the university would have given him top grades for his performance. But we are not here to enjoy a competition between ambitious students. We are here to decide the future fate of a wholly blameless, highly regarded woman, who, if I may say without exaggeration and you will most likely agree, one of the cleverest and most admired citizens not only in Europe, but in the entire world. She is the discoverer and creator of the Dynamo Theory, a scientific milestone along the lines of Einstein's theory of relativity that will re-shape the future of humanity and for which she was awarded with the Nobel Prize in Physics last year, the greatest scientific honor on our planet. Here, in Vienna, the university installed an academic chair explicitly for her, this woman sitting here falsely accused, Professor Mischa Turow, a chair she occupies brilliantly, admired and appreciated by all colleagues and students, a faculty that has contributed to restoring due honor and respect to the Vienna University. Furthermore, and in my opinion no less admirable and estimable, after decades of concentrated effort since her childhood she has gained the title World Champion in women's chess. Do you really believe such a serious, diligent and talented woman would be willing and able to commit three horrendous murders? That is completely absurd, would defy all explanation, would be against all reason. I am certain that not even our honored district attorney believes it, although his position demands he do all in his power to convince us of the opposite. Now, to address those charges made against Professor Turow. Before I go into them and repudiate them one by one, something any child could do, requiring no particular juristic talent, I would like to look into the question of why this most honorable scientist has been dragged to the prisoner's dock in the first place. To this end, I have occupied myself with the police officers in charge of investigating the fatalities in question. They have appeared before you and have made their statements. The detectives are, as you all know, Mr. Hans Stankowski and Mr. Robert Fiala of the Vienna criminal investigation department. Both men asserted that, in their opinion, based on the evidence provided and for a broad variety of reasons, the fatalities were murders wantonly, brutally and unconscionably committed by a dangerous criminal, none other than the accused. Now I have had a look at the Vienna CID's murder clearance rate. It is an impressive eighty-fiver percent. I congratulate our law enforcement authorities on their diligence. They are among the best and most successful in Europe. Mr. Stankowski and Mr. Fiala's success quota for clearing felonies, of which murder is one, crassly contradicts the numbers. Their clearance rate lies at a mere thirty percent. This means that two out of every three murderers, rapists, child molesters and other felons they investigate are still at large. One can imagine the pressure they are under to produce results for such an efficient agency as the Vienna CID. Their abysmally low clearance rate compels them to make arrests and they obviously have no qualms to fabricate evidence rather than risk a transfer or demotion to a lower salary and pension class. No one, not even government agencies financed with tax money and permanently monitored by controlling authorities, can afford to retain incompetent employees. Stankowski and Fiala know this as well as you and I and saw their redemption in the three fatalities on the Danube. Naturally, it suggested itself to ascribe the deaths to the one person present at two of the three cases which were, contrary to Mr. Fiala and Mr. Stankowski's assertions, clearly accidents such as occur all the time and everywhere, especially in a dangerously powerful river like the Danube. In one case, the falsely accused nearly left her own life, only able to save herself because she is an excellent swimmer, holding the top swimming title in her Zurich homeland. In the other case, she had done everything in her power to save him and in her anguish over her fiancé's vanishing into the Danube, a man who could barely hold himself above water in a placid lake, she was willing to jump in after him and was only held back by the grace of a valiant, quick-acting sailor. Witnesses maintaining they had seen her intentionally push Donaldson into the water couldn't possibly have done so as they were standing behind the two. A view of true events was blocked by Professor Turow and Mr. Donaldson's backs. Speaking for myself, I would not presume to be able to see through two human backs and tell you what was happening in front of them. You probably wouldn't either, ladies and gentlemen of the jury. The alleged fight between the accused and her fiancé overheard by guests at neighboring tables on the upper deck before the unfortunate accident was nothing but teasing talk between lovers. Which of you has never said to your partner, '*If you don't kiss me on the spot, I'll kill you*'? Is that a threat or a declaration of love? The answer is obvious. The same is true for all other implications, so-called evidence and witness statements in all three fatalities. How is it possible to come to such an absurd conclusion that my client murdered her dear Jonathan Brady simply because she was the last to see him alive? The indention on his head was only one of over a hundred wounds inflicted upon him in the water, probably after he was already dead, by unavoidable collisions with whirling stones, floating tree trunks, discarded metal objects and other things that may even have caused his death, but it is no proof, as the state would like you to believe, that Professor Turow inflicted it. I am no mathematician, but evidence such as this is not only a mathematical fallacy. Many witnesses, not only those called on by me, confirmed how upset, horrified and grief-stricken my client was days after both accidents that robbed her of her nearest and dearest. Such mourning cannot be feigned except perhaps in Hollywood where such scenes are produced with the help of artificial tears and appropriate makeup. But Professor Turow's tears and anguish were authentic, as you have witnessed repeatedly throughout this trial when the topic turned to the two accidents and she was forced to revisit these traumatic events. The absolute pinnacle of Mr. Stankowski and Mr. Fiala's artful rendering, however, was reached when they found the remains of a skeleton studded with multiple knife wounds in an abandoned fisher's hut on the Danube and conveniently laid the murder at my client's door because they had found her DNA in the hut. We have clearly proven that my client has been taking walks along the Danube for many years now. A dedicated nature-lover, she takes great pleasure in wandering in the lowlands, observing flora and fauna, wading through the water in rubber boots hoping to espy frogs, water birds and rodents which also has brought her in proximity to the above-mentioned hut. It is altogether normal to seek shelter in an abandoned hut when one is caught in a sudden downpour such as a summer cloudburst or thunder storm. Any one of us would do the same under such circumstances, wouldn't we? Who among us would voluntarily stand outside in the pouring rain when we see shelter nearby? My client admitted to taking shelter from thunder, lightning and rain in the hut on several occasions. Naturally she left traces of her DNA. A simple sneeze, a cough, a lost hair or merely scratching her ear would leave mucous, phlegm or skin particles, marking her presence. Does this make her a murderess when months later a human skeleton is found in the hut, making that three fatalities on the Danube? I would not wish such a fate on anyone. To be accused of murder because a skeleton or corpse was found on a place we had once spent time. Ladies and gentlemen of the jury, the district attorney has spared no effort, and as an experienced lawyer I must not refrain from reprimanding my young colleague, to practically coerce you into supporting his charges by proclaiming guilty a completely innocent person. But justice has precedence over sentencing a bill of indictment, especially one that stands on such weak legs as the one we have been served in this courtroom. As the leading judge explained to you at the beginning of these proceedings, a jury may only pronounce the accused guilty, whether that person be a homeless vagabond or renowned scientist as Professor Turow is, when they believe guilt has been proven beyond reasonable doubt. Which is utterly out of the question in this case. Nonetheless, I ask you to not acquit my client based on reasonable doubt of her guilt but rather based on her proven innocence. You have heard yourselves that all charges are not only highly dubious but that there also reasonable explanations for both accidents, not forgetting that the falsely accused herself nearly lost her own life, and that she had nothing to do with the skeletal remains in the fisher's hut. Do not acquit my client based on proven innocence because she is a well-known and respected person but rather because this is the simple truth. Even the lowliest among us deserves to washed clean of guilt when accused of a crime he or she did not commit. Put yourself, if you will, in my client's place, accused of crimes you did not commit. Imagine you had wrongly suffered such horrendous injustice after all the grief and loss you sustained prior to your arrest. I do not wish it upon you, but were the tables turned, you would expect an acquittal based on your proven innocence, as my client does, and not an acquittal based on the shadow of a doubt; a doubt that would cast more than a shadow over your future, a doubt compounding the injustices you have already suffered through no fault of your own, your months of lost freedom in prison, the defamation of your character by biased media, neighbors and friends; a doubt incurring yet another unmerited punishment. Ladies and gentlemen of the jury, I thank you for your time and place in your able hands the fate of Professor Mischa Turow, a woman who has nothing, I repeat, absolutely nothing to do with the fabricated charges against her. I put my total trust in your sense of justice and in your sound common sense."

The courtroom spectators applauded as Dr. Farbmann wrapped up his summation, his diminutive physique clearly underscoring the enormity of his intellect. Dr. Heldwein, the chairman judge, called them to order and thanked Dr. Farbmann – lending a slight nod of support to his political colleague – for his remarkable summation. He once more instructed the jury on their duties before releasing them to deliberate and adjourned the court until they returned with a verdict declaring the accused guilty or not guilty of first degree murder.

The district attorney and his attending colleagues left the courtroom in wordless defeat. Throughout Dr. Farbmann's summation, their facial coloring had progressed from an initial pallor to blanched white to ash grey. Their youthful complexions left the courtroom ancient and exhausted. Farbmann looked over at Mischa as two guards approached to lead her back to her cell until the verdict was announced. She smiled at him in grateful invitation. The district attorney had no comment for the mob of journalists and photographers waiting in the corridor. Dr. Farbmann merely admonished them to wait for the verdict and not presuppose the jury's independent decision. The select members of the press permitted in the courtroom, however, whipped out their phones and began dictating tomorrow's article to their editors.

There wasn't the slightest doubt the Nobel Prize Laureate would be acquitted, and her spotless reputation reinstated in a piece. In the wake of Dr. Farbmann's brilliant summation, it was a given that she had been sacrificed by two ineffectual criminal detectives and an incompetent district attorney attempting to save their careers. In their abysmal ignorance they had dragged her before the court on trumped-up charges, subjecting her to derision and mockery, vilified in the face of the world. No few voices were raised in indignation, demanding the three men be released from the state's service.

The jury's deliberation took less time than usual in such cases. A mere forty minutes later, the bailiff requested the participants and spectators waiting in the corridor to resume their places in the courtroom. They entered and took their seats only to rise again as the judges entered the courtroom, followed by his two assessors. The judiciary took their seats and Judge Heldwein made a small, commanding gesture with his hand bidding the attendees to sit down as well. As soon as the courtroom was more or less free of rustling and the scraping of benches, yet still pregnant with tangible suspense, he declared the trial in progress and, turning to the jury, posed the fateful question, the answer to which not only those present in the courtroom, but the entire world held their breath to hear.

"Has the jury come to a verdict?"

"We have, your Honor."

"What is your verdict?"

The jury foreman cleared his throat and waited a minute or two, reveling in the wholly new experience of standing in the limelight, fully aware that at this moment the eyes and hears of the world were fixed on him, a fleeting moment of fame soon to fade forever. Slowly, he pronounced the portentous words.

"We find the accused not guilty, her innocence of all charges proven beyond a shadow of a doubt."

A frenzy of cheering and shouting broke out in the courtroom. Even those who had previously condemned Mischa at the beginning of the trial, cursing her name loudly to anyone who would listen, joined in the joyful hullabaloo. Their idol had been resurrected! The world shall once more bathe in the radiant light of their demi-goddess! It was as if Jesus and Moses had returned to Earth, reviving the Good News.

Journalists stormed from the courtroom, the judge pounded his gavel frantically in his attempts to restore order in his once so somber courtroom. It wasn't until the journalist had left the courtroom, the doors banging shut behind them, that a semblance of order returned.

The judiciary rose, bringing the accused, the attorneys and spectators to their feet as well. The Bench chairman Dr. Heldwein, standing in the center of the triad, spoke,

"The accused is to be released immediately. The court will deliberate and declare restitution for unjust incarceration at a later date. Professor Turow, allow me to break with judicial custom and tradition and in the name of the Austrian Republic express my deepest regrets for the unpleasantness you have suffered. I wish you all the best as you resume your life's journey and hope you may soon overcome the recent troublesome events. This court is adjourned."

Mischa ran to Dr. Farbmann, pressed her hand to his, looked deep into his eyes and whispered, "My place tonight at nine. I can't wait any longer."

He smiled.

Chapter 28

The night with Farbmann – at his apartment, not hers – was not what Mischa had hoped it would be. He was not JD and would never be able to replace him, as much as Mischa wished he could. He obviously enjoyed his adventure with her, but Mischa was left unsatisfied. She kissed him tenderly, gently explaining that they were unfortunately not an ideal couple, that he was an outstanding attorney but not the man of her dreams as she had made him out to be in her profound admiration for his judicial talents. Still, after all he had done for her, she would always be there for him, was available wherever and whenever he desired her. Farbmann seemed to expect a reaction like this and looked her in the eyes like a father rebuking his dearly loved child.

"Mischa, Mischa, you worry me. I truly hope your demons do not gain the upper hand again. Keep in mind, I won't always be able to pull you out of the quicksand threatening to swallow you like I did today."

"You're waxing downright philosophical, Harald," she parried, taking on a seductive pose, offering herself again even though she hadn't a glimmer of desire for him. He was much too clever to swallow the bait, and merely stated," I had a love time with you Mischa, but have no intention of becoming one of your slaves. My life is too precious to me. You should respect that since I can only help you again when I'm alive, although I doubt even then that I could."

Farbmann was lightyears ahead of her. Maybe not on the chess board or in physics, but certainly in wisdom. She kissed him again, took a shower and dressed while he had already turned his attention to files on his next case.

Once back in her own apartment, she felt the loss of JD settle back on her heart, the knowledge that no one could replace him, reawakening her grief. He had not been banished from her heart and mind as she had hoped was the case when she encountered Farbmann's outstanding intelligence and freedom from the restrictions of moral convention. Yet, intelligence and amorality are not enough to inspire love. Love requires the inexplicable, that chimerical element eluding science and explanation. She had only found it with Richard and JD. Fleetingly with Richard, enduringly with JD.

The following day she gave a press conference at the university, announcing her intention, after all the turmoil of the past weeks and months, the trial and tempest surrounding her person, to go on vacation to an undisclosed destination where no one knew her, and she could indulge in rest and relaxation unmolested. Immediately the rumor began to fly. She was flying back to the jungles of Borneo where an ancient indigenous people had once welcomed her with open arms like a long, lost sister. No, she was off to the Danube delta on the Romanian-Ukraine border because she so loved the river and its animal life, because she so enjoyed swimming. No, no, she had had more than enough of the Danube and was retreating to a Buddhist cloister in Nepal to find peace and meaning in her life. None of this came any closer to the truth than Farbmann's convincing summation, believed by one and all and was responsible for Stankowski and Fiala's demotion as well as for district attorney Mauerfreund's transferal within the DA's office.

In truth, Mischa went that very evening to visit her best friend Rita Sokol and invite her and her partner Fred Lavalle, the talented French painter, to join her on a trip to Nova Scotia, the densely wooded, easternmost Canadian province with its many islands to explore. A former fellow classmate of hers from her university days in Switzerland, Reto von Wattenwyl -- a scientific researcher holding a prominent position at a powerful U. S. American paint and pharmaceutical corporation -- owned an expansive homestead there where they could hunt, fish, loll in the grass, swim in the lake, barbecue elk and deer meat and gaze out over the vast, unpopulated natural beauty to their heart's content. There was no better place to unwind and catch one's breath, soothing and revitalizing her spent nerves, as she told Rita. She would love to take Rita and Fred along, since she didn't want to travel alone. She needed some company to distract her from tormenting thoughts of JD and help her finally put him to rest. They needn't give a thought to the travel expenses, she would be happy to pay for everything, she assured Rita, all Rita had to do was take ten days off from the hospital. They would have a wonderful time together in Canada, could talk and joke around late into the night, romp unrestrained in pristine nature, hunt small animals, catch trout with their hands, take endless hikes and revisit their childhoods that had been so carefree for both of them. Fred could set up his easel and paint wonderful pictures, if he so desired. Reto had said she could come to the homestead any time she liked, since his spread, picture-perfectly situated between two lakes, was unoccupied the greater part of the year. It would serve his purposes well if someone were to stay at the place, air it out and light the fires, tending it for a while, chasing the foxes and wildcats from the terrace, balconies and generous outdoor fireplace.

Rita was thrilled over Mischa's offer and didn't have to think twice about accepting it. She had also had her share of stress at the hospital recently, she was terribly over-worked, and a vacation was long overdue. Canada! Images of boundless space and freedom; pure, fresh air; untouched forests; countless animals, and the solitude of the wilderness had always captivated her. She fruitlessly tried to convince Mischa to allow her to at least pay for her and Fred's plane tickets, but Mischa insisted they were her guests.

A few days later, they were on their way to Halifax, flying with British Airways. Ever since September 1998, when a fully occupied Swissair machine with 229 passengers on board plummeted into the Atlantic ten kilometers from Peggy's Cove, a small fishing village not far from their Halifax destination, Mischa had chosen other airlines when flying to lectures or chess tournaments in eastern Canada, despite the fact that Swissair was still rated as one of the safest airlines in the world. The chief investigator looking into the crash back then had discovered, with the help of scientists, ten times mores magnesium than expected in the debris, which could well have accelerated combustion leading to the inferno. They also found that a large cargo of valuable diamonds was missing from the hold. Neither of these facts were mentioned in the official report and both were struck from a Swiss television broadcast on the disaster.

Nothing is what it appears to be. This not only applied to Mischa and the Roman philosopher and scholar Boethius, who fifteen hundred years ago -- before he was decapitated in Pavia for allegedly conspiring to overthrow the Ostrogothic usurper of the throne in Rome, Theodoric -- told the parable of two philosophers walking along the beach when they espied in the distance a man clubbing another man, the latter on his knees and helpless in the sand. "Quickly!" The first philosopher cried indignantly, "We must go and deter the murderer from his intention!" When they arrived at the scene, they realized that the man with the club was not attempting to kill the other but had actually saved his life by killing a scorpion sitting on the man's shoulder and preparing to strike. Upon this discovery, the second philosopher said to the first, *"Si tacuisses, philosophus mansisses"* – *Had you held your peace, you would still be a philosopher*.

At the expansive homestead about fifty kilometers from Halifax, in the Spry Bay not far from Sheet Harbor, Mischa, Rita and Fred spent wonderfully relaxing days in utter solitude. Their next neighbor was nearly ten kilometers away, which wasn't unusual in these parts.

When they arrived at the house built of mighty round boles, they fired up the gigantic stone fireplace in the spacious living room, using the endless supply of dry wood stored for this purpose. The flames blazed, crackled and spread a comforting warmth, Christmassy long before winter. The fireplace was large enough to house two oxen and the living-room ceiling's rafters as high as a rural church's bell-tower. Taking the rifles down from their racks on the wall, they went hunting, making sure not to wander too far from the house, where they would invade the territory of bears and wolves, and kept their guns loaded and ready to fire. They bagged two hares and a rabbit, roasting them over a campfire along with the trout Rita dexterously plucked from between the stones with her hands, and enjoyed their carefree friendship. The taste of hot, smoky meat was indescribable, as was the smell of freedom and the musky aroma surrounding them.

Fred set up his easel on a knoll and painted pictures reminiscent of Monet or Picasso. The timidity and reserve Mischa had noticed when they first met in Rita's apartment in Vienna had not abated in the least, despite – or perhaps due to – Rita's love and care. She mothered him endlessly, shielded him from all harm, tended to all his needs, making all decisions for him and sparing him all the hurdles that anyone must take to learn to stand up to life's challenges. Something Fred was not at all prepared to do, which is probably why he was drawn to Rita in the first place. For her part, she loved to sacrifice herself to his needs, although he did not demand it of her. She was a natural-born mother, carrying his first child beneath her heart, a fact he was ignorant of since she had only yesterday discovered the pregnancy herself, her intuition leading her to bring along a test. She hadn't told Mischa either, but was waiting for an opportune moment when the two of them were walking by the lake or sitting on the terrace in the evening sun talking of those things women do when there is no man within earshot.

Mischa was a bit envious of Rita's happiness and her unclouded intimacy with Fred. She increasingly missed the sexual satisfaction she shared with JD and which Farbmann could not give her. Fantasies of enslaving submissive men were reawakened when she lay alone in one of the many bedrooms in the spacious blockhouse she had lived in for many days now, trying unsuccessfully to satisfy herself in lieu of a lover or slave.

The day before their return flight to Vienna, Rita took the car they had rented at the airport to Halifax to purchase gifts for friends and family and to wander around the foreign city, buying herself a few of those typical Canadian flannel shirts she always wanted to have. Unlike Mischa, Rita loved shopping. But since she knew Mischa detested aimless gadding about and senseless rummaging through shelves, tedious sliding hangars from one piece of clothing to the next on retail racks and odious browsing in antique and souvenir shops, she had told her to stay at the house and have an enjoyable day with Fred, cooking him something tasty, going with him to the lake or what occurred to her to do while she was gone. She would never have dreamed that she was gambling with her future and Fred's life, bringing the father of her unborn child in dire peril. She was convinced, as was the rest of the world, with the exception of Dr. Farbmann, that the murder charges against Mischa were built on pure speculation and the ambitions of two Viennese criminal investigators and that her supposed best friend would never do anything to hurt herself or her future husband.

How cruelly she had been deceived. When she returned from her shopping spree that evening, she found him naked, covered in blood, his body littered with countless knife wounds and doubtlessly dead on their bed. Mischa had vanished. None of her screams, wails and sobbing changed that fact. She tore the hair from her head, threw herself on his lifeless body, felt his blood on her lips and body, and still, he remained dead. Mischa had destroyed everything she had lived for.

Epilog

Interpol and co-operating police authorities combed countless countries around the globe for the Nobel Prize Laureate and World Chess Champion Mischa Turow, who, as was now evident, truly was a sadistic mass murderess. But their searches were fruitless. Only Russia refused to aid the hunt. President Kutin announced that his country would not take part in a hate campaign launched by the Western world, aimed at persecuting a Russian citizen. And by the way, he had no idea where she could be.

About the Author

Born in Milan in 1952, son of Austro-Hungarian Holocaust survivors. 1954 moved to Vienna. 1955 Joined the Jewish religious school. 1958 elementary school Kollonitzgasse. 1962 Realgymnasium Diefenbachgasse. 1965 moved to Zurich, attending Literargymnasium. Shortly after the Six-Day War in 1967, kibbutz stay in Israel. 1971 Matura, study of German studies, history and psychology in Zurich and Basel, editor-in-chief of two youth and student magazines, freelance journalist and youth leader. 1974 Literature Prize of the canton of Baselland for the short story 'Ascension', published in the volume 'Excellent Stories'. Then 5 marriages with 1 Jewess from Switzerland, Germany, France, Italy and Russia, 6 children, born between 1976 and 2012. Adventurous career as a ski instructor, car driving instructor, high school teacher, art promoter, jewelery wholesaler in Vienna, real estate agents in the US and General contractor in Valais. 1991 vice president of the Basel Chess Society, 1996 founder and president of the chess club Crans-Montana, 2016 founder and president of the Cercle d'échecs et d'art valaisan, friendship with Anatoly Karpov and Garry Kasparov. Participation in 6 ACO World Chess Championships. 2018 Swiss company chess champion. Since 2016 Publication of numerous novels, novella and short story collections in various publishers, which have been translated into several languages and presented at the Frankfurt Book Fair. Collaboration with illustrators Alexander Pavlenko and Astrid Saalmann. Readings in Switzerland, Germany and Austria. In 2019, a new novel is proposed for the German Book Prize. Readings and book presentations in English and Russian are planned in New York. Lives and writes on Lake Zurich, second home in the Valais mountains. Describes himself as a citizen of the world, Heimwehwiener and critical Swiss. Married to Natalya Yakina.

www.ingramcontent.com/pod-product-compliance
Lightning Source LLC
Chambersburg PA
CBHW020949030726
47496CB00005B/1428